THREE SISTERS

Bi Feiyu

Three Sisters

Translated from the Chinese by
Howard Goldblatt and Sylvia Li-chun Lin

TELEGRAM

First published as *Yumi* by Jiangsu Publishing House in 2003

This English edition published in 2010 by Telegram, London

ISBN: 978-1-84659-023-8

This book has been selected to receive financial assistance from English PEN's Writers in Translation programme supported by Bloomberg.

English PEN exists to promote literature and its understanding, uphold writers' freedoms around the world, campaign against the persecution and imprisonment of writers for stating their views, and promote the friendly co-operation of writers and free exchange of ideas.

A full CIP record for this book is available from the British Library.
A full CIP record for this book is available from the Library of Congress.

Printed in the UK by CPI Cox & Wyman, Reading, RG1 8EX.

TELEGRAM
26 Westbourne Grove, London W2 5RH, UK
2398 Doswell Avenue, Saint Paul, Minnesota, 55108, US
Verdun, Beirut, Lebanon
www.telegrambooks.com

Yumi

LITTLE EIGHT WAS barely a month old when Shi Guifang handed him over to her eldest daughter, Yumi. Outside of taking him to her breast several times a day, she showed no interest in her baby. In the normal course of events, a mother would treat her newborn son like a living treasure, cuddling him all day long. But not Shi Guifang. The effects of a monthlong lying-in had been the addition of some excess flab and a spirit of indolence. She seemed to sag, albeit contentedly; but mostly she displayed the sort of relaxed languor that comes with the successful completion of something important.

Shi Guifang savored the guiltless pleasure of leaning lazily against her doorframe and nibbling on sunflower seeds. She'd pick a seed out of the palm of her hand, hold it between her thumb and index finger, and slowly bring it up to her mouth, the three remaining fleshy fingers curling under her chin. She demonstrated remarkable sloth, mainly in the way she stood, with one foot on the floor, the other resting on the doorsill. From time to time she switched feet.

People did not mind Shi Guifang's indolence, but sometimes a lazy person will appear proud, and it was this that others found intolerable. What gave her the right to look so superior when all she did was crack sunflower seeds? She definitely was not the Shi Guifang of earlier days. People had once praised her as

7

a woman who eschewed the usual prideful airs of an official's wife. She smiled when she talked to them, and when eating made that impossible, she smiled with her eyes. But now, as people thought back over the past decade, they concluded that she had been putting up a front all that time. Embarrassed that she'd had seven girls in a row, she had suppressed her true nature with a show of excessive courtesy. That was then. Now the birth of a son, Little Eight, had given her the right to be haughty; she was as courteous as ever, but there's courtesy and then there's *courtesy*. Shi Guifang typified the amiable, approachable manner of a Party secretary. But her husband was the Party secretary, not she, so what right did Shi Guifang have to be so indolently amiable and approachable?

Second Aunt, who lived at the end of the alley, often came out to rake the grass that was drying in the sun. She sized up Shi Guifang with a sneer: *She had to open her legs eight times before a son popped out,* Second Aunt said to herself, *and now she has the cheek to act like* she's *a Party secretary.*

Shi Guifang had come to Wang Family Village[1] from Shi Family Bridge. During the twenty years she was married to Wang Lianfang she had presented him with seven girls, not counting three miscarriages. She was often heard to say that the three who didn't make it had probably been boys, since all the signs had been different; even her taste buds had undergone a change. She spoke of her miscarriages as if they were missed opportunities; had she managed to keep just one of them, she'd have carried out her life's mission.

On one of her trips to town she visited a clinic, where a bespectacled doctor confirmed her suspicions. His scientific explanation would have had the average person scratching his head in bewilderment. But Shi Guifang was smart enough to get the gist of it. Put simply, being pregnant with a boy demands more care, the pregnancy is harder to hold on to, and spotting is unavoidable, even when the woman manages to keep the baby. Shi Guifang sighed at the doctor's sage words, reminding herself that a boy is a treasure, even in the womb. She was consoled to learn that fate was not keeping her from having a son, which was more or less what the doctor was really saying, and that she must have faith that science also plays a role. But this did little to lessen her feelings of despair. On her way home she stared for a long moment at a snot-nosed little boy on the pier before she tore her eyes away, dejected.

That was not, however, how Wang Lianfang saw things. Having studied dialectics in the county town, Party Secretary Wang knew all about the relationship between internal and external factors, and the difference between an egg and a rock. He had his own irrational understanding of boy and girl babies. To him, women were external factors, like farmland, temperature, and soil condition, while a man's seed was the essential ingredient. Good seed produced boys; bad seed produced girls. Although he'd never admit it, when he looked at his seven daughters his self-esteem suffered.

A man with wounded self-esteem develops a stubborn streak. By initiating a battle with himself, Wang Lianfang resolved to overcome every obstacle on his way to ultimate victory. He vowed to have a son, if not this year, then the next. If not next year, then the year after; and if not the year after, then the year after that. Not in the least anxious that he might be denied a son to carry on the line, he settled in for a long, drawn-out battle rather than seek a speedy victory. Admittedly, depositing his seed in a woman was not all that difficult.

Shi Guifang, on the other hand, endured considerable dread. During the first few years of their marriage, she'd been fairly resistant to sex. On the eve of her wedding, her sister-in-law had put her lips close to Shi Guifang's ear—she could feel her hot breath—to admonish her not to open too wide and to cover herself if she desired her husband's respect and did not want to be thought wanton. In an enigmatic tone that hinted at a broad knowledge of human affairs, her sister-in-law had said, "Remember, Guifang, the harder the bone, the better it is to gnaw." In fact, Guifang had no use for her sister-in-law's wisdom. But after several girls in a row, the situation changed dramatically. No longer resistant, no longer coy, Guifang turned fearful. She clamped her legs together and covered herself with her hands. Inevitably, the clamping and covering began to rankle Wang Lianfang, who one night slapped her twice—once forehand and once backhand.

"Who do you think you are?" he had said, angrily. "Not a single boy has popped out of you, and yet you still expect two bowls of rice at every meal."

Anyone standing beneath the window would have heard every word, and if it got around that she wouldn't *do it,* she'd have been ruined. Only an ugly shrew would refuse to do it if all she could manage was girls.

A slap now and then didn't bother Guifang, but Wang's shouts made her go limp. When that happened, she could no longer clamp her legs shut or cover herself. Like a clumsy barefoot doctor, Wang would set his jaw as he pulled down her pants and, seconds after entering her, spray his seed into her body. That is what really frightened her, his seed, since every one of those little invaders was capable of turning into a baby girl.

Finally, in 1971, the heavens smiled on them. Shortly after the Lunar New Year, Little Eight was born. It was not a run-of-the-mill Lunar New Year, for the people had been told to turn the celebration into a revolutionary Spring Festival. Firecrackers and games of poker were banned throughout the village, an edict that Wang himself announced over the PA system, though even he was not altogether sure just what a "revolutionary" holiday ought to be. But that did not matter so long as someone in the leadership had the courage to make the announcement; new policy always emerged from the mouth of a member of the leadership. Standing in his living room, Wang held a microphone in one hand and fiddled with the switches on the PA system with the other. Neatly lined up in a row, the little switches were hard, shiny exclamation marks.

"This is to be a Spring Festival that stands for solidarity, vigilance, solemnity, and vivacity," Wang barked into the microphone, his words like the gleaming exclamation-mark switches he pressed while he spoke: vigilant and solemn, adding a harsh and mighty aura to the cold winds of winter.

With an old overcoat draped over his shoulders and half a Flying Horse cigarette between his fingers, Wang Lianfang went on a holiday inspection of the village on the second day of the new year—a raw, cold day. The lanes and alleys were virtually deserted, with only a few old men and children out, a dreary sight for such an important holiday. Obviously, the younger men had gathered at some secret spot to try their luck at cards. Wang stopped in front of Wang Youqing's door, where he coughed once or twice and spat out a glob of phlegm. The window curtain parted slowly to reveal the red padded jacket of Wang Youqing's wife. She glanced at the lane entrance and gestured toward her gate. The house was too dimly lit and her hand had moved too fast for Wang Lianfang to know what that gesture meant, but he turned to look just as the PA system came to life, carrying the voice of his mother, whose shouts were garbled by several missing teeth and a sense of urgency: "Lianfang, hey, Lianfang. It's a boy. Come home!"

It took Wang Lianfang, who was still looking toward the lane entrance, a few minutes to comprehend what he was hearing. When he turned back to the red jacket in the window, Youqing's wife, her face resting against the sill, was gazing at him impassively, her shoulders slumped. He thought he saw a trace of resentment on her bewitching face, which was framed by the stand-up collar of her jacket as if it were cupped in the palms of her hands. From the clamorous background emerging from the loudspeaker, Wang could tell that his living room was swarming with people. Someone put on a record, which filled the village with the valiant, sonorous, and rhythmic strains of "The Helmsman Guides the Ocean Journey."

"Go on home, you," Youqing's wife said. "They're waiting for you."

Shrugging the old overcoat up over his shoulders, Wang laughed and muttered to himself, "Well, I'll be damned."

Yumi ran in and out of the house, her sleeves rolled up to expose arms that had turned purple from the cold. But her cheeks were fiery red, generating an irrepressible glow, a sign that she was trying to suppress both an excitement and a shyness of unknown origin. The strain of mixed emotions had turned her face smooth and shiny. She bit her lip the whole time she was running around, as if she, not her mother, had delivered Little Eight. At long last her mother had a boy, and Yumi could breathe a heartfelt sigh of relief. Happiness took root in her heart. As eldest daughter, Yumi was, to all intents and purposes, more like a sister to her mother. In fact, she had assisted the midwife in the birth of the sixth girl, Yumiao, since certain things were too awkward for an outsider to handle. The arrival of Little Eight constituted the third time she'd watched her mother give birth, and that made her privy to all of a woman's secrets, a special reward for being the eldest. The second sister, Yusui, was only a year younger than Yumi, and the third girl, Yuxiu, two and a half years. But neither of them could match Yumi's understanding of the ways of the world or her shrewdness. Age among siblings often represents more than just the order of birth; it can also signal differences in the depth and breadth of life experience. Ultimately, maturity requires opportunity; the pace of growth does not rely on the progression of time alone.

Yumi was outside dumping bloody water in the ditch when her father walked through the gate. He assumed that on such a happy occasion his daughter would say something to him or at least glance his way. But she didn't. She wore only a thin knit top that, because it was a bit on the small side, showed off her full breasts and thin waist. Wang was surprised at the sight of her curves and purple arms; Yumi had grown into a woman.

Yumi normally did not speak to her father, not a word, and

he figured that had something to do with what went on between him and other women. Sure, he slept around, but his wife didn't seem to mind; she even continued to be friendly with those women, some of whom still called her Sister Guifang. But not Yumi. Though she never talked about it openly, she had her way of dealing with the women, something that Wang Lianfang learned later during a little pillow talk. Zhang Fuguang's wife was the first to let on, several years back, when she was a newlywed. "Yumi knows," she said, "so we have to be careful."

"She doesn't know shit," Wang replied. "She's just a kid."

"She knows. I'm sure of it."

It was not something Fuguang's wife had dreamed up. A few days before, she had been sitting under a locust tree with some other women sewing a shoe sole when Yumi walked up. Fuguang's wife's face reddened as soon as she spotted Yumi, and, after a quick glance, she looked away to avoid the girl's eyes. But when she stole another glance, she realized that Yumi was standing in front of her, staring holes in her. Totally calm, totally composed, Yumi sized her up from head to toe and back as if they were the only two people present. Since she was only fourteen at the time, Wang Lianfang refused to believe she knew anything.

But then a few months later, Wang Daren's wife gave Wang Lianfang a real scare. He had barely climbed on top when she covered her face with her arms and arched upward as if her life depended on it. "Party Secretary, work hard and get it over with quickly." Unsettled by her plea, he did finish quickly—too quickly. After which Wang Daren's wife hurriedly cleaned herself without a word. Wang cupped her chin and asked what was wrong. She fell to her knees.

"Yumi will be here any minute to play shuttlecock," she said. Wang blinked nervously; now he believed the rumors. But back at home he saw innocence in his daughter's face, and he knew this was a subject he could not bring up. That was the day Yumi had stopped talking to her father, and that hadn't bothered him—you can't stop sleeping just because there's a mosquito in the room. But now that Wang finally had his precious son, Yumi quietly made her existence and its significance known to him; it was an unmistakable signal that she had grown up.

Wang Lianfang's mother's lower lip quivered, her arms hung down at her sides. She was so old she could not control her slack lower lip. For women her age, unexpected happy events like this were sheer torture, for they were incapable of showing emotions on faces that seemed forever stiff. Wang's father, on the other hand, was handling it all quite well, having settled on a dispassionate response. He just puffed slowly on his pipe. He was, after all, the former director of security, a man who had seen a thing or two and knew how to keep his cool, even during happy moments.

"You're back," his father said.

"I'm back."

"Well, pick a name."

Having thought about this on the way home, Wang was prepared. "He's the eighth child, so we'll call him Wang Balu."

"Balu, as in 'Eighth Route Army'? Sounds fine," the old man said. "But 'Wang' and 'ba' together mean 'cuckold.'"

"All right then, we'll call him Wang Hongbing, 'Red Army' Wang."

The old man said nothing more, typical of a head of household in the old days. They showed approval by silence.

The midwife called for Yumi, so she laid down the basin and hurried into her mother's bedroom. Wang saw that she'd learned to hold her arms close to her body as she ran, although her braids swung briskly across her back. Over the years, he'd been so focused on fooling around and spreading his seed that he hadn't paid enough attention to Yumi, who had, it was clear, reached marriageable age.

In fact, the issue of her marriage had never been brought up. Wang Lianfang was, after all, a Party secretary, not just anyone—a fact that many families found intimidating. Even the matchmakers had passed Yumi by. All shrewd matchmakers believed the saying that an emperor's daughter never had to worry about finding a husband. Given her family background and good looks, Yumi could easily spread her arms and turn them into the wings of a phoenix.

Peasants do not have the luxury of taking winters off, for that's when they have to work on their equipment after the year's use. Everything—waterwheels, feed troughs, buckets, farming skiffs, pitchforks, shovels, rakes, flails, and wooden spades—needs attention, some to be repaired, others to be mended, sharpened, or oiled. Nothing can be overlooked or put off. The most taxing job, but also the most urgent, is repairing the irrigation system. Didn't Chairman Mao himself say that irrigation is the lifeline of agriculture? A peasant himself, the Chairman would have been a formidable farmer if he had not gone off to Beijing. He was also correct in pointing out that water is the first and foremost of the eight principles: water, fertilizer, soil, seed, density, care, labor, and management. Irrigation work usually takes place in the winter, and major repairs are especially hard on the peasants, who wind up more exhausted than when they're out working in the fields.

There is one more thing that must not be forgotten—the Lunar New Year holiday. In order to wrap up the current year and obtain good omens for the year to come, all families—from the laziest to the busiest—need a decent New Year's holiday. No one is spared from the hard work of washing and scrubbing; frying peanuts, peas, and broad beans; popping rice; dusting; repairing walls; and steaming rice cakes and buns. Pleasurable aromas permeate every house, shrouding them in steam.

Then there are the social obligations that require attention. And so, in the middle of winter, and especially during the last month of the old year and the first month of the new, a time when there is no actual farmwork, the peasants are busier than ever. As the saying goes, "Celebrate in the first month, gamble in the second, and till the fields in the third." The second lunar month is the farmers' only free time, days when they visit relatives and try their luck at gambling. They must turn to the land for survival early in the third lunar month, right after Qingming, the tomb-sweeping holiday, which falls on April 5 in the Western calendar. However important or involved other matters may be, the peasants' livelihood is buried in the ground, and it must be plowed up in the first days of spring if the farmers are to survive another year. City folk like to sing the lament, "Spring days are lamentably short," but theirs is too refined a view, embellished by sentimentality. For peasants, the meaning of that phrase—twenty or thirty fleeting days—is genuine and literal. Those good days of spring are gone so quickly they leave no time for even the briefest lament.

Yumi scarcely left the house during the second month because she was too busy taking care of Little Eight. No one forced her; she was happy to do it. A girl of few words, she carried out her duties meticulously, especially those involved in looking after the family. Eager to do well in everything, she worked without complaint, tolerated no criticism, and refused to accept the proposition that there could be a better family than hers. And yet, the absence of a male heir had been the subject of gossip swirling around her family. As a girl, she could not make her views on this matter public, though she had been anxious, worried even, for her mother's sake. But now everything was fine, because with the arrival of Little Eight, people had nothing to talk about. She quickly assumed the care of her brother and took over all her mother's exhausting duties, carrying them out with quiet, single-minded devotion. Naturally gifted in the business of childcare, she held the baby like a real mother after only a few days, cradling his smooth head in the crook of her arm as she rocked him and hummed lullabies. At first she was a bit shy and performed some of her duties awkwardly. But there are different kinds of shyness; one kind can be upsetting, another kind can be a sign of pride. With Little Eight in her arms, Yumi kept company with the married women of the village, engaging the young mothers in discussions or exchanging ideas on topics such as what to watch out for after burping the baby, the color of the baby's stool, or the baby's expressions and what they meant. While these may seem trivial and insignificant, to these women they were important topics of conversation that brought considerable pleasure.

After a while, Yumi stopped looking like a sister caring for her baby brother, and she no longer sounded like one. The proper, steady, and absorbed way she held him put everyone's mind at ease; she was so tightly bound to the baby that nothing else seemed to matter. In a word, Yumi exuded the air of a young mother, which caused Little Eight to get his kinship wrong, for as long as his belly was full he refused to cling to Shi Guifang. His dark eyes were always fixed on Yumi, and though his focused gaze may not have held any particular meaning, he never let her out of his sight. After gazing down at Little Eight for a while, she too would sometimes slip into a sort of trance for no apparent reason other than a yearning for her own marriage. At moments like that she easily lapsed into daydreams, planning her own future in a vacuum. But she remained single nonetheless.

The village was home to a few passable young men, none of whom she considered to be a good match, who clammed up if she approached when they were talking to other girls. Their eyes darted around in their sockets like startled fish. This always saddened Yumi and made her feel lonely. She believed the old people when they said that a door's high threshold has its virtues and its vices. Several of the girls her age who had been spoken for would sneak around cutting out shoe soles for their future husbands, and when Yumi spotted them doing this, instead of laughing at them, she'd steal a glance at the size of the soles and guess the boy's height. She couldn't help it. Fortunately, the girls never gloated in front of her; in fact, they felt inferior.

"This is the best we can do," they'd say. "Who knows what grand family Yumi will find?"

Encouraging talk like that secretly reinforced Yumi's belief that she was slated to have a brighter future than any of them. But when nothing came of it, her happiness seemed like a bamboo basket: its holes were revealed when it was taken out of the water. At such times, strands of sadness would inevitably wrap themselves around her heart. Fortunately, Yumi was not overly anxious; these were only idle thoughts. Such thoughts are sometimes bitter and sometimes sweet.

Yumi's mother grew lazier by the day. The physical toll of childbirth had undeniably affected her vitality. But it was one thing to hand Little Eight over to Yumi, and yet another to turn the whole household over to her. What does a woman live for anyway? Isn't it to run a household? If she shuns even the authority to do that, what is she besides a rotten egg with a watery yolk? But there were no complaints from Yumi, who was content with the way things were. When a girl learns to care for a baby and take charge of a household, she can wake up that first morning after her wedding day fully prepared to be a competent wife and a good daughter-in-law, someone who need not be in constant fear of what her mother-in-law thinks. There was another reason Yumi liked the new arrangement: her sisters—Yusui, Yuxiu, Yuying, Yuye, Yumiao, and Yuyang—had never before bowed to her authority, though they all called her eldest sister. The second girl, Yusui, was slightly simpleminded, so there was no need to worry about her. The key figure was number three, Yuxiu, who had carved out her own territory at home and in the village, employing her intelligence and her native ability to please people. And there was more: Yuxiu, who had large, double-fold eyes, fair skin, and a pretty face, could be cunning when she needed to be. Even a minor slight might send her into their father's arms to pout. Yumi could never bring herself to do that, which was why their father favored Yuxiu. But now everything had changed. Yumi not only took care of Little Eight, she had also been given charge of the household and had assumed the responsibility for keeping her sisters in line. This would not have been the case if their mother had not relinquished her authority; but now that she had, Yumi, as the eldest, was in charge. That's the way it always is.

The first sign of Yumi's authority surfaced at the lunch table one day. Yumi did not possess innate authority, but authority is something you can take in your hand and squeeze till it sweats and sprouts five fingers that can be balled into a fist. Their father had gone to a meeting at the commune, and the fact that she chose this moment to strike showed how shrewd Yumi was. That morning she had fried a new batch of sunflower seeds for their mother and, just before lunch, had fetched water to wash the dishes. She worked quietly, but a well laid-out plan had formed in her head. At mealtimes there were always so many people around the table that their mother had to keep after everyone to eat or the meal would drag on forever, making it impossible to clear the table. Squabbles inevitably resulted. Having made up her mind to follow her mother's example, Yumi decided that the lunch table was where it would all start. And so it did. With a glance at Shi Guifang, she said, "Hurry up, Mother. I fried some sunflower seeds and put them in the cupboard." Then she tapped her chopsticks against her rice bowl and shouted, "Come on, girls, eat up so I can do the dishes. Hurry up and finish your rice." That was how their mother had always done it—tap on the rice bowl and shout at the girls. Yumi's urging produced results and the speed picked up around the table. But not for Yuxiu, who actually began chewing more slowly—damned haughty and damned pretty. Taking her seventh sister, Yuyang, in her arms and picking up the little girl's rice bowl, Yumi began feeding her. After spooning in a few mouthfuls, she said, "Are you planning to do the dishes, Yuxiu?" She neither looked up nor raised her voice, but the implied threat was unmistakable.

Yuxiu stopped chewing and put down her rice bowl. "I'm waiting for Father."

No reaction from Yumi, who finished feeding Yuyang and started clearing the table. When she came to Yuxiu she picked up her sister's rice bowl and dumped the contents into the dog's bowl. Yuxiu backed away against the bedroom door and eyed Yumi without a word. The haughty look remained, but the younger sisters could tell that something was different somehow, and that Yuxiu wasn't nearly as pretty as before.

Rather than wage open warfare with Yumi at the dinner table that night, Yuxiu simply refused to speak to her. But Yumi had only to note how quickly Yuxiu was eating her congee to get a sense of what her sister was up to. Yuxiu, of course, was not about to submit easily, so she began acting up, tangling her chopsticks with those of the fourth girl, Yuying. Knowing what was going on, Yumi ignored her. Acting up like that, she knew, was a sign of desperation; Yuxiu was losing steam and needed to vent her frustration. Yuying smacked Yuxiu's chopsticks out of her hand and onto the floor, refusing to be bullied by her older sister. Calmly, Yumi laid down her bowl, picked up Yuxiu's chopsticks, and stirred them in her own congee to clean them before handing them back. Then she gently scolded Yuying: "Yuying, don't fight with your third sister." By referring to Yuxiu as third sister in front of the others she underscored the family's prized hierarchy. Now that Yuxiu was pacified, she looked pretty again. Someone had to be blamed for the incident, and that someone was Yuying, even though Yumi knew it was not her fault. But someone had to suffer an injustice to achieve a balance between two contending forces.

Yumi noticed out of the corner of her eye that Yuxiu was the first to finish her dinner. This time the cunning sister, the fox spirit, had lost her bluster. Fox spirits are known for running wild, but they have their failings. One, they're lazy, and two, they tend to pick on those weaker than them. All fox spirits are like that. If someone can tolerate those two attributes, foxes are easy to keep in line. Yumi only wanted her sister to obey her once; if she did, she'd do it again and then again. After three times, obedience would become second nature. The first time was the key. Authority is achieved when others obey you, and it manifests itself in a demand for obedience. Having vanquished Yuxiu, Yumi knew that she was now in charge of the household, an awareness that delighted her as she did the dishes. Naturally, she did not show it. Transferring what is in your heart to your face is a recipe for disaster.

Yumi had lost a lot of weight by the time the second lunar month, solar March, rolled around, and she roamed the village with Wang Hongbing in her arms. She would never call him Little Eight in front of anyone but her family; she always called him Wang Hongbing in public. Village boys normally did not hear their given names except from their teachers. But Yumi called her toothless little baby brother by his full name, investing him with a serious, more formal aura, thus distinguishing him from the sons of other families and placing him above all others. With the baby in her arms, she talked and looked like a seasoned mother, something she had learned from the young mothers on the streets, in the fields, and on the threshing ground. It was not something she came to instinctively; being highly focused, she made sure she perfected anything new before actually putting it into practice. And though she was still young, she differed from the chatty, sometimes sloppy young mothers she met, and she always looked good with her little brother in her arms. She had her own style, her unique inventions. The way she cared for the baby impressed the village women. But what they focused on was not how capably she carried her brother; rather they talked about how precocious she was and what a good girl she'd turned out to be.

But then the village women detected something new as Yumi carried Wang Hongbing around the village. Something that went beyond just caring for the baby, something far more significant. As she chatted with the village women, she'd casually take Hongbing over to the houses of the women who had slept with her father. Once there, she'd stand outside the door for a long time. This was a way to win back her mother's dignity. But Fuguang's wife was oblivious to Yumi's hidden purpose when the girl showed up at her door one day. Without thinking, she reached out to take the baby from Yumi, even referring to herself as aunty.

"Here, let aunty hold you. How would that be?" she asked.

Yumi kept chatting with the others, treating Fuguang's wife as if she weren't there, all the while tightening her grip on her brother. After two failed attempts to take the baby, Fuguang's wife realized that Yumi would not loosen her hold. But with all those people standing around in front of her house, the humiliation was intolerable. So she brought little Hongbing's hand up to her lips as if it smelled wonderful and tasted even better. Snatching the little hand away from the woman, Yumi licked every finger clean and spat at Fuguang's door before turning to scold Hongbing: "How filthy!" Hongbing laughed so hard his gums showed. Fuguang's wife paled with shock. She could say nothing, nor could the other women, who all knew Yumi's intentions.

Yumi stood in front of one door after another, exposing and warning the women inside, sparing none of them. The mere sight of her threw any woman who had slept with Wang Lianfang into a panic, and her silent accusations were more terrifying than condemnations broadcast over a loudspeaker. Without saying a word, she exposed the women's transgressions little by little and subjected them to terrible humiliation. This proved to be a particularly satisfying and ambitious feat in the eyes of the guiltless women, who were now jealous of Shi Guifang for having such a remarkable daughter. Back home, they scolded their children with more severity than usual, railing against them for being "useless things."

"Just look at Yumi," they exclaimed.

They weren't worried that their children would overlook Yumi's qualities, but that they would never match up. Also implied in this simple comment was the serious and urgent business of setting up a model for proper living. The village women's admiration of Yumi grew and grew; on their way home from work or walking down to the pier, they would crowd around her to coddle Wang Hongbing. When they were done, they'd say, "I wonder which lucky woman will get Yumi for a daughter-in-law." Expressing envy of a nonexistent lucky woman was a roundabout way of flattering Yumi. Since modesty dictated that she not respond, Yumi merely sneaked a look up into the sky, the tip of her nose glowing.

But Yumi was about to be married, and the women were still in the dark. Where did her future in-laws live? As far away as the edge of the sky, yet right in front of their eyes. Peng Family Village, which was about seven *li* away. And what about "him"? That was just the reverse: right in front of their eyes, yet as far away as the edge of the sky. This was not something Yumi was going to make public.

After the Spring Festival, Wang Lianfang had one more thing to do, and he sought help every time he went to a meeting—Yumi needed a husband. As the girl got older, it became less and less feasible for her to stay in the village. Though anxiety weighed on him, Wang told himself that his daughter must not become just anyone's wife. Marrying beneath her station would not serve her well; but more important, this would make her parents lose face. Wang hoped to find a match with a young man from an official's family, one that was naturally powerful and influential. Each time he found a suitable match in a neighboring village, he told Guifang to talk to Yumi, who reacted with bland indifference. Wang could sense that with a father like him, Yumi, a proud and clever girl, had little faith in any man from an official's family. In the end, it was Secretary Peng from Peng Family Village who suggested the third son of a barrel maker in his village, which nearly ended the conversation, for Wang knew that the "third son" of a "barrel maker" could not possibly amount to much.

"He's the young man who qualified as an aviator a couple of years ago. There are only four in the county," Secretary Peng explained. Wang bit his lip and made a sucking sound, for that changed everything. With an aviator for a son-in-law it would be as if he himself had flown in an airplane, and whenever he took a piss it would be like a day's rain. So he handed Yumi's picture to Peng, who took one look and said, "She's a real beauty."

"Actually, the prettiest one is my third daughter," Wang replied, which elicited a silent laugh from Peng.

"Your third daughter is too young."

The barrel maker's third son sent a response, along with his photo, to Secretary Peng, who forwarded them to Wang Lianfang, who then passed them on to his wife; and they ultimately came to rest snugly under Yumi's pillow. The young man was called Peng Guoliang, a name that made him a true standout. Why? Because Guoliang, which means "pillar of the state," was appropriate for an aviator. Like a pillar, he was anchored to the ground, but his head was in the sky. An uncommon name. He was not particularly good-looking, at least not in the photo. On the skinny side, he seemed older than his age. He had single-fold eyes with heavy lids and a pronounced squint. They did not appear to be eyes that could find their way home from up in the clouds. His lips were pressed tightly together, too tightly, in fact, for that highlighted his overbite, which was clearly visible even in the frontal shot. But he had posed for the photograph in full uniform at the airfield, which gave him a military air that the average person could not easily envision. The Silver Hawk airplane beside him stirred the imagination further. Despite the deficiencies in Peng Guoliang's looks, Yumi suffered a loss of pride; her self-esteem tumbled for no obvious reason as she sensed her own inadequacy. The man was, after all, someone who traveled between heaven and earth.

Yumi wished the match could be settled right away.

In his letter Peng Guoliang gave his address, including his unit, a clear indication to Yumi that her response would determine the future course of her life. This was important, and she knew she had to proceed with care. Her first thought was to have a few more photographs taken in town, but she changed her mind when she realized that he must have been happy enough with her looks to send a letter to Secretary Peng. There was no need to do anything more.

The issue now was her letter. Peng Guoliang had been somewhat vague in his, not boastful but certainly not modest. He emphasized only that "he had strong feelings for his hometown" and that when he was in his airplane "all he wanted to do was fly back home to be with the people there." The most revealing line was his positive reaction to Uncle Peng's suggestion. He wrote that "he would place absolute trust" in "any person Uncle Peng liked." But he hadn't stated outright that Yumi was the woman for him. Which meant that she had to skirt the issue as well; being too obvious indicated a lack of class, and that would never do. On the other hand, it would be worse to be overly vague; if he felt she was uninterested, the match would be lost and unsalvageable. Peng Guoliang seemed to be right in front of her eyes, yet truly he was as far away as the edge of the sky. The distance satisfied Yumi's ego, and yet it brought her sorrow as well.

After much thought, Yumi decided to write a restrained letter. Following a brief and properly worded introduction, she altered her tone:

> I definitely am no match [for you].[2] You fly high in the sky and only a fair[y] woman could be a match [for you]. I am not as good as the fair[y] women, nor am I as good-looking.

Her dignity remained intact, since it was natural for a girl to say she was not as pretty as a fairy. She ended the letter:

> Now I look up into the sky every day and every night. The sky is always the same, with only the sun during the day and only the moon at night.

At that point the letter took on a sentimental tone. Somehow, an emotional attachment was building inside her, concrete but hard to pinpoint, persistent and tormenting. As she read what she had written, she began to weep silently; she couldn't help it, for she felt deeply aggrieved, since none of this was what she really wanted to say. She desperately wanted to tell Peng how happy she was about the match. How wonderful it would be if someone could say that to him for her, to let him know how she felt. She sealed and posted the letter, though she was careful to give the return address as: "Wang Family Village Elementary

School, care of Miss Gao Suqin." Yumi was visibly thinner by the time the letter was on its way.

With the arrival of his son, Wang Lianfang felt more at ease with himself. Obviously, he would not be touching Guifang again, so all of his pent-up energy could be devoted to Youqing's wife. Wang's extramarital affairs had a long and complicated history that began when Guifang was pregnant with Yumi. Having a pregnant wife is not an easy thing for a man. During the first few weeks of marriage, he and his wife were insatiable and could not wait to turn off the light and jump into bed. But the good times came to an end when she missed her period the second month. She was enormously pleased with herself; lying in bed with her hands clasped over her belly, she announced proudly, "I got pregnant the very first night. It had to be, I just know it. I know I got pregnant our first night."

Proud, yes, but not so proud that she forgot to announce the implementation of "martial law": "No more, starting today." Wang Lianfang frowned in the dark, for he thought getting married meant that he could enjoy sex any time he wanted. It had never dawned on him that marriage led only to a pregnant wife. When he laid his hand on her belly, he sighed silently, but then his fingers took over and his hand began to move lower and lower. At the last moment, she clutched his hand and squeezed it viciously, a wanton, audacious gesture that signaled her pride of accomplishment. He had a desperate need, but he found no outlet; it was an irrepressible need that grew more urgent the more he tried to suppress it. That went on for more than a week.

Wang never imagined that he would have the audacity to do what he did then. At the brigade office one day, he pushed the bookkeeper to the floor, spread her out, and took her. His eyes must have been red from the urgent need that had been building inside him, although his mind was a total blank at the time. He recalled the details only after the fact when he picked up a copy of *Red Flag* and was hit by a shuddering fear. How, in the middle of the day, had he suddenly become possessed by that thought? The bookkeeper, more than ten years his senior, belonged to an older generation, and he was expected to call her aunty. When it was over, she got up, wiped herself off with a rag, pulled up her pants, tied the waistband, straightened her hair, brushed herself off front and back, locked the rag in a drawer, and walked out. Wang found her nonchalance perplexing. He worried that she might kill herself because of what he'd done. If she did, he would definitely lose his job as the commune's youngest branch secretary. That night he roamed the village till eleven o'clock, keeping his eyes peeled as he searched every corner, his ears pricked for any unexpected sounds. The next day he went to the brigade office at the crack of dawn, where he checked the rafters. Finding no hanging corpse was not reassuring enough. People began to stream in, and when nine o'clock rolled around, in strolled the bookkeeper, polite and cordial as always. Her eyes were not red and puffy, which put Wang sufficiently at ease that he could pass out cigarettes and engage in casual banter. After a while, she walked up with an account book and a note beneath her finger that said, "Come outside. I want to talk to you." Since it was a written communication, there was no way to gauge her emotion, and the anxiety that had melted away a short time before came rushing back. His heart was pounding as he watched her walk outside and, looking through the slats in the window, saw her return to her house. Agitated though he was, Wang managed to stay put for ten or fifteen minutes. Then, looking appropriately serious, he took out the *Red Flag* magazine, rapped the desktop with his finger as a signal for the others to keep at their studies, and walked out the door. He arrived at the bookkeeper's house alone, where his life as a man truly began. He was not quite a man when he walked through the door, and it was she who taught and guided him to the best times of his life. What kind of husband had he been? There was so much to learn. A battle between the two of them began, one that was drawn-out, difficult, and exhausting, a danger-ridden fight to the bitter end. But they ultimately pulled back from the precipice. He matured quickly, and before long she had nothing more to teach him. Then she looked and sounded terrible; he could even hear her insides collapse and break apart.

Wang Lianfang's major gain during the battle was the honing of his courage. Actually, he had nothing to fear. Not at all. Nothing bad would happen even if the women did not consent. On this point the bookkeeper had voiced criticism: "Don't pull down their pants the moment you see them. That makes them seem unwilling." Shaking that thing between his legs, she examined and criticized it: "You. Don't you know who you are? Even if they're unwilling, they need to know you're the boss. As they say, check the owner before you hit the dog, and if you don't care about the monk, at least give the Buddha some face."

There were even more gains to be had from the long, complex struggle that allowed him to see something quite meaningful. In no way an ordinary man, Wang knew something meaningful when he saw it and was expert at discovering the meanings inherent in things. Never content to be just a seed spreader, he saw himself as a propagandist as well, a man who wanted the women in the village to know that every bridegroom was overeager, since foreplay had been alien even to him. Those other men were ignorant of the depth and duration of the struggle or, for that matter, the importance of being thorough. Without Wang, all those women would forever be kept in the dark.

An additional, external factor in the history of Wang's struggle warrants a brief mention. For a decade or so, Shi Guifang never stopped being pregnant, which meant she was regularly off-limits. She would stand under a tree, one hand on the trunk and the other on her belly, and broadcast her dry heaves throughout the village without a trace of self-awareness. After a decade of this disgusting scene, Wang could hardly bear the ugly sight of her and her dry heaves. She sounded so hollow, so devoid of any viewpoint or stance; and she was oblivious to everything else around her. It was the same every time, embodying the formulaic characteristics of a traditional essay, which displeased Wang immensely. Now Guifang's only job was to quickly give him a son. But she couldn't, so what the hell was she dry heaving for? He hated those dry heaves, and the moment he heard one, he'd say, "There she goes again, another report."

Although he was told "no more" at home, Wang Lianfang did not alter the course of his struggle. And in this regard, Guifang was surprisingly enlightened, unlike many other women, who thought highly of themselves or were simply timid. Wang Yugui's wife was one of those. Wang Lianfang had slept with her only twice, and she was already displaying a degree of timidity. Standing there naked, with tears and snot flowing, she cupped her breasts, which had now been touched by someone other than her husband, and said, "Secretary, you got what you wanted, so save some, leave a little for my husband." He laughed at her strange request. Can something like this actually be saved? Besides, why are you covering your breasts? A woman's bust undergoes several changes: the golden breasts of a maiden, the silver breasts of a wife, and the bitch's teats of a mother. So what's she doing cradling those bitch's teats in the crooks of her arms as if they were gold nuggets? That'll never do.

Pulling a long face, he said, "Fine with me. There are, after all, new brides every year." But this woman became a casualty. Even her husband could not get her to have sex with him, and all he could do was beat her to vent his anger. Late at night she was often heard screaming in bed because of Yugui's fists. Wang Lianfang was finished with her. She'd talked about saving some for Yugui. Apparently she hadn't.

In more than a decade of dalliances, the Wang Family Village woman who most pleased Wang Lianfang was Youqing's wife. When he wasn't dealing with village class issues, she was the subject of all his thoughts. For him she was a true bodhisattva. In bed it was as if there were no bones in her limp body, which seemed electrically charged. Yes, indeed, he'd found a true bodhisattva. In the spring of 1971, good news cascaded down on Wang like a sow expelling a litter of piglets: first he was given a son, then Yumi found a future husband, and now he was the beneficiary of the spark plug in Youqing's wife.

Peng Guoliang's return letter traveled far. First to Wang Family Village Elementary School and then to Gao Suqin before it landed in Yumi's hand. She was washing diapers at the pier nearest the school when it arrived. In the past she had done the washing at the pier near her house, but that had changed, for once a girl has something on her mind, she prefers doing things away from home. With her back bent, she scrubbed the diapers, each of them soft and pale as if they were burdened with worry. As her hands busied themselves with work, Yumi's mind was consumed by Peng's return letter and what it might reveal. She tried to predict what he would say to her, but of course, she couldn't imagine the future. That brought her no small measure of sadness, for in the end, her fate was in the hands of someone whose inclinations remained a mystery.

And then Gao Suqin came out to wash some clothes. With a wooden bucket on her hip, she negotiated the stone steps, one slow step at a time, looking like someone in possession of rare knowledge. The sight threw Yumi into a minor panic, as if her teacher had a hold over her. But Gao looked down and simply smiled. Yumi sensed what was about to happen, though the smile was only a prelude to silence. So, it appeared, nothing was about to happen after all. What a disappointment. Yumi could only smile back. What else could she do? In fact, Yumi admired and respected Gao Suqin more than anyone she knew. Gao could speak standard Mandarin, and she turned the classroom into a giant radio, reciting lessons from inside and sending standard Chinese words out the window. She could also demonstrate complex math solutions on the blackboard. Yumi once saw her write out a long math problem that included addition, subtraction, multiplication, and division signs, as well as parentheses and brackets. One step at a time, she drew seven or eight equal signs before producing the solution, a zero.

"Why teach something like that?" Third Aunt commented. "After all that trouble, you're left with nothing, not even a fart."

"What do you mean *nothing?*" Yumi replied. "There's a zero, isn't there?"

"All right then, tell me how much is a zero."

"Zero is *something*. It's the solution to a math problem."

Now Gao was squatting beside Yumi and smiling, which turned the wrinkles in her face to parentheses and brackets. Yumi wondered what she was adding, subtracting, multiplying, and dividing, and whether the solution might also be a zero.

Finally Gao Suqin spoke. "Yumi, how can you treat this so calmly?"

The question nearly sent Yumi's heart up into her throat, but she pretended not to have understood. She swallowed and said, "Treat what?"

Still smiling, Gao Suqin lifted a piece of laundry out of the water, straightened up, and shook the water off her hands before slipping her thumb and index finger into her pocket to extract something—an envelope. Yumi blanched.

"Our second child is too young to know that he shouldn't open the letter, but I assure you I didn't read a word of it." She handed Yumi the letter, which had indeed been opened. Too stunned, embarrassed, and outraged to say anything, Yumi rubbed her hands back and forth against her pant legs before taking the letter. Her fingers fluttered as if they had grown feathers. She could barely contain the sense of pleasure that this surprise had brought her, and yet profound disappointment seeped into her bones, for her prized letter had been opened by somebody else.

Yumi walked up the bank and turned her back on Gao to read the letter twice. Peng Guoliang had called her "Comrade Wang Yumi," a formal and lofty term of which she felt utterly unworthy. No one had ever used such a ceremonial term of address for her, and it gave her an indescribable, almost sacred sense of self-esteem. Her breathing quickened at the sight of the term "Comrade" and her blouse rippled outward with the expansion of her chest. Peng's letter then described his mission in life—to protect the blue skies above the motherland and struggle against all imperialists, revisionists, and reactionaries.

By this time Yumi was barely able to stand and was on the verge of collapse from sheer joy. The skies had always been too far off to have any consequence in her life, but now things were different, for the skies were tightly bound up with and became part of her. In her mind, the blue sky now stretched far and wide until she merged with it. But the greatest impact on her came from the phrase "struggle against the imperialists, revisionists, and reactionaries," written so casually and yet carrying such bullish force. Those imperialists, revisionists, and reactionaries were not everyday landlords or rich peasants; no, they were too distant, too powerful, and too elevated—visible and yet unfathomable, mysterious and unidentifiable. Just listen to the words—imperialists, revisionists, reactionaries. Without an airplane, you could dine on healthy meals of fish and meat all your life and still not know where to find these imperialists, revisionists, and reactionaries.

Peng's letter was all but filled with ideals and vows, with determination and hatred, but toward the end, the tone changed and he abruptly asked:

Are you willing to be with me, hand in hand, in my struggle against the imperialists, revisionists, and reactionaries?

Yumi felt as if she had been dazed by a silent, staggering blow. Gone was that feeling of sacredness as her romantic feelings began to grow, little by little, then swelling into a surging torment of emotion. The words "hand in hand" were a club, a rolling pin perhaps, pressing down her passive yet willing body each time she read the letter, flattening her out, causing her to grow increasingly light and thin.

Her face paled as she leaned against a tree trunk for support, drained of energy and finding it hard to breathe. Peng had finally broached the subject, and now the matter of her marriage was settled. The thought sent tears down her cheeks. With the icy palms of her hands, she brushed the hot tears toward her ears, but her face would not dry; more tears replaced the ones that had just been wiped away—over and over and over. Finally she gave up, crouched down, buried her face in her hands, and abandoned herself to fervent sobs that evoked a sense of joy mixed with uncertainty.

Gao Suqin, her clothes rinsed, hoisted her bucket onto her hip and moved behind Yumi.

"Enough, Yumi. Just look at yourself." Then she pointed to the river with her pursed lips. "Look, Yumi, your bucket is floating away."

Yumi stood up and gazed without actually seeing the bucket that had floated ten or fifteen yards down the river. She stood there, frozen.

"Go get it," Gao Suqin said. "If you don't hurry, you won't

retrieve it even in an airplane." Finally regaining her senses, Yumi ran down the riverbank, chasing the wind and waves.

News of Yumi's impending marriage had spread through the village by that night and quickly became the sole topic of conversation. Yumi had found an aviator whose job was to fight the imperialists, revisionists, and reactionaries. The villagers had known that a girl like her would land a good husband, but an aviator went beyond their wildest predictions. On that night there was an airplane in the mind of every girl and boy, a palm-size airplane that flickered in the distant sky, dragging a long contrail behind it. This was an astounding development. Only an airplane can fly in the blue sky, of course. Otherwise, why not try to fly an old sow or an old bull? Neither a sow nor a bull could ever rise up and soar in the clouds and be so far off that it was only the size of a palm. Impossible to imagine. The airplane not only changed Yumi, but it also changed her father. Wang Lianfang had been invested with certain powers, but they were limited to events on terra firma. Now happenings in the sky also fell under his jurisdiction. Wang Lianfang had connections in the commune, in the county government, and now in the sky as well. He was omnipotent.

As Yumi's man was more than a thousand *li* away, her romance took on the unusual aura of traversing a thousand mountains and crossing ten thousand streams; this made the relationship especially moving in the eyes of others. The two began a correspondence. Exchanging letters differs from face-to-face meetings, and while it may be exhaustive and precise, it is reminiscent of the old convention that a man and woman should avoid direct contact. And so, via the posting and receiving of letters, their relationship encompassed elegance and refinement. After all, black ink on white paper constituted their courtship, created by various strokes of a pen; and the villagers found that charming. For most of them, Yumi's was a true romance—a model but also impossible to imitate. In a word, her romance was beyond the reach of everyone else.

But they were wrong. No one knew how much Yumi suffered. She could not do without those letters, but they brought her much anxiety day and night. They became a secret torment. She had completed the elementary level of primary school and would have continued on to the advanced level and, had there been one in the village, to middle school. There was neither. So she'd had only three years of schooling at the elementary level, which meant only two years' instruction in reading.

In those years, Yumi did well in most things, but the act of writing was hard for her. And no one could have anticipated the possibility that her courtship would be carried on via the written word. One after another the letters arrived from Peng Guoliang, each one creating a need for a response, making a difficult task even more so for Yumi, an introverted young woman who, like all such women, possessed a second pair of eyes that looked inward. These inward-looking eyes illuminated every corner of her heart with extraordinary clarity. But her problem was that she could not transfer the contents of her heart onto a sheet of paper. She simply couldn't. No sentence, no word, afforded her the opportunity to say what she wanted to say. And there was no one she could ask for help. Anguished, she could only cry.

If only Peng Guoliang could be there beside her, she wouldn't need words. She could talk to him with her eyes or with her fingers, or even with her silhouette. But since that was not possible, she could only bury the imagined face-to-face meeting in her heart and restrain herself. Tender feelings filled her breast like moonbeams that blanketed and illuminated a courtyard. Reaching out with her hand, she created a shadow. But she could not grab hold of those moonbeams. She tried, but when she opened her hand, all that remained were her five fingers. The moonbeams resisted all attempts to fit into a letter.

Yumi sneaked Yuye's *New China Dictionary* out of the room. But what good would that do, since she didn't know how to use it? All those unfamiliar words were like schooling fish—knowing they were just beneath the surface did not help her find the ones she wanted. It was hard, nerve-racking work. She rapped herself on the forehead. *What's the word I want? Where do I find it?* All those missing words held her back. When they simply would not come, she stared at her paper and pen, and fell into despair. Everything she wanted to say turned to tears. With her hands clasped in front of her, she pleaded, "Why won't the heavens take pity on me? Please, please, take pity on me."

Yumi picked up Wang Hongbing and went for a walk, unable to stay another minute in the house, where she was tormented by the unrelenting thought of writing a letter. Her mind was in a fog, her energy depleted. Romance—just what is it? The concept evaded her, and all she could do was talk to Peng Guoliang in her heart. Even then, the finest words she could imagine could not be transferred onto paper. They clogged her heart, bringing only pain. She felt trapped, and there was nothing she could do about it. She was awash in a turmoil caused by sadness, anxiety, oppression, and exhaustion. Fortunately, Yumi was gifted with an extraordinary ability to keep things inside. No one knew what she was going through, even though she grew more gaunt every day.

With Hongbing in her arms, Yumi arrived at the home of Zhang Rujun, whose wife had given birth to a baby—a boy—the year before. They had much to talk about. Rujun's wife, who suffered from an eye problem, was not a pretty woman and thus held no attraction for Yumi's father, a Party secretary. Yumi was sure of that.

Which women her father was involved with, and when, never escaped Yumi's sharp eye. Any woman who treated her with uncommon courtesy immediately put her on alert. She'd had a lot of that. Behind it lay guilt and flattery, an appearance of warmth that masked a sense of dread. The courtesy would be accompanied by the nervous running of fingers through hair. But the real proof was in the eyes, which darted around as if wanting to take in everything while daring to look at nothing, like those of a cornered rat. *Go ahead, be as courteous as you like,* Yumi would think, *you shameless slut. All those nice manners do not alter the fact that you're a trollop, cheap goods.* No friendly look from Yumi ever greeted those women. The funny thing was, the more obvious Yumi's frosty look, the more polite the women became; that, in turn, only increased the intensity of Yumi's look. *You deserve nothing less, you stinking whore. All good-looking women are trash.* If Wang Lianfang hadn't emptied his virility into their bodies, Mama would not have had so many girls. As for Yuxiu, the pretty daughter, Yumi predicted that she'd one day be unable to keep her belt on snugly as well, even though she was Yumi's natural sister.

Rujun's wife was different. She was not pretty, but she was a person of substance; her every action befitted a true woman. She conducted herself in an appropriate, tasteful manner, and her eyes never betrayed a hint of evasiveness. She was not an ignorant woman, which was why Yumi found it so easy to talk to her. But there was another reason why Yumi treated her so well: Her husband was a Zhang, not a Wang. All the residents of Wang Family Village shared one of two surnames: Wang or Zhang. Yumi's grandfather had told her of the fierce enmity between the two clans, an entrenched hatred that had led to many fights and at least a few deaths. One evening, when Wang Lianfang was home drinking with some village cadres, the name Zhang came up, sparking him to pound the table. "Two surnames isn't the problem," he said. "We're talking about two distinct classes."

Yumi, who happened to be in the kitchen lighting a fire in the stove, heard every word. Currently the two clans lived in peace and enjoyed an atmosphere of relative tranquility with no outward signs of discord. And yet people had died in the past, a fact that could not be brushed away. The dead had borne their rage into the grave, and one day it would sprout anew. However placid things seemed, however harmonious the surface or calm the winds, a powerful undercurrent of hostility lay hidden deep in the hearts of the Zhang clan. They always addressed Yumi's father as Secretary Wang, but just because the enmity was not in full view did not negate its existence. If every important matter were out in the open, people would not be people; they'd be more like pigs and dogs. And so Yumi used the more common forms of address with members of the Wang clan, reserving such intimate terms as "sister" and "aunty" for members of the Zhang clan. She kept outsiders close, like family, precisely because they couldn't be trusted like family.

Cradling her baby brother, Yumi had a casual conversation with Sister Zhang just inside the gate. Rujun's wife, who had been holding her own son when she spotted Yumi, quickly carried the boy inside and returned with a stool. She reached out to take Hongbing. "A change will do you good," she said when Yumi held back. "Food from a neighbor's pot always tastes better."

Yumi sat down and glanced at the end of the lane. That glance did not escape Rujun's wife, who knew that the visit, like others in recent days, had more to do with where she lived than who she was, for her house was an ideal vantage point to spot the arrival of the postman. She did not, however, let on and chose instead to sing the praises of little Wang Hongbing. There are countless ways to make a mistake; heaping praise on someone's child is not one of them. She and her visitor had been chatting about a variety of things for a while, when Rujun's wife saw Yumi sit up tall and peer over her head. Knowing that someone was coming their way, Rujun's wife lowered her head and listened carefully.

When the familiar sound of a bicycle chain did not materialize, she knew it wasn't the postman. No need to be concerned. Suddenly laughter erupted behind her, so Rujun's wife turned to see who was coming. It was a clutch of youngsters, their heads bunched together as they fought to peek at something. They were as excited as if they'd seen a table groaning with food. Slowly they approached Rujun's house as Jianguo, called Little Five, looked up and spotted Yumi. He waved and shouted, "Come here, Yumi, it's a letter from Peng Guoliang."

Not sure if she should believe him, Yumi went up to Little Five. Excitedly, he held an envelope out to her with one hand and a letter with the other. A quick glance satisfied her that it was Peng Guoliang's handwriting. It was her letter, a letter from her aviator. The blood rushed to her head. Beside herself with embarrassment, she felt as if she were being paraded through town naked. "I don't want it," she shouted. As soon as Little Five saw the look on her face, he folded the letter, stuffed it into the envelope, and licked the flap closed before holding it out to her. She knocked it out of his hand. He bent down, picked it up, and said, "It's yours, honest. It's to you from Peng Guoliang."

This time Yumi snatched it out of his hand and flung it to the ground. "You and your whole family can drop dead," she said, stunning everyone standing in the lane. This was not the Yumi they knew. They had never seen her blow up like this. It was serious. Uncle Pockface, who lived in the lane, heard the disturbance and came over, holding one finger in the air. With an angry look, he walked up to Little Five, bent down, and picked up the letter.

"Spit's no good. See, it's open again."

He sealed the envelope with pasty kernels of rice and held it out to Yumi. "Now that's taken care of," he said.

"But they all read it!"

Uncle Pockface laughed. "My son Xingwang is in the army, and when he writes home, I have to ask someone to read his letter for me."

Speechless, Yumi just trembled.

"You can have the nicest clothes in the world, but when you put them on, people will see them," Uncle Pockface said.

Somehow that made perfect sense. He smiled, his eyes turned to slits, and the pockmarks on his face went from round to oval. But Yumi's heart was in shreds. Gao Suqin had opened two of Yumi's letters, so Yumi had asked Peng Guoliang to stop writing to her care of her teacher. What good had that done? In recent days people had mentioned all kinds of peculiar things to her, some of which sounded suspiciously like what had been in his letters. At first, she'd thought she was being overly sensitive, but not now. The whole village was reading his letters before they reached her. Why wear clothes if people's eyes seemed to be growing out of her navel? Everything about her, it seemed, was an open secret. After his attempt to make her feel better, Uncle Pockface went home. But by then, Yumi's face was drained of color and two lines of tears glistened in the sunlight like long, shiny scars. Rujun's wife, who had witnessed it all, did not know what to do and was suddenly fearful. For some strange reason, she opened her blouse, freed one of her breasts, and stuck the nipple in Wang Hongbing's mouth.

Youqing's wife had come from Li Ming Village, once known as Willow River Village. The government had renamed it in honor of Li Ming, a villager who had been martyred in 1948. Prior to her arrival in Wang Family Village, Youqing's wife, whose maiden name was Liu Fenxiang, had earned a reputation as a singer who could reach even the highest notes. The natural charm and appeal of her smile allowed her to win over every listener. Her appearance, too, was special. Dark skin enhanced her beauty, which had none of the contrived qualities of city girls. A cleft chin and a perfectly round mole below her mouth and to the right gave her a slightly seductive look. But the real standouts were her eyes. Free of the sluggish, dull look of a country girl, they were lively and expressive, capable of sending suggestive messages as she gazed from side to side.

This, people said, was a bad habit she'd picked up performing in a propaganda troupe. Liu Fenxiang would shut her eyes before she laughed, causing her lashes to flutter briefly. Then she'd open her eyes, cock her head, and laugh. Li Ming villagers summed up her laughter by calling it "a wanton sound and a coquettish look, typical of a low-class woman." Thus there were two sides to Fenxiang's renown, one of them, obviously, not good. "She's a girl you want to avoid," people said in private. It was an ambiguous comment, with multiple interpretations, a case of "The mutt can't mount the bitch unless she offers herself up." In other words, once she got her claws into someone, she could do what she pleased.

There is plenty of talk like that. Everything is fine so long as it remains unspoken; but once it's out in the open, it gains credibility and can inflict mortal injury. All comments aside, Liu Fenxiang came to Wang Family Village as a bride with child; that was an indisputable fact. Some of the more perceptive women pointed out knowingly, "At least four months along. Just look at her buttocks." The father's identity was a mystery and according to the least-generous view, even she could not be sure. It so happened that during those days Fenxiang had performed with the troupe at all the nearby communes, where men had taken turns pressing down on her body. All that flattening eventually had turned to swelling. That's a woman for you: neither her belly nor her mouth can keep a secret. For Liu Fenxiang, her belly was her ruin—and cost her her good name; and Wang Youqing was the beneficiary. When this unexpected good fortune fell from the sky, he could not have been happier.

The wedding arrangements outpaced the swelling of Fenxiang's belly. They demanded both great speed and steely determination, and took less time to complete than it would to describe them. Word of Wang Youqing's betrothal didn't even make the rounds before Liu Fenxiang of Li Ming Village became a Wang Family Village housewife. She arrived without a trousseau; but even if Wang Youqing had been able to afford it, why waste rations on clothes that will fit only for a short while?

In the end, Youqing's new wife did not deliver the child. After a bad fall she began to bleed, and that night she miscarried. Suspicion—and nothing more concrete than that, since there were no witnesses—arose that her mother-in-law "accidentally bumped into her from behind" and sent her tumbling off a footbridge. It happened soon after Fenxiang joined Youqing's family, on a day when she and her mother-in-law were walking across the bridge, chatting happily like mother and daughter. Just before they reached the riverbank, her mother-in-law stumbled and bumped into her from behind. While the older woman managed to keep her feet, her daughter-in-law landed hard on the riverbank.

Fenxiang spent the next month laid up in bed, lovingly attended by her mother-in-law, who saw to it that she ate a half *jin* of brown sugar and a whole chicken every day. "Our Fenxiang sprained her hip in the fall," she told people. She was clever to a fault, and clever people have a common failing: they are given to calling attention to things that are better kept under wraps. Everyone knew that Youqing's wife was laid up from a miscarriage.

So came the strange consequence that Fenxiang entered the marriage pregnant, but never carried Youqing's child. Two years had passed since then, and Youqing's wife's figure was, if anything, slimmer than ever. Distraught over the lack of a grandchild, Youqing's mother grumbled in front of her son: "Now I see. This girl does what she shouldn't do and does not do what she should. Productive outside, lazy at home."

Stung by the comment, Youqing had no idea how to respond. Basically a decent man, he decided his only recourse was to work harder in bed, giving it his all. His "all" fell short. But his biggest mistake was to repeat what his mother had said. His wife was livid and immediately attributed the comment to her gossipy mother-in-law. Youqing was too simple and too decent to come up with anything that evil, that hurtful. Deeply angered, Fenxiang flung curses at her husband, all indirectly aimed at his mother. And, never one to let a matter drop, she demanded that his mother move out: "It's her or it's me, you choose."

On the day she swept her mother-in-law out of the house, Fenxiang fired a ruthless parting shot: "You old cunt, you'll never again hold a man between your legs." Yet, if the truth be known, her mother-in-law's comment had not been altogether unreasonable. The longer the daughter-in-law went without having a child, the uglier the villagers' comments grew, many of them aimed at Youqing himself. All mothers come to the defense of their sons, which is why his had complained about her daughter-in-law. "Youqing doesn't appear to be a virile fellow," the villagers were saying.

The truth is, Youqing's wife believed she was incurably barren. But since he had redoubled his efforts in bed, she did not have the heart to tell him. The doctor had made it clear that the miscarriage had done too much damage. But that had not stopped her from trying. She undertook a regimen of herbal preparations, staying with it for nearly four months. Nothing worked, in part because she had an aversion to traditional Chinese medicine—not the taste, but something else. The common practice was to take the dregs of herbal preparations outside and dump them in the middle of a road to be stepped on by passersby, who would crush them into the dirt; then and only then would the treatment prove effective. But Youqing's wife did not want anyone to know that she was taking the medicine, for that would make her vulnerable to all sorts of gossip. Everything had to be done in secret.

Luckily for her, as the former member of a propaganda troupe, she had promoted the philosophy of materialism and was impervious to the attractions of superstition. She merely dumped the dregs in the river. Her attempts to keep her regimen secret, however, were easily thwarted by the aromas of the herbal concoctions she cooked up, which traveled farther than the smell of an old hen being stewed. The minute she started brewing the herbs, people's heads would pop up in the yard, and they would slip gazes more lethal than arsenic through the cracks in the doorway. Over time, Youqing's wife felt more like a sneak thief than a follower of Chinese medicine, which doubled the bitter taste of whatever she was taking. In the end, she gave it up. That sort of bitterness she could do without.

Her affair with Wang Lianfang had not yet begun by the

time people started talking about them. It was not until the winter of 1970 that he began climbing onto her body. In the spring of 1971, the affair was still in its early stages. Their first meeting—out on the street—had occurred not long after her brief period of recuperation. Wang's eyes bespoke compassion, but Youqing's wife needed only a single glance to know exactly what was on his mind. Men in official positions customarily use a cordial smile as an invitation to sex, and Youqing's wife knew how to treat men like Wang. She responded with a bashful smile, confident in the knowledge that eventually he would take her to bed. It was a foregone conclusion, one that fit perfectly with the plan already forming in her mind. She would give Youqing a child; one way or another she would have his baby before having sex with Wang Lianfang, which was going to happen sooner or later. But it should be later. Men are like burglars: the easier the entry, the faster the departure. She'd learned this from experience, and the lessons of history must not be forgotten.

Wang Lianfang, on the other hand, was impatient. That became clear to her soon after they met when he desperately tried to create opportunities to be alone with her. Say what you will, he was not a man given to reckless behavior in public. Cats instinctively wait for nightfall; dogs know to hide in corners. If Wang Lianfang showed up in front of her house, Youqing's wife would go next door for some boiled water, excitedly and loudly proclaiming, "Well, look who's come to see us, it's Party Secretary Wang." In the face of such excitement, Wang Lianfang had to suppress his anger and react with a warm and friendly smile. By keeping things out in the open, Youqing's wife differed from the other women, who were almost pathologically cautious. Her way was better, effectively delaying the day when he would mount her and push her head down as a rooster does to a hen.

One day he decided to broach the subject directly: "Youqing is a fool. I wonder if I'll ever be lucky enough to enjoy the benefits of his sort of dumb luck." Youqing's wife felt her heart lurch. She was not unmoved by his comment, but she pretended that she'd missed the obvious and responded in a loud voice that made Wang very nervous. She was careful not to overdo it, since she wanted to keep him on a string and not scare him into retreating. If he lost hope, she would ultimately wind up more hopeless than he. She knew what she was—a lazy woman. Lazy people need someone to depend on. Without that, they are condemned to live out their days in a dreary anticipation of death.

The head of production had assigned Youqing's wife to the fertilizer detail, a dirty, tiring job that earned relatively few work points. The assignment had been intended as a warning. So, with a rake over her shoulder, she joined a team of men as they headed out to the fields in high spirits. Wang Lianfang was walking toward them, so greetings were exchanged. They'd continued a dozen or so steps past him when Youqing's wife suddenly turned and caught up with Wang. She reached out to brush some dandruff off his collar and fingered a loose thread. But instead of pulling it out with her hand, she leaned over and bit it off, then knotted it with her tongue and spat it out seductively.

"You don't look a damned bit like a Party secretary," she said in a low voice. "Why don't you go out and rake fertilizer for me?"

It may have been a silly comment, but it had a stunning effect on Wang Lianfang, who was so overjoyed his eyes glazed over.

Needless to say, Youqing's wife did not work with the fertilizer detail that day. Standing at the head of one row, she took off her green-checked head scarf, scrunched it up in her hands, and said, "This won't do. I'm heading back."

Hoisting the rake over her shoulder in full view of the head of production, she took off for home, swishing her hips like a set of tractor tires. No one tried to stop her. Who knew what she'd meant by "This won't do"? And what was she "heading back" to do?

By this point Youqing's wife had given up hope. There would be no more pregnancies for her. Youqing, too, had brought his efforts to an end; nothing he had tried worked. Feeling put out and unhappy, he had left for the irrigation site on the day that Wang Lianfang came by at noon. Youqing's wife had just had a good cry over how badly her life seemed to be turning out. How had it come to this?

"Where did I go wrong?"

She'd had such high hopes, loved being in the spotlight, and was eager to excel, only to see everything turn out horribly, not at all what she'd expected. The future looked dismal. Wang Lianfang walked in with his hands clasped behind his back and shut the door. He stood there looking as if he had already bedded her. Not surprised by his visit, she stood up, thinking she ought to be pleased. He could have just about any woman he wanted, and yet she had been on his mind all along; he clearly liked her.

So why not? He was the best-looking man in Wang Family Village, well dressed, always said the right thing, and had nice, clean teeth that were, she figured, brushed daily. Her shoulders sagged with those thoughts, and she cast a sad look at Wang as tears spilled from her eyes. Slowly she turned and shuffled into the bedroom, where she eased her buttocks down on the edge of the bed. Lowering her head and stretching out her neck, she began to undress. When she was finished, she looked up and said, "All right, come on."

Youqing's wife was no ordinary woman; she'd seen a bit of the world and, as such, had no reason to fear Wang Lianfang. This attitude alone was enough to make her superior to other women. Everyone was afraid of Wang, and that's just the way he wanted it. Their fear was deep-seated, not just an outward performance, which he especially liked. He had ways of dealing with people who felt differently and would not stop working on them until they feared him as much as everyone else did. But the unintended consequence of this inspired fear was that the women he took to bed either shuddered during sex or lay there like dead fish, afraid to move, keeping their arms and legs close to their bodies as if Wang were a hog butcher. Not much fun in that. But, to his surprise, Youqing's wife was not the least bit afraid of him and, more to the point, she enjoyed sex.

As soon as it began, she displayed a unique talent for taking the initiative. If it's wind you want, it's wind you'll get, and if you prefer rain, happy to oblige. She did things no one else dared to do and said things no one else was willing to say. She was a wild woman from start to finish, and when it was over, she lay on her side and wept. It was impossible not to feel sorry for her and, at the same time, hunger for more. This was a technique she employed to great effect. She was a cut of meat Wang Lianfang loved to chew on, and he was a man of considerable appetites, which she satisfied.

Utterly spent, Wang Lianfang lay on top of Youqing's wife and dozed off. When he awoke he saw that he'd left a string of saliva on her cheek. He reached for his overcoat and took a bottle of little white pills from the pocket. Youqing's wife was impressed with his preparations; obviously, he never fought battles for which he was unprepared. "Try one, my dear," Wang said with a little laugh. "It'll keep you out of trouble."

"Not me," she replied. "I plan to present Wang Family Village with a little Party secretary. You take it." No one had ever dared talk to Wang Lianfang that way.

"What nerve!" Wang said with another little laugh.

Youqing's wife turned her head and refused to take the pill, silently commanding Wang to take it instead. With a look of frustration, he did. Then she took one and watched as he spat his into his hand and laughed again. So she puckered her lips and smiled, slowly revealing a little white pill caught between her two front teeth. Wang responded with a happy display of anger, the sort of vexation to which only a man of a certain age has access. "You're making things hard on me," he said as he popped his pill in his mouth and swallowed, then opened his mouth wide for inspection. With the tip of her tongue, Youqing's wife moved the pill back into her mouth, then a gurgle came from her throat. She stuck her tongue out for Wang's inspection. Her tongue, bright red and nicely pointed at the tip like a skinned fox, moved deftly and mischievously—a bit of sexual provocation. Throwing his arms around her, Wang clamped his teeth on the extended tongue. As she quivered, she knocked the bottle of pills to the floor, where it shattered and sent its contents rolling in all directions. The pills spread like a starry night in summer and the noise gave them both a start.

"Good," she said, drawing a shout from Wang as he started in again, after which she spat out the pill she'd hidden in her mouth. No need for me to take any of those, she said to herself. I don't have that kind of luck. The thought saddened her, for it was a miserable acknowledgment that she was not doing right by either herself or by her husband. But she forced herself to drive that thought out of her mind and moved in concert with Wang. Wrapping her arms around his neck, she hung on and whispered into his ear, "Be good to me, Lianfang."

"I'll try my best," he said.

Tears formed in her eyes.

"Be good to me, Lianfang."

"I said I'll try my best." They repeated themselves over and over until she was sobbing, so choked up she couldn't utter a complete sentence. Wang Lianfang was beside himself with joy.

Wang Lianfang had gotten his first taste of what he was after; like a stubborn mule, he circled Youqing's wife, his millstone. Youqing was usually at the irrigation site, and time was of the essence. But fate controls the affairs of humans, no matter how cleverly they make their plans. What happened one afternoon proves the point: Youqing came home unexpectedly. When he walked in the door he found his wife stark naked, one leg resting on the bed frame and the other dangling over the chamber pot lid. Wang Lianfang, also naked, was standing there, stuck to Youqing's wife and swollen with arrogance. As he stood in the doorway staring blankly at the scene, Youqing was too stunned to comprehend what was happening. Wang Lianfang abruptly stopped moving and looked over his shoulder. "Youqing," he said, when he saw who it was, "go outside and rest awhile. I'll be finished soon, and you can come back."

Youqing turned and walked out. The bedroom door, the front door, and the gate were all wide open when Wang left. He closed each of them on his way out. *That Youqing,* he said to himself, *doesn't even know how to close a door.*

Liu Fenxiang now became the primary object of Yumi's attacks. She had become enemy number one. How could Yumi forgive a woman who made her father act like a bridegroom, dutifully shaving and combing his hair every morning before he went out? By then he had all but stopped talking to his wife, and the way he looked at her made Yumi shudder. Shi Guifang, who spent most of every day cracking and eating sunflower seeds in the doorway, no longer looked as if she belonged to the family. As far as Wang Lianfang was concerned, now that she'd given him a son she pretty much ceased to exist. He even started spending the night with Youqing's wife. Yumi experienced bitter disappointment on behalf of her mother, but she could only stand by and watch. It was not the sort of thing she could talk about. And who was to blame? The slut, that's who. It was all the doing of that slut. What Yumi felt toward Youqing's wife went beyond loathing.

Yumi's feelings toward Youqing's wife were complex. Admittedly, she hated her, but it was more than that. There was something that set her apart from other women: a strength unknown in the village, something the other women lacked, something they could see but could not describe. Even Wang Lianfang seemed humbled in her presence.

Liu Fenxiang was exceptional; she rose above everyone else. And it was that indescribable something that fed the people's indignation. There were, for instance, the tone of her voice and the way she smiled when she talked, a mannerism the younger women of the village gradually began to imitate. Though no one pointed it out or called attention to it, it was there, and that characterized the power she possessed. In effect, everyone in the village liked her.

The men had nothing good to say about Fenxiang, but deep down they were fond of her. Their voices changed when they spoke to her, and not even a scolding from their wives made a difference, since it would be forgotten by the next morning. Though she would be the last to admit it, Yumi was jealous. That was why her loathing ran so deep. She wanted nothing more than to carry Wang Hongbing up to Fenxiang's front door, as she had with the other women; but Youqing's wife made no attempt to be secretive and even flaunted her relationship with Wang Lianfang. Since she thought nothing of chatting with Wang out on the street, what was to be gained by standing in front of her house? The woman was so brazen it was impossible to shame her; not even the presence of Little Eight could do that.

But Yumi wound up going over to her house anyway. *You can't have children,* she said to herself, *and that is your weakness. I'll hit you where it hurts.* So, with little Hongbing in her arms, Yumi strolled casually up to Fenxiang's door, followed by a crowd of women, some with motives, others merely curious. There was tension in the air mixed with excitement. Rather than shut the door and cower inside when she saw Yumi coming, Youqing's wife strode out confidently. She did not have to try to look calm—she was truly unruffled. The first thing she did was come up and begin talking to some of her visitors. Yumi avoided looking at her, and Fenxiang returned the favor—not even sneaking a glance at the girl. In fact, the first stolen glance came from Yumi. Before Yumi had a chance to say a word, Youqing's wife was already talking to the other women about Hongbing—mainly about his appearance. She was saying that he had his mother's mouth and would be better looking if he had his father's.

It was a provocative move, heaping excessive praise on Wang Lianfang's mouth. "But he'll get better looking as he grows up," she continued. "Boys always take after their mothers when they're small. Then, after they start to fill out and head toward manhood, they more and more closely resemble their fathers."

Fenxiang kept talking. "And Hongbing's ears stick out a little too much." Yumi did not want to hear any more of that. Actually, if anything, Youqing's wife's ears protruded more than the boy's did, so Yumi turned and said rudely: "Why don't you go take a look in the mirror?"

It was a comment that would have put another woman to shame, producing an embarrassed look worse than tears. Youqing's wife acted as if she hadn't heard. The minute the words were out of her mouth, Yumi knew she'd fallen into the woman's trap by speaking first.

Youqing's wife kept talking to the other women and not looking Yumi's way. "Yumi is such a pretty girl," she was saying. "Too bad she has such a sharp tongue."

She hadn't said that Yumi was a "pretty little thing" or a "pretty youngster." No, she'd used the slightly more refined "pretty girl," as if Yumi were a virtual phoenix that had flown out of a chicken coop. She then changed the direction of the conversation by speaking up for Yumi. "If I were Yumi, I'd be the same way." In the face of such a sincere comment Yumi could say nothing. She already felt like an unmannered shrew. By calling Yumi pretty, Fenxiang settled the matter. Youqing's wife and one of the other women then turned to an appraisal of Yumi's sister, Yuxiu, ending with a comment by Youqing's wife: "Yumi is the graceful sister. Her looks grow on you." That gave the discussion a note of finality.

Yumi knew that the woman was playing up to her, though Fenxiang's expression didn't show it. Not once did she look at Yumi as she spoke, which gave the impression that she was voicing her true feelings. This actually pleased Yumi, but the woman's tone of voice angered her. She spoke as if she and she alone were the voice of authority, that whatever she said was true and therefore not open to discussion. How could something like that not make Yumi angry? Who did she think she was? She was a rotten plaything, and that was all. With a grunt of disapproval, Yumi asked sarcastically, "Pretty?" She attacked the word with ferocity, investing it with a richness of possibilities yet turning it into a dirty word at the same time and all but exterminating it.

That done, she turned and walked off, leaving a clutch of frustrated women in her wake. This first duel with Youqing's wife had ended inconclusively, with neither emerging as the victor. But, Yumi thought, *Time is on my side. You came to the village as a bride, so I've got your number. Your pinkie is stuck in the Wang Family Village door, and that is where it'll stay.*

Peng Guoliang had originally planned to return to his ancestral home during the busy summer months. But his grandfather could not wait that long—he stopped breathing shortly after the arrival of spring. As they say, "The road down to Yellow Springs waits for no one." After receiving a telegram, Peng returned to his village earlier than he'd anticipated. But after he had returned to Peng Family Village, Yumi heard nothing from him. Then, four days after the body had been placed in the coffin and the first seven-day rites were completed, Peng Guoliang removed his mourning garments and sent word that he was coming to meet Yumi. The news threw her into a panic, but it wasn't Peng's fault that the visit was unplanned. The problem was, Yumi did not have anything decent to wear. With few choices, she settled on her New Year's dress. But she'd worn that over a padded jacket, and when she tried it on without the jacket, the dress was much too big and made her look ludicrous and ugly. There was no time to make a new one, for that would require a trip into town to buy fabric. Disconsolate, she was on the verge of tears, but her happiness over the impending visit prevented the tears from flowing—and that depressed her even more.

Yumi was caught off guard when Youqing's wife stopped her on the street, as if there were no bad blood between them, as if they were meeting for the first time in days and happy to do so.

"You must hate me, Yumi," she blurted out before Yumi could say a word.

Never expecting the woman to bring it up like that, Yumi was speechless.

What a shameless woman, Yumi said to herself. No one but Fenxiang would say something like that even if they wore their pants over their face to cover their embarrassment.

"How can you dress like that when your aviator is on his way to meet you?" Youqing's wife asked.

Yumi stared at her, paused, and then said, "I'll never have to worry about getting married if men find someone like you attractive." This thoroughly shocked Youqing's wife. It was such a vicious slap in the face that even Yumi felt she might have gone too far. But how else could she even the score with so shameless a woman?

Youqing's wife took a cloth bundle out from under her arm and handed it to Yumi. She had, no doubt, prepared a little speech to go with the gift, but Yumi's comment had so unsettled her she momentarily forgot what she was going to say and she silently thrust the package into Yumi's hands.

"I wore this when I was with the propaganda troupe," she said at last. "I don't have any more use for it."

This was the last thing Yumi had expected, and it seemed somehow improper. But whatever the woman's motive, Yumi could not and would not accept the gift. She handed it back unopened. "A woman can be proud, Yumi," Youqing's wife said, "but not arrogant. The only opportunity for even the most talented woman lies in marriage. This is yours, so don't let the opportunity slip through your fingers. You don't want to wind up like me."

The reference to marriage as her only opportunity had the

desired effect on Yumi. This time Youqing's wife pressed the bundle into Yumi's arms and walked off. But she'd only taken four or five steps when she turned and, with tears glistening in her eyes and looking quite heartbroken, smiled sadly. "Don't wind up like me," she repeated. This comment surprised Yumi. Suddenly the woman no longer seemed so overbearing. Who'd have thought that she could have such a low opinion of herself? Yumi found it hard to believe that the woman could feel such bitterness, and she nearly softened her attitude toward Fenxiang. The simple act of the woman's turning back had brought Yumi pain. She had to consider the encounter as a victory, but in a way it was a lackluster one, though she could not have said why. As Yumi stood in the street looking at the bundle in her hands, Youqing's wife's words swirled in her head.

Yumi felt like throwing the gift away, but its history as a propaganda troupe costume—even though it had been worn by Youqing's wife—held a special attraction for her. It was a spring-and-autumn blouse with a turned-down collar and a fitted waistline. Though she and Youqing's wife had similar figures, the blouse seemed a bit tight in the waist. But when she looked in the mirror, Yumi nearly jumped out of her skin. She'd never looked so good—as pretty as a city girl. Girls in the countryside tend to have bent backs, sunken chests, and prominent hip bones because of the years spent carrying heavy loads on their shoulders. But not Yumi.

Standing straight and tall and graced with a full figure, she was able to wear nice clothing as it was meant to be worn. Her figure and the blouse were complementary—they each improved the other. How does the saying go? "A woman needs her clothes; a horse needs its saddle."

But the most stunning effect came from the bustline, where the blouse made her natural curves seem more prominent—as if she were wearing nothing at all. Her breasts jutted out as if they were capable of suckling everyone in the village. Liu Fenxiang must have had a lovely figure back then. No matter how hard she tried, Yumi could not keep from imagining what Youqing's wife had looked like as a young woman. And the images she conjured up were replicated in herself—and that spelled danger. Reluctantly, she took off the blouse and looked at it from all angles as she held it up. She still felt like throwing it away, but she could not bring herself to do so. A sense of self-loathing began to creep in. How, she wondered, could she be so firm in other things, but see her resolve fail over a blouse? *I'll put it aside*, she said to herself, *but I'll be damned if I'll wear it.*

Peng Guoliang arrived at Yumi's door in the company of Party Secretary Peng. When Shi Guifang, who was standing in the doorway as usual, saw Secretary Peng walking up with a young man in uniform, she knew what was happening. Standing up straight after putting away her sunflower seeds, she welcomed them with a ready smile. "Sister-in-law," Secretary Peng addressed her when he reached the door. Peng Guoliang stood to attention and saluted stiffly. With a wave of her arm, Shi Guifang invited her guests in. Her prospective son-in-law had made a wonderful first impression despite the excessively formal salute. Initially tongue-tied, all Shi Guifang could do was smile. But fortunately for her, as the wife of a Party secretary, she was not easily flustered. She flipped on the PA system. "Wang Lianfang," she said into the microphone, "please return home at once. The People's Liberation Army is here." She repeated the announcement.

The broadcast was an announcement to the whole village. Within minutes, men and women—young and old, tall and short, fat and skinny—crowded around Shi Guifang's gate. No one needed to be told what she'd meant by announcing the People's Liberation Army. In time Wang Lianfang appeared, buttoning up his collar as the crowd made room for him to stride energetically up to Secretary Peng. They shook hands.

Peng Guoliang snapped to attention and saluted once again. Wang Lianfang reacted by taking out a pack of cigarettes and handing one to each of his visitors. With yet another snappy salute, the younger man said, "Sir, Peng Guoliang respectfully reports that he does not smoke."

Wang met the announcement with a laugh. "Good," he said, "that's good." With one courtesy on top of another, the atmosphere seemed formal, tense even. "So, you're back," Wang Lianfang said.

"Yes," Peng Guoliang replied. Even the crowd outside the door appeared affected by the mood inside, for no one said a word. Peng Guoliang had impressed them with his smart salutes, all perfectly executed, smooth but decisive and resolute.

The arrival of Yumi would bring the story to a climax. She was dragged along after the women had taken Wang Hongbing from her and opened a path to her home. This was a scene they had long anticipated, and once it was acted out they could breathe easier. So they walked her home, one step at a time; all she had to do was lean back and let the others do the work. But when she reached her gate, her courage abandoned her, and she refused to take another step. So a couple of the bolder unmarried girls pushed her up until she was standing in front of Peng Guoliang.

The crowd thought that he might actually salute her, but he didn't. There was total silence. He didn't salute, and he didn't snap to attention. He was, in fact, barely able to stand, and he kept opening and shutting his mouth. When Yumi stole a look at him, the expression on his face put her at ease, though she fidgeted bashfully. Beet-red cheeks made her eyes seem darker, highlighting their sparkle as her gaze darted here and there. To the villagers outside the door she was a pitiful sight, and they could hardly believe that the shy girl they were looking at was actually Yumi. In the end, it seemed, she was a girl like any other. So, with a few lusty shouts from the crowd, the climax passed and the tense mood dissipated. Of course they were happy for Peng Guoliang, but mostly they were happy for Yumi.

Wang Lianfang walked out to treat the men in the crowd to cigarettes and even offered one to the son of Zhang Rujun, who was cradled in his mother's arms, looking foolish as only a baby can. Wang tucked the cigarette behind the boy's ear. "Take it home and give it to your daddy," he said. The people had never seen Wang be so cordial; it was almost as if he were joking with them. A chorus of laughter made for a delightful atmosphere before Wang shooed the crowd away and, with a sigh of relief, shut the door behind him.

Shi Guifang sent Peng Guoliang and Yumi into the kitchen to boil some water. As an experienced housewife, she knew the importance of a kitchen to a young couple. First meetings always turned out the same, with a pair of timid, unfamiliar youngsters seated behind the stove, one pumping the bellows while the other added firewood until the heat turned their faces red and slowly loosened them up. So Guifang closed the kitchen door and told Yuying and Yuxiu to go outside. The last thing she wanted was for the other girls to hang around the house. Except for Yumi, not one of her daughters knew how to behave around people.

While Yumi was lighting the fire, Peng Guoliang gave her a second gift. The first gift, in accordance with age-old customs, had to be a bolt of fabric, some knitting yarn, or something along those lines. But he also presented her with a second set of gifts, proving that he was different from others. He gave her a red Hero fountain pen and a bottle of Hero blue-black ink, a pad of forty-weight letter paper, twenty-five envelopes, and a Chairman Mao pin that glowed in the dark. There was a hint of intimacy attached to all of the gifts, each of which also represented a cultured and progressive spirit.

He placed them all on top of the bellows next to his army cap—its star shining bright and deep red. With all these items arrayed on the bellows, silence spoke more loudly than words. Peng Guoliang worked the bellows, each forceful squeeze heating up the fire in the stove. Flames rose into the air like powerful pillars each time he brought his hands together. For her part, Yumi added rice straw to the pillars of fire, moving in concert with Peng Guoliang as if by design and creating an affecting tableau.

When the straw fell from the tongs onto the flames, it leaped into the air first, then wilted and turned transparent before finally regaining color, creating both heat and light. Their faces and chests were reddened rhythmically by the flames; the rising and falling of their chests, too, had a rhythmic quality that required some adjustment and extra control. The air was so hot and in such constant oscillation it was as if private suns hung above their heads and all but baked them joyously in a sort of heated tenderness. Their emotions were in chaos, rising and falling in their breasts. There was at least a little confusion, and there was something in the air that could easily have led to tears, here one moment and gone the next. Yumi knew she was in love, and as she gazed into the fire, she could not stop the flow of hot tears. Peng Guoliang noticed, but said nothing. Taking out his handkerchief, he placed it on Yumi's knee. But instead of using it to dry her tears, she held it up to her nose. It smelled faintly of bath soap and nearly made her cry out loud. She managed to hold back, but that only increased the flow of tears. Up to that moment they had not exchanged a single word and hadn't touched one another, not even a finger. That suited Yumi perfectly. This is what love is supposed to be, she told herself, quietly sitting close but not touching—remote but in silent harmony. Close at hand, though longing in earnest and calling to mind some distant place—all as it should be.

Yumi's glance fell on Peng Guoliang's foot, which she could see was a size forty-two. No question about it. She already knew his sizes, all of them. When a girl falls for a boy, her eyes become a measuring tape. Her gaze stretches out to take measurements and then, when that's done, snaps right back.

Custom dictated that Peng Guoliang not stay under the same roof with Yumi before she became his wife. But Wang Lianfang was used to breaking rules and was dedicated to transforming social traditions. "You'll stay here," he announced, for he took pleasure in seeing Peng Guoliang walk in and out of the yard; his presence created an aura of power around the house and brought Wang high honor.

"It's not proper," Shi Guifang said softly.

Wang Lianfang glared at her and said sternly, "That's metaphysical nonsense."

So Peng Guoliang took up residence in the Wang home. When he wasn't eating or sleeping, he spent his time behind the stove with Yumi. What a wonderful spot that was. A sacred spot for village lovers. He and Yumi were talking by this time, though the strain on her was considerable, since words in the standard Beijing dialect kept cropping up in his speech. She loved the way it sounded, even if she didn't always understand it, because those few added words conjured up distant places, a different world, and were made for talk between lovers. On one particular evening the fire in the belly of the stove slowly died out and darkness crept over them, frightening Yumi. But this sense of fear was augmented with hard-to-describe hope and anxiety. Budding love is cloaked in darkness, since there is no road map to show where it's headed; neither partner knows how or where to start, which usually makes for awkward situations. Absorbed in this anxiety, they had maintained a respectful distance out of fear of touching each other.

Then Peng Guoliang reached out and took Yumi's hand. At last they were holding hands. She was a little frightened, but this was what she'd been waiting for. Letting Guoliang hold her hand instilled in her the satisfaction of a job well done. A sigh of relief emanated from the depths of her heart. Strictly speaking, she was not holding his hand; her hand was caught in his. At first his fingers were stiff and unbending, but slowly they came to life, and when that happened, they turned willful, sliding in between hers, only to back out, unhappily, seemingly in failure. But back they came. The sensitive movements of his hand were so new to Yumi that she had trouble breathing. Then, without warning, he put his arms around her and covered her lips with his. It was so sudden, so unexpected, that by the time she realized what was happening, it was too late. But she did manage to keep her lips tightly shut.

Oh, no, he's kissed me! But then her body felt electrified, and it was as if she were floating on water, wave-tossed, weightless, and buoyant—isolated and completely surrounded. She tried to free herself from Guoliang's arms, but they only held her more tightly, and she had no choice but to give in. She was gripped by fear, and yet she was still at ease. Yumi knew she could not hold out much longer. Her lips weakened, then parted slightly, cold and quivering. The tremors quickly spread through her body and infected Peng Guoliang. Their two bodies trembled as they pressed together, and the longer they kissed, the more they could not help feeling that they weren't kissing the right place. They kept trying to find that place, only to fail. All the while their lips were actually right where they were supposed to be. The kiss seemed to last all evening until Shi Guifang cried out from the courtyard, "Yumi, dinnertime." Yumi's acknowledgment of the summons brought the kiss to an end. It took her several moments to catch her breath. She flashed Guoliang a tight-lipped smile to show that their actions had gone unnoticed. They stood up from the pile of kindling straw, but Yumi's knees buckled, and she nearly fell. She pounded her leg as if it had gone to sleep, telling herself that falling in love was hard work.

Yumi and Guoliang moved out into the open, where they brushed pieces of straw off of each other. She carefully removed every piece from his clothes, no matter how small, making sure that nothing marred his uniform. When she was finished, she wrapped her arms around him from behind, feeling as if she had stored up great quantities of a mysterious liquid that flowed through her body in all directions. She was approaching the point of sentimentality. In her mind she was now his woman. He had kissed her, so she belonged to him, she was his. *That does it,* she said to herself. *Now I'm Guoliang's wife.*

The following afternoon Peng Guoliang reached under Yumi's blouse. Before she realized what he had in mind, he was already cupping one of her breasts, terrifying her, though the chemise kept his hand from her skin. How daring she felt. They had reached an impasse, but what can stop a hand capable of flying an airplane into the sky? The way Guoliang touched Yumi had her gasping for breath. She threw her arms around him, holding him so tight that she was dangling from his neck, nearly suffocating him. But then his fingers crept under her chemise, and this time there was nothing between his hand and her bare breast. "Don't. Please don't," Yumi pleaded, grabbing his wrist.

His fingers stopped moving, but then he whispered in her ear, "Dear Yumi, I don't know when I'll be able to see you again." That melted her resolve and saddened her at the same time. She began to weep silently as a cloud of gloom settled over her heart. Within seconds she was crying openly, but managed to choke out: "Elder Brother." Under normal circumstances she would never have called him that, but now that was what the situation called for. As she released his hand, she said, "Don't let anything keep you from wanting me, Elder Brother."

By then he was crying too.

"Dear Little Sister, don't let anything keep *you* from wanting *me*."

Even though he'd simply echoed her plea, the fact that he'd said it made it sound so much sadder; that worried her. Straightening up, she quietly gave herself to him. He lifted her jacket, exposing nicely rounded, lustrous breasts. Taking the left one in his mouth, he detected a salty taste. Suddenly, Yumi's mouth fell open as she arched her back and grabbed him by the hair.

Their last night together—Peng Guoliang had to return home early the next day and report back to his unit—they abandoned themselves to desperate kissing and touching, their bodies pressed together, writhing in agony. For days they'd been engaged in alternating attack and defense. Yumi now knew that love was not a matter of words but of deeds, the mouth giving way to the body. From holding hands they had moved to kissing and from there to touching; now the barriers were falling. Yumi advanced cautiously, and Peng Guoliang took advantage of every step to go further as Yumi yielded. She could not have stopped if she'd wanted to, and in truth, she did not want to. Finally, inevitably, Peng Guoliang told Yumi he wanted to "do it." By then she was close to fainting, but sensing a critical moment, she forced herself to be clearheaded and firm. As she grabbed his wrists, their two pairs of hands pushed and pulled atop Yumi's belly.

"I'm in agony," Peng Guoliang pleaded.

"I am too," Yumi replied.

"Do you know what I mean, dear Little Sister?"

"Of course I know, dear Elder Brother."

Peng Guoliang was falling apart. So was Yumi, but she was not going to give in this time, no matter what he said. This stronghold could not be breached. It was her last defense. If she was going to hold on to this man, she needed to keep at least one fire of desire burning in him. Wrapping her arms around his head, she kissed his hair and said, "Don't hate me, Elder Brother."

"I don't," he said.

She was already in tears the next time she said it. "You mustn't hate me, Elder Brother."

Peng Guoliang looked up, as if to say something, but all he said was, "Yumi."

She shook her head.

With one last military salute to Yumi, Peng Guoliang left. His retreating back was like an airplane rising into the clear blue sky, leaving no trace behind. When he disappeared behind an embankment, Yumi's thoughts scrolled backward.

Peng Guoliang is gone. We just met, just got to know each other, and now he's gone.

She stood there like a simpleton, but now something was stirring in the pit of her stomach, stronger and stronger, more and more aggressive—a willfulness that was impossible to keep at bay. But there were no tears; her eyes were as empty as the cloudless sky. She hated herself and was filled with heartbreaking regret. She should have said yes, should have given herself to him. How important was keeping that last stronghold from being breached? What was she saving herself for anyway? Who was she saving herself for? If the meat turns mushy in the family pot, what difference does it make which bowl it goes into?

"How could I have been so stupid?" Yumi demanded of herself. "He was in such agony, why did I refuse him?" She looked behind her. The crops were green, the trees dried up, and the roads yellow. "How could I have been so stupid?"

Youqing's wife had been under the weather for a couple of days. She could not pinpoint the cause, but something was making her listless. So she did the laundry, scrubbing clothes to pass the time. Then she washed the sheets and the pillow covers. And still she wasn't satisfied, so she dug out her summer sandals and brushed them clean. That done, she suddenly felt lazy, not wanting to move. She was bored. Wang Lianfang wasn't there. Peng Guoliang had no sooner left than Wang had to attend a meeting. She'd feel better if he were here. Anytime she was restless or bored, going to bed with Wang re-energized her. Youqing had stopped touching her, refusing even to sleep in the same bed. She was shunned by the village women, which left her nothing, nothing but Wang Lianfang. From time to time she was tempted to seduce one of the other men, but that was too risky. Wang was such a jealous lover he frowned if he even saw her having a pleasant conversation with another man. He was, after all, Wang Lianfang. But what does a woman live for? All that makes life interesting is a little pleasurable roughhousing in bed. And it's not a pleasure she can simply call up whenever she wants. Everything depends on whether or not the man is in the mood.

The sight of all that fresh laundry depressed her even more, since now she had to rinse it out. Too sore at first to bend over, she finally summoned energy from somewhere and carried a few articles of clothing over to the pier. She had barely rinsed the first piece, one of Youqing's jackets, when she spotted Yumi crossing the concrete bridge, coming her way. One look at her distant gaze and ashen face told her that Yumi had just said good-bye to Peng Guoliang, for she appeared weightless, like a shadow on a wall. It took a special girl not to just go sailing off the bridge into the river.

Yumi cannot go on like this, Youqing's wife said to herself. *It could ruin her health.* So she walked up the bank, stood at the foot of the bridge, and greeted Yumi with a smile.

"Gone, is he?"

Yumi looked down, but her gaze was a puff of smoke, ready to be blown away by the first gust of wind. She acknowledged Youqing's wife despite her callous feelings toward her, nodding as she walked past.

Youqing's wife wanted to say something to make her feel better, but Yumi was clearly in no mood to accept kind words from her. So she just stood there watching the girl's back take on the appearance of a moving black hole. Absentmindedly, Youqing's wife asked herself, *Why are you trying to make her feel better? No matter what you say, she'll soon be an aviator's wife—the pain of separation eating at her represents something worthwhile, a stroke of luck, a woman's good fortune. And what do you have? No need to do anything.*

After Yumi left, Youqing's wife ran behind the pigpen, bent over, and retched. It was lumpy and watery; she threw up more than she'd eaten that morning. Then she leaned against the wall of the pen and opened her eyes; dewy tears hung from her lashes. *I must be sick,* she said to herself. *There's no reason I should be this nauseous.* But as she thought back she realized that her discomfort over the past couple of days had been just that: nausea. She bent over again and emptied a puddle of bile. With her eyes closed, she laughed at herself.

You sorry piece of goods, you're acting like you're carrying a little Party secretary inside you, she said to herself. It was this self-demeaning comment that got her thinking. Her little relative hadn't visited her for a couple of months, but she hadn't given it a thought, hadn't dared to. She laughed again and said sarcastically to herself, *Not a chance. Do you really buy the idea that you're productive outside and lazy at home?*

"Yes," the doctor said.

"How can that be?" she asked.

He just smiled and said, "I've never seen such a woman. Go home and ask your husband."

So she counted back. Youqing had been at the irrigation site that month. She stared straight ahead. *He might be a fool, but he's no idiot. I can trick heaven over this, and maybe earth as well, but I'll never trick him. So do I keep it or not?* It would be her decision, hers alone.

Youqing's wife made a bowl of fried rice for her husband and watched him eat. She shut the door, picked up the clothes beater that she kept behind the door, and laid it on the table. "Youqing," she said, "I'm not barren." Not understanding what she was trying to say, he kept eating. "Youqing," she said, "I'm pregnant." She added, "It's Wang Lianfang's." This time he understood.

"I can't have another abortion. If I do, that might really keep me from having your child." She paused. "Youqing, I want to have this one. If you say no, I'll die with no complaints." She looked down at the clothes beater on the table. "If you can't swallow that, then go ahead, beat me to death." As he sat there with the last bite of food in his mouth, Youqing banged his chopsticks down on the table. His neck and his gaze were rigid and straight. Then he got to his feet and picked up the beater. His arm was bigger around than the beater and harder. She shut her eyes, and when she opened them again, her husband was gone.

Confused and panic-stricken, she ran out to look for him and found him in her mother-in-law's shed, where she stood in the doorway and watched as he got down on his knees in front of his mother and said, "I've failed my ancestors, I don't have what other men have." He still hadn't swallowed the last mouthful of rice, which now littered the floor around him, yellow and glossy. His wife shivered as she looked into the eyes of her mother-in-law. Then she backed out of the doorway and went home, where she dug an old length of rope out of a basket. After tying a noose, she flung the rope over a roof beam and checked to see if it would hold her weight. Then she climbed onto a stool, looped the noose around her neck, and kicked the stool out from under her.

Youqing's mother burst into the room. A clever and perceptive woman, she had seen the look in her daughter-in-law's eyes and had known that something bad was about to happen. Grabbing her daughter-in-law's legs, she pushed upward. "Youqing," she shouted. "Hurry. Hurry!"

Youqing stood there in a fog, oblivious to all that had happened over the past few minutes. He just kept looking around, trying to figure out what was going on. Finally, he cut his wife down. His mother shut the front door, then rushed over excitedly, squatted down, and opened her arms. She began slapping her own buttocks, her hands like a pair of magpies.

"I'm glad you're pregnant," she said in a soft voice. "Go ahead, have this one. It's wonderful you're not barren."

A spring wind is wild—as a spring wind ought to be. There is an old saying that, "A spring wind can cleave rocks, so wear a hat if you don't want a split forehead." That, in essence, is the power of a spring wind. Where cold weather is concerned, neither the third nor the fourth nine-day period after the winter solstice ranks as the coldest. For that, one must wait for deep autumn or early spring. The ground splits during the winter months, but since people protect themselves with padded clothing and seldom go out into the fields, the effects of the cold are seldom felt. That is not the case in deep autumn or late spring, when hands and feet have chores to do and cannot be constricted by heavy clothes. The harder the work, the more a person sweats, and thin clothes are the only answer. Winds seldom rise up in deep autumn, but early in the morning and late in the afternoon, the ground is covered by chilled dew—a silent cold, but especially bitter. What makes early spring different is the wind. While not particularly biting, it blows with great force; but most important is its patience as it meticulously whistles and howls past every bare branch from morning to night, each limb of a fine tree like a new widow. The chill of an early spring day owes its existence to the unpredictable winds.

The vast fields of wheat were green and appeared full of life. But on closer examination, every shivering leaf gave off an icy chill. In the springtime there is nothing worse than frost. Three frosty days inevitably lead to spring rains; old-timers like to say that, "Rains come three days after a frost." Spring rains are as precious as oil, but only for crops; for humans they are sheer misery. It will rain for days on end. Different from normal rainfalls; not a downpour, but a mist that wraps around you so that you cannot hide. Everything is wet, the air and the ground; even pillows retain a dampness that makes the days cold and dirty.

There was water everywhere in Wang Family Village; moisture filled the air, the wind blew. People went to bed early and slept in late, and those who knew how to economize got by on two meals a day, a tradition passed down by their forebears. During the period between harvests and plantings, they slept a lot, finding hunger easier to stave off horizontally than vertically. With less food in their bellies, it was only natural to slack off, and the pigs in their pens suffered. Unlike humans, pigs were incapable of lying down to sleep when they were hungry. And so they made loud, noisy complaints—ear-assaulting sounds, unlike the happy clucking of chickens and the barking of dogs, which have an almost serene quality, especially from a distance. Those were comforting sounds. But who can stand the noise of pigs when they sound like the transmigrated souls of hungry ghosts? Day in and day out they gave cacophonous voice to their grievances.

No sun in the sky and no moon. Darkness brought tranquility to Wang Family Village. The sky turned dark, and Wang Family Village was once again stilled.

Then something really big happened.

There had been no warning signs before Wang Lianfang was caught in Qin Hongxia's bed. Wang Family Village was quiet, all but the sows and boars in their pens, complaining of hunger. Dinners were cooking on stoves whose chimneys sent smoke into the air to merge with the evening fog; steam rose from countless treetops. All in all, it felt like a peaceful night lay ahead until the stillness was shattered when Wang Lianfang and Qin Hongxia were caught in bed, thanks to Qin's foolish mother-in-law. When it was over, people called her a dimwit, a simpleminded woman. Why all the shouting? Shout if you must, but "Help, murder!"? What was that all about?

If the mother-in-law had been a woman with her head on straight, Wang Lianfang would have gotten away just fine. Unfortunately, he was dealing with a simpleton. Everything was progressing just fine when Qin Hongxia's mother-in-law began shouting, "Help, murder! Help, murder!" Her shouts traveled far in the moist air and rang clear, alerting neighbors, who picked up whatever was handy and ran into Qin Hongxia's yard. Her husband, Zhang Changjun, an artilleryman stationed in Henan province, had resolved his organization problem—in other words, his application to join the Party—the year before and was scheduled to be discharged in the fall. Since he was away from home, Qin Hongxia's neighbors helped out whenever they could, so when her mother-in-law bellowed, "Help, murder!," how could they not come to her rescue? She stood in the middle of the yard, so breathless that she could only point to the window that she'd thrown open. The door, on the other hand, was tightly shut. Neighbors filled the yard. One crept cautiously up to the window, pole in hand, while another, emboldened by the rake he held, kicked the door open. Wang Lianfang and Qin Hongxia were frantically getting dressed, but the way their buttons were misaligned showed that they were wasting their time. Wang tried to appear unruffled, but he'd been caught in the act, and there was no getting out of it. Losing his customary calmness, he took out a pack of Flying Horse cigarettes and said, "Have a cigarette, there's enough for all of you."

Did he really think this was the time to smoke?

It was a grim situation. Most of the time, if someone offered Wang a cigarette, he checked the brand before he accepted it. Now here he was offering everyone a Flying Horse, and there were no takers. Yes, a grim situation.

The deathly stillness that night was so acute you'd have thought a murderous rampage had wiped out the village. By that time, Wang Lianfang was in town, standing in front of the commune Party secretary's desk. Wang Lianfang's superior was livid. Under ordinary circumstances he and Wang Lianfang had a special relationship, but now he was pounding the table. "What were you thinking?" he roared. "How could you be so stupid?"

Wang Lianfang went soft; his eyes were closed and he was slumping in his seat.

"Maybe I should be placed on probation," he said prudently.

That ratcheted up Commune Secretary Wang's anger. He banged the table again. "Stop mouthing shit," he shouted. "The wife of a soldier on active duty? This is high voltage stuff! This time the law's involved."

The situation had turned even more grim. Wang Lianfang

knew instinctively that unless he thought of something quick, the law really would be involved. Nothing had happened to him the first time—or the second, for that matter—but he wouldn't be so lucky this time. Everything changed when his superior said the law was involved. The commune secretary unbuttoned his tunic and stood with his hands on his hips, his elbows raising the back of the tunic high above his waist. This was how leading officials invariably reacted to a crisis, even in the movies. Wang Lianfang's eyes were glued to the secretary's back as he threw open the window and thrust out his arms: "They caught you in the act, so tell me, what am I supposed to do? What the hell am I supposed to do?"

Punishment was meted out with the same speed that the incident had been discovered. Wang Lianfang lost both his job and his Party membership. Zhang Weijun took over as branch secretary. Wise decisions across the board. Wang Lianfang met them with silence, and there was nothing members of the Zhang clan could say.

Events followed a logical course, slow when they needed to be and fast when that was required. Wang Lianfang's family crumbled in a matter of days. On the surface, of course, everything seemed normal: the bricks and tiles remained in place, needles and thread stayed by the bed where they belonged. But Yumi knew that her family had unraveled. Happily, Shi Guifang had said nothing about Wang Lianfang's affairs from the beginning, not a word. Her only reaction was to dissolve into belches. This time, she had lost face as a woman on two levels, so she took to her bed and slept for days. When she finally got up, she was a study in languor, but not the sort of languor that had followed

Little Eight's birth. That had been accompanied by a sense of pride, for it had been her own doing, happily floating with the current. This time she sailed against the tide, and she had to find the strength to deal with it. That would take hard work and perseverance. Now, when she opened her mouth to speak, a foul odor emerged.

Yumi avoided talking to her mother as much as possible, for whatever Shi Guifang said came out like a belch; obviously, the words had steeped inside her for too long. And Yusui turned out to be a huge disappointment. The little whore was old enough to know better. Yusui actually had the nerve to kick a shuttlecock around with Zhang Weijun's daughter and made matters worse by losing to a girl who was tiny all over: tiny face, tiny nose and eyes, and thin, haughty lips. The Zhangs were shoddy goods, all of them. And the shuttlecock? A bunch of lousy chicken feathers. Yusui was born to betray her family—why else would she let someone like that beat her? Now Yumi saw her sister's true character.

Nothing escaped Yumi's eyes, and she staunchly kept her composure. Even if Peng Guoliang never flew a People's Liberation Army airplane, she would not stoop to Yusui's level of contempt. If people look down on you, it's probably your fault. Since Yumi had found the strength to keep Peng Guoliang from breaching that last stronghold, she had to fear no one; as usual, she spent her days strolling around the village with Wang Hongbing in her arms. She behaved no differently now than when Wang Lianfang had been the local Party secretary.

Yumi found all those foul females beneath contempt. Back when her father was sleeping with them, they were blocks of stinky tofu, ripe to have holes punched in them by a chopstick. But now they were acting like proper ladies, like chunks of braised pork.

The rotten piece of goods Qin Hongxia returned to the village with her child after spending two weeks at her parents' home. With nice rosy cheeks, she looked as if she'd gone home for a postpartum lying-in. To think she had the nerve to come back at all! The river stretched out in front of her, but she lacked the courage to jump in and wouldn't even fake an attempt for show. She affected a bashful look as she crossed the bridge, as if all the village men wished they could take her for a wife. Some of the women sneaked a look at Yumi when Qin Hongxia reached the foot of the bridge, and Yumi knew that their eyes were on her. How was she going to deal with this? What was she going to say or do to this woman? As Qin Hongxia passed by, Yumi stood up, switched Wang Hongbing from one arm to the other, and went up to her. "Aunty Hongxia," she said with a smile, "you're back, I see." Everyone heard her. In days past, Yumi had always called Qin Hongxia "Sister," but now it was "Aunty," a change pregnant with dark hints that made any response all but impossible. At first the gathered women did not realize what was happening, but one look at Qin Hongxia's face told them what Yumi was up to. She had mischief in mind, but was clever and experienced enough not to give it away. The way Qin Hongxia smiled at Yumi was unbearably awkward. No woman with a sense of self-awareness would have smiled under those circumstances.

Wang Lianfang decided to learn a trade. After all, he had a family of ten to feed, and from now on, at the end of fall, no more perks would come his way. He lacked the constitution to farm alongside the commune members; but mainly it was a matter of face. He had no illusions about himself. He considered the loss of his position as Party secretary an acceptable price to pay for having slept with so many women. But to start hauling manure with men who had been his underlings—or digging ditches, or planting and harvesting—would have been a crippling disgrace. Learning a trade was the way to go. He gave the matter serious thought. Standing in front of his maps of the world and the People's Republic of China, a cigarette in one hand, the other resting on his hip, he narrowed his choices to: cooper, butcher, shoemaker, bamboo weaver, blacksmith, painter, coppersmith, tinsmith, carpenter, or mason.

Now it was time to synthesize, compare, analyze, study, choose the refined over the coarse, the honest over the fraudulent, examine things inside and out, and study appearance versus essence. Given his age, his strength, and the prestige factor, he settled on painter. He made a list of the qualities of the trade he found appealing.

1. It's not a very taxing job, certainly one he could manage.
2. It's relatively easy to master—how hard can slapping on enough reds and greens to cover wood be?
3. Hardly any capital is involved—all you need is a brush. A carpenter, on the other hand, needs a saw, a plane, an axe, a chisel, a hammer, and dozens of different tools.
4. Once he started work, he'd spend his time outside instead of hanging around the village all day. What he didn't see couldn't hurt him, and that would improve his mood.

5.   Painting is viewed as a respectable profession. For someone with his background, the villagers would look at him with a jaundiced eye if his job was slaughtering pigs. But not painting houses. Some red here, some green there, and from a distance it might look like he was engaged in propaganda work.

Once he'd made up his mind, he couldn't help feeling that his plans could properly be classified as being in line with the concept of materialism.

Wang Lianfang hadn't visited Youqing's wife for many days—not a long time, but dramatic changes in the situation had occurred. One day, after drowning his sorrows from noon until three in the afternoon, he stood up and decided to get a little exercise on Youqing's wife's body before leaving home. He could not be sure if he was still welcome in the beds of the other women, but Youqing's wife was his private plot, a place where he could always enjoy some of her husband's dumb luck.

Wang opened the door and walked in as Youqing's wife was snacking on dried radishes, her back to him. She immediately smelled the liquor on his breath. "Fenxiang," he said in full voice, "you're all I have." However bleak that sounded, she could not help but be moved by it; it had a warm quality. "Fenxiang," he went on, "the next time I come over, you can call me painter Wang."

She turned to face him and saw that he was not only drunk but also apparently in a terrible mood. She wanted to say something to make him feel better. But what? The incident with Qin Hongxia had cut deeply, yet she could not bear to see Lianfang in such a depressed emotional state. She knew what he'd come for and, if she hadn't been pregnant, would have been happy to oblige. But not this time. No, not this time. With a stern look, she said, "Lianfang, let's not do it anymore. I think you'd better go."

He didn't hear a word she said. Instead, he went into the bedroom, undressed, and climbed into bed. He waited. "Hey!" he shouted impatiently. He waited a while longer. "Hey!"

Not a sound came from outside the room, and so, holding up his pants, he went to see what was wrong. Youqing's wife was long gone. This was not how he'd expected things to turn out.

As he stood there holding his pants with both hands, cord in place, suddenly sober, he realized how quickly human relations can change. *All right,* he said to himself, *I see you've decided to erect a chastity archway for yourself at this particular moment, not a day earlier or a day later. Well, that's fine with me.*

"Shit!" he cursed with a sneer as he walked back into the bedroom.

He stripped again and climbed into bed, where he began singing a revolutionary opera at the top of his lungs. It was *Shajiabang.* He sang all the parts—Aunty A-qing, Hu Chuankui, and Diao Deyi. His voice was rough and loud until he came to Aunty A-qing's part, which he sang in a tinny falsetto. Unable to hit the high notes, he switched to Hu Chuankui's male role. The entire village could hear Wang's operatic offerings, but no one came over, instead they acted like they hadn't heard a thing. Wang transported an entire act to Youqing's bed, every word of it, with no mistakes. After the final scene, he imitated the sounds of drums and gongs, put on his clothes, and left.

Youqing's wife had been hiding behind the kitchen door the

whole time, so amazed and frightened by what Wang Lianfang was doing that she could hardly breathe. Once she'd managed to calm down, she was struck by a bone-chilling sadness, overcome by feelings that for the past six months she'd lived the life of a lowly dog. Her fingers and toes felt uncommonly cold as she rested her hands on her belly, wishing she could somehow dig what was in there out with her fingers.

No, she'd never do that. She shivered and looked down at her belly. "You bastard," she said, "you mangy bastard, mangy bastard, lousy mangy bastard!"

At the age of forty-two, Wang Lianfang left home to learn a trade, leaving the family in the hands of Yumi. It was a daunting responsibility, and she suddenly understood the saying that, "Only the head of a household realizes the true cost of rice and kindling." The large issues are hard on the head of the household, of course, but so are the small ones, which can be trivial, bothersome, fragmentary, and piddling, but cannot be avoided and must be met head-on. Dismissing them with a pat on the behind simply won't cut it. Take Yuye, for instance, a girl not yet eleven, who only days before had broken a window at school. The teacher demanded to speak with the head of the household. Then on the heels of that incident, Yuye knocked over a classmate's inkwell and splashed ink all over the girl's face; again the call went out to the head of the household. None of this seemed like a big deal to Yuye, who wasn't much of a talker, but thanks to busy hands and feet, frequently got mixed up in all sorts of trouble. In the past, the teachers might have given Yuye the benefit of the doubt, since there are two sides to every issue. But now her teacher was caught in a bind. Yumi was summoned to school as head of the household. She didn't say much after the first incident, just nodded when she heard the story, then went home and got ten eggs, which she took back and placed on the teacher's desk. The second time she was sent for, she grabbed Yuye by the ear when she heard what had happened and dragged her over to the office, where she gave her sister a resounding slap in front of all the teachers. Yuye's cheek swelled up and twisted her face out of shape. This time, instead of eggs, Yumi went into the sty, selected a white Yorkshire hog, and took it to school. With this escalation, the principal now got involved.

The principal, who was an old friend of Wang Lianfang, looked first at the teacher and then at Yumi, and did not know what to say to keep from offending either one. So he looked down at the hog and laughed. "Yumi," he said, "what's this all about? Are you enrolling him in gym class?" Then he turned to the janitor and gestured for him to take the animal back to where it belonged.

The principal's genial attitude put Yumi on her best behavior. "When we slaughter the pig," she said, "we'll save the liver for you, Uncle."

"I can't let you do that," he said.

"Why not? If Yuye's teacher can eat the eggs, what's to keep the principal from eating a pig's liver?" The words were barely out of her mouth before the teacher's eyes grew to the size of a hen's eggs and her face the color of a pig's liver.

Back home, Yumi took out her forty-weight stationery to write a letter to Peng Guoliang, intending to tell him how hard things had gotten for her. At this point she pinned all her hopes on him, but she stopped short of telling him what had happened at home, since she did not want him to think badly of the family. She had to tread very carefully. If Guoliang moved up through the ranks in the military, her family was assured of a second chance. "Guoliang," she wrote, "you must set your sights on getting regular promotions." But then she reread what she had written and felt it was too direct. So she tore up the letter and, after wrestling with her thoughts, wrote: "Guoliang, listen to your superiors and keep making progress."

The commune's movie team returned to the village. For days Shi Guifang had been complaining of heartburn, so Yumi chose not to go see the movie, even though it was one of her favorite pastimes; her mother never went to a movie and that always made Yumi grumble. *How come, when someone gets to a certain age, they lose interest in everything, even movies?* But now she understood that her mother simply wanted to avoid crowds. Besides, movies are so phony, nothing but groups of people passing their days on a white sheet. What does a white sheet know about keeping warm or getting cold? Such thoughts had Yumi wondering if she too was getting old and if her heart was turning cold. When that happens, age is obviously creeping up. People get old gradually, step by step, a slow death of the heart. Aging has little to do with the calendar.

As soon as dinner was over, Yuxiu sneaked a handful of sunflower seeds and was on her way out when Yumi stopped her. She had good reason for not wanting her sister to get away so early because Yuxiu was in the habit of rushing over to get a good seat for the movie. Even before the white sheet had been hung up, Yuxiu would bring a stool up to a spot in front of the projector, one of the best seats available. In truth, ability had less to do with her success in getting a good seat than the willingness of the others to let her have it. But now it would be tactless for her to expect anyone to let her take the best seat, and it could easily lead to an argument. Yumi wasn't afraid of arguments, but given the current state of affairs, the fewer the squabbles the better. So she tried to keep her sister from leaving early, stressing the need for a little decorum.

But Yuxiu would have none of it. "Don't be such a nag. Do you see a stool anywhere?" Being no dummy, Yuxiu knew exactly what to do at times like this.

"Then take Yuye with you," Yumi said.

"Why should I? She's got legs; she can walk there by herself."

"Either you take her or you don't go." No doubt about it, Yumi was now the boss. Her word was law. This time Yuxiu did not talk back. Instead, she scooped up another handful of sunflower seeds. In the end, third daughter Yuxiu took fifth daughter Yuye, second daughter Yusui took sixth daughter Yumiao, fourth daughter Yuying went on her own, and seventh daughter Yuyang stayed home in bed. Now that this had been settled, Yumi lit a lantern and carried Hongbing into their mother's bedroom. Their mother had lost weight, which showed not in the outline of her face but in its many wrinkles, row upon row of them, like tracks of flowing water; it was a wrenching picture of sadness. Yumi held a plate of the newly roasted sunflower seeds out to her mother.

"Don't roast any more, Yumi."

"Why not?"

"It's disgraceful to be seen eating them."

"Ma," Yumi said, raising her voice, "you have to eat them."

"Why?"

"To show people."

Shi Guifang smiled. Instead of saying what was in her heart, she laid her hand on Yumi's and gave it a couple of pats. To Yumi it was clear that her mother was trying to pacify her and, more important, to remind her that people must accept their fate.

Yumi stood up. "Pretend they're medicine, Ma, for our sake."

Shi Guifang patted the side of her bed for Yumi to sit down. Although she spent all day every day in the same house as Yumi, a casual talk with her daughter was a rare treat. Whatever else might be going on, having a daughter like Yumi to talk to helped put her mind at ease and dissolve some of the bitterness inside. It was a quiet, peaceful night, the kind that keeps one's heart tranquil and dispels desire. After listening for a while, Shi Guifang detected the sort of quiet that belongs to widows and orphans. Wang Hongbing was asleep in Yumi's arms, looking as adorable as ever. She took him from Yumi and gazed into his face for a very long time. He was at peace with the world, worry-free and innocent. Shi Guifang looked up at Yumi, half of whose face was framed in lamplight; she had a lovely profile that was enhanced by the light. The other half, bathed in darkness, was denied a fullness of expression, leaving her with an enigmatic, incomplete look. A burst of wind carried in the crackle of a cinematic gun battle. By leaning over and cocking an ear, Yumi could distinguish between the dive bombers and the ground fire. Shi Guifang could tell what Yumi was thinking. "Go on," she said, "go watch the movie."

But Yumi just stared dreamily at the glowing lamp wick. Shi Guifang sighed heavily, her breath bending the wick and making it seem as if it were trying to hide from her. Yumi's thoughts began to wander as if they were being transported away on an airplane. The room darkened slightly, and so did the illuminated half of Yumi's face. Her mother sat up abruptly and belched several times before smacking the bed with her open hand. "This is better," she said. "Yes, it's better this way." This abrupt outburst startled Yumi, who watched as her mother blew out the lamp.

"Time to sleep," she said.

By the time Yusui returned home with Yumiao, Yumi had dozed off. Yuying was the next to come home. Yumi woke up and sat on the edge of the bed to watch the girls wash up. The sister she was really waiting for was Yuye, a lazy little tomboy who would not wash up unless she was forced to. When she got into bed and her feet warmed up, the stench was nearly overpowering. Only Yumi was willing to sleep with her; the other girls all complained that she smelled bad.

The movie was over, and Yuye was still not home, which could only mean that she was with Yuxiu, who was probably up to no good. Yumi knew Yuxiu well. Since Yuye was with her, she could dump all the blame for coming home late on her younger sister. Yumi waited until it was all quiet outside, and there was still no sign of Yuxiu and Yuye. Finally, having run out of patience, she threw a jacket over her shoulders, slipped on a pair of shoes, and stormed out the door.

Her search took her to a haystack beside the threshing floor, where she found her sisters among a crowd of moviegoers who had lingered around a blazing lantern.

"Yuxiu!" she shouted.

"Yuye!"

No answer, although all the heads turned to see who it was. Disembodied faces silhouetted in the light of the lantern lit up the surrounding darkness, creating a strange tableau of dark and light. Not a word emerged from the expressionless faces carved into the ghostly night. As Yumi stood dazed by the sight, a premonition of dread burst from her chest. The crowd parted for her as she walked up to where Yuxiu and Yuye sat dumbly on a bed of straw, both naked from the waist down. Straw clung to their bodies, stuck to their hair, and poked out from between their teeth and the corners of their mouths. The only movement from Yuxiu was the rapid blinking of eyes that were virtually lifeless. Yumi, who knew at once what had happened, stood there staring at her sisters, her mouth hanging slack. Now that Yumi was among them, the crowd left the lantern where it was and drifted off. The outlines of their backs bled into the darkness. There was no one left, but it felt as if no one *had* left.

Yumi knelt down on the straw and put her sisters' pants back on. Both girls' crotches were soaked in blood that was mixed with another sticky substance. A strange and eerie odor rose from their pants. After cleaning them off with handfuls of straw, Yumi took each of them by the hand and led them home in the darkness. The lantern remained on the ground, throwing its light on the haystack, a mound of gold ringed by inky darkness. A passing breeze tossed Yumi's hair, which nearly covered her face. Yuxiu and Yuye shivered. They looked like a pair of wobbly scarecrows. Yumi stopped suddenly, turned, and grabbed Yuxiu by the shoulders.

"Tell me, who did this?" she asked, shaking her. "Who did it?" she shouted. The shaking sent her own hair flying. "Who ..." she screamed.

It was Yuye who answered. "I don't know. Lots of them."

Yumi sat down on the ground—hard.

Even though he was far away from the village, news of the incident still managed to reach Peng Guoliang. His next letter was but a single sentence: "Tell me, did someone take you to bed?" The accusatory tone was obvious to Yumi more than one thousand *li* away and ushered in a dramatic change in her situation. That one sentence knocked the wind out of her; suddenly, she felt cold, her strength gone. Fear gripped her. She saw a hand circle over Yuxiu and Yuye before slowly turning to point at her. Even though the sun lit up the area, she could not identify the hand as it vanished into total darkness. Not only had her fellow villagers read Peng Guoliang's letters, but they had also written to him for her. How was she going to answer him now? How could she tell him what had happened? She thought and thought until her brain virtually stopped functioning. Peng Guoliang was the family's last potential mainstay. If this airplane flew away, Yumi's sky would fall. She took out her packet of stationery and laid it on the desk. After crumpling up several sheets and ripping up several more, she began to see herself as a sheet of paper floating in the air, and no matter where the winds took her, the result was always the same—she was either ripped to shreds or trampled into the ground. Which of those passing feet would willingly pass up the chance to step on it? The curiosity of feet would determine the fate of the sheet of paper. As a veil of silence settled over the deepening night, Yumi picked up her red Hero fountain pen with its iridium nib, not to write a letter, but to start a conversation with Peng Guoliang, even though she knew it was an empty gesture. She dawdled for the longest time until she discovered that she had actually written something, lines that she found utterly shocking. When had she written that? How incredibly brazen it was—and incredibly self-indulgent. This is what she'd written: "Elder Brother Guoliang, I hold you fast in my heart. No one is closer to me. You are the love of my life." Already sensing that she was not overburdened with shame, Yumi was surprised to discover that she had the nerve to write such things.

When she wrote them a second time, she felt her chest swell. Her eyes fell on the lantern wick, which would now take Peng Guoliang's place. His warmth and brightness were arrayed before her. "Elder Brother Guoliang, I hold you fast in my heart. No one is closer to me. You are the love of my life," she wrote again; it was the only thing she was able to write, since nothing else came to her. They were, after all, words that had been hidden in the deepest recesses of her heart, and it took all the courage she possessed to bring them out into the open. Now, for the first time ever, she found the boldness to "say" them. What else was there for her to say at this point? Only this, over and over, just these few words. And so she filled five sheets of paper with them and would have filled more if she'd had them. Five sheets of paper all covered with those few words. The next morning she read every word on those five sheets of paper several times until she could no longer bear it and bathed all five with her tears.

If Guoliang cannot hear the words that fill my heart, she told herself, then everything I say will fall on deaf ears, separated as we are by tall mountains and long rivers.

So she mailed her letter, after which she looked for something to keep herself busy; but she found nothing. So she decided to simply rest, and as she sat in a chair, she fell asleep.

During the days that Yumi waited for a return letter, she turned Hongbing over to Yusui, since she wanted to wait for the postman at the bridgehead. She fretted over the contents of Peng Guoliang's return letter. If he was going to tell her he no longer wanted her, that letter must not fall into the hands of anyone else. She was prepared to take a knife to anyone who even attempted to open her letter. That would be too great a loss of face. So she waited at the bridgehead, but no letter came. What arrived in its place was a bundle that included Yumi's photographs and all the letters she'd sent to Peng Guoliang. All those ugly missives in her own hand. As she looked down at her photographs and handwritten letters, the anguish she'd anticipated did not materialize for some reason. What she felt instead was a crippling embarrassment, such a deep-seated embarrassment she felt like jumping off the bridge.

And then, at that very moment, Youqing's wife appeared. Wanting to hide the contents of her bundle, Yumi carelessly let something fall to the ground. It was her photograph. It lay there, a base, shameless object that had the audacity to smile. Youqing's wife saw it before Yumi could grind it into the roadway with her foot, and the look on her face revealed that she knew everything. Yumi was ashamed to even look at Youqing's wife, who bent down and picked up the photograph. But when she straightened up she saw danger in Yumi's eyes. Fierce determination showed in those eyes, the composure of someone unafraid to face death. Youqing's wife grabbed Yumi by the shoulders and dragged her off to her house, where she led her into the bedroom, a poorly lit room in which Yumi's gaze appeared unusually bright and extraordinarily hard. Emerging from a face that was otherwise blank, that brightness and hardness had a terrifying effect. Taking Yumi by the hand, Youqing's wife pleaded with her, "Yumi, go ahead and cry, for my sake at least."

That comment softened Yumi's gaze, which slowly shifted toward Youqing's wife. As her lips twitched, Yumi said softly, "Sister Fenxiang." Though barely audible, those two words seemed to spray from her mouth like flesh and blood, like beams of blood-tinged light. Youqing's wife was stunned, never expecting Yumi to call her that. In all the years since marrying into Wang Family Village, what, in effect, was she, Youqing's wife? A sow, maybe, or a bitch? Who had ever actually viewed her as a woman? Being addressed as Sister Fenxiang by Yumi knocked over her emotional spice bottle and filled her with even greater sadness than Yumi felt. She could not contain herself; a shout burst from her throat as she flung herself onto Yumi's body and smothered her sobs on the girl's breast. As she did so, there was a sudden movement in her belly. It was, she knew instinctively, a kick from the tiny Wang Lianfang. Thoughts of what was inside her took the edge off her emotional turmoil and kept her from sobbing or making any more sounds. If not for Wang Lianfang, she and Yumi could well have enjoyed a close sisterly relationship. But the girl was Wang's eldest daughter, an inescapable fact that closed off all possibilities. Youqing's wife could say nothing. And so, after steadying her breathing, she managed to get her emotions under control.

As Youqing's wife raised her head and dried her tears, she saw that Yumi's gaze had settled on her. The absence of any observable emotion behind that look frightened her. Yumi's face was ashen, but there was nothing unusual about her expression, and Youqing's wife found that hard to imagine. But there it was, not something that could be faked. "Yumi," she said warily.

Yumi pulled her head back. "Don't worry, I'm not about to kill myself. I want to see what happens next. You can help me by not saying anything to anybody about this."

She actually smiled when she said this, and although the smile lacked the appearance of mockery, the intent was unmistakable. Youqing's wife knew that Yumi was chiding her for being nosy. Yumi took off her jacket and wrapped the photographs and letters up in it. Then, without a word, she opened the door and walked out, leaving Youqing's wife alone and frozen in her bedroom.

See what I've done, she said to herself. *I wanted to help out but wound up being a busybody. If any of this gets out, Yumi will hate me even more.*

Yumi slept through the afternoon. Then in the quiet, late hours of the night she went into the kitchen and lay down behind the stove, where she unbuttoned her blouse and gently fondled her breasts. Although it was her hands that were moving, the sensation was the same as if Peng Guoliang were fondling her. What a shame it had to be her own hands. Slowly she moved them down to the spot where she had stopped him. But this time she was going to do for him what she had not allowed him to do.

She lay weakly on the straw, her body gradually heating up, hotter and hotter, uncontrollably, feverishly hot, so she forced herself to stir. But no matter how she moved, it didn't feel right. She hungered for a man to fill her up and, at the same time, finish her off. It didn't matter who, so long as it was a man. In those quiet, late hours of the night, Yumi was again consumed by regret. And as remorse took over, her fingers abruptly jammed their way inside. The sharp pain actually brought with it enormous comfort. The insides of her thighs were irrigated by a warm liquid. You unwanted cunt, she thought to herself, what made you think you should save yourself for the bridal chamber?

Unhappy women are all subject to the same phenomenon: marriage comes with unanticipated suddenness. During the three months of summer, the busiest season, farmers are fighting for time with the soil. Yumi shocked everyone by getting married during these busy days. Acres of wheat had turned yellow under a blazing sun, spiky awns reaching up to reflect light in all directions like static fountains. At this time of year the sun's rays are fragrant, carrying the aroma of wheat as they light up the ground and cast a veil over the villages. But for farmers, these are not pleasure-filled days, for the feminine qualities of the earth are heaving with the passion of ovulation and birthing, passions beyond their control as they grow soft in the sunlight and exude bursts of the rich, mellow essence of their being. The earth yearns to be overturned by the hoe and the plow, and thus be reborn, and to let the early summer waters flow over and submerge it. Moans of pleasure escape at the moment the earth is bathed and slowly freed from its bindings, bringing contentment and tranquility. Exhausted, it falls into a sound, blissful sleep. The earth takes on the new face of a watery bride. With her eyes shut, a blush rises and falls on her face, a silent command and a silent plea: "Come on, more, I want more." The farmers dare not slack off; their hair, their sleeves, and their mouths are covered with the smell of new wheat.

But, filled with elation, they put that smell aside, muster their strength, and rush about, picking up seedlings and planting them in the ground, one at a time, each in a spot that satisfies the earth. Bent at the waist, the farmers never cut corners, for every seedling that enters the ground depends on their movements. Ten acres, a hundred, a thousand, vast fields of seedlings. At first the little plants are strawlike, pliant, bashful, and because of the water, narcissistic. But in a matter of days the earth becomes aware of the secret it possesses and is at peace. It is languid; soft snores emerge from its sleep.

Amid this flurry of activity, Yumi's wedding got under way. Viewed in retrospect, she was in too big a hurry to get married, much the same as Liu Fenxiang. But Yumi's wedding easily outstripped Fenxiang's. She was fetched in a speedboat reserved for the exclusive use of commune officials, on which two red cut-out "double happiness" characters were affixed to the windshield.

Yumi's match had been arranged by her father. Shortly after the Qingming festival had passed and the weather began to warm, just as farmers were soaking their seeds, Wang Lianfang returned to Wang Family Village to pick up some clothes for his use elsewhere. After supper, having no place to go, he sat at the table smoking a cigarette. Yumi stood in the kitchen doorway and called to him. She did not say "Papa," but called him "Wang Lianfang."

Hearing his daughter call him by name struck Wang Lianfang as unusual. He stubbed out his cigarette, stood up, and walked slowly into the kitchen, where Yumi was looking down at the floor, hands behind her back as she stood against the wall. Wang Lianfang pulled up a stool, sat down, and lit a second cigarette. "So," he said, "what do you want?"

Yumi did not reply immediately; but after a moment, she said, "I want you to find me a man." Wang Lianfang just sat there; sensing what had happened with Peng Guoliang, he chose not to say anything. Instead, he took seven or eight drags on his cigarette, the tip of which flared up as it burned down, creating a long ash that hung from the end. Yumi tilted her head up and said, "I don't care what he's like. I have only one condition: he must be a man who wields power. Otherwise I'll stay single."

The meeting phase of Yumi's courtship proceeded in total secrecy and had a number of new twists—scheduled to take place in the county movie theater, it would be unique from start to finish. The commune speedboat came for her at sunset, a magnificent scene witnessed by many villagers from their vantage point on the stone pier. The speedboat sent waves rushing madly to the banks, fearlessly provocative as they tossed the pitiful farmers' skiffs. Yumi stepped grandly into the speedboat, but no one who saw her knew why she was leaving. All anyone in Wang Family Village knew was that Yumi was "on her way to the county town."

Yumi arrived in town for the meeting. The man she was to meet did not work there, but at the commune. Guo Jiaxing, deputy director of the Revolutionary Committee, was a ranking official in charge of the People's Militia. Aboard the speedboat Yumi had silently congratulated herself for making that vow to her father in absolute terms, a break from traditions that would have denied her such an opportunity. She was going to be a second wife, so she did not expect Guo Jiaxing to be a young man, and for that she was well-prepared. As the saying goes: "A knife is not sharp on both edges; sugar cane is not sweet at both ends."

On a personal level this made no difference to Yumi, for whom power was the key to living well. So long as the man she married possessed that power, a new beginning was assured for her family, and once that happened, no one in Wang Family Village would ever again send their stench her way. On this point she was more determined than even her father, who, she assumed, had been concerned about the difference in age, for he'd hemmed and hawed, obviously reluctant to tell her. She stopped him before he could speak, since she already knew what he wanted to say, and she didn't give a damn.

Night had fallen when Yumi entered the county town for the first time, and thanks to the blazing lamps along both sides of the street, the town appeared quite prosperous. Like a headless housefly, she was emotionally disoriented as she walked down the street. Despite the fact that her confidence was in tatters, she was driven to fight for what she wanted, to win what she'd come for, and to spare no effort to reach her goal. No longer the Yumi of the past, she had narrowed her aspirations, but was more determined, more stubborn than ever. She paused in front of a shop where fruit was suspended in the air. She had to stop for a long moment before she figured out that she was seeing a reflection in a mirror.

Then she saw her own reflection and was struck by the contrast between her homely attire and the finer clothes of the shop clerk. *I should have worn Liu Fenxiang's costume.* Thinking she wanted a piece of fruit, the boat skipper insisted on buying it for her. She reached out and pulled him back.

"Our young commune member has a strong arm," he said with a laugh.

Yet another moment of truth had arrived when Yumi found herself in front of the New China Cinema, where a red banner stretched across a high wall proclaimed: FERVENT CONGRATULATIONS ON THE SUCCESSFUL OPENING OF THE COUNTY PEOPLE'S MILITIA WORKING CONFERENCE!

Yumi now understood that Guo was attending a conference in town. The skipper handed her a cinema ticket.

"I'll wait for you out here," he said.

You definitely know how to toady up to your superiors, Yumi thought. *Who asked you to wait? I'm not married yet.* But then she had a change of heart. *Go ahead; wait, if that's what you want. I'll put in a good word for you if I get the chance.*

The movie had already started when Yumi parted the curtain. The theater was pitch black in front of an enormous color screen on which a policeman was smoking a cigarette, his nostrils, it seemed to her, as big as open wells. She had trouble believing what she saw. How was it possible to make someone as big or as small as you wanted? Gripping her ticket tightly, she looked around and started to feel nervous, unsure of what to do next. Fortunately, an usher with a flashlight walked up and showed her to her seat.

Yumi's heart raced. Happily, this was not the first time she was to meet a prospective mate, a thought that had the desired effect. Calmly she sat down between a man in his fifties to her left and one in his sixties to her right. Both seemed absorbed in the movie. Not knowing which of the two she'd come to meet, she sat stiffly without sneaking a look in either direction. The man, whichever one it was, obviously carried himself in a way that you would expect from a commune official, keeping his composure in the presence of a woman. If her father had been able to do that, they wouldn't be in the state they were in now. Yumi told herself that Guo Jiaxing must have his reasons for not speaking to her in public, so she'd be wise to keep her eyes trained straight ahead.

For Yumi, the movie was an excruciating experience, since she got so little out of it. But it was dark inside, so eventually she felt bold enough to observe her neighbors out of the corner of her eye. From what she could see, the fifty-year-old looked a little better, and if she'd had a voice in the matter, he'd be her choice. But there was no movement from that side. If only he'd brush his foot against hers, she'd know that she was right. As she watched the action on the screen, she began to worry that the meeting might not take place at all. She was tense and growing anxious. *Can't you touch my foot? What's wrong with that?*

Still, even if it was the sixty-year-old, Yumi was prepared to accept the match. As they say, "After this village there will be no more inns." There were few bachelors among the official ranks, though she would still have preferred a man in his fifties. Like a raffle player looking for a bit of luck, she sat through the movie, so fatigued at the end that she was nearly gasping for breath. She had no idea what the film had been about, although the ending was pretty predictable: the man who looked to be the bad guy turned out to be just that and was taken into custody by a member of the Public Security Bureau.

The lights came on; the movie was over. The man in his fifties got up and walked off to the left, the one in his sixties walked off to the right, both leaving Yumi sitting where she was. What a surprise that was. Neither one had said a word. Yumi wondered why. But then the truth hit her: whoever it was, he must not have liked what he saw while she sat there foolishly trying to pick him out in the dark. She was mortified. No wonder the skipper said he'd wait outside. He knew what was going to happen all along.

Yumi walked out of the theater, her confidence in shreds. The skipper was waiting by one of the posts, and she could not bear to look him in the eye.

"We're ready," he said. Yumi was so spent all she wanted was to lie down somewhere.

"I guess you can take me home now," she said, despite her embarrassment.

"I do what Director Guo tells me to do," he said with no observable expression.

When she was settled into Room 315 of the People's Guesthouse, her mind was in a fog, and she quickly fell asleep, although it didn't feel much like sleep to her. Maybe she was dreaming. At around ten o'clock there was a knock at the door.

"Are you in there?" a voice asked. "It's me, Guo."

Yumi wondered if she was hallucinating. Another knock at the door. Knowing how unwise it would be to hesitate, she flipped on the light and opened the door a crack. A man she'd never seen before pushed open the door and walked in, his face cold, devoid of expression. Fortunately for Yumi, she spotted the conference ID badge pinned to his lapel with his name: Guo Jiaxing. Overjoyed, she felt as if she'd been rescued from a desperate situation and been given a new lease on life. He hadn't gone to the cinema after all.

Yumi lowered her head, only to recall that she wasn't fully dressed. She glanced up at Guo Jiaxing, thinking she'd get dressed, but she did not like what she saw. This was not a man who had come to meet a prospective mate; he seemed more like a passerby. Yumi's heart was in her throat.

"I'd like some water," Guo said as he sat down in one of the chairs. Yumi didn't know what else to do, and for that reason, she did as he said. He took the water from Yumi, who stood there feeling foolish; by then she'd forgotten all about getting dressed. Guo neither looked at Yumi nor averted his eyes as he sat there, glass in hand. He had brown eyes, she saw, which were focused on a spot directly ahead, but with a look of indifference. He drank his water slowly, one sip after another, until the glass was empty.

"Some more?" she asked. He responded only by setting the glass on the table—his way of saying no, apparently. Unable to think of anything more to say, Yumi just stood there, not sure if she should get dressed or not.

How could anybody be that calm, that unruffled? He says nothing, he does nothing, his face has all the expressiveness of a conference hall. Her anxieties increased. *Well, that's it,* she said to herself. *He doesn't like what he sees. But wait, he may not seem thrilled, but he doesn't look dissatisfied. Maybe he's already decided it's a workable match.*

Officials are expected to act like this. As long as they think something's okay, then it's okay, and there's no need to say any more. But this was different; Yumi was, after all, a young woman, not a block of wood. Besides, they were alone, so he had no reason not to do something. She stood there feeling foolish until she too grew increasingly calm.

How strange, she said to herself. *All of a sudden I'm as calm as if I were attending the conference.* But that did nothing to lessen her fear of Guo Jiaxing.

"Time to rest," Guo said.

He stood up and began taking off his clothes, as if he were in his own home with members of his own family. "Time to rest," he said a second time. She knew what he had in mind, since he was now sitting on the bed. While that unnerved Yumi, it also shifted her brain into high gear. Whatever may or may not have been settled, this was inappropriate. Guo had undressed slowly, but then how long can it take to remove a few articles of clothing? Now naked, he lay back on the bed where Yumi had been sleeping only moments before.

She still hadn't moved.

"Time to rest," Guo said for the third time. There was no outward change in tone, but she could tell he was getting impatient.

Yumi didn't know what to do. She actually wished he'd rip her clothes off her body; rape would be better than this. She was still a virgin, and it would be unseemly for her to get naked and climb into bed just so she could marry the man. How was she supposed to do something like that?

Guo Jiaxing never took his eyes off Yumi, who, in the end,

got naked, climbed into bed, and slipped under the covers. To her, what she'd stripped off wasn't clothes, it was her skin. But she did what she had to do. Liu Fenxiang had once said that a woman can be proud but mustn't be arrogant. Yumi was naked; so was Guo Jiaxing. A subtle smell of alcohol clung to his body, a hospital smell. As Yumi lay on her side under the covers, Guo motioned with his chin for her to roll over onto her back. She did, and the lovemaking began. Too tense to move, she let him do all the work. It hurt at first—a little, not much—and it was not long before it began to feel natural. If she was reading the signs right, he was satisfied with her. He'd muttered "good" during the lovemaking, and after it was over, he said it again. Yumi could breathe easier now.

But there was a hitch. Guo checked the sheets and didn't see any discoloration. "So you're not," he said.

Such a hurtful comment! She was still a virgin since the lack of a spot on the sheets was a result of her own hand, not the actions of a man. She wondered briefly if this was just a technicality. Since she had done with her hand what she wouldn't let her pilot do, perhaps it was all the same. But she knew it wasn't. She needed to clear things up. But how? Treating it lightly wasn't the answer, but neither was overdoing it. She must be careful not to ruin everything, and all she could think to do was sit and get dressed, which accomplished virtually nothing except to make her feel better. She was empty inside and nearly in tears. But crying, she knew, would be a mistake. Guo Jiaxing lay in bed with his eyes closed. "That's not what I meant."

Yumi undressed again and climbed back into bed and lay beside Guo, blinking rapidly. Convinced that things had worked out this time, she'd have been perfectly content if she hadn't suddenly thought of Peng Guoliang. She could have willingly given in to him, but had saved herself until now, saved herself for this. An overpowering sense of self-pity filled her heart. But she forced herself to bear up under it, for she had achieved what she sought, and that was all that counted. Guo smoked a couple of cigarettes before climbing back on top of Yumi.

This time the movements were much slower, more relaxed, as he slid back and forth like a drawer in his desk. Saying as he did so, "Stick around for a few more days."

She knew what that meant, and her confidence rose. As she lay there, her head pressed against the pillow, she turned to the side and bit her lip. She nodded. "Someone I know is in the hospital," he said, more words at one time than she'd heard so far.

"Who?" she asked in order to keep him talking.

"My wife."

Yumi jerked her head around and looked wide-eyed at Guo.

"This has nothing to do with you," he said. "She's in the last stages. A few months at best. You'll move in when she's gone."

The smell of alcohol washed over Yumi. She felt as if *she* were the "last stages" wife, pinned beneath Guo Jiaxing. She was terrified. Guo covered her mouth with his hand before she could scream. Her body was rocking wildly under the blanket.

"Good," he said.

"MEN DON'T MARRY in May; women don't wed in June." In the countryside that is the taboo.

Actually, it is less a taboo than a consequence of the heavy fieldwork during the summer months. But that did not stop

Yuxiu

Wang Lianfang's eldest daughter, Yumi, from marrying herself off on the twenty-eighth of May, a mere six days after Lesser Fullness, the eighth of the twenty-four solar periods, when the winter wheat has become full, and one week before Grain in Beard, the ninth solar period. The most urgent and important task for farmers at this time is what they refer to as "fighting two battles."

The first, the "battle of the harvest," includes reaping, threshing, winnowing, and storing. The second, the "battle of the sowing," includes plowing, irrigating, leveling, and planting. Busy times.

People have only two hands, and by choosing this particular time to give her hand in marriage, Yumi showed a pronounced lack of judgment. She was well thought-of by her fellow villagers, who viewed her as a sensible girl. But in a farming village, what sensible person would choose to get married in the month of May? No wonder Second Aunt, who lived at the end of the lane, talked about Yumi behind her back. "That girl," she said, "was in too big a hurry and couldn't keep her legs closed."

Truth is, that was unfair to Yumi. She got married when Guo Jiaxing decided it was time, and his decision rested solely on when his current wife died. She left this world in late March, and the "double seven" period of mourning—forty-nine days—ended on the twenty-eighth of May, when Guo announced that he was remarrying. Not deigning to visit Wang Family Village personally, he sent a clerk from the commune on the official speedboat, who set off a string of firecrackers as he passed beneath the bridge near the stone pier. Firecrackers in May—nothing could have sounded stranger. But, undeniably, they heralded a happy event. People on the riverbank saw the pair of red paper cut-outs on the boat's windshield. The skipper was bugling the boat's arrival as it nestled up against the pier, leaving in its wake a V formation of waves that raced to both banks like the haughty dogs of a powerful master and pounced on the legs of the women standing on the pier. With shrieks of alarm, they jumped onto the riverbank with their buckets. The waves ceased when the boat was tied up at the pier and the clerk stepped out of the cabin.

It was a hasty wedding, a little shabby even, but as the commune speedboat was tied up at the stone pier, it didn't actually seem hasty or shabby; it succeeded in giving the impression of extravagance, even an air of implied superior power, since Yumi's bridal transport was to be the speedboat.

She betrayed none of the bashful confusion so common to and expected of brides to be; she was unruffled, brash and overweening, audacious and boastful. In other words, she behaved like someone with a powerful backer. She'd cut her hair short, which made her look almost athletic, ready to take on the world. She was wearing a neatly pressed red polyester top that was sheer, rich-looking, smooth, and stiff.

As she traveled the short distance from her home to the waiting speedboat, she created the unique impression of someone who was fond of both festive feminine attire and military bearing.

She looked at no one as she walked alongside the clerk, but she knew that everyone was looking at her. The way the clerk, a dignified man, bowed and scraped made it clear that he was not the groom, and the villagers knew instinctively that her husband was no ordinary man. Instead of entering the cabin when she boarded, Yumi sat on a bench in the open-air stern. The banks of the river were packed as she sat there proudly, looking less and less like a resident of Wang Family Village.

The arrival of Yumi's father, Wang Lianfang, silenced the jabbering crowds. Several months earlier, after serving as the village Party secretary for twenty years, he had lost his job and been driven out of the Party. Why? He'd wound up in the "wrong bed." The wrong bed indeed. Over that twenty-year period he had slept with many women, and had been heard to say that he'd maneuvered his way through the three generations—old, middle-aged, and young. But this last episode had constituted a major offense, a real transgression. One day, sometime later, when he was mightily drunk, he was heard to chant: "One must never screw a soldier's wife." On this day, when he reached the pier, Wang surveyed the speedboat with the flair and dignity of a village secretary; he still looked every bit the Party member. He raised his arm and, with a flick of the wrist, said, "Off you go."

The motor started up, sending waves racing to shore like dogs chasing a bone. After the boat had traveled a short distance, it turned in a wide circle and headed back; by the time it passed the pier, it was up to full speed. Yumi's short hair stood up in the wind; her blouse fluttered. She sat facing the wind, looking like one of those intrepid women in propaganda posters, a woman who could charm any man and still look death in the eye without flinching. The boat roared into the distance with the skipper sounding his horn repeatedly until only Yumi's red jacket was visible, waving like a flag.

Yumi's grandfather, grandmother, and five of her six sisters—Yusui, Yuying, Yuye, Yumiao, and Yuyang—were among the crowd of well-wishers; even her six-month-old baby brother was there in the arms of Yusui.

Her mother, Shi Guifang, had seen her only to the gate before returning to her room in the west wing, all alone in an empty and eerily quiet house. As she sat on the covered chamber pot she thought back to when Yumi was a little girl suckling at her breast. Then she recalled how Yumi would drool when she sucked her thumb, two little eyes surveying her surroundings like a thief, the glistening spittle stretching like rubber.

When Shi Guifang clapped her hands behind Yumi, the girl's large head would spin around and, because it rested on such a thin neck, would wobble a few seconds before steadying. Then she'd laugh, showing her gums, and reach out with both arms, pudgy as lotus roots, to grab hold of her mother. Scene after scene, it seemed like only yesterday, and now here Yumi was, about to be married, soon to be a wife and mother—to belong to someone else. Shi Guifang felt a crushing sadness. The only reason she didn't cry was that she didn't want to spoil her daughter's wedding day. And this was not the sole cause of her sadness; there was another even deeper one. Yumi had only told Guifang of her wedding plans a few days before. That is to say, she had kept everyone, including her mother, in the dark about her impending wedding. Shi Guifang had always assumed that Yumi and the aviator, Peng Guoliang, were still romantically involved. Several months earlier during his visit, they had grown inseparable, shutting themselves up in the kitchen and hardly ever leaving. Looking back now, it had been an unattainable dream for Yumi.

A few nights earlier, Yumi had said, "Ma, I'm getting married." What a shock that had been. Guifang had a bad feeling about it.

"To whom?" she had asked.

"The deputy director of the commune Revolutionary Committee. His name is Guo Jiaxing," she had replied.

So, a second wife. Desperate to know more, Shi Guifang did not have the nerve to ask any more questions when she saw the determined look on her daughter's face. But like mothers everywhere, she could guess what was in her daughter's heart, what fruit had been planted, and what flowers had grown. If Wang Lianfang had not suffered the calamity of losing his job and Party membership, the courtship between Yumi and her aviator would still be moving forward. And even if he'd called off the marriage, Yumi, with her good looks, would not have had to go to such extremes. She'd have found a marriage partner who would have helped erase the stain on her family's reputation. Suddenly beset by heartache, Shi Guifang covered her nose with a sheet of toilet paper. A sensible child can cause all sorts of anguish in a mother.

The third daughter of the family, Yuxiu, also stayed away from the pier. Yumi did not see Yuxiu anywhere as she searched the crowd of well-wishers before stepping into the boat. She knew why: her sister would never show up anyplace where there were wagging tongues. Truth be told, Yuxiu was the one Yumi worried about the most. They had always been at odds with each other.

117

Their mother often said that the "bad blood was a carryover from a previous life."

Yumi did not like Yuxiu, and Yuxiu felt the same way toward her. They were forever hatching schemes against each other, and over time their mutual animosity resulted in the creation of two camps among the seven sisters. Yumi commanded the loyalty of Yusui, Yuying, Yuye, Yumiao, and Yuyang; Yuxiu was a commander without an army.

As the eldest daughter, a mother figure herself, Yumi was in a position of authority. Her sisters, all but Yuxiu, did what she said. Yuxiu would not give Yumi the respect she desired. Her natural asset—her beauty—was the source of her defiance. She had beautiful eyes, a lovely nose, pretty lips, and perfect teeth. She was quite simply everything a young woman could want to be, and this was why she had developed an undisguised arrogance. She was not just beautiful; she was obsessed with her beauty, her mind focused solely on how she looked. Her hair, for instance. Although she wore braids like all the other girls, she managed to distinguish herself by leaving stray locks at her temples, which she twisted around her fingers so they would curl like melon vines alongside her ears. While that might not seem like much, it was eye-catching, different, coquettish, and reminiscent of the female enemy agents in the movies. She was a bundle of affectations, always acting a part, her attitude one of insouciance.

In general terms, the residents of Wang Family Village shared a common view of Secretary Wang's daughters: Yumi was a sensible girl, as the eldest ought to be; Yusui was flighty; Yuying was well-behaved; Yuye was stubborn; Yumiao was bad-tempered; and Yuyang was sweet. As for Yuxiu, they all agreed that she was a little fox fairy, a seductive girl. How could she fit in with her sisters? She had no qualms about being in conflict with any of the others; her bold independence stemmed not only from her good looks, but also from the fact that she had a backer.

Wang Lianfang showered his attentions on his son and was indifferent toward his daughters—except Yuxiu, whom he liked.

Why?

People were drawn to her, and that was reason enough for a Party secretary to be fond of her. With Yuxiu backed by her father, no one would have dared put her in front of a firing squad even if she had been an enemy agent. People liked to say that both the palm and the back of the hand are flesh and blood, so parents love all their children the same. It is a ridiculous saying. If you don't believe me, examine your own hand. The palm may be flesh and blood, but not the back, which is mostly bone wrapped in a thin layer of skin.

Given her natural inclinations and studied affectations, Yuxiu was secure with her father's backing. She picked on not only her younger sisters but her older sisters as well, after which she would cozy up to her father and complain about being mistreated, a girl all alone, charming and sweet, deserving of his sympathy, and eminently loveable. When there was trouble, she was usually at fault, yet she was always the first to complain, armed with all sorts of reasons or excuses. This trait, more than anything, upset her sisters, who found common cause to line up even more strongly in Yumi's camp against Yuxiu, the seductive tease.

And yet, as the eldest, Yumi needed to be prudent and adopt a well-thought-out strategy to deal with Yuxiu, especially when the family needed to unite against outsiders. She had to rally all the forces available to her, which included winning over Yuxiu to seek unity. Once Yumi had taken care of those outside forces, she'd close the door and turn her attention to dealing with the internal struggle between the two camps. She could launch a determined attack on precisely that which needed fixing. Either bringing the opposition over or beating it down would solidify her head of household status, which was her goal. While there was the appearance of two camps, in reality, it was a contest between two individuals—Yumi and Yuxiu.

In fact, Yuxiu was contemptuous of Yumi, whose greatest asset was her ability to mobilize the masses. One on one, Yumi might not have been up to the challenge. But given Yumi's pack of henchmen, Yuxiu was hopelessly outnumbered. Yumi's advantage was that Yuxiu gave little thought to numerical inferiority, for she was obsessed with her role as a fox fairy; she saw herself as a seductive serpent. With each alluring twist of the neck and flick of her forked tongue, she slithered along captivatingly no matter where she went.

The serpent's body had slithered along until the spring of 1971. Once that cold night had passed, Yuxiu was aware that the attractive serpent was a chimera.

The village was wild with joy on the day the incident occurred. The commune's movie boat had glided up to the Wang Family Village pier, and the residents were about to enjoy their first movie since Wang Lianfang had lost his position and been kicked out of the Party. It was a day of irrepressible jubilation.

Yuxiu was always happy when there was a movie. She and her sister had reacted differently to their father's troubles. Yumi appeared to be unconcerned, but that was all for show, a pretense. Yuxiu was the one who really did not care, for she had her beauty, something no one could take away. So she went to see the movie; Yumi did not. Yuxiu was smart enough to see the advantages of restraint, so she held back from grabbing a seat in the middle. Up till then, the best seats at a movie had always gone to the Wang family; no one would have dared squabble over them. Anyone who "beat the dog without seeing who owned it" was just asking for trouble.

On this evening, Yuxiu, with Yuye in tow, stood in the last row rather than work her way up through the crowd. The wife of Wang Caiguang, seeing that Yuye was too short to see over people's heads and not caring that the Wang family status had plummeted, graciously signaled them over and gave up her seat to Yuye. Years earlier, she had been one of Wang Lianfang's lovers. When the affair ended, she'd swallowed pesticide and jumped into the river, presenting a ghastly sight and having a significant impact on the village. Happily, that had been years before. As she stood beside Caiguang's wife, Yuxiu was quickly caught up in the movie, and when the night turned cold and the wind blew on her neck, she buried her hands in her sleeves to keep them warm and scrunched her neck down into her collar. About halfway through the movie, Yuxiu needed to relieve herself, but by then the winds were so strong that the screen began to billow and bend the hunched figures on it out of shape. She decided to stay put. She could wait till she got home. There is truth in the saying that, "Cold winds make for short necks, chilled air makes relief seem long."

On-screen, American bombers flew overhead and dropped their bombs on the Yalu River, making muffled sounds like those of a mother urging her child to pee. Pillars of water rose from the Yalu River; a major assault was on its way, and the movie was starting to get interesting. Then without warning, a pair of hands covered Yuxiu's eyes from behind. This was a favorite prank among local residents, and in the past, if someone had done that to Yuxiu in the middle of a movie, the prankster's lineage would have been the target of one of her withering curses. But not this time. "Hey! Whose cold claws are those?" she said with a laugh. But this time it didn't seem like a prank; the hands were pressing too hard.

Clearly upset, she was about to complain, when someone stuffed straw into her mouth. She was then hauled away and immediately set upon by many hands, which lifted her off the ground. She heard rapid footsteps. She fought, using all her strength; it was, however, a silent struggle.

The sound of exploding bombs and gunfire from the movie retreated into the distance as Yuxiu was flung down onto a haystack and blindfolded; then someone pulled her pants down, exposing the lower half of her body to the night winds. She shuddered and was shocked when her bladder betrayed her. The noise around her stopped abruptly, except for the raspy sounds of heavy breathing. All thoughts left her, everything but the will to save face. She tried to stop the flow of urine, but could not. She heard a hissing sound as it escaped. As soon as she finished, the racket around her started up again, and she heard the muted voice of a woman growl, "Don't go crazy. One at a time, one at a time." It sounded like Caiguang's wife, but Yuxiu couldn't be sure. Young as she was, she knew that her lower body was in danger, so she closed her legs as tightly as she could. Four hands pulled them apart again and held them. Then something hard pressed down on her thigh, and then it was inside her.

In the end, Yuxiu, who was crumpled up like a pile of rotting straw, was helped home by Yumi, joined by Yuye. The younger girl cried and said it hurt, but after she was cleaned up, she fell asleep. Not Yuxiu. Seventeen years old that year, she knew what had happened. She lay in bed in the arms of her older sister all night without shutting her eyes. The tears never stopped flowing, and before the night was over, her eyes were so swollen from crying she could barely open them. Yumi never left her side, drying her tears and shedding her own. They had never been so close; it was as if their mutual survival depended on it. Yuxiu spent the entire next day in bed, neither eating nor drinking, and tormented by nightmares. Yumi brought food and then took it away, over and over. Yuxiu refused to eat.

Finally, on the fourth day, she opened her mouth; her lips were flaked with dead skin. Holding a bowl of sticky rice porridge in her hand, Yumi fed her sister one slow spoonful at a time, and as Yuxiu looked up at Yumi, she abruptly wrapped her arms around her sister's waist. Weak though she was, she held on with all her might, her hands like those of a corpse. Instead of trying to pry them apart, Yumi ran her fingers through Yuxiu's hair, then combed and braided it. Finally, she told Yuyang to fetch a basin of water to wash Yuxiu's face.

When that was done, she took her sister's hand and said, "Get up and come with me." She said it softly but with authority.

Blurry-eyed, Yuxiu looked up at her sister and shook her head.

"Are you just going to hole up here? How long do you expect to do that? Our family has never been afraid of anyone, don't you know that?" Yumi said.

She opened a drawer, took out a pair of scissors, and handed them to Yuxiu. "Cut off your braids and then come with me," she said.

Yuxiu shook her head again, but the meaning behind it was different this time. Then she was afraid to go outside; now it was the refusal to part with her braids.

"What do you want to keep them for? It was your seductive manner that got you into this trouble in the first place," Yumi said, as she snatched the scissors out of her sister's hand and—*snip*—one of Yuxiu's braids fell to the floor—*snip*—then the other braid joined it. She picked the braids up off the floor and tossed them into the commode, then tucked the scissors into her waistband, took Yuxiu by the hand, and started out the door.

"Come with me," she said. "I'll cut the tongue out of anyone who says a word."

So Yumi strolled through the village with Yuxiu, who shuffled along, her limp body seemingly weightless and quite ugly. Her hair, now minus the braids, looked like a nest of straw and chicken feathers. Yumi, armed with the scissors, was her protector. One look was all it took anyone to figure out her intentions, and they dared not meet that glare; they either turned away or walked off.

She kept telling her sister, who trailed behind her, to hold her head up. Yuxiu did as she was told. Though she was drawing strength from her sister's fierce demeanor—the fox parading along behind the tiger—at least she was out in public.

Unspoken feelings of gratitude toward Yumi rose up inside her, tempered by an inexpressible sense of loathing. It was an unfounded loathing, utterly unreasonable, and yet there it was, deep in the marrow of her bones. They had fought for years, but in the end, she had no choice but to rely on Yumi's authority and her sympathy.

Why had Yumi been born a girl? she wondered. *How wonderful it would have been if she were a boy, my older brother.*

But she wasn't; Yumi was her older sister, and now she was getting married and moving away. The wedding boat was tied up at the pier, and Yuxiu had not gone to see her off. Yuxiu was afraid to. She might hate her sister, but she wished that Yumi didn't have to leave Wang Family Village. Yuxiu the fox was lost without Yumi the tiger. No longer would she find the courage to mix with people, to be in a crowd. She slipped over to the concrete bridge to the east, where she leaned against the railing and waited, looking far off in the distance. Her lovely eyes, now filled with melancholy and anxiety, were trained on the jubilant scene at the distant pier; none of that joy reached far down the river to Yuxiu. Sunlight danced crazily on the surface of the river, fragmented and blinding. The boat was coming her way, and as it neared the bridge, Yumi spotted Yuxiu. The sisters, one in a boat, the other on a bridge, stared at each other as the distance closed and they could see each other more clearly. The boat sped under the bridge, and both girls spun around to keep looking at each other, although now the distance increased and their figures grew more indistinct. Then Yuxiu saw Yumi stand up in the boat and shout something. The wind carried it up to her. She heard every word: *Don't forget to carry a knife when you go out.*

The roar of the motor faded as the boat turned at a bend in the river and disappeared from view. The waves it had created had smoothed out, and now only a bright scar was left on the surface. Yuxiu was still on the bridge, still looking down the river, seemingly focused but actually in a daze. The sun had migrated to the western sky, casting a red patina over the river and elongating Yuxiu's shadow on its surface, at once docile and quivering. She looked down at that shadow, staring at it so long that it turned into an optical illusion, looking as if it were being carried along by the ripples on the water. But by regaining her focus, she saw that it had stayed put and was not going anywhere. *If only my shadow could transform itself into a speedboat,* she was thinking, *I could leave Wang Family Village and go anywhere I wanted.*

Yuxiu was surprised to see a dozen or more little girls standing in a circle in front of her door when she turned into the lane. She walked up to see what they were doing and spotted her second sister, Yusui, in the middle, showing off a spring-and-autumn blouse Yumi had left behind, the one Liu Fenxiang had worn as the propaganda troupe's program announcer; it had a decidedly urban look—a turned-down collar and a narrow waist. Yumi would never have considered wearing any of that woman's clothes, but she hadn't the heart to throw anything that pretty away.

Yuxiu was a different matter altogether. She had kept her eye on the blouse for some time. There is a popular saying that goes "Men never turn down a drink, and women never say no to clothes." Who cares whom it belonged to? A pretty blouse is a pretty blouse was how Yuxiu looked at it. But she hadn't worn it yet, out of a fear of Yumi. Imagine her surprise when Yusui claimed it the minute Yumi was out the door. Something that nice on Yusui was like a hungry dog with a turd in its mouth—it cannot be pried out.

Yuxiu stopped at the lane entrance to observe Yusui with a squint. How could something that nice lose its charm as soon as Yusui put it on? The look on Yuxiu's face was not pretty. Obviously, now that Yumi was gone, Yusui was setting herself up as the new head of household. An ordinary girl like her ought at least to take a good look at herself. The longer Yuxiu stood there, the dumber her sister appeared, especially now that she'd ruined a perfectly good blouse. Yuxiu elbowed her way up next to Yusui and demanded, "Take it off."

"Says who?" Yusui replied, still caught up in the excitement.

"I said take it off," Yuxiu said in a tone that left no room for bargaining.

Apparently softening a bit, but not ready to give in, Yusui repeated, "Says who?"

Used to having her way, Yuxiu got in her sister's face and said icily, "Are you going to take it off or aren't you?"

Yusui knew that she was no match for Yuxiu, but one glance at the other girls told her that she'd lose face if she gave in meekly. In the end, she took off the blouse, held it for a moment by the collar then dropped it on the ground and stomped all over it.

"Take it," she screamed. "You act so high and mighty, even after all those men have had you. You piss pot! You shit can!"

Before eight o'clock in the morning, the main street of Broken Bridge is, in essence, an open-air market that sends a jumble of smells from one end to the other. But after eight, the street undergoes a transformation, becoming clean and orderly. This comes about not by fiat but by the demands of daily life, which are strictly followed and unchanging. The middle-school PA system crackles to life, heralding a solemn moment: "Beijing time—8.00 A.M." Beijing time: distant, intimate, sacred, a symbol of unity, a sign that all China's citizens live planned, disciplined lives—not only the residents of Beijing, but everyone in the country. The beloved Chairman Mao is already attending to state affairs at Tiananmen,[3] and it is time for womenfolk in towns everywhere to stop haggling over prices. The morning sun's slanting rays light up the street and are reflected off of the cobblestones, turning them red. Small pockets of quiet, bordering on total stillness, settle over the street, belying the preparations already underway. And then the general store opens its door, and the purchasing co-op opens its door. The post office, the credit union, the commune offices, the hospital, the farm-tools factory, the blacksmith and carpentry shops, the provisions branch, the grain-purchasing station, the transport office, the culture station, and the livestock-purchasing station—every unit subsumed under the nation slowly opens its big iron door for business. No longer an open-air market, the street has become an integral part of the "nation," involved in the functions and powers of "state." As these doors open one by one, a ceremonial aura quietly infuses the street, even though, not surprisingly, the townsfolk are unaware of it; it is an aura of willful indolence with a hint of solemnity. It is the moment when the new day officially begins.

Guo Jiaxing arrived at his office every day at eight. Eight o'clock on the dot. Sitting at his desk, he steeped a cup of tea, crossed his legs, and started his day with two newspapers and one magazine,[4] carefully reading every word. This could almost be mistaken for a form of study. Guo sat at his desk in town all day long, but for all practical purposes, he spent every day in Beijing, following with interest everything that happened in the nation's capital. He would never overlook who among the leading comrades moved up in the hierarchy and who moved down. The year before, for instance, seven members of the leadership had greeted Prince Norodom Sihanouk, but this year three of them had been replaced. Over the past few days, newspapers had reported that one of the three had been sent to Tanzania and a second was in Inner Mongolia, involved in "cordial discussions with herdsmen." There was no news of the third. This name, the status of which was unclear, was one that Guo would keep in mind for weeks afterward, and if too much time passed with no subsequent mention, he would bring it up with commune leaders, keeping his tone as somber as possible: "so and so" has not been heard from for quite some time, he'd say. Eventually, when "so and so" resurfaced in the papers—his name or his photograph—Guo, now relieved, would pass the news on to his comrades. He was given to equating the names in his two newspapers and one magazine with the nation. Concern for them was the equivalent of being concerned for his country. He paid attention to them not because he was ambitious and wanted to move up the ladder.

He wasn't the type. He had gotten to where he was by toeing the Party line and wanted to keep it that way. Spending the rest of his career as a commune official was what he desired, for he was a man perfectly content with what he had. His routine had become an ingrained habit formed over many years until it was part of his nature. One day was just like every other one.

Guo Jiaxing was not concerned about individual people, not even himself. In his rigid approach to life, he kept the motherland in mind and the world in view, as Chairman Mao had once said. The concepts of birth, old age, sickness, and death bored him, as did thoughts about the daily necessities—the oil, salt, vinegar, and soy sauce—of life. To him those were trivial, vulgar, insipid, meaningless things. And yet, it was trivia that in recent days had him in its grip, and he was having trouble freeing himself from it. This situation had its origins in one of the revolutionary committee's deputy chairmen. "Three flames burn in the bellies of middle-aged men," this comrade had joked when he saw Yumi. "Promotion, riches, and the death of a wife. Deputy Chairman Guo has now managed one of them."

It was an antiquated sentiment, an unhealthy remnant of the old society, and Guo was not happy when word of the comment reached him. But it made him think, and he had to admit that there was truth to it. He was not in line for promotion and had not gotten rich, but his wife had died, and by rights he should have been in the throes of depression and self-pity. And he'd expected to be. But he wasn't. No, he was upbeat, energized, vigorous, inflamed.

Why?

Because his wife had died. Out with the old and in with

the new. And there was more: his beautiful new wife, who was young enough to be his daughter, had satiny skin. While he would not have admitted it publicly, in his heart, Guo Jiaxing knew that the source of his happiness could be traced to his bed and Yumi's body.

As he thought back over the past several years, he realized what a lethargic sex life he'd had. He and his wife were an old married couple, too familiar for their own good; and having sex was like attending a meeting: first, setting up the room, then calling to order, followed by reports and finally adjournment. A seemingly significant act was, in fact, an insipid experience. And, understandably, there had been no more meetings after his wife had contracted her fatal illness. To put a fine point on it, Guo Jiaxing had not had sex for more than a year, maybe two. Fortunately, his interest and desire had not been pronounced. There's something to be said for celibacy.

Who'd have thought that spring would come to a dying tree; that the sago palm would bloom again? Guo Jiaxing would have been the last person to believe that he could be revitalized at that age, and for that he had to thank Yumi, a sex partner who knew exactly how to please him. More than that, she was very considerate. If he was lusting after her, she'd rest his head on her breasts and say, "Don't overtax your body. Slow water runs far. Besides, who would want to take a hag like me away from you? And what am I supposed to do if you ruin your health? I'd be left with nothing." Then she'd shed a tear or two to show how sad she'd be, though the effect was more endearing than sad. Guo was puzzled over how sex had become so important in his life after having given it little thought for so long—until

Yumi arrived, that is. She could not hold him off, so she moved with him until they were both sweaty. Their bed was always wet afterward, and Yumi never could figure out why sex made her sweat so much. It was hard work for her, so one day she said, "Why don't you go find a woman? You're too much for me." Obviously, that comment did not square with what she'd said in the past, but pillow talk has a way of defying logic. And Guo Jiaxing loved to hear her talk like that. It was music to the ears of this fifty-year-old man, since it meant that Guo Jiaxing wasn't old, that he was still in the prime of life. In order to recapture his youth in the marital bed, Guo secretly began doing push-ups. At first he'd barely managed one; but he was now up to four or five, and at this rate, twenty or more should be no problem by the end of the year.

As far as Guo Jiaxing was concerned, Yumi was best off staying at home to sew and wash and clean. When he told her that, she kept her head down and said nothing, as was expected from the obedient young wife of an older man. That pleased him just fine. So she became a proper housewife, serving her husband in and out of bed. Until the night she took it into her head to be slightly roguish. Her husband had gone out drinking with commune colleagues, and when he came home, thanks to the alcohol, he wanted to take her straight to bed. She said no, which was out of character. So, without a word, he undressed her. She did not resist at first, but when she was naked, she covered herself with one hand and grabbed him with the other. "I said no." She looked tantalizing, a blend of propriety and promiscuity. She was being playful, and he did not get angry. Instead, inflamed with desire, his heart snapping like a banner in a gale, he reached a point where he'd have inserted his whole body if he could. "I need it," he said. Yumi ignored him and turned her head away. "I said I need it."

This time she let go, pressed her breasts against him and said, "Get me a job at the supply and marketing co-op."

Guo's passion had nearly frozen his tongue, and he did not know what to say.

"Do it for me tomorrow," she said.

He agreed.

Yumi ran her fingers through her hair and lay back, arms and legs open for him. He was so excited by this time that the passionate lovemaking he'd been anticipating turned out to be a disappointment—he finished almost before he began.

"I'm sorry," she said softly as she lay beneath him, her arms wrapped around his neck. "I'm really sorry." She said it so many times that it saddened her and she was soon in tears.

Actually there was no need to apologize. It had not gone well, but ultimately it had no effect on his passion. If anything, it had been an intoxicating experience. He was breathing hard, experiencing a growing attachment to his young wife. She was definitely worth keeping.

The supply and marketing co-op had not been Yumi's first choice. She'd have preferred an assignment to the grain-purchasing station. And for good reason. The purchasing station was on the river, near Broken Bridge's largest concrete pier, and it was where all boats to and from the commune tied up or passed by. She figured that if she was put in charge of the scales, a position of authority, anyone who came to town from Wang Family Village could not help but notice her. She had it all worked out. But on second thought, managing scales was dirty work that would keep her out on the pier, and that was not a proper job for someone who lived in town. Clerking at the co-op was more respectable. Better surroundings, lighter work. So, after carefully weighing the pros and cons of each, she settled on the co-op. It was not a permanent position, but she'd get nearly three yuan more in wages. But then, what about the purchasing station job? That should go to someone in her family, of course. At first she thought of Yusui, but she was too empty-headed for that kind of work. No, Yuxiu was the right choice. Intelligent and attractive, she was better suited for life in town than Yusui.

But Yumi had no sooner arrived at her decision than a troubling thought surfaced. *I've been pinned down in bed, selling what's between my legs, while that little tramp Yuxiu would land a good job. She'd be in better shape than me.*

But that thought did not last. *Isn't what I'm doing the best way to win back some dignity for my family? It's worth it.*

Now Yumi's most important tasks were to keep performing in bed—doing what he liked best—and to get pregnant as soon as possible. It was critical to take advantage of his sense of newness; if she got pregnant now, managing him would be easy. If not, once the novelty wore off, who's to say what he'd do? Men are like that. What they want is sex. Feelings mean nothing to them. A woman could have a ton of feelings for a man, and that would not count as much to him as the several ounces she carries on her chest.

Yumi had barely begun working at the co-op and had not found the right moment to talk to Guo Jiaxing about Yuxiu when her sister unexpectedly came to town. She showed up at Guo Jiaxing's office before nine in the morning, her face wet with dew and sweat. Guo was at his desk reading the paper, but not taking in a word because he was dreamily recalling some of Yumi's tricks in bed. Sex was all he had on his mind. He rubbed his bald head and sighed, sounding like a man disappointed in himself.

The old house has gone up in flames and can't be saved, he said to himself. He was not really upset; the sigh was more a display of that special happiness only an aging man knows. So there he sat, happily analyzing the good fortune that had befallen him, when a girl appeared in the doorway of his office. He'd never seen her before and guessed her to be about sixteen or seventeen.

Quickly wiping the expression off of his face, he lowered his newspaper and coughed dryly. He stared at the girl, who showed no hint of fear or any sign of leaving. So, after laying the paper down on the top of his desk and sliding his glass of tea to one side, he leaned back in his chair and said gruffly, "Who let you in here?"

The girl blinked several times and smiled sweetly. "Comrade," she said abruptly, "aren't you my brother-in-law?"

That sounded so funny to Guo that he felt like laughing, but he didn't. He stood up, clasped his hands behind his back, and shut his eyes. "And who might you be?"

"I'm Wang Yumi's third sister, my name is Wang Yuxiu. I arrived this morning from Wang Family Village, and you're my brother-in-law. That's what the man at the entrance said. You're my brother-in-law." The word "brother-in-law" in her crisp voice carried a distinct feel of intimacy, the closeness of family. The deputy director of the Revolutionary Committee in charge of the People's Militia could tell at a glance that the girl was Yumi's sister; the resemblance was unmistakable. But she obviously lacked Yumi's manners and did not appear to share her sister's temperament. She was like one of those unbalanced Japanese machine guns, indiscriminately strafing the area—*tatatata*. Guo walked to the doorway and pointed outside. Then he curled his finger and said, "She's in the shoe and hat department at the co-op."

Yuxiu had arrived in Broken Bridge at a little after seven and had already taken a turn around the open-air market. This was not a casual visit. She had come with the express and unwavering purpose of putting herself in the hands of her elder sister. She could no longer stay in Wang Family Village, and the main reason was that Yusui had forced her to wear two labels: "Piss Pot" and "Shit Can."

Once those epithets began making the rounds, she could not hold her head up in the village. Worst of all, it had been her sister, not a stranger, who had coined those terms of abuse in front of a bunch of girls. There was no one else to blame. Piss Pot. And Shit Can. They had quickly become her nicknames. While a nickname isn't a real name, often it can be more *you* than your real name. It zeroes in on your flaws and your most vulnerable sore spots.

Hearing one is like being skinned alive. Even ten thousand pairs of pants cannot cover up your shame. Nicknames are poison to the person they're given to, everyone knows that. But they are not static; they have an uncanny ability to expand, and that is what Yuxiu found intolerable. Piss Pot for instance. Why not piss bottle, or vat, or jug, or jar, or ladle, or basin, or bowl, or saucer, or vase, or roof tile?

None of these had had any intrinsic relationship to Yuxiu, but that had all changed. Now they constituted a sinister threat, the ability to ruthlessly reveal the unspeakable secret of her shamed body.

These common objects could be found anywhere; and so could Yuxiu's shame. She was not being paranoid, that was not it at all. When she was talking with someone who mentioned one of those objects, the person would stop and flash an apologetic look, pregnant with meaning. It was a true affirmation, binding all those everyday objects to Yuxiu, quietly but with inescapable permanence. Once something like that attaches itself to you, it strips you naked in front of a crowd. Covering the top exposes the bottom, and covering the bottom reveals the top. Sure, the crowd feels sorry for you. Out of sympathy they keep from saying anything, pretending, as if by mutual agreement, that they didn't hear what was said. To protect your feelings, no one laughs. At least not out loud. But you can see laughter in their eyes, and that silent laughter is far more hurtful, holds greater cruelty than spoken curses. Like sharp teeth that can snap shut on you at any time, it is an embodiment of the explosive power of jaws that can crush you at will. Deadly. Too much for Yuxiu. Even the most tenacious head must bow before it. It is a situation against which no defense is possible. In her case, such indefensible situations did not always involve external forces. Sometimes they cropped up within Yuxiu herself. Shit Can is one example. It was a taboo, and so she avoided all words dealing with toilets and such, whether she was relieving herself or emptying the commode. And as the

137

restrictions grew, her freedom of movement diminished. She hated having to use the commode, for big or for small. Every time she peed, it made a despicable sound, underscoring her loss of dignity, her shamefulness. If only she didn't have to go. But she did. So she only went on the sly, each visit to the toilet making her feel like a thief. She held it in during the day and she held it in at night, and she even had nightmares about peeing that woke her up. In one of those terrible dreams she hunted for a place to pee, and this eventually led her to a deserted sorghum field. But she no sooner squatted down than a crowd of girls descended upon her. "Yuxiu," they whispered, "Shit Can." With a start she woke up. She saw people everywhere, faces with mouths and pairs of laughing eyes above them.

Worst of all for Yuxiu were the men. They never failed to give her the eye when they walked by and greeted her with salacious smiles, as if they were reliving indulgent pleasures. Such knowing looks were unspoken claims of mutual understanding, as if the men were tied to her in countless ways. In front of others, the smiles were replaced by sanctimonious looks that said, "Nothing wrong here." How sickening. That's not to say she was unaware that something had happened between them and her. But paralyzing fear kept her from bringing it into the open. They, of course, weren't about to do so either. Which made them co-conspirators—joint keepers of a secret. She was one of them.

Fortunately Yuxiu had enough self-awareness to avoid crowds unless it was absolutely necessary. That brought her a measure of tranquility, but not without a cost: she became unbearably lonely. As someone who was used to being popular, this change was especially hard to take. The only people she felt comfortable around were the most inferior, those shunned by everyone else. Either they came from families with bad backgrounds, or they weren't very smart, or they were seen as flighty. Before all this had happened, Yuxiu would have shunned them too. Now that she had no choice, she derived little joy and rather a lot of unhappiness and bitterness from her association with them. But there it was again—she had no choice.

That's not to say they didn't get along, mainly because they idolized her and were proud to be seen as her friends. They looked up to her and saw her as their model, and she found that gratifying. They followed in her wake, emulating everything she did and said, as if she had joined their ranks. Their looks of pride, however, only made them appear even more stupid. If they had a disagreement with someone else, words that Yuxiu had used became their weapon.

"That's what Yuxiu said," was their declaration of war. "That's how Yuxiu does it" would be spoken with passion, the speakers secure in the knowledge that they had nothing to fear. It removed all doubt. This gave Yuxiu a sense of accomplishment, for she placed great stock in the effect she had on people.

"Better to be the head of a chicken than the tail of a phoenix" was her motto. Everything seemed to be going well, but the good times could not last. One day she made such a fool of herself that she could no longer stay in Wang Family Village. The incident centered on Zhang Huaizhen, who lived nearby, one lane over. Although Zhang and Yuxiu had never been close in the past, she was an intelligent girl, not one to be taken lightly. Fate had dictated that she be born into the wrong family—a very bad family, in fact.

Just how bad was complicated and requires more than a brief explanation. The girl had reached marrying age, but none of the prospective matches had panned out. So the matchmaker proposed what she considered the perfect match—in this case, the grandson of a national traitor. The boy agreed and sent over a *jin* of brown sugar, another of white sugar, coupons for two *jin* of grain, a coupon for six *chi* of fabric, and two and a half *jin* of streaky pork. All in all, a generous amount of betrothal gifts. Huaizhen said no, and nothing could change her mind, not even her mother's persuasive arguments.

She returned the gifts and immediately turned into a willing mute, going all day long without saying a word. People in the village assumed that the matchmaker had said something so hurtful that the girl had stopped talking. The matchmaker, who'd suffered a great loss of face, pointed at a bitch on the side of the road and said, "You think you can open those legs of yours and win over the masses. Well, dream on." At that moment, Zhang Huaizhen vowed never to marry. From that day on, she walked around with the face of a widow, ignoring everyone who came to her door with marriage proposals.

Then for some reason she and Yuxiu became friends, able to talk freely about all manner of things. Having a friend like Yuxiu instilled a sense of pride in Huaizhen, who was transformed into a real chatterbox, never failing to sing Yuxiu's praises to anyone who would listen. On this particular afternoon, she met Yuxiu on the bridge on her way home from the fields, carrying a hoe on her shoulder.

Huaizhen was not quite herself that day, possibly because there were so many people around. Wanting to show everyone that she and Yuxiu were more than ordinary friends, she ostentatiously draped her arm around Yuxiu's shoulder just as a group of young men were walking up. Wanting to look good, Yuxiu tried to toss her hair, but it was caught under Huaizhen's arm.

"Take your arm away, Huaizhen," she said. But instead, Huaizhen hugged Yuxiu even closer, which pulled Yuxiu's blouse to the side and gave her a slovenly look. Yuxiu was very unhappy, so she wrinkled her nose and said, "Huaizhen, why is your underarm odor so strong?"

Everyone heard her. Huaizhen was stunned that Yuxiu would say something like that. Without a word, she removed her arm, turned, and walked home. By dinnertime that night, Yuxiu's calamity was on its way, although she did not know it. She was eating a bowl of rice porridge at the head of the lane when a group of a dozen or so boys from five to about eight years in age walked up to her door, each with a handful of broad beans. "*Kuang kuang kuang,*" they hollered as they ate the beans, "Piss Pot Wang, *kuang kuang kuang,* Shit Can Wang." At first she didn't pay attention and wasn't sure what Piss Pot Wang and Shit Can Wang referred to. But she quickly figured out what they meant.

The real hurt came from the word "Wang." In other words, the boys were calling her "Queen of the Piss Pot" and "Queen of the Shit Can." She simply stood there, rice bowl in one hand, chopsticks in the other, and acted dumb. She couldn't make them stop, and they were so loud that several other kids walked up to join them. Crowds are like that: as long as they make enough noise, plenty of people will join in. This particular crowd kept getting bigger and began taking on the look of a parade.

They yelled so loud that their faces turned red and their necks thickened.

"*Kuang kuang kuang,* Piss Pot Wang, *kuang kuang kuang,* Shit Can Wang, *kuang kuang kuang,* Piss Pot Wang, *kuang kuang kuang,* Shit Can Wang."

Too young to realize what they were doing, they thought that they were just having fun. But while they may not have known what they were saying, people who heard them did. Things were getting interesting. Before Yuxiu knew it, the lane was filled with people, mostly adults. As if they were watching an outdoor opera, they laughed and talked and had a grand time. Piss Pot and Shit Can.

At first the words had only hinted at something, and were little more than a verbal game. But not now. They had floated to the surface, had gone public, and had taken on fixed meanings. They had become slogans invested with deep emotional impact. Everyone who witnessed the incident knew that.

Meanwhile, Yuxiu stood there not knowing what to say or do, and her face underwent a slow change. She felt a greater shame than if she had been standing there naked. She might as well have been a dog. The sun was about to set behind the mountain, and the sky above Wang Family Village turned blood red. As she stood in the lane, Yuxiu felt like biting someone, but she didn't have the strength. The soupy rice had long since dribbled down her chin. "*Kuang kuang kuang,* Piss Pot Wang. *Kuang kuang kuang,* Shit Can Wang! *Kuang kuang kuang,* Piss

Pot Wang. *Kuang kuang kuang,* Shit Can Wang!" It had a nice ring to it, like a chant.

Before she left home, Yuxiu swore that once she walked out the front door, she would never again set foot in Wang Family Village. She'd be ashamed to show her face in this place. She had no interest in settling scores with its residents. If everyone is your enemy, it is the same as having no enemies. When there are too many lice, you stop scratching.

Yuxiu accepted what had befallen her. She could let everyone off the hook but the little whore Yusui. Thanks to her, Yuxiu was no longer able to hold her head up in Wang Family Village. If the little whore had never uttered those evil, hurtful words, none of this would have happened. The girl would have to pay, especially since she was her own sister. This was one score Yuxiu was determined to settle. And once she'd made up her mind, she swung into action.

One morning before the sun was up, Yuxiu got out of bed and tiptoed up to Yusui's bed with a kerosene lantern.

The little whore really was a simpleton; she looked dumber than other people even when she slept, with her arms and legs spread all over the place like a dead pig. Yuxiu set down the lantern and took out a pair of scissors. In a matter of seconds, Yusui was bald on one side, not neatly, but as if a dog had gnawed on her hair. It changed her appearance so much that she looked like a different—and very strange—person.

After laying the locks of hair in Yusui's hand, Yuxiu slapped her sister twice and ran. She'd barely made it to the door when she heard odd noises coming from Yusui. Seeing her own hair in her hand must have scared the little whore silly, especially

143

since she had no idea what had happened. All she could do was scream.

Yuxiu ran as fast and as far as she could, and when she conjured up the bizarre image of Yusui holding clumps of her own hair in her hand, she had to laugh. Soon she was laughing so hard her body seemed to get lighter and she could barely breathe. Few people were as stupid as Yusui, the little whore. It took her forever to realize that her cheeks were stinging. The little whore's head must be filled with pig guts.

Once she had settled into a room in the commune compound, Yuxiu uncharacteristically turned into a hardworking, almost servile resident. Yumi could tell that her sister had come to Broken Bridge not because she was clever enough to anticipate Yumi's plan. Not at all. The little fox fairy had dragged her broken tail to town because she couldn't stay another day in Wang Family Village. That was a fact.

Yumi would know what sort of fart was coming whenever Yuxiu fidgeted. Pleased with the change in her newly servile sister, she saw no need to tell her about the purchasing station, not yet. Better to give her time to put her lazy past behind her and get rid of her haughty ways. Things had changed, and Yumi was beginning to place a bit of hope in Yuxiu. Time for her to learn how to get along in this world. The girl's flirty nature had been a constant worry, but no longer.

Rape is never a good thing, but in this case, it had led to a radical shift in behavior when Yuxiu realized that she needed to change for the better. A terrible incident had produced positive results.

Yuxiu had not yet fully recovered from her frightful ordeal;

she still had a ways to go to feel as safe and secure as Yumi did, and as the days passed, the heaviness in her heart actually increased. She had left home with one thought—to get as far away from Wang Family Village as possible—and had never considered the prospect that Yumi might not want to take her in.

If that happened, however remote the possibility, she would have no place to go, and now that she had taken the fateful step, fear over that grim scenario began to set in. To complicate matters, there was Guo Jiaxing to deal with, not to mention his daughter, Guo Qiaoqiao; and that made her situation even more grim.

It did not take Yuxiu long to realize that her fate was not in the hands of Yumi, but in those of Guo Jiaxing and, quite possibly, his daughter. Yumi may have considered herself important in Wang Family Village, but in this house she enjoyed no discernible authority. None, actually. This came across most clearly at the dinner table, where Guo always sat at the head in his rattan chair, facing south. He was in the habit of smoking a cigarette before the meal, scowling as if he were angry at someone.

Qiaoqiao was different. A sophomore in high school, she was known for her antics and the loud, coarse language that emerged from her mouth. But at home she was a different person. She'd pull a face as long as a carrying pole and, like her father, appear to be angry at someone. That someone, obviously, was Yumi. When the rice bowls were filled, Yumi sat between Guo Jiaxing on her left and Qiaoqiao on her right, an arrangement that put her on tenterhooks, afraid that she'd do something wrong. When she reached out with her chopsticks to pick something out of a dish, she'd sneak a look first at Guo Jiaxing, then at Qiaoqiao, to check out the looks on their faces.

Yuxiu had spotted this right off. Yumi was afraid of Guo Jiaxing in a strange way that managed to attach her fear to his daughter as well. She was forever trying to win over the girl, but invariably failed, and that drove her to distraction. That knowledge was why Yuxiu was so scrupulous in waiting on the father and daughter. If she indulged them to their satisfaction, Yumi would not be able to send her packing.

Yuxiu had a good idea of how to deal with Guo Jiaxing. Any man his age was susceptible to flattery from a pretty and flirtatious girl. For proof of that she needed to look no further than her own father, Wang Lianfang.

If anything, she was even more confident where Qiaoqiao was concerned. All she had to do was demean herself in Qiaoqiao's presence, thereby convincing the girl of her own superiority, to win the day. Granted, it was not something Yuxiu did with pleasure, but she had only to remind herself that she was used goods, and in that case, what was there to be unhappy about?

Yuxiu worked especially hard in front of Guo Jiaxing and his daughter, always bowing and scraping for their benefit. Qiaoqiao was touched by the first thing Yuxiu ever did for her: coming in early in the morning and discreetly emptying the girl's chamber pot.

Qiaoqiao was not only a foolish girl, she was also a slob. She compounded her slovenly appearance by eating and drinking as much as she could every day, which made for a full chamber pot. Yuxiu could not even guess when the girl had last emptied it on her own, and when she picked it up, the vile contents splashed over her hand. That action produced instantaneous results—Qiaoqiao actually spoke to her.

Yuxiu was off to a terrific start. When it was time to eat, her shrewdness served her well. Keeping her eye on everyone's rice bowl, she was quick to act as soon as one was empty.

"Here, let me, brother-in-law," or "Don't get up, Qiaoqiao, I'll get it for you." Her cunning also manifested itself in how she acted during meals when she adopted a strategy that was the opposite of Yumi's. It was a gamble, but at mealtimes she put on a happy act. Pretending she was in high spirits, she talked nonstop, asking all sorts of comical, even silly questions. She'd cock her head in front of Guo Jiaxing and bat her eyelids.

"Brother-in-law," she'd say, "do all members of the leadership have double-fold eyelids?"

Or "Brother-in-law, are all communes 'common' or could some be 'uncommon'?"

Or "Exactly where is the Party? Is it in Beijing, the 'northern capital,' or in Nanjing, the 'southern capital'?"

Those were the kinds of questions she asked meal after meal, and she was never prettier than when she was asking them. Her face was bright, her look one of naiveté and innocence with a trace of seduction. Some were honest questions, things she truly didn't know, and others she made up for effect. It was exhausting work, racking her brains for things to ask. Fortunately, her father had been a Party secretary for twenty years, which supplied both a rich source of topics and the courage to put them into words.

Yuxiu's foolishness embarrassed Yumi, who tried to stop her. She was surprised to learn that Guo and his daughter actually found Yuxiu's questions intriguing and pleasing to the ear. She put smiles on their faces. Qiaoqiao even spit out a mouthful of rice several times from laughing so hard. Yumi, who never thought something like that could happen, was secretly pleased. Guo himself pointed to Yuxiu with his chopsticks after a hearty laugh and said to Yumi, "She's a fascinating little comrade."

Yuxiu was given a room behind the kitchen, facing the living quarters; from there she secretly observed Guo and his daughter as much as possible, waiting for the opportunity to divulge her desire to stay in Broken Bridge. The timing had to be perfect, and she needed to do it just right. She would have one chance, one beat of the drum. If she blew her chance the first time around, there would not be a second. She could not afford to be haphazard.

Sunday. There were no classes, so Qiaoqiao was home. Yuxiu decided to do Qiaoqiao's hair before lunch, something she did with instinctive imagination and creativity. After Yuxiu gave Qiaoqiao a shampoo, the basin was filled with greasy water. It was disgusting.

Even before she was finished, Yuxiu developed a loathing for this idiotic cunt, who was beneath contempt; she'd have liked nothing better than to shove the girl's face into that basin of pig grease and drown her. But her fate was tied to the girl, so she forced every finger on both hands to be obedient and docile. After the girl's hair was clean and dried, it was time for Yuxiu to comb and braid it.

Until now, Qiaoqiao had always worn a single, thick, unattractive braid, which gave her a hard, somewhat imperious look. Yuxiu thinned her hair with scissors, then parted it down the middle and gave Qiaoqiao a pair of small braids, which she coiled up and fastened at the ends. The tips of the braids rested just above her ears and bounced slightly when she moved—a mischievously chic look like that of the typical spoiled daughter of a traitor in the cinema. Without those two braids, Qiaoqiao, who was a bit of a tomboy to begin with, could easily have been mistaken for a boy. But now, thanks to Yuxiu's grooming, she at least looked like a girl and was clearly pleased with the results.

As she stood off to the side, Yuxiu said in a voice dripping with envy, "I'd love to have hair like yours, Qiaoqiao." She sounded sad, and once flattery reached that level of emotion, a recipient would have to be made of wood not to be moved. As expected, Qiaoqiao loved the sound of that comment. She beamed, grinning from ear to ear like a clam. All you could see on her face was her mouth. One look told Yuxiu that this was her chance.

She sighed. "Wouldn't it be wonderful if I could be your personal servant, Qiaoqiao? But no such luck, I'm afraid."

Qiaoqiao was admiring herself in the mirror, first from one angle, then another, marveling over how nice she looked.

"That shouldn't be much of a problem," Qiaoqiao blurted out.

Yuxiu carried on a cheerful conversation with Qiaoqiao during lunch, which sounded strange to Guo Jiaxing, since that wasn't like his daughter, who was never chummy with Yumi. But she obviously was with Yuxiu.

After losing her mother at such a young age, no wonder the poor girl saw Yumi as the enemy. Guo couldn't recall ever seeing her in such a good mood, and he was so happy he ate more rice than usual.

As she handed Guo Jiaxing his rice bowl, Yuxiu knew that her moment had arrived.

"Brother-in-law," she said, "Qiaoqiao and I have agreed that I'm going to be her personal servant. I'll stay here—but you have to supply three meals a day." She said it like a spoiled, winsome little girl. But she knew that this was the critical moment and waited nervously for his reaction. Holding his bowl in his hand, he took a look at Qiaoqiao's head. He had a pretty good idea of what was going on.

As he shoveled some rice into his mouth he mumbled, "Serve the people."

The words made Yuxiu's heart lurch. Her hand shook. But she knew that everything was okay. Thinking her sister was joking, Yumi dismissed what had just happened. But Yuxiu turned to her and said, "Well then, dear sister, I'll stay."

So it hadn't been a joke after all. Like a medicinal plaster, the little scamp had found a way to stick around. Yumi didn't know what to say. Qiaoqiao put down her bowl and left the table, and as she watched the girl walk away, Yuxiu reached over and grabbed Yumi's wrist, squeezing it tightly as she whispered, "I know my own sister wouldn't want me to leave." The real message in this comment was a plea. Yumi knew that, and she still could not abide the way Yuxiu had used her cunning to her advantage. But what could she say in light of Yuxiu's sisterly comment? She just pursed her lips and shot a glance at Yuxiu, slowly chewing her food as she said to herself, *You can't stay in Wang Family Village, you little whore, so you come here to upstage me with your slick ways.*

Yuxiu lowered her head. Everyone present would have been

surprised by how fast her heart was pounding at that moment. She was on edge. As she shoveled food into her mouth, her heart leaped into her throat and she nearly choked. Tears threatened to spill from her eyes. *I got what I came for, a place to live,* she thought. Seeing her sister's empty bowl, Yuxiu jumped up to refill it. But Yumi put it down and announced, "I'm full."

So Yuxiu now had a place to live, and though she hadn't given a thought to how her sister would feel about that, Yumi actually had high hopes for her and was content to let her be on her own. But Yumi found Yuxiu's budding friendship with Qiaoqiao troubling. Guo's foolish daughter was difficult to deal with, and Yumi realized that she was afraid of Qiaoqiao.

Normally, Yumi feared no one, but now she found that the girl had her exactly where she wanted her. Qiaoqiao was not the calculating type, not someone adept at playing tricks. Not Qiaoqiao. She was openly ruthless and tyrannical. She said what was on her mind and did what she felt like. That was just the sort of person Yumi found difficult.

Yumi recalled, for instance, how Qiaoqiao had come home from school one day shortly after the marriage, and Yumi had tried to show the girl how kind a stepmother she could be. In front of a crowd in the government compound, Yumi greeted the girl. "Back from school already, Qiaoqiao," she said with a smile as she reached out for the girl's schoolbag.

Qiaoqiao rewarded her by calling her a "dumb cunt"—hardly expected, especially in front of all those officials.

For Yumi, it was a disastrous loss of face. That night in bed she told Guo Jiaxing what had happened. "Why would she do that?" Yumi asked. "It was as if she'd seen the devil herself."

Showing a remarkable lack of interest, Guo said in an offhanded way, "She's only a child."

"A child? She's not much younger than me." Actually, Yumi didn't say that; she just thought it. This was not something she dared to say aloud. She was disheartened. Barely older than the dense Qiaoqiao, she did what was expected of a stepmother, but her dignity was in shambles and she had gained nothing for her effort. But that's how parenting works sometimes. When you lose a mate, the natural reaction is to feel you've let your child down, and so to compensate, you spoil the child, who then becomes self-indulgent and undisciplined. As Yumi lay beside Guo Jiaxing, her chilled heart was filled with grievances. In the final analysis, men cannot be trusted. They flatten themselves out on top of you to satisfy their desire and exaggerate their emotional involvement. They are calculating in their choice of whom to be close to and whom to keep at arm's length. A man is one thing before he pulls out and something altogether different after—bitterly disappointing.

Yumi wanted a heart-to-heart talk with Qiaoqiao so she could make it clear that she didn't expect the girl to call her "Mother." She knew she could never be the girl's mother. But she could call her "Aunty", couldn't she? And if that was too much to ask, how about elder sister? Or she could settle simply on Yumi. But not a peep out of Qiaoqiao.

Daughter and stepmother spent most of every day together in the same rooms, and Qiaoqiao would not speak to her, as if a single sentence would split her lips. She just glared at Yumi, treating her like a mortal enemy, refusing to give her a chance, unless, that is, Yumi liked the idea of being cursed. Qiaoqiao's mouth was typical for a girl born to a mother who did not have the chance to bring her up right. There was nothing she wouldn't say. Where had she picked up these things? You had to hand it to her. Yumi sometimes felt that her devotion to her "daughter" fared less well than feeding a broom—at least a broom acknowledges the effort with a bit of noise. Yumi could only sigh. She did fine as a second wife, but was a failure as a stepmother.

For some reason, Qiaoqiao and Yumi were natural enemies, like a mouse and a cat or a weasel and a dog, and Yuxiu could not have been happier. She derived considerable, if inexplicable, satisfaction from seeing anyone attack Yumi. Yuxiu's heart flowered despite her attempts to suppress it, and that always led to smiles of pleasure. In Yumi's presence she maintained a humble, modest attitude, but it was all an act. What she felt inside was a sense of liberation like that of an emancipated peasant. If Qiaoqiao called to her, instead of answering right away, she would cast a glance at Yumi before walking somewhat reluctantly, almost furtively, up to Guo's daughter as if she were afraid of offending Yumi. In reality, she was putting her sister on notice, confusing her by digging a hole so deep that Yumi could not see the bottom and would forever be kept in the dark. In this way, Yuxiu created a mysterious relationship with Qiaoqiao, a cleverly concealed alliance in which they worked together with one mind. If Yumi asked about something, Yuxiu would feign ignorance and pretend to rack her brains. "That can't be," she'd say. Or "Don't ask me" or "You don't think she'd tell me, do you?" Or simply, "I forget."

Once again, Yuxiu had a backer. Whenever Yumi tried to size

up her sister, there was a sense of vigilance in her gaze—exactly what Yuxiu had hoped for. So long as Yumi hated her, saw her as a competitor, and was on her guard against her then that was proof they were equals. Yuxiu did not want her sister to feel sorry for her. To keep that from happening, she relied upon Qiaoqiao. *I don't mind demeaning myself in front of others, but I cannot yield to Yumi,* thought Yuxiu. How strange that they had been born as sisters.

Yuxiu's job was to wait on Qiaoqiao. In general that meant taking care of the girl's appearance, and under Yuxiu's tutelage, Qiaoqiao had a change of attitude: *I'm not a boy; I'm a girl, like any other girl.* Her expectations in regard to her femininity rose dramatically. But she was too clumsy to improve her appearance on her own. Yuxiu, on the other hand, was an expert.

In light of Yumi's objections, Yuxiu did not dare to pay too much attention to her own appearance, so she applied all her styling techniques to Qiaoqiao's hair, accessories, buttons, and braided ornaments. She had that special knack and an assertive attitude that gave her a sense of accomplishment, belying a deep-seated sorrow, which was manifest in her attention to detail.

Qiaoqiao was a girl transformed, and if her father had not been a deputy director, people would have criticized her for looking like a vixen. Yuxiu worked especially hard on the girl's nails. She managed, somehow, to acquire some garden balsam flowers, which she ground into paste, added some alum, and dabbed meticulously on Qiaoqiao's fingernails, coat after coat; then she turned her attention to the girl's toenails. When she was finished, she wrapped the nails in broad-bean leaves. Several days later, the effects were spectacular: Qiaoqiao's fingernails and toenails had changed color. They were bright red, beautiful, translucent, and remarkably eye-catching. Light bounced off them whenever she waved her hand or wiggled her toes.

There was something different about Qiaoqiao every day. The changes were visible and fundamental, and could be summed up in the saying, "A girl undergoes dramatic changes at eighteen." The people in the government compound took notice. The most visible and fundamental change in Qiaoqiao was in her eyes and her actions—the way she carried herself. In earlier days, her most notable attribute had been rashness; she had impressed people as a guerrilla fighter, wild and reckless. That image was a thing of the past.

Now there was room for twists and turns in both her expressions and actions. Somewhat affected, to be sure, but feminine. She and Yuxiu were often seen entering or leaving the compound together, walking side by side like best friends, as sweetly paired as devoted sisters. That had been Yuxiu's fondest desire. Everyone in the compound knew who Yuxiu was. That's Yuxiu, they'd say. That's Director Guo's young sister-in-law. A pretty young thing.

But Yuxiu had a cold edge and a bit of arrogance. She seldom stopped to chat with anyone. When she was alone, she walked with a light step, her head cocked to one side so that half of her face was covered by her hair and only one eye was visible. That left the impression that she was sulking for no apparent reason, which invested her with a haunted beauty. If startled by an unexpected encounter, she would sweep her hair behind her ear while a smile spread slowly across her face. That smile, unique to her, became famous in the compound. Rather than explode on her face, it formed in measured stages, from slight to broad, the corners of her mouth slowly retreating—silent and flirtatious, revealing a restrained coquettishness, an almost wanton and yet refined quality.

None of this escaped Yumi's eye. Yuxiu did not dare to put on her seductive, fox-fairy act in front of her sister, but she had not changed. She was like the dog that can't stop eating shit. In fact, she was getting worse. Sooner or later, Yumi would sound the alarm. But not yet, given her relationship with Qiaoqiao. But then again, Yumi knew that she must say something because of that relationship. When she did, the results would be less than ideal. They would be back to being sisters, two girls "born to be enemies."

Qiaoqiao came home early one day, having chosen not to participate in the school's afternoon of manual labor. She told Yuxiu to bring the photo albums out into the yard, where they looked at the pictures together. Yuxiu took pride in her assumption that she'd become a part of the family, that she'd made her way into its private places, its closely held secrets. It was a privilege denied Yumi. Yuxiu was treated to photos of Guo Jiaxing as a young man, Qiaoqiao's mother as a young woman, and Qiaoqiao herself as a little girl. She took after neither her father nor her mother, but had inherited the least attractive features of both. They all came together to produce her homely face. But Yuxiu heaped compliments on every photo, her flattering words filling the air. On one page she spotted a young man who bore some slight resemblance to Guo Jiaxing but was better looking, with softer eyes, moist like a young mare's. With the refined, cultured look of someone with high ideals, he was dressed in a neatly pressed tunic. Yuxiu knew it could not be Guo Jiaxing—the aura was different. "Is this a picture of Director Guo as a young man?" she asked disingenuously.

"Are you kidding?" Qiaoqiao asked. "That's my older brother, Guo Zuo. He works in an automobile factory in the provincial capital." Now Yuxiu knew: Qiaoqiao had an older brother who worked in an automobile factory.

Before Yuxiu could learn any more, Yumi came home and spotted the two girls with their heads together, holding something secretively. They were never that intimate with her. What were they looking at so intently? Her curiosity piqued, she leaned over to get a look. But Qiaoqiao must have had eyes in the back of her head because—*bang!*—she slammed the photo album shut, stood up, turned, and walked off alone to her room.

Rebuffed in front of Yuxiu, Yumi spun around and went quickly to her own room, where she leaned unhappily against the window and silently observed Yuxiu, who noticed the look on her sister's face through the window—it was a mixture of humiliation, anger, and helplessness. Instead of lowering her eyelids, Yuxiu looked off in another direction so she wouldn't have to see that sight. *It's none of my business,* she told herself. But as Yumi saw it, Yuxiu was being provocative.

"Yuxiu," Qiaoqiao yelled from her room. "Come here!"

Yuxiu headed to the east room, first shaking her head as a sign of reluctance—for Yumi's benefit, obviously. *This has to stop,* Yumi said to herself, alone at the window. *I can't let Yuxiu keep living off of one person and helping another.*

Yumi held her feelings in until it was time to make dinner. She went into the kitchen and looked out into the yard—it was empty. After a few perfunctory swipes on the counter with a dishcloth, she turned to her sister. "Yuxiu," she said, "you're my sister." Coming out of the blue like that, anyone hearing this would not know what to make of it. But as she picked up a large spoon to stir the rice porridge, Yuxiu knew what was on Yumi's mind; she could hear it in her voice. The sudden comment may have sounded forceful, a strict warning, but it seemed weak. The atmosphere in the kitchen took a strange turn that would test both sisters' tolerance.

Without looking up, Yuxiu kept stirring the porridge and said, after pausing a moment to think, "I'll listen to you. Tell me what to do, and I'll do it." But what sounded submissive was actually a honey-coated rebuke. She had gained the advantage by feigning innocence and had turned the tables on Yumi, who was stuck for a response. What could she tell Yuxiu to do with Qiaoqiao in the picture? What could she *dare* ask her to do? She stood there, dishcloth in hand, stymied. A long moment passed before she said to herself, *All right, Yuxiu, go ahead, do what you want.*

On the surface it had been a trivial dispute, but one of enormous significance, especially for Yuxiu, for whom it was a turning point. Yumi had sounded the alarm for Yuxiu only to discover that it was actually sounding for herself. Undeniably, the day would come when Yuxiu would openly oppose her.

One of Yuxiu's tasks was to shop for the day's groceries. Seldom feeling obliged to rush home, she took advantage of the outings to wander around town, often gravitating to the supply and marketing co-op. It was her favorite spot. In the past, when she lived in Wang Family Village, she had always gone to the co-op simply to linger and take in its ambiance. Well-suited to people seeking a place to rest or be a tourist, it owed its attraction in part to well-stocked shelves, but even the process of buying something was itself interesting. The cashier sat high above the salesclerks, who stood beside a steel cable, each with its own metal clasp. When a clerk wrote out a sales ticket or was given cash, she clasped it onto the cable and flung it upward like a tiny locomotive making its way up a suspended track, all the way up to the cashier. A moment later, the little locomotive whizzed its way back, carrying change or a receipt. Magical, inscrutable, wondrous.

Yuxiu carried a secret in her heart from when she was a little girl filled with envy: she had a fascination with the cashier sitting high above the others. The woman had been sitting in that spot for years, and the way she clicked her abacus fascinated Yuxiu. Her fingers reminded Yuxiu of a butterfly or a bewitched moth that skimmed the surface of water then darted off. When the woman's fingers stopped, they looked like a dragonfly resting lightly on a lotus leaf, creating indescribable beauty. So soft it seemed to contain no bones, the cashier's hand formed Yuxiu's childhood dream. Too bad she isn't pretty. Wouldn't it be wonderful, she often mused, if she could sit up there one day?

Yuxiu would make herself up like a lovely snake crossing a river, a sight for everyone in the commune, young and old, when she slithered around. An ambitious child who harbored secret plans, she'd believed with all her heart that she would not spend her whole life in Wang Family Village, that she would not hang herself from that particular tree. She'd always had faith in her plans for the future. Now, of course, that faith had died; her plans would not pan out after all. And so for her, the supply and marketing co-op was a place of shattered dreams and a broken heart. But people are strange creatures because sometimes they actually develop a fondness for just such a place and cling desperately to it with no thought of ever leaving.

Unhappy that Yuxiu liked to loiter and waste time doing nothing, especially at the co-op, Yumi told her to stay away from the place. Yuxiu asked why. Yumi's answer was simple and straightforward: "It's no place for you."

Yumi's hard work in bed was not wasted effort. Sex is like that; you reap what you sow. She was pregnant. She didn't tell anyone, but she could feel the changes in her body, things she'd never felt before. More than being just the addition of something inside, the changes affected her entire body so deeply that it felt as if she had been reborn as a different person.

Emboldened by this development, she enjoyed increased confidence in her dealings with Qiaoqiao. Naturally, she did not openly display her newly felt sense of authority, especially in her face. Instead, she held it inside her, where it took on qualities of magnanimity, steadiness, and self-assurance. After the child was born, Yumi would stop feeling inferior and put upon in front of Qiaoqiao even if the girl's father continued to back her in all matters. Both children would be his, and it would be unthinkable for him to be close to one child and distant from the other—or to state a preference. That simply would not happen. Once you held your own child in your arms, that sort of distinction was not possible. A mother's value rests with her son, as they say. The problem was Yuxiu, and Yumi needed to watch her carefully. Who did Yuxiu side with? Where did she stand? Her position in all this would figure prominently in Yumi's future and in her fate.

Yumi decided to be magnanimous, only to discover that, to her surprise, Yuxiu had begun moving in a new direction. She was spending less time at home, always running off to somewhere, usually in the afternoon. Yumi knew that her sister was not one to sit around and wait for things to happen, and it only took a few days of keeping a close eye on her to see what she was up to. As soon as Yuxiu had free time, she was off to the bookkeeper's office, where she had grown cosy with bookkeeper Tang, a comrade well into her forties whom everyone nonetheless called Little Tang. She had chubby cheeks and fair skin, the sort of face that proclaimed springtime the year round. She was like a sunflower, quick to smile and as likable as she could be. Yuxiu called her Little Tang like everyone else, but made it unique by adding the word "aunty"—Aunty Little Tang—thereby displaying her familiarity with proper etiquette. This created a special bond between them.

Needing to know what had turned her sister and Little Tang into bosom buddies, Yumi strolled over to a spot outside the bookkeeper's window one day, and there they were: Yuxiu and Little Tang, each sitting in front of half a watermelon and scooping out tiny pieces with paper clips. They saved the seeds by tossing them onto the glass-covered desk. They nibbled and talked and laughed, taking pains to keep the noise down, whispering even though they assumed there was no one else around. Obviously, theirs was an uncommon friendship. Yuxiu, her back to the window, was oblivious to the watchful look in Yumi's eyes. It was bookkeeper Tang who spotted her outside the window. She stood up and said to Yumi: "Come in, Mrs Guo, have some watermelon." There was so little melon left that the invitation was meant as a courtesy. But it did not seem false to Yumi, who actually felt rather good about it. To her surprise, people who lived and worked in the compound were given to calling her Mrs Guo behind her back. It was a refined form of address. Rising water lifts the boat, and Yumi was struck by a sense that her identity had changed. She smiled.

"Yuxiu," she said to her sister, "why don't you invite Little Tang over to the house sometime?" That was, she felt, just the right thing to say, for it affirmed her status, as it was something only "Mrs Guo" could legitimately say. Feeling extremely flattered, Little Tang smiled as she manipulated the melon seed in her mouth with her tongue, twisting her face out of shape.

On the way back home, Yumi realized why she'd been smelling melon seeds in the kitchen lately. *That's where they came from. And when they're ready, she runs to bookkeeper Tang's office to share them and talk some more. That is what's been going on.* Apparently, Yuxiu was like a black snow-boot cat, welcomed everywhere she showed up. Active and social, she'd put roots down all over the compound in a matter of days. If this kept up, what would she need a big sister for? How was Yumi going to control her? Extreme care was called for. Yumi began to worry, and was right to do so.

Yuxiu was spending time with Little Tang neither for the melon seeds nor for the conversation. No, she had other plans. She needed a skill, and that is precisely what she could learn from Aunty Little Tang. What she'd do once she'd mastered the abacus wasn't clear, and only time would tell. But a skill, any skill, opened doors, and Yuxiu knew she had to plan for her future. Relying on Yumi was definitely not the answer, nor did it appeal to her.

She chose not to reveal her plan to Little Tang for fear that Yumi would find out about it and would not be supportive. Better to observe and learn on the sly. She knew she could do it. Her knitting skills had been formed the same way. She hadn't taken any special lessons in the basic stitch, the knit and purl, the cross stitch, the V stitch, the spiral stitch, or the Albanian stitch. After quietly and covertly observing others, she had picked it all up with ease and then had produced finer knitting than anyone. She had a sharp mind and nimble fingers. But the abacus presented a special challenge. After Yuxiu spent several days observing, the clicking sounds came through clearly enough, but she could not quite figure out what was happening. Imagine her surprise when Little Tang brought up the subject on her own.

"Yuxiu," she said one day, "why don't I teach you how to have some fun with an abacus?"

That was totally unexpected, and Yuxiu blurted out, "I'm too dumb to learn something like that, don't you think? Besides, what good would it do me?"

Little Tang smiled. "It'll be a nice diversion for me," she said. And so it began.

Not wanting to be too ambitious, Yuxiu said she'd worry about addition and subtraction first. She asked Little Tang to leave multiplication and division for another time since she didn't know how to do them even on paper.

Little Tang told her not to worry, that adding and subtracting were all that she needed. She didn't know how to divide either and had never found any need to learn. She said that adding a little here and taking away a little there was, in a nutshell, what bookkeeping was all about. That comment told Yuxiu that Little Tang likely knew what Yuxiu had in mind. Since the bookkeeper didn't bring it up, Yuxiu knew she'd better not either.

Yuxiu was a bright student, but this was actually not her first contact with an abacus. Her third-grade math teacher had introduced the class to a large model abacus that hung from the blackboard with the beads tied with string to keep them in place. But Yuxiu had lost interest after the first lesson and had spent the rest of the time in whispered conversations with the other students. Having a clear goal is the only way to learn something, Yuxiu was thinking. That's what makes it interesting.

Little Tang discovered that Yuxiu was not only smart, but she had a first-rate memory as well; she soaked up knowledge and it stuck. The complicated rhyming words for the abacus were a case in point: Yuxiu had them memorized within days, much faster than Little Tang had been able to do.

"I have a good teacher," Yuxiu said in response to Little Tang's praise. Any teacher lucky enough to have a bright apprentice often displays more enthusiasm than the apprentice. Little Tang expected Yuxiu to come by every day, and when she didn't, she let her disappointment show.

From the beginning, the master-apprentice relationship was secondary to the friendship. Little Tang began inviting Yuxiu to her home near the government-run rice mill. On her first visit, as they entered the mill compound, Yuxiu saw a sheet-metal smokestack attached to a generator room; it was, she discovered, the source of a sound she had been hearing every night. Each cloud of steam that belched from the smokestack made a distinctive popping sound. Little Tang showed Yuxiu around her house with obvious delight, especially the bedroom, where she proudly pointed out her Red Lantern transistor radio, her Butterfly sewing machine, and her Three Fives alarm clock,[5] all highly prized, Shanghai-produced status symbols that designated their owners as well-off. They meant nothing to Yuxiu, who could not tell good products from bad. Trying to enlighten her was like talking to a brick wall, but none of that lessened Little Tang's enthusiasm.

For their conversations, Little Tang and Yuxiu preferred the bedroom over the living room. They'd sit on the bed and talk quietly about nothing in particular, and Yuxiu was struck by how quickly their friendship had blossomed. Despite the difference in ages, they were soon more than casual friends. Little Tang even revealed some shortcomings of her husband and her child to Yuxiu, who, sensible girl that she was, defended them against Little Tang's criticisms with quick words of praise. That, of course, delighted Little Tang. "Ai," she'd sigh fretfully, "you don't know what they're like." It was a meaningless comment since Yuxiu had not met either of them.

But then one day Yuxiu met Little Tang's son and she could hardly believe her eyes. He was a head taller than she and muscular, yet possessed a shy nature that belied his appearance. Since Little Tang had always referred to him as Little Wei, Yuxiu had expected to see a middle school student. In fact, he worked in the rice mill and was a core member of the local militia. Little Tang called him over using his full name—Gao Wei—and introduced him to her guest: "This is Yuxiu."

At that moment she no longer sounded like Little Tang the government clerk but spoke with the propriety and authority of a mother. Then she reverted to her normal tone as she said to Yuxiu, "This is my slow-witted son." The immediate change in tone put Yuxiu out of sorts since it seemed to imply that she and Little Tang were of the same generation, the one ahead of Gao Wei. Quickly recovering from her discomfort, Yuxiu said, "You shouldn't say that, Aunty. He doesn't look slow-witted to me."

Taking that as a cue, Little Tang turned to her son. "Yuxiu has been saying all sorts of nice things about you, Little Wei."

By calling attention to what was best left unsaid, Little Tang had Yuxiu looking for a hole to crawl into. Obviously uncomfortable around girls, Gao Wei was ill at ease; he blushed but didn't dare walk away. Yuxiu's face also reddened, and the thought struck her that Little Tang was a different person at work than she was at home, where she ran the house in all affairs, big and small. No wonder the boy was the way he was. Yuxiu now saw her friend in a different light.

While it could be said that Little Tang was a capable, resourceful worker—although her motives were not always transparent—it was clear to Yuxiu that Gao Wei's mother had plans for the two youngsters. Yuxiu had thought that she was being clever by secretly learning how to use an abacus from Little Tang, but all the while Little Tang was throwing her net far and wide and luring Yuxiu into it. It was Yuxiu who had fallen into a trap, not Little Tang. *That's what living in town can do for you,* Yuxiu thought admiringly.

Gao Wei's looks seemed all right to Yuxiu, but the crucial factor was that he worked in a factory. Pairing up with a worker was something she'd always thought was beyond her reach. Not that she wasn't a good catch. But there was always the unpleasant fact that she had been raped. That was something Aunty Little Tang did not know, and if she ever found out, any match with her son would be brought to a screeching halt. That would be an enormous loss of face for Yuxiu, and that thought brought bitter disappointment. *At my age, I can't avoid the troubling fact that people will try to get me married.* Panic set in, and her thoughts grew confused.

She slept badly that night. As the night wore on, Broken Bridge was as quiet as a deep, bottomless well. The puffing of the mill generator seemed louder now. Unlike kerosene generators, the steam noises were not continuous but were more like the beat of a hammer, with pauses between each *pop.* Up till now, Yuxiu had enjoyed that noise since it sounded distant and not at all annoying; the muted *pops* were friendly and usually induced a deep, untroubled sleep.

But not on this night; instead, they pounded against her eardrums. Better, she thought, to tell Little Tang the truth. She couldn't keep it hidden all her life, could she? But a second later she cursed herself for such idiotic thoughts. Once the word was out, there would be no hope for her. Not only would this match become impossible, but she would have given people something to use against her forever. She mustn't let that happen. She had suffered enough over that in Wang Family Village and had learned her lesson. Besides, while a match may be what Aunty Little Tang had in mind, nothing definite had been said, so why jump the gun?

Yuxiu climbed out of bed in the morning feeling sluggish. She'd decided to stop going to the bookkeeping office. But on second thought, that was a bad idea. No, she'd keep going. Little Tang hadn't actually broached the subject, though she'd hinted at it, so if Yuxiu put on a bashful act, that would show that she knew what was going on. Wouldn't that be the same as a voluntary confession? No point in doing that. If she revealed what she knew, she'd be stuck with no exit strategy, and that would only make things more difficult. Feigning ignorance was still her best option. Given her current situation, how could she even think that this might work out? It was a mismatch from the very beginning. Where could you find anyone willing to eat sugar cane that someone else had already chewed on?

Yuxiu suddenly had a clear picture of exactly who she was. As a female, her value had dropped to virtually nothing. This brutal fact made her sadder than any self-inflicted humiliation ever could. For her, the future held only despair and misery, with no tears to shed. At that point she cocked her head and said to herself, *Don't give it any more thought.*

So Yuxiu went back to the bookkeeping office, willing to gamble, to take a chance. No matter how she looked at it, an opportunity had presented itself, and she'd be crazy not to grab it. Before setting out for the office, she took pains to make herself up nicely, going so far as to secretly borrow a pair of Qiaoqiao's red hair ornaments and pin one above each ear. Feeling fetchingly pretty, she quietly went up to Aunty Little Tang, trying to act as if everything were perfectly normal, though Yuxiu was not without a sense that she might be overdoing it. It was an awkward moment.

Her smile came quickly and left just as quickly. She said very little before lowering her head and concentrating on the abacus—on which she made one mistake after another. When Little Tang noticed the ornaments in Yuxiu's hair, she understood that the girl had caught on, that she knew everything.

She's no fool, she said to herself. *No need to beat a drum.* Little Tang laughed derisively in her heart. *You foolish girl. What good does it do to make yourself up for me?* Her plans for Little Wei appeared to be a foregone conclusion. That was not to say there was nothing to worry about—the girl's rural residence registration, for instance. No matter how you looked at it, marrying someone from the countryside was a step down. On the other hand, if Little Wei married the sister-in-law of Director Guo, that would form a welcome bond between Little Tang and the director. Nothing wrong with that. But then her thoughts took another turn: *I'd actually belong to an older generation than Director Guo.*[6] That thought raised her spirits and brought on a case of nerves at the same time. *So what now? How is this going to work out?*

Not much happened over the next few days. Other than Yuxiu's progress in her study of the abacus, there were no substantial developments in the personal realm. But, eager to get things started with Little Wei and Yuxiu, Little Tang began looking for the right time and the right place. Once that was settled, she could remove herself from the picture.

Children have to make their own happiness. It is important

for them to go public on their own. Boys and girls can't always play games of hide-and-seek. Strike while the iron is hot. That's the line in "The Internationale": "We will succeed if we strike while the iron is hot," which can only mean that all people advocate exactly that. So Little Tang invited Yuxiu back to the house, to which she reacted with a look of reluctance. Yuxiu knew what was coming and was not sure how to deal with it. But Little Tang took her by the hand and, without waiting for a response, set out for home. Given her experience in such things, Little Tang knew what she was doing. Since shyness is expected of a girl in such circumstances, a little arm-twisting is called for. The more you twist, the better your chance of getting her to go along. This time, instead of taking the long way around, Little Tang headed straight to the rice mill compound, half of which was taken up by red and green brick buildings that served as rice storehouses. As she gazed at the buildings with their red or green roof tiles, Yuxiu was impressed by the imposing size of the government mill.

"This is where Old Gao works," Little Tang said. Yuxiu knew that Old Gao was Gao Wei's father, Little Tang's husband.

"He isn't the head of his section," Little Tang commented as if she were talking to herself, "but his word carries as much weight as the best worker." Yuxiu tensed when she heard this. She knew Little Tang well enough to guess that she was hinting at something directly related to Yuxiu and her future. What she heard in the comment that Old Gao's word carried weight was that Little Tang's word carried more weight than his and that her fate was in Little Tang's hands.

There is something extraordinary about a government office,

Yuxiu mused. Whoever works in one can make decisions that determine other people's futures.

Yuxiu's breathing quickened and her mind worked at warp speed, all because of her prospects there at the mill. With growing confusion, she walked into Little Tang's house. Gao Wei was waiting for them, just as Yuxiu had expected. That saved her from a case of nerves. He'd apparently been waiting for some time and seemed anxious, but he was trying to hold it in—the embarrassed look on his face bordered on anguish. Yuxiu, poised by comparison, was in control of her emotions. They sat in the living room, Gao Wei facing south, Yuxiu facing north. Little Tang, facing east, kept them company by engaging in meaningless small talk. The atmosphere was both casual and strangely tense. They sat like that for a short while before Little Tang stood up as if something had just occurred to her and said, "I was going to buy a watermelon, but it slipped my mind." Yuxiu quickly got to her feet, but Little Tang gently pushed her back down.

"You sit there. Just sit and talk," Little Tang said, picking up a nylon mesh bag on her way to the door. She'd barely stepped outside before she came back to shut the door behind her. Yuxiu turned her head, and their eyes met just as Little Tang smiled at Gao Wei, a special, proud smile unique to mothers who are happy for their sons. "You two have a nice chat, I'll be right back."

Yuxiu and Gao Wei were alone in the room; the steam generator supplied the only sound. The silence, which had arrived abruptly, had a special, almost threatening quality. It was immediately apparent that neither Yuxiu nor Gao Wei had been prepared for that silence as they looked in vain for a way to dispel it. They were both being sternly tested by the somber atmosphere—this showed especially in Gao Wei's face, although Yuxiu was not doing much better. Wanting to say something, she all but forgot where her mouth was. Fear began to register on the face of Gao Wei, who abruptly stood up. "I ... I," he stammered. That's all that emerged as his breath came in labored spurts. Poor Yuxiu didn't know what to do, and she was suddenly reminded of the heavy breathing around the haystack the night she was raped.

Gao Wei took a step, but it wasn't clear if he was going over to open the door or walk toward Yuxiu. Terror engulfed Yuxiu. She jumped to her feet, her palms jutting out in front, and she cried, "Don't come any closer! Stay where you are!" The suddenness shocked Gao Wei, who did not know what to do. His only thought was to flee. But Yuxiu beat him to it. She bounded to the door, jerked it open, and ran for all she was worth. In her state of alarm, she missed the gate and was stopped by the wall. She pounded her fists on it. "Let me out of here!" she screamed.

Little Tang, who had not gone far, heard the scream and rushed back to see Yuxiu pounding on the wall. Wondering what was going on, she took Yuxiu by the arm and led her to the gate, where the girl broke free and fled, leaving Gao Wei and his mother standing in the yard. Gao Wei stared blankly at his mother for a long moment before he could speak. "I didn't do anything," he pleaded in his defense, looking deeply ashamed. "I didn't touch her."

Little Tang dragged him into the house and surveyed the living room carefully. There was no sign of anything amiss. She was sure that her almost pathologically shy son would never have laid a finger on the girl. She'd have been happy if he were bold enough to do something like that. So what went wrong?

She sat down, crossed her legs, and tossed her nylon bag onto the table. "Forget about her," she said. "I knew all along that she was the hysterical type. What nerve! A girl from the countryside trying to pass herself off as something special in my house!"

Yuxiu hated herself.

How could I have done something like that? Everything was going fine until I ruined it. Now I won't even be able to master the abacus.

She was crestfallen.

Aunty Little Tang had been so good to her, but after botching things so badly, Yuxiu would not be able to face her again, let alone talk to her. She shuddered at the thought of seeing Aunty Little Tang. Imagine Yuxiu's surprise when she ran into her the next day in the market. If she hadn't known better she'd have thought that Aunty Little Tang had planned the encounter. It was too pat to be a coincidence. All Yuxiu wanted was to get away, but it was too late. Little Tang stopped her. Thinking she wanted to talk about what had happened the day before, Yuxiu decided to say something to avoid the subject, but Little Tang was the first to speak. "Yuxiu," she said with a ready smile, "what are you fixing for lunch?" Before Yuxiu had a chance to reply, Little Tang pulled her basket over to look inside. It was empty. "On a hot day like today, the leeks will be tough. You don't want any of those for Director Guo. His teeth are bad."

Yuxiu conjured up an image of her brother-in-law brushing his teeth in the morning, and how he first took something out of his mouth. Probably false teeth. "Ah," Yuxiu murmured as she nodded and smiled.

Little Tang acted as if there'd been no incident the day before—as if it had never happened. Apparently, she was not going to talk about yesterday—not now, not ever. This was good news to Yuxiu, although she could tell that Little Tang's speech was a bit crisper than usual and her smile broader. Even the crow's-feet by her eyes stood out more than usual. Yuxiu knew that the smile was intended to inform her that their friendship had run its course. It was over.

All Yuxiu could do was smile, no matter how much effort it took and how much it pained her. Then she said good-bye to Little Tang and stood in front of the leek-seller's stand in a daze. And as she stood there with all of the confusion of the marketplace around her, she heard the steam generator. It sounded far, far away and sort of unreal. A hard-to-describe sadness and feeling of regret washed over her. As she forced back the tears, she wondered what had come over her the day before. *What got into me? What was I thinking? I must have been out of my mind! I ruined the best chance I'll ever have. And I didn't even learn how to use an abacus.*

Forgetting about leeks, she absentmindedly followed a small street to the town's vast, mist-covered lake at the far southern end. *Just as well,* Yuxiu thought. *A clean break. He wasn't mine to begin with, so no harm done. Even if I'd become Gao Wei's wife, there'd be trouble if they ever found out what had happened to me.* She told herself it was a lost cause and vowed to forget about it. But she couldn't figure out why her acceptance of that fact made her feel even worse. Was there anything in this world that could restore Yuxiu's maidenhood? She'd gladly trade her right arm for it—even one of her eyes.

Now was not the time for Yumi to tell Guo Jiaxing that she was pregnant because an atmosphere of hostility existed in the house. Guo Qiaoqiao and her father had heated arguments every day, and neither one would give in. Guo wanted to send his daughter to work in the countryside after her sophomore year in high school. That would not only make him look good, but it would also solidify his status in the commune hierarchy. A year or two of fieldwork would lay a good foundation and establish Qiaoqiao's credentials for whatever she did in the future.

It is important for the young to have wide-ranging goals. Guo tried to pound this concept into his daughter's head with fatherly concern, citing his son's experience as a case in point. Guo Zuo had gone down to the countryside to work alongside the peasants as one of Mao's "educated youths"[7] and had gained entrance into the Party. When the call went out for factory workers, he was hired at a government-run factory in a big city.

But Qiaoqiao would have none of it. A few days earlier she'd fallen under the spell of an attractive, well-dressed woman in a movie about textile workers and was dead set on getting a job as a spinning machine operator at the Anfeng Commune textile mill. But how could Guo let his daughter take a job in a small textile mill run by the collective? She could wind up with a case of arthritis if she wasn't careful. But he had another objection, one better left unspoken, and that was the fact that Anfeng Commune was located outside the town of Broken Bridge and thus beyond his influence, which could make things difficult in the future. Yumi guessed that this was his real concern, but she kept that to herself. Where Qiaoqiao was concerned, the less she was involved the better.

Guo Jiaxing sat in his rattan chair in the living room; Qiaoqiao stood in the doorway of her bedroom. Neither spoke. The silence lay heavily in the room for a long time before Guo Jiaxing lit a Flying Horse cigarette and said, "You need to join a rural production brigade. Can't you get that through your thick skull?"

"No!" she said as she leaned against the doorframe, pouting. "Let's say I do what you want. What if you lose your grip on power? Who'll take care of me then? I don't want to spend the rest of my life on a farm."

Yumi's heart skipped a beat. The girl might seem dull-witted, but she was smart enough to worry about her long-term prospects. That was the last thing Guo expected to hear from his daughter.

What kind of talk was that! Guo pounded the table in anger, startling Yumi. *Qiaoqiao is a foolish girl after all,* Yumi thought. One doesn't use words like "what if" and "lose power" when talking to an official. How could she not have known that? Yumi heard her husband push his chair away and tap his finger on the tabletop.

Once he got his anger under control, he said in a loud voice, "The red flag will never be taken down." With the mention of the red flag, the situation turned so grim that Yumi grew fearful. She'd never heard her husband use that tone of voice before; he wasn't merely angry, he was furious.

Silence returned to the living room for a long moment. Then Qiaoqiao slammed the double door of her bedroom—*bang,*

bang. That was followed by her shouting from inside: "Now I see. After Mama died you got yourself a concubine and joined the ranks of the feudalists, capitalists, and revisionists. Now you want to send me to the countryside so you can please your concubine!"

Yumi heard every word and all she could think was *This girl is outrageous. Now she's dragged me into the middle of this.*

Guo's face was dark with anger. With his hands on his hips, he stormed outside, where he spotted Yuxiu, who was quietly observing him from the kitchen. He pointed at her through the window.

"I forbid you from backing her up anymore!" he ordered. "Who does she think she is, the mistress of a feudal household involved in class exploitation?"

Yuxiu tucked her head into her shoulders at the warning just as the skipper of the commune speedboat opened the front gate. When he saw the anger on Director Guo's face, he stood there and waited.

Suddenly Qiaoqiao burst out of her room and ran toward the skipper. "Come. Take me to my grandmother's house."

He stayed put.

Guo Jiaxing turned to his daughter. "You haven't taken your final exams," he shouted as if this had just dawned on him. His tone softened a bit. Qiaoqiao ignored him. She walked through the gate, dragging the skipper by the arm; he kept looking back nervously until Guo Jiaxing dismissed him with a weak wave of his hand.

With Qiaoqiao and the skipper gone, an air of calm settled over the yard, abrupt and unexpected. Guo stood there, smoking furiously. Yumi slipped quietly out the door and stood beside him. Obviously heavy-hearted, he sighed deeply. "I've always stressed the importance of ideology," he said to her. "And now, you see, we've got a problem."

Yumi answered his sigh with one of her own. "She's just a child," she said to comfort him.

"A child?" He was nearly shouting, still in the grip of anger. "At her age I'd already joined the new democratic revolution."

As Yuxiu watched the scene through her window, she could tell that Yumi was ecstatic regardless of how she tried to pretend otherwise. She did a good job of covering it up. *My sister is like water, always finding a way to flow downward. She manages to fit in perfectly without leaving the slightest gap,* Yuxiu said to herself, admiring her sister for a talent that she herself did not possess.

Yumi looked at Guo and kept her eyes on him as they filled with glistening tears. Then she took his hand and laid it on her belly. "I hope we never make you angry like that," she said.

Orientation is important at all times and allows for no mistakes—ever.

Take flattery, for instance. Ever since coming to Broken Bridge, Yuxiu had taken pains to wholeheartedly "serve the people" in the person of Guo Qiaoqiao. Now it looked as if she'd bet on the wrong number and had lost more than she'd gained—this was something that she felt with great intensity. Since Yumi was pregnant, her status in the family was assured, probably even enhanced. From now on, she'd be the one for Yuxiu to look to, it seemed. Even if Qiaoqiao grew increasingly imperious, she would not stay home forever, and Yuxiu berated herself for not thinking far enough ahead. Fawning on someone is hard work; just being shameless isn't enough. Strategy and tactics are the essence of fawning. And tactics are tied up with orientation. Yuxiu had lost her way, but that wouldn't last. Qiaoqiao's departure left only one path open. Yuxiu had set herself adrift, and now she had to find her way back to shore. It was time to get on Yumi's good side.

But, as they say, last night's food loses its taste, and the grass behind is no longer fresh. Yuxiu's attempts fell flat with Yumi. Nothing illustrated that better than the act of serving rice. After Qiaoqiao left, Yumi refused to let Yuxiu wait on her, preferring to do everything herself. Most of the time she acted as if Yuxiu weren't even there, which had the desired effect.

Yuxiu felt as if she'd been kicked out of a production brigade. The difference this time was that she did not blame her sister. There was no way around it—the fault lay with her. She'd stood with the wrong unit, had chosen the wrong orientation, and in the process had caused her sister considerable pain. She could not blame Yumi for being disappointed in her; it was totally deserved. It was now up to Yuxiu to behave differently, to talk less and do more. If she worked hard at reforming herself, she could show her sister that she was a new person. And once her sister saw that new person take shape, her anger would dissolve and she'd be in a forgiving mood. Then she'd let Yuxiu wait on her. Despite all that had happened, they were still sisters, and that gave Yuxiu all the confidence she needed.

Yuxiu was right to think that way, but she chose the wrong tactic. Yumi was giving Yuxiu the cold shoulder in hopes that she would reflect on her behavior and admit that she'd done wrong. What Yumi needed was an open admission of mistakes.

It was all about attitude. And by attitude she meant that Yuxiu should stop thinking about saving face. As long as she adopted the proper attitude, Yumi, who was, after all, her older sister, had no interest in embarrassing her and would be happy to have her continue to live with them. But this was lost on Yuxiu, whose desire to turn over a new leaf was undermined by the frown that seemed permanently fixed on her face. Yumi saw that as a sign of resistance, even of outrage over the treatment of Guo Qiaoqiao. That sort of obstinacy was not what Yumi had hoped for. *Well,* she said to herself, *all right, if that's how you want it. Since you're hell-bent on doing it your way, don't blame me for making things hard for you.*

Yumi wore an unusually stern expression. With Qiaoqiao now out of the house, she would bang her rice bowl and chopsticks down on the table, adding to the heavy atmosphere. Yuxiu was stymied. One day passed, then another and another, driving Yuxiu to the point of distraction. She spoke as little as possible, and her darkening mood increased the impression of defiance. Admitting mistakes is never easy because you need first to determine what the person you're dealing with is looking for. Only after you know that can your attitude be considered proper.

The day for Yumi to lay her cards on the table finally arrived, but Yuxiu was still in the dark. Guo Jiaxing had gone to a meeting out of town, leaving the sisters home alone. The house was oppressively still, an outbreak of close combat threatening to erupt at any minute. Right after breakfast Yumi summoned her sister from the kitchen. Yuxiu rushed into the living room, water dripping from her hands. One glance told her that something was wrong. Yumi was sitting with her legs crossed in the rattan chair, a seat normally reserved for her husband. She didn't say anything right away, and Yuxiu's heart sank. She stood in front of Yumi, who ignored her and contemplated her own feet. Then she reached into her purse, took out two yuan, and laid the money on the table. "This is for you, Yuxiu," she said. With her eyes on the money, Yuxiu breathed a sigh of relief.

This was a welcome development, not what Yuxiu had expected. "I don't want any money," she said. "I don't need to be paid for waiting on my own sister." That was just the right thing to say.

But it had no effect on Yumi, who then took out a ten-yuan bill and fingered it for a moment before laying it next to the two yuan. "Give this ten yuan to Mama."

With that, Yumi got up and went into her bedroom, and as she stood alone in the living room, Yuxiu realized what was happening. "Give this ten yuan to Mama." Yumi was telling Yuxiu to go back to Wang Family Village, wasn't she?

In the grip of panic, Yuxiu followed her sister into the bedroom. "Sister," she said.

Yumi ignored her.

"Sister!" Yuxiu called out again.

With her back to Yuxiu, Yumi crossed her arms and gazed out of window. "Sister," Yuxiu repeated, controlling her emotions. "I can't go back to Wang Family Village. If you force me to go, I'll have to kill myself."

Clever as always, Yuxiu knew that this was exactly the right thing to say. To begin with, she was telling the truth, but it also represented strength in weakness. That is, while it sounded feeble, almost like begging, hidden in it was the power of coercion when directed at her own sister.

With a faint smile, Yumi turned and said with due politeness, "Go ahead, Yuxiu, kill yourself. I'll find you some nice woolen funeral clothes."

This shocking comment took Yuxiu's breath away. Her indignation was no match for the crippling shame she felt. She stared with a dazed look at Yumi, who returned her gaze. The length of time that the two sisters stared at each other, unblinking, was protracted and grim; it carried the dual significance of ending the past and creating a new beginning.

Yuxiu blinked and her gaze began to soften. Softer and softer, weakening even her legs until she fell to her knees in front of Yumi. She knew perfectly well that the effect of kneeling lasted forever. Once you go down on your knees, that's where you will stay, always inferior.

Still Yumi said nothing. As Yuxiu knelt, tears spilled from her eyes; she kowtowed, touching her head to her sister's feet. Time passed slowly. Then, dropping her arms, Yumi crouched down and began gently stroking Yuxiu's hair, over and over as her eyes also filled with tears, big translucent drops that ran down her cheeks. Cupping Yuxiu's chin in her hand, she said, "How could you lose sight of who we are, Yuxiu? Have you forgotten that we're sisters? I'm your big sister." There wasn't a false note in what she was saying. She wrapped her arms around Yuxiu and held her close.

Enough had been said by then that Yumi felt it was time to get everything out in the open. And so, she talked in fits and starts, starting with the day of her engagement, all the way up to her plans to bring Yuxiu to town to see if she could make something of her life. Tears of sadness accompanied every word. "Yuxiu," she said, "our brother is just a baby, and of all the girls in our family, you're the only one who has a chance. How can you not know what's in my heart? Why must you act like a seductress? Why do you always fight me?" There was a bleak quality to Yumi's voice. "You have to amount to something, Yuxiu, you just have to. Show the people of Wang Family Village what you're made of. Please don't disappoint me anymore."

Yuxiu looked up at Yumi, and at that moment she knew she was not her sister's equal; she had let her down terribly and was unworthy of her.

She burst out crying. "I've been a terrible sister and I'm so sorry."

"Have you no feelings for family?" Yumi said. "Not this family, our family?"

Yuxiu sobbed as she let go of her sister's legs and listened carefully. Guilt and remorse told her that this time she'd really and truly grown up and had become an adult. She vowed she'd never again do anything to disappoint her sister, no matter what. She buried her head in Yumi's bosom and said what was in her heart. "Everything, it's all been my fault, and I swear I'll never disappoint you again. If I do I know I'll die a horrible death."

The sun at noon that Sunday was blazing hot, so Yumi decided to air the winter clothes—which had been stored in a chest during the rainy season—since fastidious homemakers always aired their clothing under the summer sun to prevent mold.

Yuxiu rummaged through closets and opened chests, adorning the yard with lines of colorful clothing and filling the air with the smell of mothballs, an odor that Yumi had actually liked in years past. But this year was a little different—the smell did not please her, probably as a result of her morning sickness. Almost everything smelled different these days. Sitting in the living room, hands resting on her belly, she felt good about herself, perfectly contented now that she had claimed final victory. By the look of things, she would have the last laugh.

What she had to concern herself with now was how to get Guo Jiaxing moving in the right direction to find a job for Yuxiu. She sat in his rattan chair all afternoon, half asleep, lazily fanning herself with a dried palm frond and gazing through half-closed eyes at the clothing in the yard. Eventually her eyes closed and the fan dropped to the floor. Yuxiu rushed over, picked it up, and waved it over her sister for a while until she woke up. *Life is not perfect,* Yumi thought. *But everything is going smoothly—like a lovely maiden's features—so why not enjoy my pregnancy? This is my chance to take it easy.*

Yuxiu kept going back out into the blazing heat; the shimmering sunlight was harsh and blinding. She squinted as she turned the pieces of clothing in the yard with light, nimble movements. Standing amid the piles of clothes with the weight of the heat on her, she smelled the powerful odor of mothballs that permeated and spread under the sun. She breathed in deeply as her spirits soared. That feeling came not only from the mothballs, but from something else as well. After years of contending with Yumi, she had fallen to her knees before her sister in the end. Her unconditional surrender had brought happiness, a different kind of bliss.

When it gains the quality of habit, submission can be

addictive and can make a person content with her lot and turn her into someone who is willingly compliant. And it feels better with the passage of time. Qiaoqiao's absence from home, of course, played an important role, and the longer she stayed away, the simpler life became. Yuxiu assumed that Qiaoqiao would not be returning anytime soon, certainly not until the blowup over being sent down to a production unit in the countryside had died down. But even if she did come home, it wouldn't be long before she was off to work in the textile mill. So Yuxiu allowed herself to envision a hopeful future. She began to hum a song she'd heard in a movie and a few tunes from a local opera.

Shortly after three in the afternoon, a knock at the gate interrupted her reveries. Most of the time the gate was left open, but Yumi had decided it wasn't a good idea for the people who worked in the government offices to see all that nice clothing— expensive woolens, fine silks, khakis, and an array of knitting yarns—displayed out in the open. So she'd closed the gate and bolted it. It's always best to get rich quietly.

Since the clothes had belonged to Guo Jiaxing's first wife, Yumi had every right to own and wear them. Even if she chose not to wear all of them, she could send some back to Wang Family Village to be altered and handed out as new clothes for her sisters. They would be the beneficiaries of nice things to wear, and Yumi would gain considerable face. The sisters would enjoy the fruits of her magnanimity.

Yuxiu went up to the gate and opened it. A young man she'd never seen before stood there; a faux leather briefcase with the word SHANGHAI stamped on it was sitting on the step beside him. He was good-looking and obviously cultured; his shirt, with a pen in the pocket, was tucked into his pants. To still be so neat and trim on such a hot day spoke of a rare vitality. Yuxiu and the young man stood on opposite sides of the gate sizing each other up for a long moment.

"Big sister," Yuxiu called out, "Guo Zuo's home." By the time she'd reached down and picked up the briefcase, the young man was standing beneath the eaves next to Yumi, who stared at him, momentarily at a loss for words.

"Oh!" she blurted out finally and stepped down into the yard, where she managed another "oh."

"You must be Yumi," he said with a smile. He looked to be roughly the same age as she was, which caused her embarrassment. But he treated the situation better than she had imagined he would. She waved her fan in front of him a couple of times. By then Yuxiu had walked up with a wash basin. Yumi dipped a towel in the water, wrung it out, and handed it to him. "You're sweaty. Here, wipe your face."

Guo Zuo had called Yumi by her name, which she found pleasing. That eliminated the possibility of all sorts of awkwardness and introduced an instant rapport that would make it easier for them to get along. He appeared to be a couple of years older than she, and while their roles in the family were mother and son, they were actually of the same generation. Yumi liked what she saw; he had made a good first impression. *There is certainly something to be said for sons,* she told herself. *Qiaoqiao is a strange, unpleasant girl who does not know what's good for her. This one is much better behaved.*

Once he'd wiped his sweaty face, Guo Zuo looked cool and fresh as he sat in his father's rattan chair, picked up his father's cigarettes, and lit one. He took a deep drag as Yumi told her sister to gather up all the clothes in the yard while she went into the kitchen to make a bowl of light soup with noodles. However one looked at it, Yumi was the mother, so she needed to act like it. By the time Yuxiu had steeped some tea for Guo Zuo, he was quietly reading a thick brick of a book. Yuxiu, who had been in a decent mood to begin with, was now feeling even better. So good, in fact, that the seductress abruptly resurfaced. It had been a long time, and she welcomed the return of her old self. She might not have been able to put these feelings into words, but there was no mistaking the sense of delight they brought.

She wasn't singing now, but there were songs in her heart, and the arias from the local operas were accompanied by gongs and drums. Her spirits were on the rise, thanks to this happy turn of events. On each of her repeated trips in and out of the room, she cast a glance in Guo Zuo's direction, intentionally or not. It was an impulsive act that she couldn't resist.

Guo Zuo noticed. He looked up at Yuxiu, who was standing just beyond the door under the blazing sun, wearing a straw hat with a wide brim on which a saying from Chairman Mao was printed: MUCH CAN BE ACCOMPLISHED IN THIS VAST WORLD. When their eyes met, Yuxiu smiled at him for no apparent reason. She was happy and exuberant, and this seemingly vacuous display was a genuine expression of the feelings that flowed from her heart. The sun, which had migrated to the western sky, lit up her teeth and made them sparkle.

There have been so many changes, Guo Zuo thought. *It no longer seems like my house. The place feels so full of life.* When his mother died, Guo Zuo ought to have come home for the funeral and stayed for a while, using up his accumulated vacation days. But his father was busy delivering the body to the crematorium the day after she died, and when he returned home, he wrote a long letter to Guo Zuo, filled with serious philosophical issues. Guo placed great importance on expounding upon materialism and the dialectics of life and death. So Guo Zuo did not return home.

But now he was back, not for a vacation, but to recuperate from a work-related injury. During a training exercise for an outpost team he had suffered a concussion and was sent home to recover.

When Guo Jiaxing returned from the office, father and son greeted each other with simple nods of the head. Guo asked his son a question or two; Guo Zuo replied in the same perfunctory manner, and that was it—nothing more was said.

What an intriguing family, Yuxiu said to herself. *Blood relations who treat each other as comrades. Even their greetings are in the same hurried manner, as if they were making revolution or promoting production. There can't be many fathers and sons like this.*

Guo Zuo stayed close to home, spending his waking hours walking or lying around or sitting in the living room with a book. *An enigma like his father,* Yuxiu thought. But it took only a few days for her to see that she was wrong. Unlike his father, Guo Zuo had a penchant for conversation and enjoyed a good laugh. On a day when both Guo Jiaxing and Yumi were at work, Guo Zuo sat in his father's chair with a book resting on his knees as he smoked a cigarette, the blue smoke curling into the surrounding silence then fanning out until only a tail was left, which flickered briefly and then disappeared. After a nap, Yuxiu walked into the living room to straighten things up and pour Guo Zuo a cup of tea. He appeared to have just gotten up from a nap himself; marks from the straw mat still creased his cheek like patchwork corduroy. That struck Yuxiu as funny, but she smothered her laugh in the crook of her arm when he looked up.

"What's so funny?" he asked, puzzled.

Yuxiu dropped her arm; the smile was gone, replaced by a look of innocence, as if it had been nothing at all. She coughed.

"I haven't even asked you your name," Guo Zuo said, closing his book.

Yuxiu blinked a couple of times and, with her dark eyes fixed on his face, raised her chin and said, "Guess."

For the first time Guo Zuo noticed that her eyelids were as wide as leek leaves and deep—utterly bewitching with their double-folds.

"That's a tough assignment," he said, looking stymied.

"Well," Yuxiu said to help him, "my sister's name is Yumi, which means I have to be 'Yu' something. The 'mi' in her name means 'rice,' and you wouldn't expect me to be called 'da mi'—big rice—would you?"

Guo Zuo laughed and struck a thoughtful pose. "So, it's 'yu' what?"

"Xiu," Yuxiu said, "as in 'youxiu,' you know, 'outstanding.'"

Guo Zuo nodded and went back to his book. She had assumed he was in the mood to talk. But he wasn't.

How can a book be that engrossing? Yuxiu wondered. She took a corner of the book between her thumb and forefinger, bent over, cocked her head, and read, "Spar—ta—cus." She kept staring at it, knowing the Chinese characters, but having no idea what she was reading.

"Is that a translation from English?" she asked.

Guo Zuo smiled, but didn't respond.

"It must be," she said. "Otherwise I'd understand it."

Again he smiled, but this time he nodded and said, "Yes, it is." *The girl's not only pretty,* he thought. *But she possesses a sort of unlettered intelligence and a bit of unsophisticated cunning. Very interesting and quite amusing.*

With the scorching sun shining in the yard, it had been an enjoyable afternoon, but the weather changed abruptly. Gusts of wind rose up, followed by a rainfall that quickly turned into a downpour. Large drops bounced off the ground and the kitchen roof, and the house was promptly shrouded in a dense mist that formed a watery curtain just beyond the living-room door.

Yuxiu reached out through the curtain; Guo Zuo walked up and stuck his hand out next to hers. The insane torrent stopped as quickly as it had begun; it had only rained for four or five minutes. The watery curtain was replaced by beads of water that fell one at a time, creating a tranquil, lingering, dreamlike aura. The brief rainsquall had cooled the air, a welcome respite from the heat. Yuxiu's mind wandered, her arm still suspended in midair. Her thoughts were miles away; she seemed to be staring at her hand, but saw nothing, although her dark curly lashes blinked rhythmically in concert with the beads of water dripping from the roof and also created a tranquil, lingering, dreamlike aura. Then she came back down to earth.

She smiled at Guo Zuo through a veil of embarrassment that seemed to come out of nowhere, reddening her face, deeper and deeper, and forcing her to avert her eyes. She had, she felt, just taken a mysterious journey somewhere.

"I guess I should call you aunty," Guo Zuo said. That simple statement reminded her that there was an established relationship between her and Guo Zuo—aunt and nephew. An aunt at her age? The question was: did becoming his aunt bring them closer together or increase the distance between them? She mulled over the concept of "aunt"; to her it implied intimacy, and as it wound its way around her mind, she began to blush again. Afraid he would notice, but secretly hoping he might, she experienced feelings of elation mixed with threads of sadness that made her heart race.

Once the ice is broken, conversation comes more easily. And so it did for Yuxiu and Guo Zuo, who were able to talk comfortably about many things. Her favorite topics were urban life and movies, and he always had ready answers to her questions. She was bursting with curiosity. Guo Zuo could see that even though she was a country girl, she was ambitious and had an expansive mind—she was a bit on the wild side, having the sort of impudence typical of someone who has no desire to spend the rest of her life in farming villages. There was a deep yearning in her dark, exceedingly soft eyes, which were like the feathered wings of a night bird that, having no feet, does not know where to land. Yuxiu, who spoke only the local dialect, wanted him to teach her how to speak Putonghua, the national language.

"I can't speak it either," he said.

"I don't believe you." She cast him a sideways glance.

"Honest."

"I said I don't believe you." She tried to look angry, but could not mask the look of reverence in her eyes as they swept over him. He, on the other hand, seemed flustered and appeared eager to leave. With her hands behind her back, Yuxiu blocked his way, shifting her body seductively.

"I really can't," Guo Zuo said, his voice taking on a serious tone. Yuxiu made no response. With a smile, he repeated insistently, "Honest, I really can't."

But Yuxiu would not give up. By now *Putonghua* was no longer the issue; what mattered was the conversation, which is what she'd wanted all along. But not Guo Zuo, who stood with a silly grin on his face, which she found irritating. She turned her back on him. "I don't like you," she said.

Though Guo Zuo could not be bothered by the fact that Yuxiu had stopped paying attention to him, it was not something he could simply put out of his mind. Those four words—"I don't like you"—irritated him. It was the sort of irritation that confused him; it forced him to reflect on things and left him unsure of how he felt.

Whether he wanted to or not, he began noticing things about Yuxiu; during dinner that night he made a point of looking her way once or twice. That did not please Yuxiu. Actually, it distressed her. Knowing she had the temperament of a child, Guo Zuo reminded himself that he was a member of a unique family, and that it was important to avoid doing anything that made people unhappy.

The next day, after Yumi left for work, Guo Zuo placed his book in his lap and struck up a conversation with Yuxiu. "All right, I'll teach you."

Not only did Yuxiu not squeal with pleasure, but she let his offer pass without comment as she prepared some vegetables. Instead, she chatted about mundane personal things, such as whether or not he enjoyed living away from home, how he liked the food where he was, who did his laundry for him, and if he ever felt homesick. All grown-up matters that made her sound like a caring aunt, not at all like the day before. Guo Zuo wondered how she could be one person one day and someone else the next.

Since he had nothing special to do, he got up and stood beside her to help with the vegetables. She smacked the back of his hand, hard enough to make it sting. "Go wash your hands," she said sternly. "This is my job, not yours."

That stopped Guo Zuo, but only for as long as it took him to catch her meaning; he washed his hands. When she was finished, she washed up, walked over to him, and put out her hand.

"What's this for?" he asked.

"Slap it."

Guo Zuo bit his lip. "Why?"

"I slapped yours a minute ago, so now you slap me back."

That made him smile broadly. "Forget it," he said.

"No."

"I said forget it." He drew the words out.

Yuxiu stepped closer and said, "No."

Her tone was sly and capricious, and he wasn't sure how to deal with her. That excited him. Now he had only one option— do as she said. This was beginning to look like playing house, except that it was a flirtatious game. After he slapped her hand, Yuxiu took the cigarette out of his other hand, put it up to her lips, and breathed in a mouthful of smoke. Then she shut her eyes and mouth to send two identical streams of smoke slowly out of her nose. The smoke lingered in the air as she returned the cigarette, opened her eyes, and said, "Did I look like a secret agent?"

He found that strange. "Why would you want to be a secret agent?"

"Because they can be so alluring," she said in a hushed voice that carried a touch of mystery. "Who wouldn't want to be someone that gorgeous?" She was not joking, and danger now seemed to lurk somewhere between them.

Guo Zuo reacted nervously, but was more aroused than ever. He tried to sound serious, but did not do a very good job. Somewhat paternally, he said, "Keep talk like that in the house."

Yuxiu laughed. "I don't need you to tell me that," she said. Then she added charmingly, "For your ears only." Her conspiratorial tone implied a special bond, a closeness and mutual understanding between them.

Her eyes widened. "You won't tell your father what I just said, will you?" she asked nervously.

His smile failed to allay her fears. She wanted a promise.

"Let's take a vow," she said, holding out her thumb to seal the deal. "A hundred years of silence." She linked her pinkie with his. One hundred years sounded too long, so she changed the vow: "Let's say 'fifty years of silence.'" This had the appearance of a pledge of faithfulness, which obviously pleased them both. Their thumbs separated, but the feeling persisted and led to melancholy, followed by a barrage of disconnected thoughts.

Guo Zuo was obviously a happy man. Spending time with a

girl like Yuxiu was a first for him. She was even happier than he was, since talking openly and freely with a young man was new to her as well. Given Guo Zuo's age, a girl like Yuxiu was expected to avoid such situations. But no such expectations accrued to an aunt. What was she expected to avoid? Nothing.

Yuxiu, wittingly or not, began treating Guo Zuo not as a nephew, but as an elder brother, which then made her a little sister, an intoxicating thought. Aunt served as an effective cover. It not only protected elder brother, but even more importantly, it protected little sister as well. It was something special—indescribable and strange, but firmly implanted in their hearts.

A once solemn and respectably sedate home came alive—but, of course, only secretly, almost underground, in dark corners and in the hearts of certain family members. Yuxiu discovered early on that Guo Zuo had plenty to say whenever it was just the two of them, and sometimes his face lit up when he was talking. But when Guo Jiaxing and Yumi returned home, he clammed up. Like his father, his demeanor connoted procedure, policy, organization, discipline, and the spirit of formal meetings.

The only sound at the dinner table was Yumi's voice urging Guo Zuo to eat or the clacking of her chopsticks when she placed food in his bowl. For Yuxiu, this seemingly subtle difference was both obvious and heartening. It was as if she and Guo Zuo had reached a tacit understanding. The silence around the dinner table held special meaning for her, bringing with it an anxiety that created a strange sense of happiness amid extraordinary bewilderment; although she did not realize it, the silence had developed into a shared secret known only to heaven and earth.

People find secrets moving, for they have the power to inspire and achieve a tear-inducing tenderness. Secrets slowly seep into the deepest recesses of themselves and then spread outward. When they reach their outer limits, they quietly split apart and move in directions that cannot be put in order, like spilled water that cannot be recovered.

Yuxiu had a feeling that there was something odd about her, something baffling. Guo Jiaxing and Yumi would no sooner be out the door than she and Guo Zuo would come to life. The oddest thing about it was her preposterous actions. When Guo Jiaxing and Yumi were on their way to the office, she retreated to the kitchen to change her clothes and attend to her hair, combing out her short braids and plaiting them with great care until not a strand was out of place. After neatly securing them with butterfly clips, she moistened them with water till they were a deep black and slippery smooth. Finally, she made sure that her bangs were neatly trimmed so that they fell loosely over her forehead like thin tassels. Her grooming completed, she sat at the mirror and inspected herself closely, not returning to the living room until she was satisfied that everything was perfect and that she was as pretty as she could be. Then, taking a seat, she wordlessly removed the dead leaves from the vegetables for the noon meal—all this under the scrutiny of Guo Zuo, who sat opposite and slightly to one side of her.

The tension in the room was palpable. Silence reigned. The air felt viscous, as if it were trying hard to circulate but not succeeding. But, as they say, there's tension and there's tension. Sometimes it has the quality of deathly silence, at other times it is full of life and replete with the power to stir things up. It is easy to shatter, and extra care is needed to stabilize it. He did not speak. Neither did she.

Actually, she did speak. A girl's hair speaks for her quite eloquently, strand by strand. Can there be a single strand that does not tell of what is in her heart? When Yuxiu combed her hair, confusion filled her head with hesitation, warnings, and embarrassing self-reproach. She knew she was flirting with mischief, that seduction was afoot, and she steadfastly commanded herself to stop, just as Yumi would have done. But something deep down inside would not let her. Though she could not know it, she was experiencing the first awakenings of love. With the coming of spring, light rains fall, and the heart begins to bud. Leaves appear recklessly. Though weak and easily battered by the wind, every plant is born with a stubborn streak, and even if it is pinned beneath a stone, it will squirm until its head emerges and finds a way out, little by little.

Hot though the days were, every once in a while Guo Jiaxing still sat down to drink with members of the leadership. He was not much of a drinker and preferred not to do this. But Director Wang, his superior, liked to drink and chose to hold meetings in the evening, which invariably turned into banquets. Truth be told, Director Wang's capacity for alcohol was limited, so he never drank too much. But that did not lessen the delight for someone who loved a party as much as he did, which is why the various leaders spent so much after-hours time together.

Director Wang maintained a high standard of behavior where drinking was concerned. He could never be accused of trying to get anyone drunk, but he often remarked that one must drink, and his favorite sayings were, "The key is to never lose your fighting spirit" and "Drinking is a good test of that fighting spirit." For him, it was something a man cannot do without, which was why Guo Jiaxing had to join in.

Something had come over Guo in recent days. When he reached a certain level of inebriation, he wanted to make love as soon as he was home in bed. If he was still relatively sober, the desire would not be strong enough, and if he'd had too much to drink, sex never entered his mind. But when he had reached that precise point and not gone beyond, he was ready to go home and perform. Just where that point was he could not say, but he knew when he reached it.

On this particular night, he'd had just enough to drink—he'd reached that point—and he was feeling potent. Everyone was asleep when he got home. He turned on the light and silently studied Yumi as she slept. After a moment she woke up to the sight of her husband with a peculiar grin on his face. She did not have to guess what he had in mind. At times like this that grin would go through several unique phases—his cheeks would move a bit, then stop, then move a bit more, and stop again, before finally settling into a real smile. And that smile told her he was ready to do it.

With her head resting on the pillow, Yumi experienced an awkward moment. She had no interest in dousing his passion, but thought about what the doctor had said a few days before. "Everything is fine, Mrs Guo," she'd said, "but you must avoid pressure on your abdomen." If her husband was not to be denied, the doctor went on, make sure he went about it "lightly" and "not too deeply." Yumi understood perfectly, but blushed nonetheless. *No wonder everyone says that doctors are coarse people,* Yumi said to herself. *That seems right to me—the woman didn't even try to be tactful.*

Yumi chose not to tell Guo Jiaxing what the doctor had said. Nothing in the world could have made her say those words. He'd fathered two children so this was something he ought to know.

He did. That night he did not press down on her, he didn't actually "do it" in the full sense of the word. But his hands and his teeth were so savage, so sharp and painful that he broke the skin on her breasts in several places. Yumi kept opening and shutting her mouth from the pain, but she didn't try to make him stop. Experience told her it was a bad idea to make a man lose his temper in bed. So she let him have his way. He was soon breathing so hard it sounded painful. He touched and kissed her over and over, but nothing worked, so he groped and kneaded in agony in the dark.

"This is no good," he muttered, breathing his liquor breath on her face. "This isn't working."

Yumi sat up and thought long and hard before deciding to put him out of his misery. She got out of bed and took off his pants. Then she knelt on the edge of the bed, leaned over, and took him into her mouth. This came as a shock. He had known lots of women and had plenty of experience in bed. But this was a first for him. He thought about making her stop, but his rebellious body would not let him. Meanwhile, Yumi's determination did not slacken as she moved along with him. Guo Jiaxing was powerless to stop this scene from being played out; that night Guo had sex in what for him was a very strange way.

Yumi, her lips pressed tightly together, turned, lifted the lid of the chamber pot, and vomited loudly. Her husband's

199

problem had been solved, and the effects of the alcohol had evaporated. Nearly paralyzed with euphoria, he loved her with all his heart at that moment. He took her in his arms like a father holds his child. Gazing up at him and wiping the corners of her mouth with toilet paper, she smiled and said, "A bit of nausea, I guess."

When Guo awoke early the next morning he saw that Yumi was awake and that she'd been crying; her cheeks were wet with tears. Thoughts of the stirring events of the night before ran through his mind as he gazed at her and wondered if it had all been a dream. "Let's not do that again," he said as he patted her on the shoulder. "No more of that."

She buried her head in his chest and said, "What do you mean, no more of this or that? I'm your woman." That simple comment moved him in ways he'd never felt before.

"Then why are you crying?" he asked as he looked into her tear-streaked face.

"For myself," she said. "And for my foolish little sister."

"What does that mean?"

"Yuxiu keeps pestering me about getting her a job at the grain-purchasing station. She says it wouldn't be any trouble for someone as powerful as her brother-in-law to arrange. That made sense to me, so I said okay without checking with you first. Over the past few days I've been thinking that no one has the power to blot out the sky. You already found me a job at the co-op, and now I'm asking you to find one for your sister-in-law. That would be too high-handed. She can swear at me for all I care, but the thought of my family looking down on me is something I could not stand. They'd say that when she married the director of the Revolutionary Committee, she forgot where she came from and wouldn't even help out her own sister."

With thoughts of the previous night in his head, Guo knew he could not deny his wife's request. He tilted his head and blinked a time or two. "Wait a few days," he said thoughtfully. "A few days. It would look bad for her to get a job so soon after you. I'll put in a word for her one of these days."

The private conversation between Yuxiu and Guo Zuo came to a sudden halt, plunging the room into total silence, for neither wanted to begin talking again, as if there were a fuse in the air that would send up smoke if they weren't careful. They did not know how or when it started. Yuxiu stole several glances at Guo Zuo, as their gazes turned into wary mice that were sticking their heads out at dusk, each one scaring the other and sending them both scurrying around. The night before, after intuiting what was on his mind, she sneaked a look at *Spartacus* and saw that he'd stopped at page 286. That morning he had resumed his reading, engrossed in the book for over an hour before getting up for cigarettes. The moment he left, she tiptoed over and picked up the book, only to see that he was still on page 286. This discovery made her heart flutter with unease. Obviously he was pretending to read, though his mind was elsewhere, and she assumed that he was thinking of her. She'd thought she would be happy to learn how he felt, but no, the realization actually produced a sharp pain; with tears brimming in her eyes, she tiptoed back to the room behind the kitchen, where she sat lost in thought on the edge of her bed.

Except for mealtimes, Yuxiu avoided the living room; she was, after all, the aunty. That went on for several days and everything seemed fine, but Yuxiu was, in fact, waging an intractable war with tranquility—a silent, lethal, and exhausting war. She wished there could be someone else in the house to liven it up and bring real peace to her. But her sister and brother-in-law had to work. After they left, the house was empty except for Guo Zuo and, of course, her. The house turned as still as the glass in the windowpanes, bright yet hopelessly fragile. Besides the steam generator at the mill, she heard nothing but her own heartbeat.

Shortly before noon what was making her so anxious finally occurred. Guo Zuo came into the kitchen unannounced. She felt her heart tighten and pound shamelessly. He stood there quietly and awkwardly, not looking at her. Then he took out an emerald green toothbrush and laid it on a stool, saying, "Don't use your sister's toothbrush. Sharing a toothbrush is unsanitary." His voice carried palpable concern. He then left the kitchen and resumed reading in the living room.

Yuxiu held the toothbrush in her hand and stroked the bristles with her thumb, which created a downy feeling that was replicated in her heart. She quickly lost herself in the feeling and, without being conscious of it, picked up a tube of toothpaste, squeezed some of its contents onto the brush, and began to brush her teeth. In a daze, she kept brushing the same spot with the same motion. When Yumi came home more than an hour earlier than usual, she was surprised to see her sister standing by the bed brushing her teeth because Yuxiu normally used Yumi's brush in the morning after she was done with it.

"What's wrong with you, Yuxiu?" she asked softly.

"No," Yuxiu replied, making little sense, as she was caught between swallowing and spitting out the foamy paste.

That aroused Yumi's suspicions, so she lowered her voice even more. "Why are you brushing your teeth again?"

"No," Yuxiu said. This really got the attention of her sister, who spotted the new brush.

"Buy a new brush?"

With foamy liquid now spilling out of the corners of her mouth, Yuxiu said, "No."

"Then who gave it to you?" Yumi persisted.

Yuxiu stole a quick glance through the window into the living room. "No."

Following Yuxiu's gaze, Yumi spotted Guo Zuo, who was reading in the room, and she knew at once what was going on. But she just nodded and said, "Hurry up and make lunch."

That night Yumi lay quietly in bed, breathing evenly. Her eyes were closed, but when Guo Jiaxing started to snore, and she heard his breathing level out, she opened her eyes and clasped her hands behind her head. Yuxiu had hurt her feelings quite badly. Apparently she was an incorrigible flirt who had inherited Wang Lianfang's lecherous genes. Yumi knew that the girl was hopeless and that she couldn't depend on her. No matter where she went, trouble followed. Owing to her promiscuous nature, Yuxiu stopped dead in her tracks whenever she saw a man. This could not continue, and it was up to Yumi to stop it. A nephew and his aunt! Could anything be worse? If they got into trouble and people heard about it, the Wang family would be disgraced. And what about the Guo family? Things like that cannot be hidden. Good news never gets out the door, but scandals travel far. No, she had to send Yuxiu home as soon as the sun rose. She couldn't stay another day.

But Yumi had no sooner made up her mind than she hesitated. Yuxiu could not go back to Wang Family Village after all; Guo Zuo could follow the fox fairy home, where there would be no one to watch them, a recipe for disaster. So sending her home would not solve the problem. Yumi sighed, rolled over, and saw that this was becoming a big headache. The only answer was to send Guo Zuo away. But how could she convince him that it was the thing to do? She couldn't possibly talk to Guo Jiaxing about it; things would get ugly if she could produce no evidence of a problem. Unable to find a workable solution, Yumi slipped out of bed.

Guo Zuo was still up. He habitually went to bed late and slept in late. The earliest he'd consider going to bed was ten o'clock, even if he had to fuss about until then. Casting a glance into the kitchen, Yumi opened the door to the west room, and the light quickly went out in the kitchen. Now she knew what Yuxiu had been up to every day right under her nose. Shameless! Yumi cursed silently before putting a smile on her face. She stood in front of Guo Zuo. "Still reading?" she asked.

Guo Zuo lit a cigarette and mumbled a response. She sat down across from him and said, "You read all day long. Can there really be that many books to read?"

"Yes," he replied, absentmindedly.

Guo Zuo, I never expected you to be the playboy type, Yumi said to herself. *You're nothing like your father.*

She chatted casually as the night deepened and the sound of the generator grew more distinct. He obligingly answered all her questions. Then, as if it had just occurred to her, she asked about the boys he'd gone to school with. "Keep an eye out for someone suitable, will you?" He just stared at her, not knowing what she was getting at. With a sigh, she said, "For my younger sister."

So that was it: Yumi was asking him to help find a husband for Yuxiu.

"So long as he has a solid background and isn't incurably stupid, I wouldn't care if he was missing an arm or a leg."

Guo Zuo laughed awkwardly. "You must be joking. It's not as if your sister would have trouble finding a husband."

Yumi held her tongue and, with a grief-stricken look, turned away. Her eyes glistened with tears. Finally she managed to say, "Guo Zuo, you're a member of the family so it's all right to tell you. Yuxiu—we really don't expect much for her." He tensed and waited for her to continue: "Yuxiu, she was spoiled by seven or eight men. It happened this past spring."

His mouth opened slowly. "That's impossible," he blurted out.

"It's all right if you think that makes things hard. I don't expect much anyway," she said.

"Impossible," he repeated.

As she dried her tears, Yumi stood up, looking sorrowful. "Guo Zuo, no woman would make up something like that about her own sister. I realize I shouldn't ask for your help, and I understand perfectly, but please keep it a secret." Guo Zuo's eyes lost their focus as the cigarette in his hand burned down dangerously low. Yumi turned, walked slowly back to her room, closed the door behind her, and climbed into bed. She drifted off to sleep.

Guo Zuo cut his visit short, leaving one morning without saying good-bye to anyone. But the afternoon before he left, he did something totally unexpected—he took Yuxiu by force in the kitchen. He had often asked himself if he'd really fallen for her, but had not been able to produce an answer. He avoided the issue and found his justification in Yumi's comment: "Yuxiu, she was spoiled by seven or eight men. It happened this past spring."

The more he thought about it, the greater the pain he felt, until his pain turned to anger mixed with affection and other unrelated emotions, including rabid jealousy and a certain inability to accept what he'd been told. It was on that same night that he decided to have sex with Yuxiu; after seven or eight men, one more shouldn't matter. Startled by his own thoughts, he tossed and turned that night, reproachfully calling himself a no-account bastard. He rose early the next day and, in a half-awakened state, spotted Yuxiu brushing her teeth in the courtyard.

Oblivious to the turmoil Guo Zuo had experienced the night before, she brushed with an exaggerated motion while looking around with her pretty marelike eyes. When their eyes met, he looked away as sadness swept through his heart. He managed to hold off all that morning before packing up his stuff and making up his mind to leave. When he was done, he saw Yuxiu still in the courtyard, now washing clothes. She was leaning over the washboard, her hands busy with the wet clothes, the board pressed up against her belly, her breasts swaying with every movement. He felt an indescribable force rise up inside him. Unable to control himself, he bolted the door to the courtyard, walked up and wrapped his arms around her from behind, shocking them both. With her in his arms, he felt awful, but this feeling then manifested itself in rash actions. Planting his lips on the nape of her neck, he began kissing her frantically. She was too stunned to react. When she finally realized what was happening, instead of struggling, she placed her wet hands over the backs of his and caressed them tenderly. Then she spun around and draped her arms around him. The courtyard seemed to turn and move as they held each other tightly before ending up in the kitchen. He wanted to kiss her lips but she avoided his mouth; then he grabbed her head, trying to push her face up to his, but she held on and he failed. His arms, too, failed to bend her legs or her neck. After a while, however, her neck went limp and he pulled her face around little by little until they were looking at each other. "Is it true?" he asked with red-eyed indignation, wanting to know if what Yumi had said was true. But, unable to ask her outright, he had resorted to a vague and seemingly nonsensical question.

Not knowing what he meant, Yuxiu became confused. Her mind went blank while her body felt an urge to do the one thing she feared most. So she nodded like a little sister then shook her head like an aunt. She kept nodding and shaking her head weakly, as if her body were asking and answering its own questions. Then she stopped nodding; she just shook her head, slowly and weakly at first, but soon she did it with heartbreaking determination. Tears began to well up, stopping her from moving because she knew they would stream down her face if she continued to shake her head. A bright yet confused gaze shone through her tear-veiled eyes before she suddenly cried out. He covered her mouth with his lips and pushed his tongue inside, blocking her cry and forcing it back down into her, where it died.

Their bodies clung together, but their minds were on different things. Thoughts flashed past quickly and violently as Guo and Yuxiu focused on the other person and forgot themselves. Moving fast and almost savagely, he began to undress her; a piercing fear flickered in her mind, a fear of men, a fear for her lower body. She was shaking as she fought, so violently that even the weight of his body could not suppress her. On the brink of total collapse, she opened her eyes and realized that it was Guo Zuo. Her body went slack like a sigh. What had been a tremor turned into an undulation, waves rolling in with a simplicity that was impossible to recollect. Afraid she might be carried away alone, she wanted Guo Zuo to take her with him, to float away together. She wrapped her arms tightly around him and pressed her body against his.

Yumi began to show when September arrived, but it was the warm weather and thin clothes that highlighted her curves. When she walked, she leaned backward, her feet splayed outward, which made her appear to be affecting a look of superiority by holding her head high and thrusting out her chest. Her office mates joked that she "now looked like an official's wife." Yuxiu was led by her sister—head held high, chest thrust out—to the grain-purchasing station. Although still languid, Yuxiu was happy that at least she had a job with a monthly wage. She had wanted to be a bookkeeper, but Yumi spoke "on behalf of Director Guo," hoping that the organization would place Yuxiu on "the front line of production," in charge of the scale and that she "would make the organization happy with her work." So that was what Yuxiu ended up doing. September was the purchasing season, which meant that people from Wang Family Village came frequently and Yuxiu saw them each time.

At first she was anxious, for they all knew of her shameful past, but it did not take long for her mind to be at ease. Envy was written on the face of everyone from Wang Family Village when they saw her, which satisfied her vanity. She could literally look down on them in their boats from her vantage point on the shore. Things were not the same anymore, and that realization gave her confidence, particularly since the villagers were turning over their grain to the nation, and she sat there, more or less a representative of the nation.

As she sat behind the scale, Yuxiu's thoughts naturally turned to Guo Zuo. She wondered what he was doing. She thought mostly about that afternoon. But "that thing" meant little to her. After so many men, what did one more matter? What saddened her was his departure; he should not have left so suddenly and in such haste, without a word to her, as if she would have clung to him and not let him go. He had broken her heart. Yuxiu was not stupid and would have refused even if he had wanted to marry her. She was ruined and had enough self-awareness not to try to tie him down.

What made it hard was missing him. At first she just missed having him around, but after some time, her body longed for him and that mystified her. She had been afraid of "that thing", but after Guo Zuo, and after such a long time, how had she come to want it as if it were an addiction? It was an unusual longing that would come with a vengeance, as if claws were gouging her heart. But Guo was nowhere to be found. She tossed and turned in bed and finally pressed down on herself with a pillow; she felt better, but only slightly. Gasping for breath, she was convinced she was a slut. Why else had she become so shameless?

One night her longing took on a new guise; it was her mouth that longed for something, a strange longing, a craving that made her wish she could stuff a handful of salt into her mouth. In the end, she got out of bed and tried some salt. It took her breath away, but it didn't help. Opening the cupboard, she made a careful inspection, but turned up nothing to eat but garlic, leeks, soy sauce, vinegar, MSG, and sesame oil. She decided on the vinegar, the sight of which made her drool. A small sip energized her immediately, the tart taste reaching down into her heart and taking the edge off of her hunger. Problem solved. Relieved and comforted, she tipped her head back and took one big gulp after another, realizing that she was more than just a slut—she was also a glutton. No wonder the old folks in Wang Family Village said, "A male glutton is poor for a lifetime, a female glutton has loose pants."

Unaware of what was happening in her body, Yuxiu was not convinced that she was pregnant until the third month, in mid-October. Still young, she was little bothered by morning sickness, which lasted but a short time, and since she was busy with work at the purchasing station, she ignored the symptoms. Her first missed period ought to have alerted her that something was out of the ordinary, but at the time she was preoccupied with Guo Zuo. She carried on imaginary conversations with him, quarreling, then making up, then quarreling again. Immersed in thoughts of him all day along, she forgot about herself. When her period didn't come the second month, she was momentarily concerned, but then she reflected on what had happened in the spring. She didn't get pregnant after being raped and didn't think she would this time, because Guo Zuo had been the only one.

More men meant more virility. How could a single man be more virile than all those others combined? Comforted by the false certainty that nothing would happen, she teased herself that being pregnant with Guo's child would give her the perfect excuse to go see him in the provincial city. That thought put her in a happy mood; although she couldn't be certain, she was convinced that everything would turn out fine, that her period would come in a few days. When it still hadn't arrived nearly a week into the third month, she began to feel uneasy, yet continued to hope that luck was with her. When the pregnancy was confirmed, she was, of course, afraid, but still she hoped for the best, anticipating a miscarriage. Deep down, however, her heart grew increasingly heavy, and her mind filled with apprehension, up one minute and down the next, as if she were stumbling along on a gimpy leg.

By the middle of October Yuxiu's concerns multiplied. She knew she had to come up with a plan. The most important thing was that Yumi could never know; for if she did, Yuxiu would be as good as dead. There was only one path out of her predicament—to get rid of the thing inside her. And the best way to do that was to go to the hospital; but she'd be exposed if she did, which would make things worse than if she didn't go at all. She decided she had to find her own solution, the first of which was to jump up and down. She recalled how, back in Wang Family Village, Wang Jinlong's wife had miscarried as a result of jumping up and down after a fight with her mother-in-law. She'd slapped herself on the buttocks, then leaped around, cursing until she cried out and lost the baby.

That's what I'll do, I'll jump up and down. And Yuxiu began carrying out her plan right away. Whenever she had a free moment, she'd find a secret place with a cement floor and jump forty or fifty times; she then increased it to seventy or eighty times and eventually to just under two hundred. She jumped higher and higher, but after two weeks, all that happened was that her appetite improved. So she told herself that she ought to slap her buttocks the way Jinlong's wife had done; so she did that four or five times, only to be disappointed by the false efficacy of a shrew's behavior. She had to find another solution. She was reminded of Zhang Fagen's wife, whose miscarriage had been caused by medicine prescribed by the co-op clinic when she had the shakes from malaria. Zhang's wife had lost a three-and-a-half-month-old fetus, which, according to the barefoot doctor, was caused by the quinine pills; the medicine bottle had indicated that pregnant women should avoid taking them. Now she knew how to take care of her problem—get hold of some quinine pills.

Despite being a common medicine, it took a great deal of effort to acquire them. She made some new friends, whom she called older sister or aunt, and after four or five days, she got what she needed. Her mind was finally at ease that morning when she went to work and took the pill bottle with her. She sneaked into the public toilet, where she dumped a handful of the pills out of the bottle and tossed them into her mouth. Denied water to help her swallow them, she had to chew the pills, crunching away as if she were eating fried broad beans; tears welled up in her eyes from the bitterness. She forced the pieces down, which filled her with assurance and happiness, before returning to sit behind the scale and carry on conversations with the other workers. The medicine began to work after about as long as it takes to smoke a cigarette. Her lips turned purple and her eyes lost their focus; her neck hung limp and lolled around like a sick chicken's. Her mind, though, was still lucid; afraid that the others might try to send her to the hospital, she got up with a smile and walked toward the warehouse. She had to hold on to the wall when her body began to fail her and groped her way inside to climb onto sacks of grain before she passed out. Yuxiu slept till dark, during which time she had countless strange dreams. At first she dreamed that she had cut open her belly, taken out her intestines, and wound them around her neck before she began to squeeze out one of Guo Zuo's fingers from them. She kept squeezing, producing nine fingers, which she held in her hands and said, "Guo Zuo, these are all yours. Put them on." Guo took a look and picked one out to affix to his hand, which was missing a finger. Staring at the extra fingers in her hands, she wondered why there were eight more. Why? She didn't know the answer. Guo Zuo just stared at her. She panicked and woke up to find him standing in front of her. Greatly relieved, she leaped with joy. "You're back," she said. "I dreamed about you. I just dreamed about you." But, in fact, she was still dreaming.

Yuxiu was seriously ill for several days; as she waited for what she hoped for, she felt only half-alive. But her underwear remained clean—no sign of her problem being solved. Obviously, the quinine hadn't worked either.

Yumi, who was also pregnant, had grown lethargic and

increasingly ill-tempered, forever ordering Yuxiu around for one thing or another. Yuxiu waited on her sister attentively, but her weakened state meant that she didn't always satisfy Yumi, who became even more demanding. Knowing she could not reveal her secret—if Yumi became suspicious, trouble was sure to follow—Yuxiu put on a happy face and did as she was told. Several times she was on the verge of collapse, but her strong will pulled her through. Her underwear, however, remained disappointingly pristine.

Even after all she'd been through, Yuxiu's belly finally began to show. It wasn't noticeable to others, but she could feel the bulge. What worried her most, of course, was that others might spot the difference, so to be on the safe side, she began dressing in autumn clothes as soon as October arrived. She put on a spring-and-autumn blouse she'd brazenly borrowed from Yumi, and she walked into Yumi's bedroom and stood before the dressing mirror to examine the lower hem. Worried that it seemed to flare outward, she thrust out her chest and grabbed the hem with both hands, tugging and pulling until she was satisfied with what she saw, both from the front and from the side. But when she let go, the blouse stuck up like pouting lips. To deal with the damned thing, she stood before the mirror, twisting this way and that way for quite some time until her hands froze at the sight of Yumi, who was coolly watching her in the mirror.

Yumi had been watching Yuxiu fuss over herself with great concentration, evidently trying out flirtatious and seductive poses. She opened her mouth to say something, but then changed her mind and looked away. *Yuxiu will never change. She's barely started working, and she is already playing tricks. The little bitch simply refuses to cover her rear with her tail, preferring to stick it into the air and wag it whenever a male dog comes sniffing around. Doesn't she know how that looks? Of all a woman's afflictions, a flirtatious nature is the hardest to change.*

Yuxiu guarded her secret well until Little Tang, a woman with keen, perceptive, all-seeing eyes, stumbled on it. At noontime one day, Yuxiu went to the public toilet as usual. She was squatting there, holding her belt—actually nothing but a cord—in her teeth when Little Tang rushed in. Yuxiu wanted to greet Little Tang but, caught off guard, she overreacted and before she could say a word, the cord fell into the pit. Tang squatted down and chatted with Yuxiu for a moment, and when she stood up, she handed her own pant cord to Yuxiu. It had little value, but the gesture meant a great deal. Yuxiu refused it out of politeness, and in the process accidentally showed her belly. She was extra careful as always and sucked her belly in the moment it was exposed. But she was too young and inexperienced to realize that she had a light brown stretch mark that ran up to her navel. The significance of that mark escaped her, but not the worldly Little Tang, who reacted with surprise. She knew at once what was hidden behind that mark and glanced quickly at Yuxiu.

That brief look of research and exploration confirmed her suspicions. Four months, give or take, and by the look of it, a boy. Little Tang laughed to herself derisively, *Congratulations, Yuxiu.* Then, with a sideways glance, she scolded the girl, "Why have you stopped coming to visit? You're always so sweet, calling me 'aunty this' and 'aunty that,' but you've obviously forgotten all about me."

With a solicitous smile, Yuxiu tied her pants and left with

Little Tang, responding to her with pleasantries. *Obviously,* she thought, *I'm too petty. I've been avoiding Little Tang all this time, and she has forgotten what happened and still considers me a friend.*

It was midday the next time Yuxiu visited the accounting office. Little Tang had run into her in the dining hall and asked her to come by since Little Tang had to work on the books. Suffering from drowsiness, Yuxiu had wanted to take a nap, but she could not turn down Little Tang's warm and insistent invitation. So she went and sat down to eat fruit candy across from Little Tang for ten or fifteen minutes until the bookkeeper finished her work. Then they began to chat, just like before, with no sign of past unhappiness. Yuxiu was sleepy but happy, and Little Tang seemed as concerned as ever about the girl. But then she abruptly stopped talking and kept quiet for a long moment before resuming earnestly, "Yuxiu, apparently we're still not close enough. You don't treat me like a real friend."

The sudden change of tone confused Yuxiu, who could only blink and stare at Little Tang. "Yuxiu," she said, going straight to the point, "if you're in some sort of trouble, you shouldn't hide it from me. I ask you, who besides me can help you? And who besides you would I help?"

By then her eyes had fallen on the area beneath Yuxiu's breasts, quickening Yuxiu's heartbeat as she felt a slashing sound rise from her belly, as if Little Tang's gaze had opened it up, sending her secrets oozing out like intestines. Yuxiu paled as Little Tang quietly went over to shut the door so they could have a private heart-to-heart talk. When she returned, Yuxiu sat frozen, avoiding the woman's eyes. Little Tang walked up behind her, laid her hands on the girl's shoulders, and gently patted her. Feeling a warm current rise up inside her, Yuxiu turned and wrapped her arms around the waist of Little Tang, who knew exactly what was going on.

"Whose is it?" she asked softly. Yuxiu looked up and shook her head over and over; she wanted to cry, but knew she couldn't, so she just let her mouth hang slack. She had never looked so ugly before, which aroused Little Tang's sympathy. She bent down and whispered into Yuxiu's ear, "Whose is it?"

Yuxiu began crying so hard she could hardly breathe; strings of snot hung from her nose. As her own eyes reddened, Little Tang took Yuxiu's hands in hers.

"Aunty, please help me," Yuxiu pleaded in a choking voice.

Little Tang wiped tears from both her and Yuxiu's faces before repeating softly, "Whose is it?"

"Aunty, I beg you. Please help me."

Little Tang did not ask about the baby's father again, to Yuxiu's enormous relief. And she set out to help the girl in many areas. Nutrition, for instance.

She warned Yuxiu that pregnancy was too important an event in the life of a woman, married or not, to be careless. They'd talk about what to do about the child later, but Yuxiu must take care of herself, for if she didn't, and her health suffered, no amount of fish or meat could bring it back. Yuxiu just nodded, listening to Little Tang without a word, since she had no ideas of her own.

Tang prepared chicken broth, pork-rib soup, carp soup, and pig's foot soup that she sneaked into the accounting office. She made Yuxiu drink it all down, then forced her to eat the meat. She spent a good deal of her own money on Yuxiu's health and cared for her with the stern, strict manner of a loving mother, with no room for bargaining.

Yuxiu might have been young and impetuous, but by being forced to eat and drink, she realized how lovingly Little Tang treated her, just like a mother, and she often cried as she ate. Whenever that happened, Little Tang cried with her, sometimes even harder than Yuxiu. Yuxiu was no longer worried about the future, for now she had someone to lean on. She cried mainly because of Little Tang, the sort of friend only rarely encountered; with a friend like that, Yuxiu could ask for nothing more. She did not feel the same depth of gratitude and emotional attachment toward her own mother that she felt toward Little Tang, who told her not to worry. "Leave it me," Little Tang said, all but thumping her chest for emphasis.

Being young, Yuxiu had a healthy appetite, and before a month had passed, she realized to her horror that her belly was growing at a frenzied pace and was now bulging noticeably. The baby inside, as if responding to her encouragement, had begun misbehaving, kicking here with little feet and thumping there with tiny hands. She reacted to the movements with an indescribable sense of affection, but this was overshadowed by panic. That little lump inside her was a person, one who slashed and gladdened her heart at the same time. Yuxiu went to tell Little Tang, even pulling up her top to show her belly there in the bookkeeping office. Surprised by what she saw, Little Tang sighed and said, "It's all my fault. I was too anxious and gave you too much nutrition too soon." But how could anyone blame Aunty Little Tang?

Yuxiu's special nutritional regimen came to a halt that day, but her belly was like cadre assignments, which always grow, never shrink. Since her fall clothes could barely cover her belly, she cleverly wrapped it with a sash she fashioned out of lengths of fabric.

"Aunty Little Tang, you won't tell anyone, will you?" she asked, clearly anxious. Little Tang was so upset she turned her back on Yuxiu and wept once again. Knowing she'd said the wrong thing, Yuxiu apologized abjectly for doubting her and, with great effort, managed to stop Little Tang's tears.

The ideal solution, in Little Tang's view, was to go to the hospital, but timing was the key. Obviously, going too late was out of the question, but too early was nearly as bad. That sounded right, but Little Tang could not decide when the timing was right, and, since Yuxiu could not possibly know, she placed her faith in Aunty Little Tang. All she could do was nudge Little Tang every once in a while, but not too often, for fear that this might be misread as a lack of trust. Little Tang, for her part, had her own difficulties. She told Yuxiu that she'd gone to the hospital several times without entering and beat a hasty retreat the moment she saw the doctors. If she'd said what she was there for, Yuxiu's secret would be out. "You have no idea how bad doctors are at keeping secrets. They'll talk for sure," she said. That sounded convincing and reasonable to Yuxiu, who was appreciative of Aunty Little Tang's attention to every little detail.

But a few days later, Yuxiu decided that she no longer had the luxury of worrying about that. "Go ahead, tell the doctors," she said. "They'll need to know sooner or later anyway."

The days turned progressively cooler until the air was downright cold; for Yuxiu, that was a blessing. If not for the early arrival of winter, the changes in her body would have been obvious. So heaven had kindly dropped the temperature precipitously after a wintry rain, making it natural for her to put on her yellow overcoat. The weather warmed up for a few days after that, but the overcoat was not so out of place that it invited questions. That, unfortunately, was the only good news. Emotionally, the pressure did not lessen; if anything, it got worse because she learned that she could no longer rely on help from Little Tang.

Little Tang made a special trip to see Yuxiu, and the moment Yuxiu saw her puffy eyes, she knew that something was terribly wrong. Little Tang told Yuxiu everything, how she'd gone to the hospital and sought out the director, but before Yuxiu's name even came up, the director turned suspicious. She said, "He asked me if my son had been 'fooling around' and 'made someone's belly big.'" She continued, "I'm a mother myself, what could I say?" Little Tang looked miserable and felt guilty about her selfishness as a mother; she was so unhappy she could not look Yuxiu in the eye.

Despite her feelings of despair, Yuxiu was mature enough to understand Little Tang's predicament and knew she could not ask her to sacrifice her son for her sake. No mother would do that, for this was a matter of "personal conduct," something that could have a permanent impact on a person's future. Yuxiu had acted improperly at Little Tang's house once, leaving a bad impression. She felt terrible about the incident, and now, if Gao Wei were to be held responsible for what she'd done, heaven would strike her dead. Finding it impossible to lend any more help, Little Tang sobbed silently in front of Yuxiu, who felt guilty in the presence of Little Tang's tear-streaked face; self-loathing rose up inside her; her conscience was under attack. Little Tang's assistance had turned into a dead end, which meant that Yuxiu had reached a dead end, too. She wiped the tears from Little Tang's face and said to herself, *Aunty, I'll have to wait till my next life to repay your kindness.*

This, in fact, was not the first time Yuxiu had thought about taking her own life. It was not a good end, but it was a way out. Seen from any angle, dying was a solution. She'd frightened herself when the thought had first occurred to her, but then a door opened in her mind and the fear disappeared. *Once you close your eyes,* she thought, *you won't know anything anymore, so what's there to be afraid of?*

The idea brought relief and cheered her up a bit, to her surprise. With her mind settled, she began to consider the possibilities, the first of which was the well in the yard in front of her office building, a deep, dark well. But she gave up on that after much thought, because the blackness of the well seemed scarier than death. So what about hanging? No, she couldn't bring herself to do that either. Back in Wang Family Village, she'd seen a hanging corpse with blood oozing from the nostrils, upturned eyes, and a protruding tongue; it was a horrible sight. Yuxiu was too pretty to do that to herself, for even if she were to turn into a ghost, she wanted to be an attractive one. In the end, it came down to the water right there in front of the purchasing station. It was a good location, wide-open with clear water; it was where she worked, and the retaining wall was neat and well constructed.

Now that her mind was made up, she was no longer in a hurry to die. Relieved, she wanted to enjoy a few good days. If she lived another day, she'd enjoy life one more day; in fact, it would be a stolen day, since she considered herself already dead. Finally she was able to get a good night's sleep and relish what she ate. The rice tasted better, the noodles tasted better, the steamed buns tasted better, even the peanuts and radishes tasted better; every bite brought her pleasure and enjoyment. Water tasted sweeter than ever. Yuxiu had a revelation: life is good. There were so many things to enjoy, why hadn't she noticed them before? Once she began to take notice, every second and every minute felt different; she savored them all and, feeling the enticement of life, was suddenly unwilling to part with it. She began to cherish life again, which in turn brought her heartache. The biggest enemy of death is not the fear of death but the desire to live. It's great to be alive. It's wonderful to be alive! If not for her embarrassing belly, she'd rather, as the saying goes, "Plod along in this world than be buried in the earth beneath it."

But her belly kept growing, bigger and bigger. Even with the overcoat, she still had to wrap it with a sash every morning, and she could not be too careful; the slightest misstep would be disastrous. Having her belly cinched like that did not actually hurt, but sometimes it made breathing difficult, which was worse. She could exhale but not inhale, since the air she sucked in was blocked, and that caused great discomfort. After all, breathing is different from everything else; you cannot stop, you rely on it every second of your life. For Yuxiu, some aspects of life had become the worst kind of torture. After nightfall, she'd relax a bit by secretly untying the sash and taking deep breaths; she felt wonderful and free, and it seemed that every pore in her body was thanking her. No amount of gold or silver could have bought such comfort. But feeling comfortable was one thing; her appearance was another.

She could not bear to look at herself. *You call that a figure? Is that really Yuxiu?* She was a startling, scary sight to herself. She could not see her feet. They were blocked by a bulge, a protrusion that stretched her belly into a round, thin, inky, ugly balloon that would pop if pricked with a needle. With the belly unbound, the naughty little imp inside was so happy it couldn't keep its little paws quiet. It even knew how to tease her. When she put her hand on the left side, it would rush over to kick that spot, as if to remind her that it was still there. When she moved her hand to the right, it took no time for the imp to rush over and give her another kick, as if inviting her to come in for a visit. So she moved her hand around, left and right, here and there, sending the imp into a flurry of movement until, exhausted and upset, it began to ignore her.

She whispered to herself, "Come, come over to Mama." Never imagining that she would say something like that, Yuxiu was shocked and stunned by how she had blurted out the word "Mama." She froze at the thought. But Yuxiu *was* going to be a mother. Tender feelings rose up inside, causing her shoulders to sag, as if she were gradually swirling into herself, one eddy after another. She seemed to be on the verge of total collapse as she thought to herself, *Yuxiu, you're soon to be a mother; you're going to have your own child.* Her heart constricted, nearly crushed by the thought. She could not face herself; she simply couldn't. She sat vacantly on the edge of the bed for a long time before snatching up the sash, wrapping it around her belly, and pulling at it, tighter and tighter, as if to crush herself. "Don't move again. Do you hear me?" she said to her belly. "It's your fault, and I'm going to crush you."

While she wanted to hate the baby, nothing could subdue the love she felt for it; they were bound by flesh and blood. Sometimes she'd think about only herself and at other times about the baby; she was happy sometimes and anguished at others. In the end, she could no longer tell how she felt. She was lost. She had originally planned to enjoy a pleasant New Year's holiday, since it wasn't far off and wouldn't last long. When it was over, she'd steel herself and end it all. But she abruptly changed her mind because she could not and would not live on. She was too tired and near the point of exhaustion and fatigue; a single day began to feel like a year. If she couldn't go on, then why force the issue? Why not end it early and save herself all that trouble? So one evening, when dinner was over, she finished her chores, hummed a few lines of Henan opera, and chatted briefly with Yumi. Then she locked herself in the room behind the kitchen, where she began combing and braiding her hair, making sure the braids were tight so they would not come loose in a strong wind or become unraveled from the motion of rolling waves. It would be terrible if her hair spread out in the water and gave her a crazed look. When her hair was done, she wrapped her wages in a piece of cloth and tucked the bundle under her pillow so Yumi could buy some nice clothes for her. She laid down the house key, turned out the light, and walked over to the cement pier at the grain-purchasing station.

The night sky was black; the air freezing cold. The wide river flowed past the station; a lake stood off in the distance. Nothing stirred on the surface of the water except the flickering lights on a couple of fishing boats, creating a static, gloomy chill. Yuxiu shivered as she walked down the cement steps all the way to the water's edge, where she dipped her right foot in to see how cold it was. An icy chill bored into her bones and quickly spread through her body. She pulled her foot out and stepped backward. But only for a moment. *Don't tell me you're afraid of the cold,* she mocked herself. *You're here to die, so go ahead.*

She took four steps into the water, stopping when it reached her knees and looking out at the eerie dark surface; there was nothing to see, but she sensed an empty vastness, a submerging depth. Tiny wavelets beat at the legs of her pants like small hands grabbing at her. Tiny hands that filled the watery depth reached out for her, each with many furry fingers cramming their way into her heart. A bone-piercing panic sent her back to dry land, where, because of her big belly, she fell the moment she reached the steps. Sprawled on the ground, she gulped down mouthfuls of air before she could get up and walk back toward the water. This time she did not get far before her thoughts grew tangled and she was gripped by fear. She managed only two steps.

Throw yourself in, she demanded. *Go ahead, do it and everything will be fine.* She couldn't do it. The terror of dying is the most intense right at the moment before death. Yuxiu shook all over, desperately wishing there was someone to push her. Standing up to her knees in water, she exhausted her courage and returned to dry land in despair. Death, naturally, begets greater despondence than life. But sometimes the reverse is true.

The purchasing station held a secret, which was that everyone at the station knew Yuxiu's secret. And that meant that all of Broken Bridge held a secret, which was that everyone in town knew Yuxiu's secret. She assumed that no one knew, but they all did. This is generally how private matters are treated. It is as if they were screened by a sheet of paper so flimsy it cannot withstand a simple poke but so sturdy that everyone will avoid it. Only country folk are so uncouth and impatient that they need to get to the bottom of things at once. Townsfolk aren't like that at all. Some things are not meant to be poked open; exposing them spoils the fun. What's the hurry? You cannot wrap fire in paper; sooner or later it will burn through and everything will be exposed. That is more spectacular, more appealing.

So everyone in Broken Bridge waited patiently; they were in no hurry. One fine day our comrades will reveal themselves, so let's wait and see. It won't take long. Why be in such a hurry if they're not? Really, there's no need.

The winter of 1971 was bitterly cold, particularly at the purchasing station, where the open space let the wind blow in from all directions. During lunch breaks the older employees preferred to stand in front of the wall, facing the sun for warmth. But not the younger ones—they had their own ways to keep warm. They gathered in groups in an open space to play shuttlecock or jump rope or play hawk catching a chicken.[8] Yuxiu told everyone that she did not know how to play shuttlecock, but she actively participated in jumping rope and worked hard at hawk catching a chicken, because that was a way to show that she was like everyone else. She tried her best, but her bulging clumsiness was revealed for all to see. It was a sight they enjoyed. She did relatively well jumping rope, since that was something she could do alone. Hawk catching a chicken was different because it required the cooperation and coordination of all the "chickens." As part of the group, Yuxiu's obvious difference made her the weakest link, and this always led to the group's defeat. But the people preferred watching her play hawk catching a chicken over jumping rope, especially when she was last in line. The sluggish "tail" became the hawk's favorite target. But it was in no hurry to catch her; instead, just when it was about to get her in its clutches, it turned and attacked from the other side. As a result, Yuxiu was forced to keep dashing around without ever being able to catch up with the rest of the "chickens."

Her neck stretched out ahead of her as she was constantly being flung out of the team and onto the ground. It was an amusing sight to see her sprawled on the ground, where she took in little air no matter how hard she breathed. All she could do was open her mouth wide while more air went out than came in. It was even more entertaining when she tried to get up; lying flat on her back, she smiled like a flower in bloom but could not pick herself up. She looked like an overturned turtle that can only paw the air as it tries but fails to right itself. At such times, she had to roll over and then bend forward to push herself up onto her knees. Everyone laughed at the childish movements; so did she. "I've put on some weight," she'd say. No one would respond, unwilling to agree that she'd gained weight or refute that she'd gotten heavier. Consequently, her comment turned into a pointless monologue, devoid of any real significance.

The very pregnant Yumi took Yuxiu back to Wang Family Village for a short visit before the New Year's holiday. With the aid of a small, fast boat, they left in the morning and returned that afternoon. Yumi's return failed to cause a stir this time, for it was neither extravagant nor an attempt to grandstand. She didn't even leave her parents' house. When the boat was about to leave the pier, the villagers saw, to their surprise, Yumi and her entire family emerge dressed in new clothes. The Wang family now was enjoying a sudden rise in prosperity and influence. Though Yumi no longer lived in the village, the residents felt her presence everywhere; her understated moves and gestures were self-confident without seeming arrogant and exerted a powerful sway that carried a dominating authority. That was how Yumi conducted business these days—letting her actions speak for her. Her silence was more compelling than words.

The visit home reminded Yumi of Guo Qiaoqiao and Guo Zuo, who should have returned to Broken Bridge by then. She was worried and had reason to be. Qiaoqiao, after all, was Qiaoqiao. As for Guo Zuo, he was a nice enough young man, but he might have trouble dealing with Yuxiu, a fox fairy incarnate. Yumi could not watch over them all the time, and what if something funny were to happen? In fact, Yumi was more worried about Guo Zuo than Qiaoqiao. Unquestionably, she'd have preferred not to see either one of them, but this was their home, and they had every right to return to it. And when they did, she had to put on a happy face in the role of stepmother. Many days had passed, but there was no news from either Qiaoqiao or Guo Zuo, and this had transformed Yumi's concern into what might have seemed like anticipation. But whether she wished it or not, neither of them had returned home. What puzzled her was that Guo Jiaxing never mentioned them and acted as if they didn't exist.

Since he didn't talk about them, Yumi found no need to, but still she felt uneasy. Once, when she could hold back no longer, she mentioned them to Yuxiu, who replied glumly, "They're not coming back. Qiaoqiao has already started work at the textile factory." That was all she said, and she had mentioned only Qiaoqiao, so how would she know that "they" wouldn't be back? Yuxiu had left before her sister could follow up with more questions. In any case, Yuxiu's prediction proved to be accurate. Qiaoqiao was nowhere to be seen even on New Year's Eve, and there was no sign of Guo Zuo.

Good news arrived shortly after the holiday, brought by none other than Yumi's baby. She had a girl, and everyone was happy, including Yumi, even though deep down she was disappointed. She'd hoped for a boy, having resolved even before she was married that her firstborn would be a boy. That determination was rooted in what had happened to her mother, who had spent half her life pregnant, giving birth to seven girls in a row. Why? So she could deliver an heir. Yumi had often thought that if she'd been a boy her mother would not have had to go through so much and that things in her family might have been drastically different. But most everything is difficult when you start out, and now it looked as if her mother's misfortune might repeat itself with her.

Convalescing in bed, Yumi felt bitter; angry at her daughter and at herself, though she could tell no one. Fortunately Guo Jiaxing was happy, exuding a genuine delight with having a child late in life. *He's actually smiling,* Yumi thought to herself. *When has he ever shown such a cheerful side?* That thought brought her some consolation. A mother gains status through her children, and now that Guo Jiaxing was fond of his new daughter, a good life was in store for Yumi. That alone made it worthwhile; and besides, she could have another child. What really surprised Yumi was the affection that her sister showed for the girl. Falling madly in love with the new baby, Yuxiu cradled her whenever she could, wearing a contented look that could belong only to a mother. After close observation, Yumi was convinced that Yuxiu was not putting on an act just to please her. She was truly fond of the baby—she could not have faked the look in her eyes, for eyes never lie. *Who would ever have expected the little whore to love a child so much? How strange.* No wonder people say you should not judge a person by appearance alone.

For her monthlong confinement Yumi asked that Yuxiu be given a leave of absence from the purchasing station—where a work slowdown had already begun—so she could stay home and take care of Yumi. To be fair, Yuxiu was devoted to the child's needs, especially at night. Once mother and child were home, Yuxiu began sleeping in her clothes so she could respond as soon as she was called.

Obviously, the fox fairy had learned her lesson and grown up. Secretly overjoyed, Yumi moved Yuxiu's bed out of the kitchen and turned everything over to her at night except for breast-feeding. The major task, of course, involved diapers, and Yuxiu's reaction to them pleased Yumi. Yuxiu didn't mind the dirty diapers. Diapers are a good measure of whether one genuinely likes a baby or not. Most women can ignore the filth only when it is their own baby; if it's someone else's, they find it intolerable. But Yuxiu acted like a loving aunt and, in fact, seemed more like the baby's mother than Yumi in some ways. She had virtually grown up overnight. Her overcoat was sometimes soiled while she was changing the baby, but she simply wiped it off with a damp cloth and said nothing. It got so dirty that it was nearly unrecognizable. To get Yuxiu to wash it, Yumi tried to give her a wool coat belonging to Guo Jiaxing's first wife. But each time Yuxiu merely turned and clapped her hands at the baby.

"Baby's shit is aunties' sauce, and aunty wants it at every meal," she said.

She and Yumi had grown closer, chatting during lulls in the day's busy schedule like true sisters. This had never happened before. Yumi marveled at the change in their relationship. They were sisters who, by definition, ought to be close and yet had been mortal enemies, and now they were growing close like sisters ought to be.

As they cared for the baby, there was no end to what they talked about. Yumi even brought up Yuxiu's prospects for marriage.

"Don't worry. As your older sister, I've been keeping an eye out for you," Yumi said. Yuxiu rarely responded when that subject came up. "Nothing to worry about. It's something every woman has to go through," Yumi said as she tried to console Yuxiu because she had experienced it all herself.

Touched by her sister's concern, Yuxiu nearly wept; she felt like burying herself in her sister's embrace, telling her everything, and having a good cry. But she held back each time. She was worried that one day she might break down and tell Yumi, whose temper she knew too well: Yumi could be as nice as a bodhisattva when things were going well, but if she learned the truth, she could turn against her. Yumi had the capacity to do cruel things.

On the surface, the baby Yuxiu carried in her arms was Yumi's, but she treated her as if she were her own, hers and Guo Zuo's. It was a puzzling illusion. Yumi's daughter slept soundly in her arms while her own unborn baby was as good as dead, even though it was alive and kicking inside her at the moment. Yumi and Yuxiu were sisters, and both of their babies had been fathered by men of the Guo family. Yuxiu could only sigh. What disconcerted her most was when her baby moved while she was holding her little niece. With a baby in her arms and another one in her belly, she was disturbed and taunted by the churlish, clinging, willful movements inside her. At moments like that, she felt as if she were falling apart; but she didn't dare cry. All she could do was open her eyes wide and look around, even if she had no idea what she was searching for. She just kept at it, but in vain, since there was nothing for her.

Yuxiu decided upon death after all. *What's the point in clinging to life like this? How could you be so gutless? How could you have so little self-respect? Only death will save face for you and your child. Yuxiu, have some self-respect, will you?* So she went to the pier once more. The weather was not good that night, with winds howling all around her, turning the night even bleaker and more savage than before. Some of her determination evaporated the moment she stepped out the door, but this time she was calmer, imbued with an approach befitting someone who was not afraid to die. Having been there before, she calmly stood at the water's edge. The first time is hard, the second time easier.

She truly believed she'd be successful this time. It occurred to her that she ought to untie the sash and set the little one free to run a bit; not to do so would be too cruel. But her foot had barely touched the water when violent spasms erupted in her belly. The little imp, startled, incensed, and outraged, was wreaking havoc. She pulled her foot back and blurted out, "My poor baby." The baby was hurling its anger at Yuxiu, who froze and felt her steely determination soften bit by bit. The fetus kept moving, but its movements then turned gentle as if it were helplessly pleading with her. She sensed a knot tighten inside as something surged up into her throat; she opened her mouth and threw up. Yuxiu backed up onto the bank, vomiting until there was nothing left. The look in her eyes hardened. Suddenly angry, she looked up and said with a contemptuous ferocity, "I haven't an ounce of self-respect. I'm not going to die. If you think you can put a knife in me, go ahead and try."

Life gets easier when your heart is dead or paralyzed. No knife falls from the sky, and life goes on. Life is not a millstone that requires daily turning; it keeps going on its own, and you must simply follow along. Yuxiu treated herself as if she were the baby's bed and blanket, telling herself that even deities cannot do anything to you so long as you don't call yourself human.

The third lunar month soon arrived. Trying to keep her mind blank, Yuxiu often dozed off sitting behind the scale. One afternoon, her father arrived at the purchasing station, having hitched a ride on a boat from Wang Family Village. With a faux leather briefcase in hand, he stood before Yuxiu smiling broadly. She looked up and snapped out of her somnolence the moment she saw him. Craning his neck forward, he beamed proudly at his daughter. Not expecting to see him there, Yuxiu was puzzled but nonetheless happy. Even so, she did not want the others to see her father's affectionate look, so she pulled a long face and asked, "What are you doing here?"

Without answering her question, Wang stepped on the scale. "See how much I weigh."

She looked around and said, "Get down."

He ignored her. "Come on, tell me how much I weigh."

"I said get off that." Yuxiu was clearly unhappy, but her father would not relent. He just kept smiling.

"How much do I weigh?"

"Two-fifty," she said, using a term that meant dimwit, which only made him smile even more broadly.

"Little tramp," he said. Without getting off the scale, he turned and explained quite redundantly to the people around them, "She's my daughter, number three." He sounded proud, with a hint of tenderness. Then he stepped off the scale and began to chat with her co-workers as he passed out cigarettes. He asked about their family backgrounds, their ages, the year they joined the revolution, the number of their brothers and sisters. He was smiling the whole time and seemed pleased by the answers he got. Making a circle in the air with his arms, he rallied everyone: "You must stand together." He sounded like a man giving a report on current affairs and political missions. Everyone puffed on the cigarettes and wordlessly turned to look at Yuxiu. This had no effect on Wang, who, still smiling, took out his cigarettes and passed them around again.

Wang Lianfang stayed at Yumi's place in the government compound, which upset Guo Jiaxing, though he could not say so because Wang was, after all, his father-in-law. So Guo moped around with a long face; but as that was his customary look, it was hard to tell what he was thinking.

Wang did not care that Guo Jiaxing ignored him or that Yumi did as well. His granddaughter was the only one whom he wanted to talk to, reading *People's Daily* to her as she lay in her cradle. She gradually got used to Wang's voice and would cry and fuss if he stopped reading the paper. She would quiet down only when he resumed this important activity. Whenever he could, he'd sit down beside the cradle and wave the paper in his hand. "Listen up, comrades. Ah—be good. Let the meeting begin. The meeting is called to order."

On one warm Sunday afternoon Yumi, Yuxiu, and Wang Lianfang sat in a circle around the baby in the courtyard to catch some sun. Guo Jiaxing was a man without Sundays—he preferred his desk at the office, where he stayed whether he was busy or not. Even with the warm spring sunlight bathing the courtyard, Yuxiu was still in her overcoat—as overdressed as a corpse. Being small-boned and young, she had kept her figure, especially with the sash wrapped tightly around her belly; her appearance had hardly changed. To be sure, there were signs that aroused Yumi's suspicion—quite a few, in fact.

For one, Yuxiu quickly gained back all the weight she had recently lost. She had a remarkable appetite for a while, and then for some time she was suddenly absentminded and sleepy-eyed. If she dropped her chopsticks, she'd grab another pair from the table and use them to drag those on the floor closer instead of bending over to pick them up. All these were clues, any one of which could have led to the discovery of her problem, but Yumi didn't pay much attention, mainly because it hadn't occurred to her that she ought to. That is how it is with so many things; we find evidence to match the reality only after the fact, though the more we pay attention, the more problems we discover.

Yuxiu had managed to hide her situation for so long primarily because she and Yumi were together every day. Yuxiu's added weight is a case in point. She was much heavier than she'd been before, but since she hadn't gained the weight overnight, it was almost impossible to detect; the weight gain slowly and gradually became a sort of quiet transformation.

Yumi felt her scalp itch from sitting under the lazy sun for so long, while Wang Lianfang was in a "meeting" with his granddaughter. The more she scratched her head, the worse it seemed to itch. Deciding to wash her hair on the spur of the moment, she called out to Yuxiu, who had gone inside. The girl was more lethargic than ever; she'd been listless all morning and took to bed whenever she got the chance. But Yuxiu was not lazy; she had a bellyache that made her walk with a pained look when Yumi told her to get some water. After setting the basin up, Yuxiu began to wash Yumi's hair, but her mind was elsewhere and her fingers lacked consistency, hard at work one moment then slackening off the next. She even had to stop for a minute, and when she did, she made a muffled noise as if her throat were blocked. Nothing emerged but her labored breathing. Growing impatient, Yumi said, "What's wrong with you, Yuxiu?"

Yuxiu mumbled a response, and it wasn't until she was rinsing her sister's hair that Yumi realized that something was definitely wrong. Yuxiu should have dumped the water before the second rinse, but she didn't; instead she crouched down and remained motionless, her eyes staring straight ahead. Her lips were quivering wildly as if they were being seared by boiling water. Yumi noticed beads of sweat on her sister's forehead.

"Why are you still wearing that coat?" she asked.

But instead of answering, Yuxiu backed up slowly, a willful look in her eyes. When she reached the wall, she leaned against it for support and slid down to a sitting position as she closed her eyes; she opened her mouth wide, but no sound emerged. Then she reached under her coat, her hands a flurry of motion as she unknotted, tugged, and pulled at the sash. Her eyes were still shut and her mouth hung slack as she dragged the sash out little by little; the more she pulled, the more she held in her hand, like a magician. Finally she exhaled and made a guttural noise that, to Yumi's ears, sounded like agony but could have been ecstasy. But that was all—Yuxiu did not make another sound.

Sensing that something might be terribly wrong, Yumi walked up to her sister, water dripping from her hair, and tugged tentatively at the overcoat; Yuxiu did not resist.

"Stand up, Yuxiu," Yumi said sternly.

Her eyes still shut, Yuxiu merely twisted her neck from side to side, so Yumi pulled her up.

"Stand up, I said."

Yuxiu struggled to her feet, but with the cord untied, her pants slipped to the ground the moment she got to her feet. Yumi lifted Yuxiu's coat and undergarment, exposing a giant belly that presented a terrifying sight under the harsh glare of the sun. "Yuxiu!" Yumi cried out.

Cocking her head to look at Yumi out of the corner of her

eye, Yuxiu continued her labored breathing and, holding on to her sister, slowly sank to her knees.

"It's all over for me, sister," she said softly.

Yumi grabbed a handful of Yuxiu's hair.

"Whose is it?" she asked.

"It's all over for me, sister," Yuxiu said again.

This time Yumi pulled Yuxiu's hair back to make her sister look up at her. "Whose is it?" she demanded furiously.

Wang Lianfang was standing behind Yumi.

"Stop asking, Yumi. He'll be part of the next generation of revolutionaries."

The following morning, Yuxiu gave birth to a baby boy at the county People's Hospital. Yumi had begged the doctor to abort the child, but she'd refused, saying it was too late and too risky. True to her reputation, Yumi did not panic. With a letter from Guo Jiaxing to the head of the hospital, she took charge, and everything went smoothly. But she had her own issue to deal with: she needed to know the identity of the baby's father.

On the way to the hospital, she had grilled Yuxiu while they were on the speedboat, even slapping her a dozen times. When her hands were sore from slapping her sister, Yumi had tugged at Yuxiu's hair, ultimately pulling out a handful; Yuxiu had remained stoically quiet the whole time. The corners of her mouth had begun to bleed, and even Yumi had not been able to bring herself to slap her any more, yet Yuxiu had refused to tell her what she wanted to know.

"I've never seen a slut like you!" Yumi had screamed at her sister. After seeing her into the delivery room, Yumi sat quietly on the bench in the hallway with the speedboat skipper, utterly exhausted. Reclaiming her daughter from the skipper, she sighed and shut her eyes weakly. But then they snapped open. She glanced over at the skipper, slowly stood up, turned, and kneeled before him. Stunned, he tried to pull her up, but she said, "Skipper Guo, please, for our sake, don't tell anyone. Please, I beg you."

The skipper got down on his knees, "Don't worry, Mrs Guo," he said, flustered. "I give you my word as a Party member."

Yumi sat down again, her mind now busily figuring out what to do with the doctor and the baby. How should she deal with the baby? And was it a boy or a girl?

Everything went smoothly, and Yuxiu had her baby half an hour later. When the doctor walked out and pulled down her mask, Yumi went up, grasped her hands, and asked, "Is it a boy or a girl?"

"A boy," the doctor said. Yumi fell silent as an unspeakable bitterness and sadness surged inside her. *You did well for yourself, you little slut,* she thought.

The doctor stood there looking at her and waited. Yumi's lips quivered before she sighed and said, "I think we'd better give him away."

After taking care of the details, Yumi walked into the ward and stood before Yuxiu with a grim look. Yuxiu's bloodless face looked paler than paper, but although she appeared to be drained of energy, she took her hands out from under the blanket and said softly, "Sister, let me see my baby."

Yumi had not expected such a blatant request, and her face turned dark purple.

"Yuxiu," she blurted out, "how can you be so shameless!"

Yuxiu, still breathing hard, swallowed and said stubbornly, "Sister, please." Her weak fingers clutched Yumi's arm, but Yumi flung her sister's hand away.

"It's dead, I tossed it down the toilet. What made you think you could give birth to anything worth keeping?"

The light went out in Yuxiu's eyes when she heard her sister's words. Reluctant to give in, she propped herself up on her elbows but lacked the strength to sit up. Her head drooped down from her weak neck, a tangle of hair hanging in front of her face.

"Sister, help me up," she said, cocking her head. "I want to take a look, just one look, and I'll die happy."

Yumi pushed her away and sneered. "Die? I don't mean to mock you, Yuxiu, but you could have done that long ago if you'd wanted to."

Yuxiu managed to hold herself up on her elbows for another minute before finally flopping back down in complete surrender, her energy spent. She lay there motionless, fixing her lovely, unblinking eyes on the ceiling; the light in those eyes was strangely clear and unusually bright.

As she looked down at her sister, despair and an almost unbearable sadness rose up inside Yumi; she tried but failed to hold back her tears. Covering her face with her hand and clenching her teeth, she said, "You've brought me nothing but shame."

Yuyang

NO ONE WANTED to run 3,000 meters. What did 3,000 meters mean anyway? It meant you had to forgo food and water like a jackass and stumble blindly around seven-and-a-half laps on the 400-meter track. Yuyang, who had no physical ability worthy of mention and was not gifted with the height, speed, or strength of her classmates, had a stocky, solid build and, at best, a bit of awkward stamina. Anyone with a sharp eye could tell she was a country girl with little physical training—her arms and legs lacked coordination and flexibility. Like most girls from the countryside, she was not endowed with any special talents; her grades were passable, but that was about it. Her looks were even less memorable. How could her homeroom teacher ever notice a girl like her? And yet, the young teacher was a sports fan so athletic wins and losses meant a great deal.

He entered Yuyang in the 3,000-meter race, though he didn't expect much of her—a case of hitting a date tree just for the sake of making contact with something. But if she came in sixth place, it would add another point to their total. She might not be able to brag about any particular talent, but for the collective honor of Section Three of the class of '82, she had an obligation to work and sweat. Pang Fenghua, another girl in the race, curled her lip and said to Yuyang confidentially, "Now you see how much the teacher values us, always giving us the most glorious tasks. Let's not disappoint him."

Like Yuyang, Fenghua was a country girl who had passed an exam to attend school in town. The two girls had similar backgrounds, though Fenghua often appeared more worldly. Whenever the teacher criticized her, her tears flowed as easily as pee, gushing so much that the teacher had no choice but to take pity on her.

Yuyang could tell that Fenghua had more nerve than she. Her eyes might scrunch up as the tears streamed down, but she never lost her poise and knew exactly what to say to make a point. That was something Yuyang could never hope to accomplish. Of the two of them, Fenghua was more confident, mainly because she had a nicer face, even though anyone would be hard-pressed to call her pretty. As if that weren't enough, Yuyang could see that Fenghua was a natural-born flirt.

Feeling something akin to stage fright, Yuyang stepped onto the track and immediately froze, making a fool of herself. The starting pistol sounded after the starter yelled, "On your marks." All the other students rushed ahead, necks stretched to the limit as they fought for position, pushing and shoving to take the lead, all but Yuyang, who stood there like an idiot. She didn't know that in races above 800 meters, only "on your marks" was shouted and "get set" wasn't used. How was she supposed to know that? So, after all the others had taken off, the starter walked up with his pistol and said in a pleasant voice, "Are you done thinking? Do you need more time?" Then he shouted, "What are you still standing here for? Go—run." Startled into her first step—it was more like a leap—she drew laughter from the spectators.

She had begun the race in utter disgrace. And she was surprised to see that Pang Fenghua was already five or six meters ahead. During lunchtime, Fenghua had dragged her along to see the homeroom teacher to tell him with a pained look that she was "inconvenienced" and could not run. The teacher was visibly displeased, but he could say nothing about a female student's physical condition. Gazing into his eyes, Fenghua changed her tone: "I'll do the best I can, but don't be upset with me if I don't do well." So reasonable, so accommodating. The teacher nodded and patted her on the shoulder to show his appreciation.

The second the starting pistol fired, Fenghua took off like a racehorse with no sign of being "inconvenienced." But then she quickly slowed her pace and contorted her face in apparent agony. She kept running slowly, making each step seem like a struggle. Yuyang recalled how Fenghua had managed to skip a physical education class recently using the same excuse. The little whore had been inconvenienced twice in one week like a faucet. She knew how to get what she wanted—she was shameless.

In fact, after counting the days, Yuyang realized that her own misfortune was only a couple of days off. She'd felt bloated during lunch, but Yuyang would never let on to anyone; it was not something she could talk about. When she was on the second lap, she realized that Fenghua had a reason to be shameless. Yuyang was in agony. She could hardly breathe, and the heaviness in her chest made her wish she were dead. Fenghua, on the other hand, had gotten what she wanted; she ran one-and-a-half admirable laps before collapsing in the arms of the homeroom teacher. Yuyang saw it all. Fenghua looked so frail, with her seemingly weightless arms draped around the teacher's neck as if she were presenting him with a Tibetan *hada*. Her eyes were shut. She was so delicate, all she lacked was a pillow; she might as well have been the teacher's own little girl.

Meanwhile, Yuyang struggled, as Fenghua, after drinking a glass of sugar water, was talking and laughing with classmates. Yuyang would have loved to give up halfway too, but the homeroom teacher was yelling at her sternly from the bleachers. Standing straight as a javelin, his arms crossed, he was watching her with a worried look on his face. She was in agony, and she was afraid, but she had to soldier on, one step at a time, for the collective honor of her class.

Yuyang had no idea where she finished, which, in reality, did not matter. When a second ring was draped around her neck after the second lap, the first six girls, maybe even the first twelve girls, had already crossed the finish line. Some were being congratulated, others were pouting like spoiled children. By now there was little happening on the track, but Yuyang kept running, silently, diligently—her neck thrust out like a little turtle's.

Sheer embarrassment made her want to stop at one point, but a resonant, lyrical sound came through the PA system to encourage her, awarding high praise to her "spirit." Yuyang felt that she was no longer herself; her torso was gone and so were her arms and legs. All that remained was her spirit, an involuntary force that propelled her forward. She was undeniably slow, but her second wind kicked in, revitalizing and keeping her going. The boundless power of her spirit made it impossible for her to stop even if she'd wanted to. She believed that she could keep at it till dark and reach her symbolic Yan'an[9] before daybreak, just as long as someone first brought her two bowls of rice and a glass of water.

By the time Yuyang crossed the finish line, the spectators' attention had shifted to the field, where some of the students had gathered. A tall boy from the class of '81 was trying to break the school's high-jump record. He was the track and field star—in fact, the star of the school in general. Knowing that everyone's eyes were on him, he felt especially inspired and energetic. He kept running his fingers through his hair, taking deep breaths, and making charming but bogus motions with his sticklike arms. Finally, after four or five sets of those, he took off running, but stopped just before he reached the crossbar and trotted past it, eliciting shrieks from the bleachers. Then he lowered his head, as if deep in thought, and returned to the starting point, where he once again ran his fingers through his hair, took some more deep breaths, and repeated the charming yet bogus motions. This was the moment when Yuyang crossed the 3,000-meter finish line. Except for the judge who was recording the finishes, no one noticed.

She received nothing for finishing; no one was there to give her an arm to lean on, and she did not get a glass of sugar water. Burning with shame, she cowered on the sidelines. That's when the cramps started, reminding her that she was more than just spirit, since spirit would not have to put up with cramps. It was a sharp, intense pain. She bent over and saw something that looked like a worm on the inside of her thigh—a red worm, warm and soft, crawling down slowly, and the farther it went, the longer and thicker it grew. Shocked by the sight, she stood there in a daze before bolting toward the dormitory building.

Yuyang was alone in her room, curled up in bed like a shrimp. The pain was more emotional than physical because the 3,000-meter race was over before she'd had a chance to use all of her strength. She was convinced that if it had been a 10,000-meter race, she might have come in first or at least have been among the top finishers. It wasn't until that moment that she realized that the track and field meet actually held meaning for her. She realized that she was too ordinary; she had nothing to attract attention, nothing she did better than anyone else. If she'd done well in the race, things might have been different, and the teacher would have seen her in a better light.

Come to think of it, Yuyang had accomplished only one thing in her entire life: being admitted into the teacher-training school, which had brought her many days of glory. The news had caused a sensation in Wang Family Village, where it made the rounds several times shortly after the old principal opened the admission letter. "Wang Yuyang? Who's that?" Commune members had to ask around before finally making the connection between Wang Yuyang and the seven daughters of Wang Lianfang. All but the oldest, Yumi, and the third daughter, Yuxiu—who had left the village more than a decade earlier—were simply too ordinary. Older villagers recalled how different the Wang family had been back then. The girls would step outside and cut a dashing figure, and Wang Lianfang had served as secretary of the local Party branch instead of being the sorry drunk he was now. He had impressed everyone as an authority figure when he made announcements over the PA system, blaring constant references to "our Communist Party" and "the Wang Family Village branch office of the Chinese Communist Party," so full of himself that he might as well be treated to a cow's cunt at every meal.[10] To hear him speak, no one would have believed that he was a local villager; instead, they'd have thought he had trekked thousands of miles through hailstorms of bullets and forests of rifles while overcoming tremendous difficulties, traversing snowy mountains and grassy plains, and crossing the Yangtze River and the Yellow River before arriving at Wang Family Village.

Yuyang was the seventh and youngest girl, which normally would have made her the baby of the family, but no such luck. Her father had refused to give up and mustered a bit more strength before returning to bed to give it another go, which had led to the birth of a son, Little Eight. That had rendered the youngest daughter inconsequential. At best she'd been a necessary preparation for her parents' project of producing a baby boy, a rehearsal, a trial run. In a word, she was an extra, born to be disliked and shunned by her parents. In fact, she wasn't even brought up by them. At first Yumi took care of her and after Yumi was married, Yuyang had no choice but to move in with her grandparents.

She was clumsy—verbally and physically—and antisocial. That actually saved the parents and grandparents trouble and worry. She did, however, possess one unique quality, which the teacher discovered as soon as she entered school—she loved to study. Stubbornly burying her head in books, she was willing to put in all the necessary effort and expend the required energy. She might not have been at the top of her class, but she was solid and pragmatic, and could commit page after page of her textbooks to memory. Her admission into a school in town gave the old principal a lot of face. He insisted that she share some of her learning experience so, standing with her back to the wall in the teachers' office, Yuyang rubbed the sole of her shoe against the wall nervously until she managed to force out a sort of golden rule: memorize. How simple the plain truth can be. The old principal grabbed her hand and said excitedly, "Practice is the way to verify truth. We must spread Yuyang's wisdom around. Starting next semester, we'll rally the students to learn from Yuyang—memorize." His excitement prompted him to retroactively award her a Three-Good Student certificate, while counseling her to keep all three things foremost in her mind when she went to town. He raised his middle and ring fingers, as well as his pinkie, to indicate good health, good grades, and good work.

Yuyang spent that summer fully vindicated in Wang Family Village. She was lonely every day, but it was a special kind of loneliness, different from what she'd felt before. In the past, loneliness had been the result of being neglected by others, being forgotten and ignored. In the summer of 1982, she was still alone, but it was the solitude of someone who stood out like a crane among chickens. She was standing on one foot as she silently tucked her head under a wing on which snowy white light glinted off of every feather. It was a cheerless solitude that drew together a unique beauty and pride, the restful moment before she spread her wings and soared into the sky. At any moment she could turn into a cloud and glide toward the horizon. What made her proudest was that it even prompted her big sister to make a trip home from Broken Bridge. Yumi told people that she had come home to see "our little Yuyang." Though they were sisters, the two of them had nothing much to do with each other. In Yumi's eyes, Yuyang had always been just a child. On her infrequent visits home, Yumi would send her sister off with some hard candy, telling her to go out and play.

But this time Yumi came home as the wife of an official, her hair wound into a bun at the back of her head. She had put on weight and had a new tooth that gave off a golden glint even though it was copper veneer. Highlighted by this golden sparkle, her smile signaled affection and magnanimity. And it exuded happiness. In order to show off her gold tooth as much as possible, Yumi smiled a lot, the broader the better. Although she was now the wife of a commune cadre and could play the exalted role of an official's wife, Yumi spent her own money on a two-table banquet to which the village leaders and Yuyang's teachers all came. Yuyang was allowed to sit at the table, which marked her status at the first formal banquet she had ever attended. Feeling shy and proud at the same time, she smiled with her lips pressed tightly together. In reality, of course, Yuyang's presence at the table was symbolic because Yumi was busily in charge, taking over and tossing down one cup of liquor after another. Having developed a remarkable capacity for alcohol, she appeared brash and aggressive, even drinking a cup "on behalf of Yuyang." She drank so much that everyone assumed she was drunk. But no, she kept up the pace, one cup after another, and by the time the banquet was over, the people in Wang Family Village knew that Yumi could hold her own around a table. She managed to put away more than twenty ounces of strong liquor and still played two hours of poker with the village cadres. She threw down her cards one at a time with a loud snap, always on the attack and showing no mercy.

After three rounds of poker, Yumi crawled under Yuyang's mosquito net, where the younger girl was fast asleep. Nudging her awake, Yumi began counting out money under the oil lamp so Yuyang could see—five-yuan bills with consecutive numbers, so new they could slice cakes of tofu or slap someone in the face. It was not money she'd won at poker, but bills she'd brought back especially for Yuyang. She counted out ten of them, plus coupons for twenty-five *jin* of grain, which could be used anywhere in the country. It was a large sum of money, possibly enough to kill for. Thrusting the fifty yuan and grain coupons at her sister, Yumi ordered Yuyang in a gruff, but somehow tender manner, "Take this, little girl."

"Just put it there," Yuyang said sleepily.

"Open your eyes, sleepyhead, and tell me what you see."

Still half asleep, Yuyang did not seem impressed.

"Let me sleep."

She shut her eyes, and Yumi stared at the back of her sister's head. She was surprised by the girl's reaction. Not only had her foolish baby sister dismissed Yumi's generosity, but she had already begun to talk like a city girl who knows the value of understatement in important matters. Without another word, Yumi stuffed the money and grain coupons under her sister's pillow, blew out the light, and lay down next to Yuyang, whose back was to her. But she'd had too much to drink to fall asleep right away. Her thoughts were on her sister's accomplishments. Relying only on the pen in her hand, Yuyang had made all the strokes necessary to get into town. That was no small feat; it was actually quite remarkable, something no one would have dared predict a few years earlier. *A foolish girl can enjoy foolish good fortune,* Yumi thought to herself. The timing was perfect for a little girl who was destined to make a name for herself.

The day after the track meet was a Sunday, when most girls stayed in bed late, even if they were fully awake. They wanted to lie there and think their own thoughts. Better to be lazy than to get up, even for breakfast. They lay in bed for the sake of lying in bed; not to do so would be wasting an opportunity. Imagine their shock that Sunday when they learned that a thief had taken things out of Pang Fenghua's case. No one knew when it had happened, but sixteen yuan in cash and four yuan's worth of meal coupons had gone missing.

Fenghua had the commendable habit of counting her money and meal coupons when she took a tube of toothpaste out of her patent leather case each morning. On this morning, she discovered that the cash and coupons were gone. It was a considerable sum to lose, which made it a serious incident.

At 10:15 Beijing time that Sunday morning, every student in Section Three of the class of '82 was called together before many of them had eaten breakfast. Yuyang did not even have time to brush her teeth and wash her face. The homeroom teacher was there, and so was Director Qian of Student Affairs, but not Pang Fenghua. She stayed behind in her room to give a statement to the police. Students who saw her on their way out of the dorm said she was sitting on the edge of her bed, hair hanging down, eyes puffy. She looked sad and drained of energy. The policeman poured her a glass of water. She didn't touch it. This time her grief was genuine, unlike the day before out on the track. It was not a look she could easily fake.

When everyone was present in the classroom, the young

homeroom teacher stood straight as a javelin at the blackboard looking unhappy. He was waiting for Director Qian to speak. But Qian just pursed his lips, which deepened the lines around his mouth. He hadn't said a word from the moment he walked into the classroom, but finally he lit a cigarette, inhaled, and slowly blew the smoke out. Then he spoke.

"My name is Qian, you know, 'money,'" he said. "Anyone who has the guts can step up and steal me."

His comment elicited laughter that quickly died out—he did not look like he was joking. Then he went quiet for a long time, during which two rays of light shot out of his eyes like the searchlights in black-and-white movies. The lights sliced across the face of every student with an inaudible swish, and if one of them shied away from the searching look and lowered her head, he warned her, "Raise your head and look me in the eye. Don't look away."

Director Qian's devotion to all aspects of student affairs—life, work, and thought—was famous among teacher-training schools, even at the provincial level. For two straight years he had been awarded the title of "Advanced Worker at the City and Provincial Levels." The certificates hung proudly on his office wall. During the reign of the Gang of Four, he'd been imprisoned, and after his rehabilitation, his superiors had planned to "bring him up" to work in the bureau. But to their surprise, he had turned down the offer, insisting that he'd rather work "down below."

He said he was passionate about school and passionate about education, so he stayed put and began his second spring at the school. He spared no effort on behalf of his students, working diligently to make up for lost time. In his own words, he was in charge of matters as important as someone's death and as trivial as the disappearance of a needle. No one could "trick the mosquitoes into taking a nap" because he was a master at managing student affairs, all of which could be summarized in one word: "seize." Seize the work, and seize the individual. He wrapped one hand around his wrist as he explained to all the homeroom teachers how to seize a person. You take the matter and, more important, the person, in hand and squeeze, forcing submission. That does it. Thanks to his graphic, vivid description, the homeroom teachers caught on immediately.

Frankly, every student at the school was afraid of Director Qian and tried to avoid him at all costs. But when they did encounter him, they realized that he wasn't so scary after all. He'd call students over and ask nicely, "Would you say I'm a tiger?"

No, he was not a tiger; he was a hawk, a predator that could spot prey even when it didn't see him. Once a problem arose somewhere, a special odor attracted him, and he cast his shadow on the ground, soundlessly circling above. At this particular moment, the hawk was perched on the Section Three classroom podium, eyes fixed on the students below. He was talking again, but not about the theft, not directly, and the confused students were properly intimidated, even shaken, by the righteousness in his voice.

"What kind of school did the principal and I decide to set up?"

He began with a serious and fundamental question.

"I want you to know that I was in complete agreement with our principal," he continued, answering his own question, "when he said, 'We must have steely discipline and steely character.'" He poked the podium with his index finger to remind the students of the meaning of "steely." What is steel? Of course, "you've all seen it" so there was no need for Director Qian to repeat himself. Focusing on the common metal, he slowly worked his way up to the matter at hand.

"How can steel be so durable? Because it has been refined and is unalloyed. If there are impurities, it will fail and the building will collapse." Then another question: "So what must we do? Very simply, we must identify the impurity and expunge it." The classroom was so quiet that the girls could hear their own labored breathing. Some girls' faces turned red from trying too hard to regulate their breathing. In conclusion, Director Qian said, "Now I'm giving you a word of caution: honesty begets leniency; resistance begets harshness. Dismissed."

But Pang Fenghua's meal coupons and cash were not missing at all. She'd been in such a hurry Saturday morning, thanks to the 3,000-meter race, that she'd taken them out and put them in a small pocket sewn into her underwear; then, once she'd started running around the track, she had forgotten about them. She found them Monday while doing her laundry. They still carried the warmth from her body.

But she had sounded the alarm and alerted the police, and thus could not bring herself to reveal the truth. Crouching in the bathroom, she cried a second time, her face the picture of genuine sorrow and grief. No one could bring her out of her crying fit; in fact, the more people tried, the harder she cried. In the end, even the other girls began to cry with her. Who could blame her? Something so terrible would make anyone cry.

Fenghua went to see the young homeroom teacher that night.

He lived in the teachers' dorm, but all the other teachers were out playing ball while he stayed behind to correct homework. She stopped and held on to the doorframe with both hands until he turned and gestured for her to sit down in the only available seat, the single bed beside his desk. Still looking grief-stricken, she lowered herself slowly, wriggling her hips to locate the edge before finally settling onto the bed. The teacher found the graceful way she sat enchanting. Fenghua was not especially pretty, but her hips had an alluring quality that was not lost on the teacher, whose sympathy for her redoubled. He swallowed hard. "Any new clues?" he asked.

With her eyes fixed on him, she shook her head silently, looking wan and obviously distressed. He sighed, realizing how difficult it must be for her now that her money was gone, so he took out his wallet and offered her ten yuan.

"This should tide you over for a few days."

Deeply moved by his gesture, she stared at the money as tears welled up in her eyes. Her gaze slowly moved up until their eyes met, hers now brimming with tears.

"Teacher," she said, but she was unable to go on and began to weep.

She threw herself down on his pillow and sobbed, her shoulders heaving. He got up and sat beside her, cautiously reaching out to pat her on the back. She twisted her shoulders, sending a signal: "Leave me alone." But how could her own homeroom teacher leave her alone? So he patted her some more, touching the bottom of her heart and bringing forth even more tears. This time she did not twist her shoulders, but she increased her crying to the point that her whole body seemed to be choking on tears. His heart was breaking.

This went on for two or three minutes until Fenghua recovered, quietly got up, and wordlessly took the money before she sat down in his chair. She slipped the money under the glass tabletop of his desk and picked up his handkerchief to dry her eyes. Then she turned and, looking straight at him, smiled briefly; but she hurriedly shut her mouth and hid the smile behind her hand. Without warning, she stood up and walked to the door. There she spun around to see him still sitting on the edge of the bed, staring blankly at his handkerchief.

The case remained open because the police had found no clues of any value after taking Fenghua's testimony, which made it impossible to proceed. On Monday afternoon, the students in Section Three noticed that the police car that had been parked outside the administrative building was gone. With more important things to do, the police could not possibly waste any more time on a trivial matter like this. But Director Qian said that they must solve the case, and that meant increased responsibility for everyone at the school if they were to get to the bottom of this. So the teachers in the security and student affairs sections divided up the labor and produced an organizational plan. They formed a special-case unit that was in operation day and night, and spread the net far and wide—a dragnet that would snare even the most cunning fish.

At an administrators' meeting, Director Qian said that seizing the thief was not as important as making this incident an example—using it as a negative teaching model in the service of thoroughly rectifying the students' thoughts and behavior.

According to him, the school had taken a downward turn. Some of the boys were letting their hair grow long, and a few of the girls had begun wearing bell-bottomed pants. "You call that a hairstyle? And what about those pants? I'm forty-three years old," he said, "and I've never seen the likes of this." They also had to be on guard against the actions of the off-campus juvenile delinquents who wore froglike shades and hung around the school gate with a Sanyo cassette player blasting decadent music by Teresa Teng—"Sweet Wine in Coffee" and "When Will the Gentleman Return?" What kind of crazy music was that? These were all signs of danger that had to be dealt with early and decisively.

"What are we running here?" Director Qian asked. "It's a teacher-training school. All signs prove that unhealthy societal influences have already seeped onto our campus. We must eliminate them now. Don't expect them to die on their own. We must be vigilant, we cannot let down our guard."

So Director Qian devised a policy he called "outside loose and inside tight." "Outside loose" meant that they must continue the normal operation of school affairs and give that particular student a false sense of security to draw her out, like enticing a snake from its den. "Inside tight" required everyone to keep their eyes open and "not let go of that thread, even for a second."

"Outside loose" proved hard to maintain with everyone so tense. Yuyang was a case in point. What exactly had she done after finishing the race? Danger lurked in her inability to explain why she had returned to the dorm alone. After two days of indecision, she went to see her psychology teacher, Ms Huang Cuiyun, who was also the assistant Director of Student Affairs. It was a wise move, for if she hadn't, it would have been virtually impossible to prove her innocence after her period was over. She explained the situation to Ms Huang, telling her that she'd gone back to the dorm because of her "special condition." After hearing her out, Ms Huang took her into the girls' toilet, where she told her to drop her pants and show her the pad. Obviously, she was telling the truth—that was something no one could fake.

Ms Huang, a woman in her forties who had been mistakenly condemned as a rightist,[11] had been sent from the county level to teach at the school after her rehabilitation. Unlike Director Qian, she was friendly and approachable, always ready with an easy smile, like a mother, or, perhaps, a big sister. Though she was an assistant director, she told the girls to call her Teacher Huang not Director Huang, and for that she earned respect and credibility from the teachers and students alike. After checking Yuyang out, she smiled and asked, "So what does this prove, Wang Yuyang?"

Yuyang pondered the question and had to agree that it really didn't prove much. The special condition only confirmed that she had returned to the dorm alone, which conversely proved that she had been at the scene of the theft. Sweat beaded the tip of her nose as she stood there dumbfounded before blurting out, "I didn't do it."

"Before the thief is found," Teacher Huang softly replied, "everyone is a suspect, even me. That's a possibility, isn't it?" What more could Yuyang say since even the teacher included herself among the suspects? Aggressively defending herself at this point would reflect badly on her attitude.

The scope of the investigation kept changing—sometimes

it expanded, sometimes it contracted, but nothing came of it. Four days quickly passed without a breakthrough. During those four days, the girls in Section Three gained a keen and personal understanding of the terms "steely discipline" and "steely character." Steel was a metal they came to know well. It was expressionless, wordless, silent—but heavy and hard, with an oppressive power. They developed a fear of steel because its absence of motion was always temporary. Once it began to move, no one knew what might happen. They also learned that at a certain temperature anything could turn to steel—an event, time, or a mood. Once any of these became steel, they turned heavy and hard and lodged in the hearts of all the Section Three students. Gloom lay heavily over their classes, where everyone walked softly, afraid of bumping into the steel—*clang*. Another possibility was that steel would silently take a large chunk of their flesh.

In relative terms, Wang Yuyang felt more pressure than the others, and not just from the school administration; it came largely from other students, even from herself. Not knowing what she'd done or what others might be thinking she'd done and not being particularly articulate to begin with, she decided not to say anything. But that made it difficult to hold her head up in public. She could be numb to the pressure, but she couldn't work the same magic on her fellow students, whose eyes were deeply penetrating. More significantly, their imaginations were equally penetrating. A rumor was already spreading that Wang Yuyang and Director Qian had entered a stage of stalemate as they waged psychological warfare, waiting to see who would blink first; either the east wind would have the upper hand or the west wind would prevail.[12] The other girls all knew that this was the calm before the storm; it was just a matter of when.

The storm struck without the usual warning signs. Tranquility had reigned, though only among the school administrators; the turmoil among the students had never ceased. As the saying goes: "The trees want to stop moving, but the wind keeps blowing." At nine o'clock Saturday morning Beijing time, Director Qian, followed by Teacher Huang and the homeroom teacher, walked into Section Three's classroom; all the girls were present. Director Qian was all smiles, uncharacteristically relaxed, as if he'd shed a heavy load. Teacher Huang, on the other hand, seemed depressed. Her usual amity was gone, and she seemed to be under substantial strain. One look at Director Qian and the students knew that the case had been solved and that the affair had come to an end. But their anxiety was palpable as they waited to hear a name; the atmosphere was oppressive. Yuyang swallowed, so did the other students. There was plenty of reason for them to be nervous. A chunk of steel was about to drop from the sky, and before it fell, who could predict whose head it would strike?

The students were touched the moment Teacher Huang opened her mouth to speak. Her voice was low, a bit raspy, but they could tell she was trying hard to turn her grief into strength. She began by talking about her son and daughter, the former a student at Beijing University and the latter a student at Nanjing University. Saying she was proud of her children, she spoke in a soft voice, her gentle expression brimming with motherly love and concern, which, for no apparent reason, elicited sorrow from everyone in the room. The students were in a fog, confused over why she was talking about her family at this critical moment.

Nonetheless, from her speech they could tell how much she cared. A meeting had been held the night before, and it had been decided to expel the "recalcitrant, unrepentant student." With a misty gaze coming from her reddening eyes, Teacher Huang said forcefully, "I did not agree."

She began to reminisce, recalling the dark days when she had been treated unfairly. There had been her son's dangerously high fever in the countryside, which, since he'd had a seizure, had required half an hour of emergency treatment; and there was the nearly fatal food poisoning her daughter had suffered at the age of four. All these sad moments in her life evoked sympathy. She began to cry as she turned to Director Qian. "Is there a child anywhere who never gets sick? Is there one who never makes a mistake?" Qian could say nothing. Like a gentle breeze and a spring shower, her words caressed and sprinkled the students' minds, drizzle by drizzle, bit by bit, and drenched their hearts. Lowering their heads, they shed tears of remorse. Teacher Huang dried her tears and continued, "I've asked the school's Party committee for one last chance, two more days. I'm convinced that the student who made the mistake will repent by admitting it; that she'll go to the post office and mail me the money and coupons, things that do not belong to her. As a mother and a Party member, I promise you that we will handle the matter internally so long as you send everything back. Please believe me, my dear children. Don't trust to luck in this matter. The police have taken fingerprints from Pang Fenghua's case. They know and we know who has touched it. Once the police come to campus to make an arrest, it will be too late." She was anxious, fervently and tearfully hoping that the guilty student would own up to what she'd done. "Please believe me, my dear children, this is your last chance. You don't want to break your mother's heart."

Her plea was so ardent, her expression so intense that she actually choked on her words several times, nearly crying out loud. Those words warmed the hearts of the students, brightened their eyes, and stoked their courage. The result was immediate. A money order arrived Monday morning after the second period. But Teacher Huang was caught in a bind, a truly serious bind. The original plan, elementary and simple, had been to find the thief by matching the handwriting on the money order. Who could have predicted that there would be not one, but four money orders? No matter how you looked at it, the pilfered twenty yuan could not possibly have returned quadrupled. By comparing the handwriting with that on student essays, Director Qian and Teacher Huang found three matches: Kong Zhaodi, Wang Yuyang, and Qiu Fenying. The fourth sample could not be immediately assigned because it had been written with the left hand. Slamming the four money orders down on Qian's desk, Teacher Huang said, "Take a good look. Can you tell who it was?"

Qian smiled and sighed. "Old Huang, you've had twenty years of political experience, positive and negative. When someone comes forward to take the blame, what's the problem?"

Slapping the back of her right hand against her left palm, she said, "What I mean is, what do we do about the eighty yuan?" Qian fished out the one with unidentifiable handwriting and placed it before her. "Cash this and return the money to Pang Fenghua."

"What about the other three?"

Qian put the three money orders in his drawer and locked it. "Leave them here for now."

"Sixty yuan is not a small amount, and we shouldn't let it go to waste."

"How would we be doing that? How?" Qian asked.

Confused, Huang asked cautiously, "What exactly are we going to do with the money?"

"Look at you. What can I say? With some matters, we mustn't be too detail-oriented. Sometimes it's better to leave an issue hanging rather than try to resolve it. That's all I'll say for now. So put this aside and don't mention it again, all right? It's over."

The stolen money had been returned, and everyone in the school now knew they could breathe a sigh of relief. "I didn't do it. It wasn't me."

What better result could they have hoped for?

None.

Their relief was followed by anticipation as they waited to learn the identity of the thief, but the outcome was disappointing. Four or five days passed, but no punishment announcement was put up on the bulletin board, a clear indication that the theft had indeed been dealt with internally. Yuyang was filled with gratitude and happiness for escaping what can only be described as a "near death." And yet, gratitude and relief aside, she felt somehow wronged. Why? She had confessed to something she hadn't done by sending in money. On the other hand, what options did she have? The police had taken fingerprints, and she could not recall whether she had ever touched Fenghua's case. Maybe yes, maybe no. But common sense would dictate that not touching it would have been just about impossible because the girls shared a dorm room.

What if the police had retrieved Yuyang's fingerprints and publicized the fact? She'd have been in hot water, and that was a risk she could not afford to take; it was simply too much of a gamble. She told herself that it was better this way, since no one could be sure of anything. The other students could play their guessing game if they wanted to, so long as she avoided an outright disaster. As the saying goes, "Take a step backward and you can see the whole world."

In any case, Yuyang finally managed to get a good night's sleep, and what could be better than that? But why hadn't anyone spoken to her yet? Was this what they meant by "internally"? It must be. So the leaders had kept their word and she had reason to trust them. She should stop her second-guessing now that they had decided on leniency; otherwise she would not be worthy of their good faith.

Responding to the new situation and conditions at the school, a security team was formed the day before the new year arrived. A special fund was set up to purchase yellow army overcoats for each of the security guards, who were also given army belts. At the inaugural meeting, Director Qian made it clear that the coats and belts were public property and were to be returned upon graduation. The guards were instructed to treat their new uniforms with care. Completely ignoring his admonition, the students carried their coats over their shoulders and cinched the belts around their waists in order to show that they were special. That, of course, was perfectly understandable since it was an honor to be chosen for the school security team. These items showed that the users were class activists and had been elected democratically by secret ballot and then screened carefully by the school administration. Only one student, boy or girl, could be selected from each class.

Director Qian called a meeting for the team, stressing the importance of their mission to protect the school and ensure the integrity of the people's property. He stood up and shouted, "Can you do that?"

"We can," they replied in unison, the boys' deep, powerful voices merging with those of the girls, which were crisp and resonant, and seemed to linger forever in the rafters of the auditorium. Pang Fenghua's was among them.

How in the world had the loss of money increased Pang Fenghua's popularity on campus? It was as if she'd not only lost money but had found some and returned it, or had done something quite courageous. Naturally, it didn't make her smug; on the contrary, she was more humble than ever, a perfect example of an outstanding student who excelled both in her studies and her temperament. All that went to show how much she had changed, which caused Yuyang to wonder why she couldn't be lucky enough to lose a little money. Things like that simply didn't happen to her.

Fenghua had received enough votes in the security team election for a second-place finish. Even Yuyang had voted for her. In retrospect, Yuyang realized that this made no sense. She just went ahead and cast her vote—people are strange animals.

Normally, in accordance with the principle of democratic centralism, Fenghua should not have been counted as being elected to the security team, but after centralizing, the homeroom teacher allowed her to join, saying that the student who'd received the most votes, a member of the athletic committee, was needed to work elsewhere. So Fenghua was on the team. She put on the army overcoat and leather belt, cutting a striking figure—brave and imposing—like a soldier or a policewoman.

Now that Fenghua was involved in school security, the homeroom teacher summoned her to his dorm room for a talk. He said that he expected her to be more active in all aspects of school functions, to become a true activist, and thereby to serve as a role model. He invited her to sit down, but she declined; instead, she stood by his desk, her finger rubbing the glass top under which the ten-yuan bill remained next to the teacher's class schedule. It hadn't been touched.

Her finger flitted back and forth, and she couldn't stop smiling. Every sweep of that finger rubbed against the glass covering the ten-yuan bill. The teacher got up, paced the room, and shut the door. When he sat down again, Fenghua was overcome by a sudden unreasonable anxiety, and the smile disappeared from her face. Her fingers now moved mechanically over the desk as she cast her eyes upward, an absent-minded look on her face. The silence dragged on for a long time, since the teacher said nothing. Then, without warning, Fenghua blurted out, "You must have fallen in love in college, didn't you?"

What she was asking—not to mention the fact that she'd addressed him as "you" and not "teacher"—echoed like a thunderclap.

"What kind of question is that?" he said sternly. The silence returned briefly until he spoke up again. "Who'd have fallen for someone like me?"

"That's silly, teacher," she said. "Teacher, you're talking nonsense," she added even more strongly. At this point she dared not look at him. Fenghua's gaze returned to the money under the glass. "Why don't you put that away? Are you that rich?"

He laughed. "One of my students ran into some hard times, but she wouldn't accept my help."

She smiled. "Who was the ungrateful wretch?"

She lifted the glass, fished the money out, turned, and walked out the door. Caught off guard by her actions, he sat frozen in his chair and stared at the door, which seemed to sway before his eyes. He was lost in thought, caught in flights of fancy.

The following morning, the homeroom teacher strode up to the podium only to find Fenghua's seat unoccupied. A few minutes later she walked in—or, more accurately, sauntered in. She wore her army coat, and around her neck was a bright red, eye-catching scarf, obviously brand new.

"Sorry I'm late," she said.

"Please, come in," the teacher said. All quite proper and expected, as was the way she went over and took her seat— nothing out of the ordinary. But the teacher appeared inspired by the bright red scarf, having seen a connection between it and the ten yuan. His eyes lit up, and he was energized. "Why do we say, 'Capital came into this world dripping in blood and filth'?" he asked in a booming voice. "Please open your books to page seventy-three." His voice bounced off the walls. Only he was conscious of this—he and also Pang Fenghua—for it touched on no one else in the room but them. Even among all those prying eyes, it was their secret. And it was wondrous, exquisite.

Wei Xiangdong, in charge of daily concerns for the school union, was the head of the new security team. He stood out as a unique case at the school. A former student who was kept on as a teacher, he could boast no special quality except for a willingness to work hard. Mild-tempered and rather timid, he shocked everyone, himself included, at the onset of the Cultural Revolution, for no one ever expected that he had—and was willing to use—hard fists and that he was capable of decisive action; but he did and that quickly moved him up the ladder. Due to his actions, the school entered a new stage in the revolution—as they say, "A single spark can turn into a prairie fire."[13] However, this new stage did not last long because history quickly exposed his true nature. Not a good person, he was someone actively engaged in beating, smashing, and looting during the revolution.

When the old Party secretary was released from prison after the Cultural Revolution and resumed his position, the teachers thought that Wei would be in for a bad time. This did not happen.

"Let us not engage in class retaliation," the Party secretary said. "Instead, let us unite in favor of stability. Class retaliation is not the correct attitude for historical materialists." That public statement altered Wei's fate.

After seventeen self-examinations, twenty-six tearful demonstrations, and nine solemn vows, he was returned to the school and assigned to the security section. Being the sole person in that section, he was also appointed as a member of the school union committee, which was responsible for duties related to daily life. The union was an interesting place because the position of chairman was traditionally assumed by the vice principal.

In practice, however, Wei was in charge, although the vice principal's name was on the door of the chairman's office. As a result, the school union stopped being a true union[14] and became the security section, an organ of the dictatorship. The daily duties conducted by the union all related to women: distributing birth control pills, condoms, sanitary napkins, and shampoo to the female faculty. Wei worked hard, and that, of course, was good. But most important was how he adjusted his attitude to fit each situation, whether the position was high or low. A true man knows when to be humble and when to be assertive.

Once, at a section meeting, he announced to the female faculty, "From now on, don't think of me as a man, no, don't even treat me as human. I am a feminine product you can use whenever you want." With words like these coming from a big, husky man like Wei, the teachers laughed so hard they nearly doubled over. If it had been any other man, they'd have called him a scoundrel, but coming from him, the words sounded different. It was no easy matter for a rugged man like Wei to bounce back after taking such a fall, but he developed a cordial relationship with the female faculty. When the teachers came for their items, for instance, he'd say, "Here you are, Teacher Zhang, 3.3 centimeters long for your husband. Teacher Wang, this one is yours, 3.5 centimeters."

Talk about shameless! How could he be so coarse? *I'm coarse, I admit it, but what's wrong with that? I* am *coarse.* Back and forth they bantered and flirted. Instead of detesting him, the women actually welcomed someone who had a sense of humor and was eager to help. Who doesn't like to joke and laugh? Who doesn't want to be happy and cheerful every day? Who wants to constantly frown and live a life centered on class differences?

It was only logical for Wei to be in charge of the school security team, but the leadership followed strict organizational procedures in appointing him. Director Qian recommended Wei, but that required the personal consent of the Party secretary before it was approved. As someone who was capable of getting the job done, he was the ideal man. One semester he caught a pair of thieves on campus. Rather than beat or berate them, he tied their hands behind their backs before pasting medicinal plasters from the school infirmary over their eyes and letting them loose on the sports field, where they could walk, jump, or run, but not get away.

Groping around with their feet, as if they were trying to catch fish underwater, they cut a pathetic figure. Seven hours later, they knelt down and wailed, a sight that drew laughter even from the old Party secretary, who privately admitted that Wei had a knack for educational discipline. While the head of the school security team was not a particularly important post, it gave him the ideal opportunity to expend his excess energy and showcase his talent, all to the benefit of the school. Naturally, in light of his special circumstance, he had to be employed "under supervision"—the degree of which would be determined by Director Qian.

"What do you think, Little Wei?" Director Qian asked him as they sat in the student affairs office. Wei was less than a year younger than Qian, but Qian always called him Little Wei to mark the distinction between leader and subordinate. Little Wei was standing before Qian like a student.

"I'll do whatever Director Qian asks me to do," he said sincerely.

"Give me frequent reports," Qian said.

"I will."

Qian was pleased. He was a man who did not like flattery. If you tried it on him, he saw right through it. On the other hand, he appreciated people who worked for and talked to him respectfully. Clearly pleased, he said, "You may go now."

"Head of the school security team" was a vague phrase that could or could not be considered a job title. But that was not important; most important was the group of troopers under Wei's supervision, the people he would deploy. His job was no sinecure, but it was one that moved him into a leadership role. And that made him inordinately happy.

Soon after he took up his post, Wei began meeting with the students one-on-one, his favorite mode of carrying out his duties. During evening study period, Wang Yuyang watched as Wei called Pang Fenghua out of the classroom and then saw the two of them carry on a long and serious yet cordial conversation in the hallway. Yuyang reminded herself to be careful and not to talk too much in front of Fenghua, now that she'd become one of the more active students. But then she considered her own place in the class. She really didn't amount to much; she was like a squirt of urine in the Yangtze River. With or without her, it made no difference, and nothing either good or bad would come to her, so why worry? That thought put her more or less at ease, but it was a special kind of ease; it was neither painful nor scratchy—not bitter and not sweet, sort of sour.

Yuyang was experiencing a hard-to-describe sense of loss.

She knew she was jealous of Fenghua. Never one to compete with others, she nevertheless secretly felt that she was a match for Fenghua; but now, though hard to believe, she paled in comparison. The other girls in class were whispering that, thanks to special tutoring by their homeroom teacher, Fenghua had even learned to understand Misty Poetry.[15] That was no small feat. Obviously she'd made considerable progress.

But Yuyang had underestimated herself. Good luck was about to make a visit; she just didn't know it yet because Wei was still deliberating. With his experience in management and discipline, Wei had little faith in the school security team, for the team members, though unquestionably enthusiastic about their mission, had a serious flaw: they were out in the open, and the other students were on their best behavior around them. That made them ineffective when it came to monitoring their fellow students' thoughts and souls. In order to fully understand them and truly take control of their actions, Wei would need to find suitable informants from the inside—"an eye that can see ten thousand *li*" or "an ear that can hear what travels with the wind." This sort of person should not be too prominent, too showy, or too noticeable in either a positive or negative way. Wei was convinced that he would be well informed in regard to the political orientation of the school if he could develop one such student in each class. Naturally, these students were to remain anonymous heroes, reporting to him and him alone.

Yuyang could not believe that Teacher Wei even knew who she was. He'd called out "Wang Yuyang" in a loud, clear voice, and had even waved, so obviously he was trying to get her attention. This unexpected recognition from the teacher was flattering, but it also made her nervous. The stolen money incident was closed, yet it remained an unstated sore spot for her, and she was still afraid of being called on by the teachers.

Wei summoned her to the general duty office. Lacking the nerve to take a seat on her own, she stood with her eyes lowered, but after a brief and simple chat, she realized that Teacher Wei was a genial person and not mean at all, despite the fact that he was tall and big-boned, which gave him a rough appearance.

Unlike Director Qian, who always looked glum, Wei seemed to be outgoing and laughed easily. Finally he broached the subject. "We have been secretly observing Wang Yuyang with the intention of making her someone we should cultivate." Teacher Wei had said "we," not "I," which meant that he represented the gigantic, tight-knit, behind-the-scenes leadership—mysterious, sacred, and impossible to see in its entirety. He pointed out in a somber voice that as a target of cultivation Wang Yuyang was still lacking in certain areas. In her current state, she wasn't quite up to par. She was, for instance, inadequate in the area of "one heart and one mind" dedication. Although he was subjecting her to criticism, there was a kind-hearted message in his words that implied anxiety over turning iron into steel and potential into substance, and this underscored his expectations and hopes for her.

He was stern yet earnest, hinting at a different kind of organizational trust. No one had ever extended a helping hand of that magnitude or indicated this kind of enthusiasm and trust to Yuyang before, and it moved her profoundly. With myriad emotions surging inside her, she fell into a daze as Teacher Wei gave her instructions and an assignment. From now on she was to give a weekly written report to "us" on any and all anomalies, even those involving members of the security team, whether on campus, in class, or in the dorm. In other words, Pang Fenghua might be on the security team from the perspective of organizational procedures, but she was, in reality, under Yuyang's surveillance and control. It was too appealing for words.

The conversation with Wei lasted only twenty minutes, but those twenty minutes were immensely important to Yuyang, a landmark that woke her up and convinced her that she was not dispensable, not useless. She was, in fact, regarded with trust and esteem by the people who counted. The most enthralling quality of her job was that it required secrecy and underground activity. With the knowledge that she'd been given considerable responsibility, she suddenly felt grown up. On her way out she kept turning over what Teacher Wei had said to her; his words echoed in her ears. He'd told her to "observe more, listen more, record more, talk little, and make yourself less noticeable." How kind his words had been. She'd never sought the limelight, not because she hadn't wanted to, but because she was too shy and didn't know how to. Now, however, everything was different; keeping out of the public eye was an essential feature of her mission.

Real student life began after nine-thirty at night. During the long daylight hours the students could not be themselves. Their time was divided into filing cabinet drawers, into which were placed daily meals, calisthenics, eye-health exercises, and rest periods. The biggest drawer was further divided into class times. There was a bit of flexible time in the late afternoons, but that was like a cupboard for odds and ends. This chunk of time might have appeared enjoyable, but it was monotonous, taken up by group activities, physical education, or the arts, which after a while, became repetitive. Once the evening study period was over, the students tidied up, rinsed out a few of their things, washed up, and climbed into bed before beginning their real activity. If you looked at the dormitories from a distance you'd find them quite attractive during this time. Every window was lit like a scene from a fairy tale. Then at nine-thirty Beijing time all the windows went dark. At lights-out, the campus quieted down, the dorms included; only the soft nightlights in the bathrooms remained on. The windows turned pitch black as indoor activity began to die down; but this did not mean the day was ending. On the contrary, it was just beginning.

In the brief span of time before they fell asleep, the students lay in bed in the dark, full of energy. Their minds, bright and shiny as if washed clean, became sensitive, sharp, and discerning, capable of philosophical research or poetry composition. The students became transient philosophers and momentary poets. Their tongues sharpened, and even the shiest and least articulate among them seemed to possess a supercharged mouth that emitted the blue flame of wisdom. They chattered away, talking about everything—ancient and modern, domestic and foreign, trivial and outdated—covering interpersonal relationships, the future, their resentments and rancor, their happiness, and anything they could think of.

Of course, everything was twisted, colored by pubescent exaggeration, passion, and sorrow. Lying calmly under their blankets, they spoke with naive sophistication interspersed with mature recklessness. In fact, they were honest, exposed, and transparent, convinced that they knew everything, that whoever considered them naive would suffer when the time came. Understandably, their conversations tended to center on the school and their classes, young Zhang and young Li in their classrooms, Mr Zhang and Miss Li among the teachers, Old Zhang and Little Li at the eatery by the campus gate. With their eyes shut, the students appeared to rest, but their faces were no less expressive than when their eyes were wide open and were often even more colorful and intense. Since the door was bolted, their conversations assumed a private, secretive air. But that was an illusion. Each room had eight mouths, and the following morning, eight would become sixteen, sixteen would become thirty-two, and in no time the secrets would be public knowledge. But this bothered no one.

If the conversations got really animated, the girls would open their eyes and look into the darkness, which had no effect on their cleverness. Their voices would grow louder with uproarious talk or wild laughter. At such moments, a shout would rise up from the teacher on night duty downstairs: "Who's talking up there?"

Sometimes the general became specific: "Room 323. Do you hear me? Room 323." The disturbance would die down again as everyone shut their eyes, savoring the best part of the conversation with happy, contented smiles.

Yuyang lived in 412, a standard room with five girls from the cities, plus Pang Fenghua, Wang Yuyang, and Kong Zhaodi. The most active and conspicuous girl in the room was Zhao Shanshan, who played the violin and the piano, was the class's literary mainstay, and, predictably, was on its arts and literature committee.

A favorite of the teachers, she was outstanding in every respect except for her predilection for giving her classmates nicknames, starting with the boys. She had a gift for giving names that were right on target in mocking the subject's unique features. The name sometimes sounded contrived at first, but the more one mulled it over, the more one had to agree that it was the perfect nickname. She said that one of the boys was like a camel except for his lack of fur. Sure enough, many of his movements did resemble a camel. When the girls ran into Camel on the street, he'd nod and they'd smile knowingly. *He does, he looks like a camel.* In this wondrous world, seeing is believing.

Her victims included Mantis, Hound, Frog, and Toad. As for so-and-so, he definitely resembled a rooster, but only if you looked at his profile when he thrust out his neck, alert and jerky. Of course he was a rooster. The boys in class were unaware that she'd turned them into zoo animals.

After naming her way through the boys in the class, she hadn't yet exhausted her talent, so she moved on to the girls—with Wang Yuyang as her first target. There was nothing malicious in her choice of Yuyang; she simply was in love with all the attention and wanted to show off her clever tongue. One night, when she was washing up, she abruptly asked the other girls if they knew what Wang Yuyang looked like. Trying to supply an answer, the girls silently scrolled through all the animals they could think of, but none reminded them of Yuyang. Shanshan waited till lights-out to reveal the answer: Wang Yuyang was a steamed bun. That drew the girls' focus away from animals. Yes, Yuyang's back, especially the nape of her neck, did look like a steamed bun. So it was settled—Yuyang was Steamed Bun. As Yuyang lay in bed feeling hurt, she did not say a word. Shanshan was clearly picking on her—as if she were pushing Yuyang's head down and sticking her nose up her bottom. The following morning Yuyang did not show up in the cafeteria; the thought of seeing steamed buns enraged her. The day dragged on till nightfall, when she blurted out, apropos of nothing that was being said at the time, "Zhao Shanshan, you're an oily fritter."

Shanshan turned over and said nonchalantly, "How could I be an oily fritter? I don't look anything like one. Hey, everyone, do you think I look like an oily fritter? Of course I don't."

"Then you're gruel," Yuyang said.

If anything, that was even less likely, and Yuyang knew it. Who in the world could look like gruel? Shanshan ignored her.

Without the anticipated echo from the other girls, Yuyang felt shamed and did not know what to say.

Kong Zhaodi came to her rescue: "Let's get some sleep. I'm on duty tomorrow." Since both girls were from the countryside, Kong Zhaodi and Wang Yuyang shared a private sense of a united front; they knew they had to team up because the city girls were simply too haughty. By rights, Pang Fenghua should have been the third element in the united front, but having come from a small town, she was a special case.

Admittedly, her town was considered rural, but Fenghua had grown up eating commodity grain, and her family possessed a city household registry. So strictly speaking, she was not a country girl. That, however, did nothing to make the five city girls in the room treat her as one of their own. To them, she was country. As a result, Fenghua wavered between the two fronts, one side being too lofty for her, the other too demeaning. Since Fenghua lacked a clearly defined tendency or a firm stance, Yuyang could not expect any help from her. Now, having received no positive feedback in the wake of her retort, Yuyang felt even more injured. She felt worthless, her self-hate as strong as her loathing for Zhao Shanshan.

In the end, Pang Fenghua was forced to join the rural united front after Zhao Shanshan got carried away and gave her the malicious nickname "Taken." It began with a pair of shoes. One morning as she left the dorm, Li Dong put a pair of shoes with stretchable openings on the window sill to air out, but when she returned that afternoon, they had been replaced by a pair of sneakers. Li Dong knew immediately that Fenghua had made the switch. Tossing the sneakers on the floor, Li Dong commented casually, "Whose worn shoes are these anyway?"

That was all Zhao Shanshan needed to engage her clever tongue: "Didn't you just say it yourself, Li Dong? Worn shoes are surely taken." Li Dong, no longer upset, was pleased. It had to be Pang Fenghua who was "taken" like worn shoes. The nickname not only appeased Li Dong but was witty and had a negative implication, since it referred to loose women. This was how Pang Fenghua got her nickname, though its use was restricted to the small circle of their dorm room. It was clever, but not something one brought up casually. If it spread beyond the dorm, it would not only be considered thoughtless and indiscreet, but in terrible taste for girls their age.

Fenghua had returned a bit later than usual that night since she'd gone to the homeroom teacher's office before the evening study period was over. She was increasingly drawn to what he had to say even though he tended to ramble, often incoherently, as if he were shrouded in clouds and fog. She understood every word, but not everything he said when he strung the words together, which she found endearing, since they sounded to her like Misty Poetry. And she discovered that their relationship itself was beginning to resemble Misty Poetry: filled with meaning, having no beginning and no end, and marked by an anxiety that yearned to be made clear. But the means to put this into words seemed forever beyond her reach.

In recent days the homeroom teacher had been on an emotional roller coaster, suffering mood swings from extreme happiness to intense sadness. There did not seem to be any reason for these mercurial changes, and, while Fenghua asked herself what was going on, she was smart enough to guess what was happening. Like her, he had a restless heart, and she worried about him, felt bad for him, and would have liked to share his anxieties. And yet, she experienced an indescribable sweetness, an irrepressible pleasure that was simultaneously sheer torture. In fact, nothing inappropriate had happened and nothing probably would in the end; but that was precisely why she felt such a yearning, such concern. Immersed in a welter of emotions, she felt like crying, but no tears came.

She returned to the dorm five minutes before lights-out, washed up inattentively, and climbed into bed. Experiencing similar mood swings to her teacher, she was confused and bewildered. Then Zhao Shanshan walked in, bringing with her a burst of cold air. The lights in the room went out almost immediately, so even though it was clear that something was wrong, no one could tell what it was in the pitch darkness.

Even so, Shanshan managed to display how she felt by the noisy way she washed up, splashing water and banging against the enamel basin. Apparently Wei Xiangdong of the school security team had not had anything good to say to her. Shortly after Pang Fenghua had left to go to the homeroom teacher's office, Wei had summoned Zhao Shanshan to talk about her penchant for giving her classmates nicknames. He had refrained from scolding her, but she was more terrified than if she'd actually received a reprimand, for Wei apparently knew everything she did in the dorm room. That little bitch Pang Fenghua had taken advantage of the homeroom teacher's favoritism and ratted on her.

Trying to contain her anger, Shanshan climbed into bed without a word. Even though the lights were out, her roommates could feel her blinding anger. "Don't think I don't know," she said in a menacing growl, instantly altering the atmosphere in the room. "Don't think I don't know," she repeated.

Pang Fenghua, whose thoughts still lingered on the homeroom teacher, emerged from her reveries and detected a threat in Shanshan's comment because Fenghua did indeed have something to hide.

"What's the matter, Shanshan?" she asked uneasily.

"Don't think I don't know," Shanshan repeated as if reciting a poem. Of course everyone knew that her pointed comment was targeted at someone. "Don't think I don't know," Shanshan said one last time, intending to clear up an ambiguous situation, but actually making it even more ambiguous.

A strange, amorphous, dark object was thrashing around in the room. No one knew what Shanshan knew exactly nor did they know what the connection was between what she knew and anyone else, especially Pang Fenghua. It was mysterious; it created suspicions. But not with Yuyang, who lay beneath her blanket, for she knew; she knew everything. And as she lay there quietly, she began to feel hot, so she stretched out her left leg and found a cool spot; her big toe rested against that spot. It was refreshing; it felt good.

Following a winter rain, the days grew cooler; actually, they became downright cold. Yellowed, withered leaves hung on the parasol trees, but there was nothing leafy about them. Even more of the leaves had fallen to the ground, where they were plastered to the road surface by the rain. What really caught people's attention were the fuzzy acorns that still adorned the tips of the branches. From a distance, the campus looked like an orchard filled with fruit trees. But no harvest was in the offing; only winter was in the future, and indeed it was already the end of November.

On the other hand, late November actually began instilling the vitality of spring in the students; the campus turned lively despite the cold air, harsh winds, and dreary rain. A casual flip of the calendar revealed that 12–9 was barely two weeks away.[16] How could any school leave December 9—a revolutionary moment, a time when blood roiled, the day when the wind, the horses, and the Yellow River roared—off their schedule?

On that day the red sun shone brightly on the East as the god of freedom sang with loud passion, as described in a poem posted by Chu Tian, a student in the class of '81.

You
12–9

Are a torch
You
12–9
Are a bugle
You're sonorous
You're aflame

December 9 was a holiday for the great mass of students; it was a holiday for Zhao Shanshan, a holiday for Pang Fenghua, and a holiday for Wang Yuyang. A holiday required celebration because that was what people did. There was nothing particularly memorable about their school's form of celebration, which was to gather the students on the athletic field between classes for singing contests. The holiday would not be considered celebrated until they had all sung, had enjoyed a good and festive outing, and had seen the top three prizes awarded. Of course, the prizes lent the celebration a special character because every class fought hard to win them; and it wasn't just the students who wanted to win. The homeroom teachers wanted to win, so did the music teachers. Section Three of the class of '82 had fired blanks at that year's sports meet, having come in fourth among the six sections of that class.

It was an utter failure that naturally made the homeroom teacher even more fervently hopeful about the singing contest. Having graduated from college in 1982, he did not plan to spend the rest of his life at the school; he intended to take the graduate school entrance examination. On the other hand, his reputation was on the line, and he could not take the contest lightly. He'd received his degree in political education from the provincial teacher-training college, and upon graduation, his counselor had impressed upon him the importance of honor and reputation.

"What is work?" the counselor had asked. "It is winning honors and gaining recognition. So don't be shy or timid. Nothing happens when everyone wins honors, but if you are the only one who does, then a staircase will appear before you, allowing you to ascend to a higher level and see what others cannot see. That will be especially beneficial when the time comes for promotions, housing assignments, evaluations, selection as a representative, and marriage. If everyone has it, but you don't, then you have wasted your energy. Your exhaustion will be a sign of poor health and nothing else. So you must strive for honors and recognition. You can break your skull and shed your blood, but you must turn around and start over. Never, ever be shy and timid."

The homeroom teacher had already had a taste of what the counselor had talked about. On the night of the sports meet, the teacher whose class came in first even found a new way to smoke a cigarette. With his head held high and his chest thrust out, he looked less like a smoker than a tiger ready to conquer the world. With its defeat at the sports meet, Section Three must win back its honor at the singing contest, so the homeroom teacher called a pre-battle meeting to spur on the students.

Section Three began preparing for the contest earlier than the other sections. To keep the practices secret, the teacher found a nearby factory warehouse to rehearse in. This time they enjoyed a number of advantages. To begin with, Zhao Shanshan played the piano, which eliminated the need for the music teacher to accompany them. The extra points that earned would give them an edge with the judges. Unfortunately, the teacher held an unfavorable—actually, a quite bad—opinion of Shanshan, who had been picking fights with Pang Fenghua. What had Shanshan meant when she called her Taken? It seemed clear that Shanshan was targeting him and that he had to be very careful. Yet, for the sake of the big picture—winning the contest—he had to put up with things the way they were and wait to "execute" the problem case after the contest.

"To execute" was the homeroom teacher's favorite expression; it denoted a grand, decisive tone that conveyed a sense of power and authority. When he uttered the phrase, he sounded unwaveringly resolute, as if the culprit would be shot on the spot and the problem solved. Or he might "execute a class" representative who failed an assignment. Who doesn't fear being "executed"? His temperament demanded that he "execute" Zhao Shanshan as soon as possible because the brassy girl, bolstered by her belief that she was the backbone of the class's arts and cultural activities, was nearly out of control.

During the selection process for choral director, he had tested Shanshan. Knowing that he preferred Pang Fenghua, Shanshan insisted on Hu Jia's being the director, going so far as to say that there was a problem with Fenghua's deportment.

What kind of talk is that? What does she know about deportment anyway? Ridiculous. Absurd. His face darkened to show his displeasure. So Shanshan was out as a member of the committee for cultural activities, and when the contest was over, he'd have to "execute" her.

The music teacher was very accommodating, and Section Three's choral practice at the warehouse was taking shape. The forty-eight students were lined up in four rows representing the four vocal parts; the separate vocal sections intersected, corresponded, and contrasted with each other to produce a musical performance with such depth and breadth that it seemed created, not by forty-eight students, but by thousands of singers. It was the unified strength of a social class; better yet, it was the unified strength of a nation that permeated with the intensity of boundless hatred and bottomless anger mixed with the flames of struggle and resistance. Standing off to one side, the homeroom teacher pulled a long face as he hugged his elbows and stood as straight as a javelin about to be hurled. He was happy, but he kept gnashing and grinding his teeth; that, of course, might well have been the effect that the singing had on him. In art, hatred and anger are infectious; that is what art is all about.

After the music teacher had lined the students up, the homeroom teacher sought the assistance of the dance teacher in an attempt to "replace the old with something new." The dance teacher added a bit of choreography and some standard gestures, such as a sudden clapping of the hands or the abrupt thrusting of fists into the air. The addition of this high-spirited movement to the resonating tempo gave the song a rhythmic flair that elevated its power; the performance now exuded a dauntless, do-or-die quality. The dance teacher's ingenuity was fully displayed in the lyrical segment when he asked the students to stand with their feet apart and let their arms hang to their sides, their balled fists turned inward. With their chests thrust out, they swayed from side to side, shifting their weight from one foot to the other. Though their feet were firmly planted on the floor, they looked as if they were forging their way through fire and water together. And yet the gentle movement, done with juvenile clumsiness, evoked a tender feeling, like willows in a spring breeze, and conveyed a deep affection, a longing, and a tribute to the motherland. These winsome actions, achieved in a uniform manner, were breathtakingly beautiful.

But most of the boys were too shy to make the necessary gestures, and as they were trying not to laugh, the do-or-die determination was lost. Several practice rounds fell short of the desired results. The athletic committee member, a tall, strapping student, was the worst, for he came across as especially bashful and awkward when he balled his fists and swayed back and forth.

"Sun Jianqiang, watch what you're doing," the homeroom teacher shouted.

As a smile crept over his face, Sun Jianqiang looked as if he'd rather die, and that made the teacher redouble the severity in his voice. "Sun Jianqiang!"

That effectively brought the practice to an abrupt end and stopped the swaying of the willows in the spring breeze.

"What's wrong with you?" the teacher asked, glaring at the boy.

"Can't we scrap this? It's hard to do and it's ugly," the student said.

As his face darkened, the teacher ordered, "Get over here."

So Sun Jianqiang stepped out of the formation and did not pass up the opportunity to make a face at Pang Fenghua along the way, which did not go undetected by the teacher. Since he always made a point of passing the ball to the teacher whenever they played basketball, the boy did not take the teacher's annoyance all that seriously. He knew how to deal with the teacher; they were like friends. So he walked up and struck a casual pose, rocking back and forth to express his "I don't care" attitude.

"Tell me, what do you mean by ugly?" the teacher demanded.

"It's too girlish and sissy-looking," Sun said with a red face. The boys laughed; so did some of the girls. The homeroom teacher sent a look to the music teacher that really was ugly before he turned around and roared at Sun, "Get out." He pointed to the warehouse door.

Momentarily taken aback, Sun realized that he'd been executed, and the loss of face was more than he could bear. He spun around and walked off, pointlessly muttering something under his breath. The teacher pointed a finger at the boy's receding back like a pistol—the coup de grâce for Sun Jianqiang. The teacher screamed, "You're no longer on the athletic committee. And don't ever come back here."

Now that Sun was out, there was a gap in the chorus line, and as the teacher continued to fume, the singing practice came to another halt. Facing the chorus as the conductor, Pang Fenghua signaled the teacher with her eyes, asking what to do about the empty space. The Section Three students were well aware of the teacher's decisive nature; he meant what he said and said what he meant. It would be impossible for him to backtrack now, especially since the outburst had occurred in front of the whole class. With his hands on his hips, he walked over to Fenghua.

"Keep practicing," he said. He was still angry, but it was clear that he was thinking as his eyes lingered on the empty space left by Sun Jianqiang's departure.

The students started up again; after gesturing with their

hands, fists, and elbows, they began to sway to the left then to the right. They swayed with renewed effort, but without producing the desired effect. The earlier harmonious motion could not be recaptured, and with it went the imposing air and the spirit of resolve. The teacher's eyes swept over each student's face before landing on Yuyang, whose awkward movements were lackluster at best. With her eyes downcast, she looked ashamed; not only did she fail to look off at a forty-five-degree angle with deep longing, as required by the choreography, but she bit her lip. And she forgot to sing.

The teacher walked up, grabbed her by the elbow, and yanked her out of the formation. Then he gestured for the remaining students to close up ranks, returning symmetry to the chorus and filling Sun's space at the same time.

"Good, very good. Now you're making progress. Keep it up," he said, clapping his hands and sighing happily.

With two students having been "executed," the rest of the team increased their spirit and morale; they raised their voices as the veins bulged on their necks. From where he stood behind Pang Fenghua, the teacher also began to gesture, a sort of de facto conductor. Yuyang remained off to the side, knowing that she'd been executed but unsure of what to do now. So she just stood there stiffly, hoping for something to happen.

Afraid that the teacher would give her the coup de grâce, she made sure that she didn't turn her back on him, but she didn't want to stay where she was, either. That was just too awkward. She seemed to be waiting, but in vain, since the teacher had no intention of letting her rejoin the chorus. He'd forgotten all about her. So there she stood, biting her lip, her eyes downcast.

And then she made an accidental discovery: the ugly round tips of her cloth shoes looked horribly unsophisticated. Taking two steps back, she tried to hide her shoes, but to no avail. Now she was truly ashamed, ashamed of her countrified appearance. Luckily, she was no longer the dumb little girl she'd once been, and she knew how to get out of this. She walked up to the teacher. "Teacher, I don't feel well. May I be excused?" He was too engrossed in his conducting to hear her, so she repeated, "Teacher, I'd like to be excused."

Now he heard her, and without even turning to look, he waved her away, assigning the responsibility for consent to his wrist. As she walked off, she forgot to swing her arms because her fists were still balled at her sides. The stiffness in her movements nearly caused her to goose-step out of the warehouse. The dozen or so steps sapped all her energy, each one stomping on her heart.

Sun Jianqiang was relieved of duty that evening. Without a word of explanation, the homeroom teacher simply put up a new list of committee members, replacing Sun's name as athletic committee member with that of the Section Three class representative, and added "also serving" in parenthesis next to that name. A class meeting was called during the evening study period, and the teacher gave a short speech expressing his wish that the students not "give up on themselves" and not be "too clever," for "nothing good" would come of either of those. He did not have to name names for them to know whom he was referring to. Sun Jianqiang was not likely to be passing the ball to the teacher on the basketball court anytime soon. But he was not the intended target of the phrase "too clever," since he could hardly be called even a little clever. That was meant for Zhao Shanshan, whom the teacher glanced at during his speech. Shanshan was not stupid, which she proved by lowering her head. Now she knew that she would not fare any better than Sun if she didn't get behind Pang Fenghua or find a way to get on her good side. Her date of "execution" was not far off; she was living on borrowed time.

Yuyang was dejected at not being allowed into the chorus to celebrate 12–9, but she refused to let herself sink into defeat. So she went to the library to study, and when she found that she was unable to focus, she picked up a detective novel by Agatha Christie and was immediately hooked. Reading a novel a day, she soon finished the entire series. They had different story lines, crime scenes, and modi operandi, but the same deductive method was used to catch the murderer in each one. Logic was the starting point and the central technique in moving the plot forward to its climatic ending. Grouping Christie's novels together, Yuyang realized that, except for the mustachioed Belgian detective, Hercule Poirot, everyone connected to the crime was a suspect because they all had motive, time, method, and opportunity. Everyone was involved in the crime, and no one could claim innocence. Feeling that her eyes were wiped clean by the novels, Yuyang gained a renewed understanding of underground work and was emboldened to carry out her mission. She believed that the systematic reading would enable her to do an even better job pleasing Teacher Wei and putting those in the organization at ease.

Yuyang did not take the novels back to her dorm or to the classroom—better not to take books like that out of the library, where an air of research and contemplation gave this reading legitimacy. Exerting extra effort, she jotted down her reactions in a notebook as she read along. In addition to the contents of those notes, she gained something concrete—she met and eventually got to know Chu Tian of Section One of the class of '81, the school's most famous poet.

Not noticeably handsome and a bit on the skinny side, Chu had an unremarkable appearance. Compared to the other boys, he stood out only because of his hair, which was not only longer than everyone else's, but was also unusually messy—like a pile of chicken feathers. The hint of suffering on his face gave him an ascetic air and in turn made him unique. He hardly ever spoke to anyone, for he was arrogant and proud beyond words, and Yuyang had heard that the average student could only dream of getting to know him. Chu Tian, whose real name was Gao Honghai, was a country boy; but he was now Chu Tian, no longer Gao Honghai. The new name gave him a complete makeover, turning a tall, reedy youngster into someone not quite real and transcendent, as vast and as distant as the sky. His unique airs set him apart and instilled in him the sort of artistic temperament that was seen as so important by the teachers. In fact, Chu Tian had a very low sense of self-esteem, but his neurotic and reserved manner sent out a sparkle—a cold, haughty, superior, and conceited sparkle that was, naturally, the glittery evidence of his supremacy. Yuyang never dared look directly at him, and deep down she revered him, especially after reading his poem on the bulletin board. She was amazed at how he had referred to 12–9 as "you," as if he were pointing to a person.

He was audacious, presumptuous, and willful, and yet he

sounded so urgent and insistent, as if he could summon up such things at will. Just listen, and imagine him pointing with his left hand:

> You
> 12–9
> Are a torch

Then he points with his right hand:

> You
> 12–9
> Are a bugle

Who else but Chu Tian could use "you" in such a heroic and carefree manner, and make it sound so spontaneous and ingenious? And what did he mean by "You're sonorous, You're aflame"? That was magical, inconceivable. The lack of punctuation only increased the singular quality of his poetry.

She had heard that an elderly teacher had once questioned Chu Tian about the lack of punctuation. He had replied with only a sneer, turning the teacher's face so red that it looked as if it were about to explode. When the teacher proctored an exam, he kept a close check on Chu Tian, hoping to catch him cheating so he could give him a warning.

But Chu Tian did not need to cheat, for he excelled in every subject except physical education. He was part of the landscape—someone of interest at the school, coming and going alone, ignoring everyone. No one meant a thing to him, not even Director Qian. With her own eyes Yuyang had seen Chu Tian walk past the director, head held high as he refused to acknowledge the man's existence. And yet, the famous and intractable Chu Tian actually spoke to her; in fact, it was he who started the conversation. She was sure that no one would believe her.

It was noon. Yuyang stood at the magazine rack, holding *Poetry Journal* in one hand and picking her nose with the other. Chu Tian was standing beside her, staring at her intensely. She looked up, saw him, and dropped the magazine. He bent down, picked it up, and handed it back to her.

With a cordial smile that had no hint of superiority, he asked, "Like poetry?"

Finding it impossible that he would actually be talking to her, Yuyang turned to see if someone was standing behind her before she responded with a nod. He smiled again. His teeth were uneven and discolored, but at that moment they seemed bright and sparkling. She wished that she could smooth her hair, but it was too late, for he'd already floated away. Yuyang stared until Chu Tian disappeared behind a door before realizing that her face was burning hot and her unreasonable heart was pounding wildly. *This is none of your business, heart.*

She stood there, savoring what had just happened, asking herself over and over, "Like poetry?" Her mind refused to concentrate, and when she returned to her seat, she picked up her pen and began to doodle:

Like poetry
Yes
Like poetry
Yes
Like poetry
Yes
Like poetry

Yes
Like poetry
Yes I do
Like poetry
Yes yes I do

She looked down at her notebook, shocked to see that she was writing poetry. This was poetry. What else could it be? Sadly, she realized that she had been a poet all along. What a pleasant surprise—she was already a poet.

The new poet sat in her seat with a blank look on her face, but she could feel her heart flutter as she recited silently:

You—Chu Tian
Are a torch
You—Chu Tian
Are a bugle
You're sonorous
You're aflame

She was amazed when she finally recovered her senses. She remained motionless while the wind blew wildly against the branches outside.

Once you meet someone, it seems that you're always running into each other. That is exactly what happened to Yuyang and Chu Tian. They ran into each other over and over—in the cafeteria, on the athletic field, and, of course, in the library. But mostly it happened when they were headed somewhere. It was invariably accidental, but to Yuyang, the repeated encounters began to take on a special meaning and became a secret that she buried deep in her heart. Girls of her age are good at keeping secrets; they keep a tidy record of neatly categorized secrets in a corner known only to themselves, with a tender wish for two hearts to beat in unison. *Like I'm a part of you and you're a part of me.*

To Yuyang, the campus seemed to have shrunk now that it felt as if there were only the two of them. Life on campus had a miniature quality that enabled her to manipulate it. For instance, she might be walking along on campus when she'd have a sudden premonition that she would run into Chu Tian. So she'd turn or look around and there he'd be.

There was even an extreme example. One day when she was in her dorm room, she was suddenly restless and felt an urge to go out for a walk. She went downstairs and had barely taken a dozen steps before—there he was again. He wasn't looking at her, but she was overwhelmed, yes, overwhelmed, nearly to the point of tears. She was positive that heaven was on her side, secretly helping her; otherwise, how could such coincidences take place? Chu Tian was intentionally keeping his eyes averted, which had to mean that he was thinking about her. She knew she wasn't pretty, but he was a poet, and poets have tastes that cannot be judged by ordinary standards. His attitude toward her only confirmed the fact that he was different from everyone else.

Every encounter felt blissful to her and constituted a moment of sheer joy. The feeling could even be characterized as intoxication, though that is an uncommonly vile thing that always stands in opposition to you. Intoxication is invariably brief and disappears before you know it. Then comes the endless, bottomless waiting while you yearn for it to happen again, like an addict.

And so intoxication is a void, a boundless entanglement and a lingering that accompanies a sense of loss and heartache, as well as an unending anticipation and waiting. Intoxication is essentially a different kind of suffering, a dull torture.

But for Yuyang defeat was nullified by patience, and even more by a sense of excitement.

She asked herself what was happening to her. It took a long time, but she finally realized that what she felt for Chu Tian was, simply stated, tender affection. She was attracted by his chicken-feather hair, his solitude, his knitted brows, and the way he walked. Everything about him demanded that someone bestow tender affection on him and cherish him. Yuyang knew she was the only one who could do that. If a rock were to fall from the sky and threaten Chu Tian, she would shield him with her body. She wished she could find a way to let him know that she was prepared to stop at nothing to make sure nothing happened to him.

Yuyang had never thought that she could be so daring, that she could act improperly, shamefully even. Where had she found the courage to be so bold? On this particular evening, she followed Chu Tian with her eyes until he entered the library. Then, after hesitating in the doorway for a moment, she walked in and found him seated on a bench in the reading room. Sitting down next to him, she took out a book and pretended to be engrossed in it. It did not matter what she was reading; what mattered was the reality that she was sitting beside him, shoulder to shoulder.

Since they were in the library, no one could spot anything untoward, especially because she sat with her eyes lowered, as if everything were perfectly normal. But her face burned red the whole time, and that made her very unhappy. Whoever said "The eyes are the window to the soul" was an idiot. For a person in love, it is the face, not the eyes, that is the window to the soul. Her window was bright red, as if the character for happiness had been painted on her face. How could she hide her feelings from anyone? She couldn't. Chu Tian turned his head when she gave a dry cough. She knew he'd done that, which instantly changed everything in her—body and soul. Her heart skipped a beat before it began to sink, darkly and slowly, to an indescribable place, while her body turned strangely light and drifted upward.

The air in the reading room compressed, yet the light felt moist as it caressed and gently stroked her. She felt like crying, but not out of sadness. No, she wasn't sad; she just wanted to cry and cry until her body fell apart, which was the only way she could explain how she felt inside. But she composed herself, then took out from her bag the brand-new hard-bound notebook that she'd recently bought. Opening it to the first page, she began to copy in neat handwriting the poem Chu Tian had posted on the bulletin board:

You
12–9
Are a torch
You
12–9
Are a bugle
You're sonorous
You're aflame

She added a dash and his real name, Gao Honghai, and conferred on his name the sort of significance one associates with names like Gorky, Shakespeare, and Balzac. Unsure if the "Hong" in his name was the character for "red" or for "flood," she settled on the latter since it was more common for a boy to have "flood" in his name. After finishing the task, she wrote her name in the lower right-hand corner of the cover followed by, after a moment's reflection, her year and class, as well as her dorm room number. Originally she'd thought she'd be nervous, but she wasn't and, in fact, was uncharacteristically calm. With a somber look, she pushed the notebook away from her before getting up and walking out. It was at that moment, when she was leaving the library, that a panicky feeling began to spread through her body, all the way to her fingertips. But there was nothing she could do about that now, so she ignored it.

Two days later Chu Tian returned the notebook to her—in the library, of course. He didn't even try to be discreet; instead, he walked up and set it down in front of her. No one noticed. She opened it to see his autograph. She'd been wrong; it was "red" not "flood." As she hurriedly shut the notebook, a mysterious door in her heart was broken open, and in rushed a flood of unreasonable things. Scared and nervous, she felt she might faint then and there. *I must be in love,* she thought, *this has to be love.*

She was in love—Yuyang was sure of it. After that secret exchange, her chest always tightened when she ran into Chu Tian, while he, too, appeared awkward, tossing his hair repeatedly to fling it off of his forehead. That was totally unnecessary. *Why are you tossing your hair?* Yuyang wondered. *You don't have to do that; your hair will never be too messy for me. Will you still be Chu Tian if your hair is neat?* He didn't have to do that, and she'd tell him so when she got a chance.

Yuyang might not have been articulate, but she wasn't stupid. She quickly figured out his daily routine, including his tendency to stroll along the athletic track at least once a day, usually after morning calisthenics or before the evening study period. With fewer people at those times, the field was more spacious, a perfect place for a poet's solitary walk and an ideal spot for the pursuit of romance.

Twelve minutes before the study period began one evening, Yuyang finally mustered the courage and pretended to go for a walk, arriving at the field only to find it empty. Puzzled, she looked around, convinced that she'd seen him head this way after dinner. Where could he have gone?

Undaunted, she tiptoed around behind the cement bleachers, where she spotted Chu Tian, which set her heart pounding furiously. Standing alone in the weeds, he was not composing a poem; no, he was standing with his legs spread as he aimed a stream of urine at a tree, straining to send the liquid pillar as high as his head. In order to reach new heights in his urinary endeavor, he pushed with his buttocks and dug in his toes for leverage. Yuyang's mouth fell open. She was shocked by the discovery that the solitary Chu Tian, the proud and unrestrained poet, would be secretly engaged in such sordid, despicable behavior. She stood still, not daring to make a sound, until she managed to turn around and flee. When she reached the entrance to the field, she turned to look behind her. Chu Tian emerged and froze like a pole nailed to the track, apparently knowing that she'd witnessed his disgusting act. They could not see each other's eyes, but they were obviously looking at each other. The ideal image of her poet was shattered; her heart crumbled. As the evening deepened, a dusky color built up between Yuyang and Chu Tian, blurring their outlines and carrying them farther and farther apart. Bracing herself by resting her hand on an iron gate, Yuyang took in big gulps of air as tears roiled in her eyes.

Yuyang fell out of love. But that had no effect on her classmates, who put on an outstanding performance at the singing contest. In fact, Section Three of the class of '82 had a great deal to be proud of. Whether they won or not was secondary; what mattered most was the unprecedented solidarity among the students who formed a combat-ready bloc. Under the centralized leadership of the homeroom teacher, they cooperated with and supported each other, creating a brand-new, positive classroom atmosphere. But of course, none of this had anything to do with Yuyang, although, from a certain perspective, it did seem linked to her. When it was time for Section Three to go on stage, everyone stood up, emptying all the seats but two, one of them occupied by Sun Jianqiang, the other by Yuyang. She was not prepared for that. Even Sun, normally thick-skinned, could not hold his head up. His neck went limp and his head fell forward, his ears reddening. Yuyang looked up only once during the performance and saw little but Sun's red ears. She, too, could no longer hold her head up, for everyone at the school, including Chu Tian, must have seen that she, Wang Yuyang, was not qualified to celebrate 12–9. It was a public humiliation, a display of disgrace. Keeping her head between her knees, she kept scratching the ground with her fingernail, but she had no idea what she was writing or sketching. Maybe she was trying to dig a hole so she could crawl into it and cover herself with dirt. She felt like crying, but lacked even the courage to do that; fortunately she managed to hold back her tears, since crying under these circumstances would have been an even greater loss of face. What would the homeroom teacher think of her then?

Zhao Shanshan was engaged in a flurry of activities. After she applied her makeup, her sparkling eyes were beyond description. Looking at Shanshan from a distance, Pang Fenghua had an anxiety attack, and she was incredulous when Shanshan walked up and offered to make Fenghua's eyebrows longer. When was the last time Shanshan had even acknowledged her presence? But Shanshan was for real, for she'd already raised Fenghua's chin and was elongating her eyebrows all the way up to her temples.

Shanshan then redrew Fenghua's lip lines to make her mouth smaller and show off its outline. After changing the color of Fenghua's eye shadow, Shanshan held up a small mirror for Fenghua to see how she looked.

"Silly girl, see how pretty you are."

Fenghua glanced away and spotted the homeroom teacher, who was gazing attentively in their direction. Still caught up in her low self-esteem, Fenghua said, "Shanshan, we country girls can never get rid of our country look."

Shanshan rapped Fenghua's head with her knuckles, which hurt; it was as if only pain could help her explain what she wanted to say.

"How could you be a country girl? What makes you think that? Just look at you. You have such good qualities."

Shanshan's earnest words entered Fenghua's ears and went straight to her heart. She was deeply moved. Fenghua had always been concerned that she looked like a country girl, but everything was fine now that an authoritative description of her had been formed.

She was so emotional she felt a need to repay Shanshan's kindness, but before she could say anything, Shanshan gave her a kind reminder: "When we're on stage, don't wait for me to nod to you. You have to give me the signal, all right? Remember, you're the conductor."

Fenghua just stared at Shanshan and, with a sudden sadness rising up, wrapped her arms around the girl's waist. "Shanshan, I've been so jealous of you, but I promise I won't be any longer. I mean it. Let's be sisters." Shanshan knew she meant it.

Knowing that people tend to degrade themselves when in the grip of emotion, Shanshan still did not like what she was hearing. Fenghua was flattering herself. *How dare she claim to be my sister. Who does she think she is?*

Shanshan turned and saw that the homeroom teacher was watching her. This time, he looked away before she did. Turning back, she took Fenghua's hands and said, "It's our turn." Feeling a bit lost, Fenghua stared straight ahead, a blank look on her face. But she was convinced that a friendship between Shanshan and herself had taken hold. There had been, she thought, a definite improvement in their relationship. Now she was an integral member of Shanshan's group.

Section Three did not just win; it scored a resounding victory with a huge lead over the class that came in second. When Shanshan went onstage to receive the award, the homeroom teacher signaled his approval with a tilt of his chin. He was the first to applaud. Except for Sun Jianqiang and Wang Yuyang, everyone in Section Three was bathed in a holiday mood. Luckily those two were overlooked, since the others were too happy to be reminded of them. Why would they give them even a passing thought? The homeroom teacher did not have to say or do anything for the students to know how he felt about their accomplishment.

They weren't children, after all. Taking advantage of the happy moment, Shanshan dragged Fenghua over to the homeroom teacher's dorm room that evening. Fenghua, who hadn't wanted to go, stood hand in hand with Shanshan outside the teacher's room, wearing a stylish red hairclip that was a gift from Shanshan.

The teacher was happy to see them and had plums ready as a treat, as if he'd known they'd come. "You've done well," he said, drawing a bashful smile from Shanshan, who was sitting on the bed next to Fenghua, still holding her hand.

The teacher lit a cigarette, but he looked like a new smoker as he puffed on it in an awkward, exaggerated manner. But that did not stop him from chattering away; in fact, he all but monopolized the conversation. His Misty Poetry-style of talking was replaced by plain everyday conversation that was easily understood by both girls. That went on for five or six minutes before Shanshan jumped to her feet, suddenly reminded of something urgent. Fenghua stood to leave with her, but Shanshan said, "You stay. I just remembered that someone's waiting for me." A note of self-reproach crept into her voice.

Fenghua insisted on leaving with her, but relented when Shanshan stood firm. Any more insistence would have seemed planned. The room abruptly quieted down when only the two of them were left.

"I never realized how nice Zhao Shanshan can be," Fenghua said quietly.

"Yes, Zhao Shanshan has been behaving nicely lately," the teacher commented after a brief silence.

Not knowing what else to say, they sat quietly, trying to think of something to talk about. And that created an atmosphere of nervous tension. They weren't, of course, really nervous. These were unusual circumstances; they both felt a desire to do something, yet dared not take another step, for that would be crossing a line. Saying that a warm, tender feeling filled their hearts better describes the moment.

Avoiding Fenghua's eyes, the teacher focused on the red hairclip. "I see you like red," he said with a smile. Fenghua lowered her head and concentrated on rubbing her hands.

"Red really isn't a good color," he said.

Without looking up, she batted her eyelids and said, "And why is that? You have to take responsibility for what you say."

His chest heaved with a silent laugh. "For something like that? What responsibility do you expect me to take?"

"If the girls in my class say I'm not pretty, I'll come looking for you."

Surprised that she had the nerve to say that, he had to laugh. "I meant red isn't a good color for you."

"Why not?"

"It just isn't."

Fenghua looked up and glared at him, pointing with her

chin. With her eyes fixed on his face, she blurted out harshly, "Bullshit."

Panic-stricken at her outburst, she quickly covered her mouth, but was surprised to see that he was not offended. On the contrary, he appeared to like the way she talked; his smile seemed to indicate that he was glad to hear that kind of talk from her. She could tell that the word brought him unexpected happiness. People often forget themselves when they're happy, and the teacher was no exception.

"What did you just say?" he asked softly. "Say it again."

Emboldened by what he must be thinking, Fenghua leaned forward and replied in an even softer voice, "Bullshit. You're full of shit." Her voice was so soft that she seemed to be only mouthing the words.

He reacted to the unique whisper by smiling and saying in a honeyed voice, "Be careful, or I might sew your mouth shut."

Falling out of love is the same as falling ill, and Yuyang's illness was a serious one. She was weak and lethargic. Everyone in her class was elated over winning the singing contest, but their euphoria only made her more aware of her own insignificance and inferiority—yet another kind of humiliation. Preoccupied over her disappointment in love and the pain of that humiliation, she had completely forgotten an important task—she hadn't sent a written report to Teacher Wei for two weeks in a row. His displeasure and anger were clearly on display when he pulled the curtain shut after calling her into the duty office. He got right to the point by giving an accurate diagnosis of Yuyang's problem before asking her to talk about it: she was dispirited and her thinking must have been contaminated by something unhealthy.

As she sat across from her teacher, she felt ashamed and terrified, aware that he'd seen through her, so she looked down at her feet and held her tongue. In fact, she had been watchful since the day she had met Chu Tian, and had cautioned and castigated herself, but to no avail. Unable to control herself, she'd fallen in love with a young hooligan. The results would have been devastating if Chu Tian hadn't destroyed himself in her eyes, if he hadn't exposed his hooligan nature.

After being silent for as long as it took Wei to smoke half a cigarette, Yuyang finally shed tears of remorse and courageously looked up at the teacher. "I'll tell you everything," she said through her tears.

Wei Xiangdong took swift and decisive action. Eleven minutes later, Gao Honghai, alias Chu Tian, was standing in Wei's duty office, where he was told to take the "three-against" position—pressing his nose, his belly, and his toes against the wall. While he was flattened up against the wall, he was told to trace the shameful course of his inner journey as a means of "exposing" his problems. Think, and think hard. The three-against punishment lasted forty-five minutes, which meant that Gao told on himself for three quarters of an hour, after which he was ordered to turn around. Wei then switched on all the lights in the office and brought over a desk lamp to shine in Gao's face; a round patch of lime on his nose made him look like a Peking Opera clown.

"Have you thought through everything?" Wei asked. Gao

kept quiet and began to wet himself, drenching his shoes and making a puddle on the floor.

"Have you thought through everything?" Wei repeated.

"Yes," Gao responded softly.

"Then talk."

So Gao talked, telling a shocking story. Stripped of the façade of a poet, he exposed his filthy and sordid inner world, for he was "in love" with eight girls at the same time: Wang Qin, Li Dongmei, Gao Zijuan, Cong Zhongxiao, Chan Xia, Tong Zhen, Lin Aifen, and Qu Meixi. Every night after lights-out, he confessed, he began to think about them one by one.

He even had poetry as proof:

Your long hair flying in the wind is the darkness in my heart
Intoxicating me in a dream I savor while we're apart
I want to touch in the distance only your back
You're my little bird you're my butterfly
Oh splashing rain my tears to start

This one was dedicated to Li Dongmei. With his eyes fixed on Gao, Wei breathed hard, but that went unnoticed by Gao, who was drunk on his own poetry. His eyes grew misty as he worked himself up to give another example, a poem to Qu Meixi:

I'm lost
Oh I'm lost
In the distant stream
You are the bride of my dream
I want to get closer and closer to you but you hide from me
I can only scream

Gao recited another poem and then another, clearly self-satisfied and completely unaware of the menacing look on Wei's face. With his eyes fixed on Gao, Wei felt his anger mount until he slammed his fist on the desk and shouted, "No more rhymes. Stop it. Just talk."

Gao's recital came to an abrupt end as he hunched his shoulders. Then he slowly relaxed and wordlessly looked at Wei, as if in a daze.

The following morning Gao did something utterly shocking in his classical essay class when the teacher was explicating Su Dongpo's "Red Cliff Lament." The teacher, a man in his fifties, spoke with a southern accent that made his "n" indistinguishable from his "l," and his "zh," "ch," and "sh" indistinguishable from his "z," "c," and "s."

He had a high-pitched voice that tended to turn shrill when he was excited, giving it a soaring quality and himself a self-indulgent air. His eyes emitted searing heat from behind his glasses. In order to explicate the line "When he first married the younger sister Qiao, he showed a resounding air of gallantry," he began to cite allusions that would involve the phrase, "If the east wind brought Zhou Yu no aid."

He turned around to write, "The two Qiao sisters would be locked up in Tongque Terrace in late spring" on the blackboard when Gao Honghai stood up and commanded in a severe voice, "No rhymes."

The teacher spun around and asked cautiously, "What did you say?"

To everyone's surprise, Gao slammed his fist on the desk and shouted in a voice that seemed to have the power to swallow the world, "No rhymes!"

Taken by surprise, the teacher suppressed his anger and said patiently, "Comrade Chu Tian, you write free verse, so you don't have to rhyme, but classical poetry is different. This is not a question of whether you can or cannot; it's a matter of the formulaic structure and rules of classical prosody. Understand? You have to rhyme."

Enraged, Gao Honghai insisted stubbornly, "No rhymes!"

Unreasonable, disrespectful, disruptive. The aggrieved teacher froze. Fortunately, the bell rang, which gave him a chance to voice his anger in the way he announced, "Class dismissed." He picked up his notes, but Gao would not give up. Growing fixated on the teacher, Gao repeated the command over and over:

"No rhymes!"

His patience exhausted, the teacher grabbed Gao with his bony hand and dragged him to the student affairs office, where he screamed at the director, "It was Su Dongpo who rhymed, not me! How could I avoid it? This is ridiculous!" He was visibly agitated, but the student affairs director had no idea what had caused the teacher's outburst.

"What happened?" the director asked calmly.

The classics teacher was so hot under the collar his face had turned purple. "If I don't teach well and you're unhappy, just tell me. But you can't do it this way. It's Su Dongpo who rhymed. I repeat: it wasn't me!"

Still confused, the student affairs director shifted his questioning eyes from the classics teacher to Chu Tian just as the principal walked by. The classics teacher pulled the principal over and continued even more shrilly, "He can complain if I'm not doing a good job teaching the class, but not like this!"

By now a crowd of students and teachers had gathered. The principal raised his chin.

"Calm down and tell me what happened," he said.

The teacher dragged Gao over and pushed him up to the principal: "Let him tell you."

The steam had left Gao by then, but he refused to give his mouth a rest.

"Ridiculous!" the teacher mumbled to himself.

"No rhymes!" Gao said, catching his second wind.

"Ridiculous!"

"No rhymes!"

"Ridiculous!"

"No rhymes!"

The teacher sputtered and began to tremble. "You ... you ... cra ... zy ... lu ... na ... tic." With that, he spun around and stormed off.

The teacher's outburst had given the principal a sense of what had happened, so he leaned over and, with one hand behind his back, reached out to touch Gao's forehead.

With astonishing arrogance, Gao knocked the principal's hand away and intoned a poem with a sad and gloomy look:

Five fingers
A hand the man had
When you balled your fist
I was so very sad

The principal smiled, intending to smooth things over. "Didn't you just rhyme?" he asked.

"No rhymes!" Gao said.

The principal turned and whispered in the director's ear, "Call for an ambulance."

Gao tried to escape when the ambulance arrived, but five male students from the school security team pounced on him. Shouting angrily, he fought to break free, but the team wrestled him to the ground and restrained him. A doctor in a white smock came up and promptly gave Gao an injection, a wonderfully useful shot; this created a lively, comical scene that was witnessed by everyone in sight. The hardworking crystal liquid quietly did its job, and Gao slowly crumpled before their eyes. His belly heaved a few times with increasingly less force each time, and that was his body's last attempt to struggle. His eyes glazed over as if he were blind, and his mouth hung slack like a beached fish's; a long stream of drool oozed from it. The students were convinced that Chu Tian would never again be *Chu Tian;* he could only go on as *Gao Honghai.*

Yuyang stole the first thing in her life on the evening Gao Honghai was carted away in the ambulance. At nine-twenty-eight, shortly before lights-out, she slipped into the dining hall unnoticed. She'd made a meticulous calculation, knowing that her timing had to be perfect—not a second too early nor a second too late. She walked bent at the waist, feeling her thumping heart ready to burst from her chest, but she managed to control herself and tiptoe over to the rack with the boys' bowls. She looked and listened carefully to make sure no one saw her before turning on her flashlight to begin searching the rows of bowls. Finally she located Chu Tian's enamel rice bowl, which was stenciled with the dark red English letters CHT; she had stolen so many glances at the bowl that the three letters were seared on her heart. Now for the first time it was inches away.

She grabbed Chu Tian's stainless steel spoon and put it in her pocket, then she killed the light and ran off. When she was almost out the door, she bumped into a dining table and felt a piercing pain in her knee. But she fled the room, not daring to check her injury, and made it back to Room 412 in the girls' dormitory just as the lights went out. All conversation stopped as soon as she walked in. Without washing up, she climbed into bed and pulled down the mosquito net before taking the spoon out of her pocket. After a momentary hesitation, she put it in her mouth and tasted the coldness of the stainless steel, which seemed to reach all the way down to the deepest recess of her body. She felt the hard steel and its smooth, curved surface, and hot tears welled up in her eyes. Her knee was also hot and burning, and was probably bleeding by now. Pulling the blanket up to cover her head, Yuyang buried her face in the pillow and sobbed so hard that the bed frame began to quake.

"What's so funny, Yuyang?" Kong Zhaodi asked from the upper bunk. "Aren't you going to share it with us?"

When he wasn't busy working, Teacher Wei Xiangdong's favorite activity was chatting up the female teachers. You might say that flirting with the female faculty had become his hobby. No one could have anticipated the trouble that would ultimately emerge from his mouth. As the saying goes, "Mistakes inevitably arise when one talks too much." Qi Lianjuan, a chemistry teacher who had been married for two years, had never come to Wei for the "item." But her belly remained stubbornly flat.

As someone given to vulgarity, Wei betrayed himself with

his mouth one day when he cracked a joke regarding Qi. Most of the time Qi was one of the more open-minded, easygoing teachers on the faculty, but what Wei said that day upset her. His attempt at humor occurred when there were several other teachers around.

"Teacher Qi," he said during the conversation, "it's time for you to have a baby, don't you think?"

He continued, "If your husband is lazy, there's always me to help out. If not you, who else would I help?" He smiled.

If it had been one of the other teachers, she'd have punched and pinched him, but that would have only enhanced their friendship. They would be closer than ever.

But not Teacher Qi, whose face reddened slowly, culminating in a deep purple. Unable to bear the loss of face, she turned and walked off after tossing a comment at Wei. "Who do you think you are, you shameless ass?"

It was an awkward moment for everyone, especially Wei, who made a few lame excuses as the gathering broke up. Qi's husband, the son of a ranking cadre, had stayed on at the school after graduation. He was socially inept, like a stick of chalk, a man who could manage a few words only if you pushed him; if not, nothing emerged. A lab worker with mediocre talents, he was lucky enough to marry a smart woman with a sharp tongue. After losing the verbal battle, Wei returned to his office in the student union, out of sorts.

He lit a cigarette in the duty office, but the knot in his heart still remained as Qi's comment played itself over and over in his mind:

"Who do you think you are?"

A harmless comment, but hurtful to him, for he knew who he was. Or, more accurately, he knew who he wasn't; he wasn't a man or a woman. He was the conventional "third sex," for he had been impotent for years, a fact known only to him and his wife. In a clinical sense, the affliction could be traced back to the summer of 1979. Before that, he had performed well in bed.

In fact, the bed had been his revolutionary domain, a place where he could "start a campaign" anytime he pleased, and his wife, Tan Meihua, was the target. The pained look on her face spoke volumes. All he had to do was say "Hey," and she would spread herself on the bed, an event that was repeated every two or three days. All she asked of him was to drink less and to be gentler when he was drunk.

But for him even that little bit was too much to ask. Sex isn't throwing a party, or writing an essay, or painting a picture, or embroidering flowers; the last thing you want is refinement, restraint, timidity, or politeness. No, sex is an insurrection, with one side triumphing over the other. Though understandably unhappy, his wife did not dare let her feelings be known. How could she talk about it with anyone? People would have called her stupid and smutty. Luckily for her the heavens were just and Wei lost his virility. He was a changed man, and she, it seemed, was a different woman, since now she could boldly say no.

Although one's post may be little more than an empty title, it can have real consequences. As Wei's status at school changed, so did his status at home, but the change was subtle and occurred slowly over time. In any case, his wife felt that she could now be a different person, feeling a sense of liberation that propelled her to rise above him. In turn, the subtle change in their relationship returned to take root in their bedroom dynamics. This is common among couples; what starts out in bed often ends up in bed.

The ill-fated moment came in the summer of 1979 when Wei experienced a failure, a rare occurrence. It was an alarm signal, and yet he paid little heed. That failure was the beginning of a terrible situation, for over the ensuing months his appendage rebelled and failed, and rebelled again, only to fail one more time until it met with total destruction and never rose again.

It was during a winter snowfall when he comprehended the severity of the situation as that beast between his legs turned into a gentle little bird. On the outside, nothing extraordinary had happened in the previous two years; life wasn't all that bad even after he had lost his official position.

In reality, however, everything changed, especially in bed. Wei was worried and puzzled. Don't they say that one feels free with no official duties? Then why for him was it soft with no official duties? Energy wasn't the problem, and he could not figure out what had happened to him. He was, after all, someone who had seen the world and weathered many storms, so on another snowy evening he laid his cards on the table. "Why don't we get a divorce?" he said to his wife.

She responded with unusual vigor: "Do you think those two ounces of hanging flesh are all I want from you?" She meant well, but that stung even more, since it implied that she'd given up on his "two ounces of flesh."

But Wei did not let his dejection show. At moments like this, a man must be resilient; he had to carry on and look energetic. He appeared to be more cheerful and outgoing, which was why he enjoyed chatting up the women at school. He favored topics with a sexual undertone as if that were the only way he could show he still had it and that nothing was amiss. But when he was alone, he knew he really didn't have to wear himself out acting like that. No one would know anyway, particularly now that he no longer had extramarital affairs. Of course, he couldn't even if he wanted to. So who would know? No loss of face there. Still, while Wei could control his thoughts, he could not keep his tongue from wagging in front of the women teachers. It felt good to talk about it even if he could no longer do it.

To his surprise, his loose talk turned out to be a real blunder this time. *Doesn't Teacher Qi have a sense of humor? I'll have to talk to her about that.*

Qi's husband showed up at his door that night with murder in his eyes, which were as red as a rabbit's. He held a kitchen knife in one hand and a cleaver in the other. His arms shook and his lips trembled. Wei knew what this was all about the moment he opened the door, and he smirked inwardly at the sight of Qi's husband.

What do you think you're doing? You're out of your league here. You want to play games? Well, you've come to the right place.

Smiling, he said, "Little Du, why are you being so formal when visiting a colleague? And there's no need to bring gifts. Come in, come in and have a seat." Draping one arm over Du's shoulder, Wei escorted him inside and shut the door. Then he took the knives from him, laid them on the table, and offered him a cigarette while he brewed some tea.

Wei sat down, crossed his legs, and started chatting in an amicable tone. He told Du that his wife was doing a good job at school and that the responses from other comrades were encouraging; everyone liked and respected her.

After that, Wei changed the subject and told Little Du about plans for the school. "Construction of a natatorium and an all-weather athletic field and the renovation of the library's second floor will all begin next semester. Everything is moving in the right direction. Since society is taking great strides toward progress, we have to do the same. Everyone knows that making no progress is the same as backpedaling, a truth that can be applied to any place and time."

Wei, who had not occupied a leadership position for a long time, was surprised to discover that talking like this made him feel like a leader again. He had regained the tone and gestures of an official. But the crux of the matter was that a leadership mentality had come back—the damn thing had returned.

For his part, Little Du acted respectfully. Wei was somewhat unfocused, but that did not affect his speech, which became more lucid and decisive as he went along; his professional level had not fallen, and he was now sure that he could be entrusted with leadership work at the section level. Little by little, Little Du's anger subsided; he had lost his righteous edge and began nodding his head in response.

Finally, Wei stood up, smoothed the front and back of his jacket, and picked up the knives, which he wrapped in a copy of *People's Daily* before handing them back.

"Stop by whenever you like, and next time no gifts. There's no need for that." Du was about to say something, but was stopped by Wei, who added with a smile, "My door is always open."

After seeing Little Du off, Wei turned and saw his wife, her face contorted by a sneer. He returned to reality as the illusion of being a section-level leader evaporated. He felt like explaining but didn't know where to start, so, with a nod, he said, "It's all right. I cracked a joke about Teacher Qi this afternoon. Everything's fine."

Her face stayed frozen in the sneer. "I know everything's fine. How could I not know? You may not be good at much, and now you'll never again have a 'lifestyle issue.'"

Wei's face darkened at her insinuation. "Tan Meihua!" he shouted.

She ignored the tone of rebuke as she turned and went into the bedroom, closing the door with a final comment, "A dog never gets out of the habit of eating shit."

Deeply hurt, Wei Xiangdong felt a deep loathing for Tan Meihua and for his home life. But he was Wei Xiangdong, a man who knew how to turn grief into vigor by redoubling his devotion to work.

Wei had requisitioned an extralong flashlight with added weight and heightened brightness, and every night after nine-thirty he took it along to inspect the athletic field, the brush behind the bleachers, the art studio, the music room, the grove of trees to the left of the laboratory, the dining hall, and the area around the pond. For the most part, he seldom had to turn on his flashlight, for little escaped his keen eyes, even in the dark. He'd developed a sort of sixth sense so that most of the time, even when there was no sign or evidence, his innate perception helped him identify a spot where a couple was kissing or touching in the dark. Once he verified it, his flashlight would snap on, sending a blinding searchlight across the night sky and nailing the suspects to the ground. More precisely, the white light acted like a loudspeaker or a hood descending upon the suspicious objects. The dark mass on the ground would separate immediately to reveal itself—a panicky boy and girl exposed by the powerful flashlight.

As a whole, the undercover school security team, represented by Wang Yuyang, was a functioning aspect of Wei Xiangdong's project. Secret lovers or signs of a budding love on campus did not escape his attention. The only blemish on his record was his failure to catch any of the transgressors in the act. If he ever did, he would not stop at punishing one couple to warn the others, or as the saying goes, "Kill a chicken to scare the monkeys."

If he caught one, he'd punish one, and if he caught two, he'd punish two. Where romance was concerned, Wei was pigheaded to the point of obsession. Viewed from a certain angle, this was not loathing; it could even be seen as a kind of affection, a fondness. He wanted to catch them, and he wanted to punish them, expose them in broad daylight.

Yuyang worked hard, but the quality of her work was low. Her reports were generally worthless and covered only trivial matters, to Wei's disappointment. On the other hand, he liked her more than the others. Why? Because the intelligence she gathered was generally accurate and undiluted. She never used her power to serve her own interests or to attack or to exact revenge. This was a work ethic deserving of emulation. Some of Wei's undercover agents performed much worse than she. Zhang Juanjuan of Section One of the class of '82, for instance, or Li Jun of Section Four of the same year were highly problematic. Zhang Juanjuan would send in false reports on anyone she didn't like and abused her power for personal gain. What displeased Wei most were the lies. She had once given a vivid description of a romantic liaison between so-and-so and so-and-so, who "sneak out to the grove every night for a quarter of an hour."

Wei had lain in wait at the grove twice, each time emerging empty-handed. It turned out that Zhang had fought with the girl in question and had reported her to take revenge. That had to be stopped. So he called her into the duty office, only to have her stick to her story, insisting that she'd reported the facts. Teacher Wei had not gotten there in time. For the first time, he lost his temper with an undercover agent and felt like slapping her. Zhang's eyes reddened. She even managed to shed a few tears, as if suffering a great injustice.

By comparison, Yuyang was much better. For Wei, her sense of duty was secondary to her playful loveable side. He'd always thought that she was a simple girl, like the knot on an elm tree, but in fact, she could be a lot of fun, even a riot when she shed her timid self.

This he discovered one evening behind the library when he found her playing with a Pekinese dog belonging to Teacher Gao. It was a furry, pudgy animal with short legs that made jumping difficult. But Yuyang knew what to do. Teasing the dog by putting her finger in its mouth and pulling it out, over and over, she leaped into the air, higher and higher. This excited the dog and it stood up on its hind legs and tried to bite her fingers. Quite a sight. The dog looked like a clumsy but obedient child. When it licked her fingertips, she let out an exaggerated, energetic scream as if there were no one else around. And, of course, no one else *was* around. Yuyang kept at it over and over, as did the dog; neither was bored by the monotony of the game. They must have been playing for quite awhile before Wei spotted them because Yuyang had taken off her winter jacket and had on only a thin sweater.

The sweater, which was too small, seemed to wrap itself tightly around her. What caught his attention was not the size of the sweater but her curves, her vigor, and her vitality. Though not tall, Yuyang was well developed; her breasts moved in a lovely and compliant way, as if they were too dim-witted to know what was good for them. Her bangs were so soaked with sweat that they stuck to her forehead in a shiny crescent.

Wei moved closer, clasped his hands behind him, and squinted at Yuyang and the dog, his eyes brimming with tenderness. Unaware of his presence, Yuyang kept lifting, leaping, and screaming. And as the game continued, she got bolder and let her fingers remain in the dog's mouth, which prompted Wei to blurt out, "Careful or he'll bite."

Startled, she withdrew her fingers, scraping them against the dog's teeth in the process. They began to bleed. But she paid no attention to the wound; instead, she spun around and stood at attention in front of Wei.

From her bright red face, he could tell that she was nervous and ill at ease. Her shining eyes darted around, unsure of where to focus.

"Just look at you," he scolded, but with a hint of affection in his voice. He came up and took her hand; after a cursory glance at the wound, he led her in the direction of the infirmary. The dog, obviously unwilling to let her go, trotted along behind them like a ball of yarn. Wei turned and gave the dog a kick, sending it somersaulting through the air before hitting the ground. With a series of loud yelps, the dog twisted itself around and waddled off.

At the infirmary, Wei picked up a cotton ball soaked in rubbing alcohol.

"Be brave," he said. "This will sting."

Yuyang looked up at him, not knowing what to do or say, so she did as he said. He kept sucking in air, as if each dab were sending a sharp pain deep into his heart and into his mouth instead of hurting her. After taking care of her wound, he looked out of the window just before he slapped her on the rear.

"Now be a good girl, and stop playing with that dog," he said. Then he mumbled, "What a silly girl." He sounded like her father, or maybe an uncle, but definitely someone from Wang Family Village.

"Now be a good girl, and stop playing with that dog." "What a silly girl." These two brief comments left a powerful impression on Yuyang, and she was deeply touched.

Shortly before the winter break, something extraordinary happened to this "silly girl"—she became pregnant. Yuyang herself was unaware of it and would never have known if Wei hadn't called her into the duty office. The moment she walked in the door she could tell that something was wrong. She'd been treated well by Wei from the beginning; he'd never frowned at her, and the lines around his eyes had felt like sunshine to her.

But things were different this time. He sat in his chair with a stern look, signaling with his chin for her to shut the door and sit down.

She did as she was told, and her heart filled with anxiety.

She wasn't really afraid because she was secure in the knowledge that Teacher Wei was fond of her. Thinking she'd forgotten to report something important, she asked cautiously, "Has something happened on campus?"

Wei came right to the point: "Something has happened to you."

"No," she said, feeling confused. "I'm fine."

Wei slapped his hand down on the desk and produced a letter. "One of your schoolmates has written to expose you, saying that you are involved with someone and that you have gotten yourself pregnant," he said.

Yuyang's mouth fell open. She stared blankly for a moment as she tried to comprehend what he was saying. When she did, she nearly fainted.

"Who said that?" she demanded.

"I need to investigate the allegation," he replied calmly. The conversation could not continue because the tune "The Well Water at the Frontier is Clear and Pure," sung by Li Guyi, was blaring through the PA system. It seemed both far off and close by at the same time. In Li Guyi's falsetto, the words were like sighs or labored breathing, and the singer sounded worn out from expressing so much emotion. This created a strange atmosphere in the room, as the words started to seem both progressively distant and increasingly distinct.

"We can go to the hospital, or I can check it out myself," Wei said.

Yuyang lowered her head, a welter of thoughts racing through her mind, as she tried to decide what to do. In the end, being checked by Teacher Wei seemed the better option, since he'd been so nice and would not bring false accusations against a good person like her. So she carefully drew the curtains and walked boldly up to him.

Wei was still seated, but he'd turned sideways and had opened his legs wide like a welcoming bay. At the last moment Yuyang's courage left her, and she clutched the cord holding up her pants, unable to untie it. With an air of official indifference, Wei said, "We can always go to the hospital."

His words, hinting at compromise, calmed her mind, yet the blood rushed to her face. *True gold does not fear fire, and an upright body never fears a slanting shadow. Go ahead and check.*

Standing between his legs, she untied her pants and draped the cord around her neck to let Wei press his hand against her belly and move it around slowly. Assured that this was a scientific search for the truth and confident that she knew what that truth was, she had nothing to fear.

Yuyang was innocent—that was proven beyond all doubt. In the spirit of never sparing a single culprit or falsely accusing an innocent person, Wei gave it his all, body and soul, and conducted a thorough inspection that exhausted him; he was sweating and breathing hard. Fortunately the final result allowed Yuyang to breathe a sigh of relief when he patted her buttocks and said, "Good girl." She was not convinced until he repeated the words, "Good girl."

As she stood there, she felt like crying, for what can be more comforting than the trust of the organization? As she retied her pants, she concentrated on trying to guess who had written that shameless, slanderous letter. Had it not been for Teacher Wei, the consequences would have been unthinkable. Even though he'd been a bit rough and had hurt her more than she wanted to admit, the end result was worth all of her forbearance. Now, like Agatha Christie, she began to analyze, deduce, and evaluate the people in her class and discovered that every boy and girl was a suspect. But who could it be? She vowed to find and expose that despicable person.

Yuyang may have been exonerated by the inspection, but the one who truly came out a winner was Wei Xiangdong, who experienced an unexpected consequence. While rubbing Yuyang's belly, he discovered, to his amazement, that a certain appendage had regained its life and revived—and with that he recovered the ability and courage to conquer all difficulties. There is justice in the world, after all; heaven rewards those who work hard.

The elated Wei tried to show off in bed that night but got nowhere. He had been able to do it earlier, why not now? The damned thing was importunately shameless—betraying and splitting him once again. What a tragedy!

As he rested the back of his head on his folded arms, Wei's dejection seemed to reach into the marrow of his bones and send a searing pain straight to his heart. Suddenly distracted, he could not get Yuyang out of his mind. From that point on, she became his obsession.

The winter break was three weeks long, but to Wei Xiangdong it seemed endless. Listless and lethargic, he was reminded that he was neither man nor woman, but had become a true third sex. Now that the students were away, the campus seemed forlorn. It was bad enough that he couldn't see Yuyang; what made it worse was that there was no one to report to him or to expose others, no one to order around, and no work to take charge of. Life lost its appeal, and he found it difficult to go on.

Worse yet, the weather was awful beyond words, with nonstop snowfall and days too cold for the snow to melt. The packed snow was a terrible thing, the reflected light inexplicably souring Wei's mood. The light turned night into day, bringing everything out into the open: no secrets, no hints, and no suggestiveness. Even the normally dark grove was exposed and transparent. Flashlight in hand, Wei roamed aimlessly in the snow, feeling utterly bored. The nights were worse than the days, since there were no more dark corners where people could engage in unsavory acts. He sighed and headed home.

The campus came to life once the winter break ended. Nearly all of the students had put on weight; the boys were heavier than before, the girls even more so. Their faces were a size larger than they'd been only weeks earlier. Rosy, flushed faces told the experienced teachers that the girls had eaten and slept themselves into a fleeting plumpness that would disappear within days.

With the extra weight, the girls looked healthier, and the improved skin tones made them prettier than ever. But when they lost the excess weight, they'd no longer be the scrawny girls of before. Those days would be over. They say that a girl's looks change at eighteen. That seemed to be the case at the school. But this could have been the sixteenth or seventeenth change on the road to the transformation from little girls into women. Their eyes and the way they carried themselves displayed a new temperament, and this made their metamorphosis complete.

But not Yuyang. She actually had lost weight, for she hadn't eaten or slept well over the winter break. A movie played continuously in her head, one with unspeakable scenes. She kept feeling that her lower body was exposed and that a hand was stuck to it. She tried to blot it out of her mind, but the hand had the unerring ability to find her like a shadow that cannot be severed, not even with a knife. It found every opportunity to reach out and slither over her body like a snake. Back in the duty room, she hadn't felt the humiliation, but shame reared its ugly head once the break began and she had returned home. Lacking the courage to discuss it with anyone, she could only bury it deep inside. But humiliation is a strange thing. The deeper you bury it, the smaller its teeth, and yet its bite is sharper.

Yuyang's sense of humiliation brought her more than pain; she was consumed with outrage. The anger she felt toward the slanderer went beyond loathing. She racked her brains trying to ferret out the culprit. Over the three-week break, this thought consumed all her time and energy. Using logical deduction and imaginative power, she set her mind on finding the slanderer. First she made a list of all the students in Section Three of the class of '82 and examined each of them whenever she could. Everyone was guilty, and everyone was innocent. When she finally settled on someone, she'd change her mind the next day. Who was it?

Who was it? Two days into the semester, Pang Fenghua tripped herself up and revealed her foxtail. She had developed the habit of skipping the last rung on the ladder to the upper bunk whenever she was in a hurry or in a good mood. That was what she did that morning, except that this time she let out a scream and fell into the lower bunk, where she rolled around. Startled, the other girls crowded around her but saw nothing out of the ordinary. Yuyang, thinking that she might have twisted an ankle, held up Fenghua's feet to check and was greeted by a frightening sight. Two thumbtacks were stuck in one of her heels and the force from her jump had pushed them deep into her flesh. All Yuyang could do was hold Fenghua down and pull them out, which left two punctures in her heels that immediately began to bleed.

Her face contorted with pain, Fenghua slapped Yuyang.

"You put those in my shoes! You did it!" Her outrageous accusation was groundless, since everyone had been given a box of thumbtacks for a sketching class that semester.

What made Fenghua assume that it was Yuyang who had put the tacks in her shoes? Two of her own tacks could have fallen into her shoes. Covering her mouth with her hand, Yuyang felt tears well up. No one said a word; Fenghua's wails were the only sounds in the room.

Everyone knew that Fenghua hadn't really meant it, that pain and anger had made her lose her temper, but that was not what Yuyang was thinking. Through her teary eyes, she finally saw through Fenghua.

What made her assume that it was Yuyang? Why had she thought that Yuyang had sought revenge? She had something to hide, which meant that she had written the slanderous letter.

Yuyang managed to force back her tears as the corners of her mouth curved upward, almost as if she were smiling.

Very well, Pang Fenghua, very well, Yuyang thought to herself as she let go of Fenghua's foot, turned, and left the room without a word.

Fenghua was frightened because she had slapped Yuyang

for no justifiable reason. Yuyang might look like an open book and be easy to get along with, but it was hard to say whether or not she'd report her. Fenghua was also unsettled by the look in Yuyang's eyes and her smirk, so she hobbled over to the homeroom teacher's room that evening, where she burst out crying the moment she saw him.

After hearing her out, he sighed.

"It's all my fault," he said with a look of torment. "I've spoiled you." Then he added, "How could you have done that?"

That effectively brought a halt to their conversation. With neither of them saying anything, the room was quiet except for the buzzing of the transformer in the fluorescent light. Fenghua kept her head lowered and picked at her fingernails. Her teacher was too fond of her to sit and watch her suffer, so he reached out for her hand, which he examined, front and back, before he said with a smile, "I didn't realize you could be so ferocious."

That stopped her tears; she retreated, pulled her hand back, and held it behind her. She swayed uneasily as she bit her lower lip and looked ashamed. With a stern look he said, "Don't do that again. Don't ever—or *I'll* slap *you*." He raised his hand threateningly, never expecting her to look up, take a step forward, cock her head, and push her face right up to him.

"Go ahead, slap me," she said softly.

Caught off guard, he didn't know what to do. His hand was suspended in midair.

"Do it." Her eyes, only inches away, stared down at him. "You don't dare. You don't have the nerve, do you?"

His arm began to drop, but then he froze like a statue, and so did she. This was totally unexpected—for both of them—and it was torturous, for they both yearned for the next step though neither knew what that would be. They heard each other's heavy breathing and felt the blood race through their veins as they breathed on each other like snorting horses.

What happened next took them both by surprise. He wrapped his arms around her and pulled her to him; it looked impulsive, and yet it was completely natural. His lips fell on hers as she stumbled toward him, confused and not realizing what was happening. Neither had any experience doing this, so their kiss was awkward and rushed. It wasn't anything like a real kiss; it was more like bumping lips together. They were frightened and yet dying to try it out, so after touching lips, they quickly separated.

But that touch was a lethal one—now there was no fear to stop them. They went ahead with the next kiss, a serious, proper one. Their lips seemed glued together, and before it was over, tears were streaming down the teacher's face while Fenghua nearly fainted.

"My life is over," he said, finally revealing what he'd been hiding in his heart.

Fenghua felt a sadness well up inside her, and she went limp. "Take me with you and we'll die together," she said with her eyes shut.

The paper-thin curtain separating them had finally been torn open to reveal a welcoming intimacy. They had been in love all along, a secret, private, heartbreaking love. But now the most important thing shifted from love and the expression of that love to something else, something they had to face and confront together: their only hope for the future was to never let their love come to light.

The consequences of public exposure were unthinkable; that thought paralyzed them. They stared at each other, and the more they stared, the stranger the other one looked. Unable to gaze any longer and incapable of believing what they'd done, they nearly stopped breathing from the anxiety, as if they were in a minefield where any misstep could be fatal. Still breathing hard, the teacher listened at the window to make sure no one was within earshot.

"Do you understand?" he asked mournfully. She stared at him through teary eyes and nodded. How could she, his student, not understand? Not completely convinced, he said, "Tell me you understand."

She burst out crying. "I do."

Love is essential, but sometimes it is even more essential to hide and shun it so as to escape watchful eyes. They made a pact to stop seeing each other and to wait until she graduated. With their arms around each other, they gave voice to their love with unusual vows. Over and over they vowed to stay apart while fantasies filled their heads over what awaited them after her graduation. But they tried not to think about that, for the uncertainty brought only sadness.

Vows are loud and clear, firm and vigorous, but it doesn't take much for them to become laughable or unrealistic. The teacher and Fenghua both forgot one thing: people who are in love cannot control their feelings. They simply couldn't do it. It was as if their lives were in danger and they needed to be together every second of every day. So they continued to see each other, to shed endless tears, and to repeat their vows, as if they were meeting not because they missed each other but because they needed to review and reaffirm their promises.

"This is the last time, absolutely the last time," they'd say, but it didn't help. They felt that they were on the verge of insanity.

Fenghua's eyes brightened like clear glass one moment and darkened like frosted glass the next, depending on whether they could meet. Try as she might to be calm and control herself, she couldn't hide her abnormal behavior from Yuyang's watchful eyes. Fenghua used every trick she knew to hide what was going on, but in the end it was all in vain. Yuyang knew what was going on in Fenghua's life more thoroughly and in greater detail than Fenghua herself. Here is what Wang Yuyang recorded in her diary.

Wednesday: Pang Fenghua left the classroom at 8:27 P.M. and returned to the dorm at 9:10; she was sobbing under her blanket after lights-out.

Saturday: 4:42 P.M., the homeroom teacher and Pang Fenghua had a brief conversation in the hallway before going their separate ways. Pang Fenghua did not eat in the dining hall and did not return to the dorm until 9:32. At midnight, she turned on a flashlight to look at herself in the mirror.

Saturday: Pang Fenghua washed her hair at 6:10 P.M., left the room at 6:26, and did not return until 9:08. Her eyes were red as if she'd been crying.

Monday: Pang Fenghua complained of a headache during evening study period and asked to be excused, leaving the classroom at 7:19. She was not in the dorm room when study period was over; she returned at 9:11. Her spirits were high and she was very talkative. After getting into bed, she sang "The Waves in Honghu Chase Each Other" softly.

Saturday: Pang Fenghua washed her hair and brushed her teeth at 6:11 P.M. Left the room at 6:25; returned at 9:39.

Saturday: Pang Fenghua washed her hair and brushed her teeth at 6:02 P.M.; she left the room at 6:21. At 7:00 the homeroom teacher came to inspect the dorm, talking loudly at the door of Room 412, but he did not enter. He left at 7:08. Pang Fenghua returned at 9:41.

Sunday: Pang Fenghua was lost in thought in front of a mirror. She had a wound on her neck; it was oval in shape, like a human bite. Fenghua muttered to herself, "What lousy luck to be scraped by a branch." She was lying; a scrape from a branch looks different.

Naturally Fenghua's name did not appear that way in Yuyang's diary; it was represented by the letter P. Pang Fenghua was now just P. As mysterious as P might be, she would not come to a good end. How could she? She simply couldn't. Yuyang was not just keeping a record; she was also analyzing the data. Using impeccable logic, she compared the times listed in the diary and reached a definitive conclusion—Pang Fenghua was in love. When Saturday rolled around, she gave herself a thorough cleaning, including her teeth.

Except for going out to see someone, why else would she do that? That was point one.

Point two: Fenghua's love interest was still unknown, but in Yuyang's view, it could very likely be the homeroom teacher. Leaving other possible signs aside, Yuyang noticed that he had been ignoring Fenghua for a while. He never asked her a question during class, and sometimes he even avoided looking in her direction. That was a new wrinkle, one that could only invite suspicion. When someone tries too hard to hide something, they usually wind up drawing attention to it.

Point three: except for Saturday, which clearly was their meeting day, they occasionally saw each other on Mondays or Wednesdays. Yuyang had yet to determine where they met, and that was something she needed to work on. She had to increase her surveillance, but she was confident that the secrets would be exposed like sprouting seeds. All she had to do was follow and observe Fenghua a while longer. As time went by, it became easier to detect a routine in her movements, and routine meant regularity. That would help explain the situation. Regularity is the biggest and most powerful thumbtack that, with adequate pressure, can pin you to the pillar of shame and humiliation.

To be absolutely accurate, Yuyang began tailing Pang Fenghua and digging up dirt on her simply as part of her job; she had no particular motives of her own. After a while, though, she found to her surprise that she had developed a fondness for the job. It was a good job, to which she became so powerfully addicted that she didn't think she could give it up. She was convinced that even if Pang Fenghua had not offended her, she'd still have enjoyed the work.

Nothing escaped her attention; she saw everything. This was a special gift, an extra reward from life that gave her an extraordinary sense of accomplishment. No wonder Wei Xiangdong wanted to cultivate "all-hearing ears" and "far-seeing eyes." She found it easy to like whatever he liked. It was simply perfect; her life was filled with all sorts of activities, colors, trepidation, and stirring emotions when she hid in dark corners to ferret out others' secrets. She was grateful to life and to her job.

And yet Yuyang was not happy, not really. Something still weighed on her; it was the money order, a zombie that had come back to life and opened its eyes to glare at her. She saw it, an eerie blue light: the light of death. It was during the afternoon extracurricular activities period when it re-entered her life. Teacher Wei walked up and asked her to come with him to the duty office. She did not want to go, not now, not ever, for whenever she saw that building, she was reminded of how she'd bared her body for Teacher Wei. But she had no choice; she had to go, especially when Wei mentioned the money order, so she followed him without a word.

The money order lay on Wei's desk. He said nothing, nor did she. But as she looked down at it, a sense of calmness came over her, and she sneered inwardly as she realized what he had in mind. He might be older and appear proper, but what he wanted was simple enough—to touch her.

How repulsive.

It was at that moment that Yuyang began to despise him. How she looked down on him now! Though her fear had not abated, she now knew that she had the psychological advantage, so she waited calmly, thinking to herself: *Let's see what you've got to say. Let's hear how you conduct this transaction. Even if I'm willing to go along, I want to see the money order and verify its authenticity, then I want to see it turn to ashes before you can have what you want from me. I tell you, Wei, I've seen through you.*

Without betraying his feelings, Wei took out a lighter. To light a cigarette?

No. Instead, he held the money order in one hand and the lighter in the other as he walked up to her. She examined the piece of paper and decided that it was indeed hers, with her handwriting. The lighter flicked on and the yellow flame licked the money order, which curled in the flame, turning first to smoke and then to ashes.

Yuyang stared blankly at it, trying to sort things out as the ashes settled to the floor. Wei put his foot down and erased everything, sending "ashes flying when the smoke dies down", in the words of Su Dongpo. That was not what she'd expected, so she stole a glance at Wei, who remained composed. Guilt feelings crept up inside her as she reproached herself for mistaking his good intentions as an evil scheme.

Tears of remorse wetted her face. Wei laid his right hand on her left shoulder and patted it twice, which served to increase her guilt. She covered her face, but a loud thump made her open her eyes. To her astonishment, Wei was kneeling in front of her, silent tears flowing from his upturned face. It was an ugly sight to behold; his mouth was open, his arms raised in the air. He inched forward on his knees and wrapped his arms around her legs. "Yuyang."

Now she was truly frightened. No. Stunned.

"Yuyang, help me! Please help me, Yuyang."

Her will softened, and so did her legs. She slumped to the floor and blurted out, "Please don't be like that, Teacher Wei. I beg you. You can touch me wherever you like."

Yuyang did not expect to bleed so much. She shouldn't have; where had all that blood come from? It stained a towel, but in the end it stopped, though the pain remained. And she was not the only one who was shocked by the bleeding.

Wei cried again, his forehead drenched in sweat and his hand covered in blood. But he ignored her as if nothing interested him except the blood on his hand, as if the blood was Yuyang, for he kept saying tearfully to his fingers, "Yuyang, ah, Yuyang! Yuyang, ah, Yuyang!" The way he called out her name was touching. "Yuyang, ah, Yuyang! Yuyang, ah, Yuyang!"

All night long she was tormented by a terrible dream in which she was surrounded by a tangle of snakes. There were so many of them, like baskets of noodles, knotted, twisted, and snarled. They were sticky and slimy, writhing, roiling, surging, and slithering. Worse yet, she was naked and the snakes glided over her bare skin, cold and chilly. She wanted to run, but couldn't. She could only move her hands. But finally she was running, with the teachers and students cheering her on, and the loudspeaker blaring, "Yuyang, ah, Yuyang! Yuyang, ah, Yuyang!"

She ran as if her life depended on it until she reached the finish line of the 10,000-meter race.

Why wasn't she ashamed of her nakedness? How could she be so shameless?

Then the PA system crackled to life, and someone was talking. It was Wei, waving a red flag in one hand and holding a microphone in the other.

"Pay attention, everyone," he shouted. "Look carefully. Yuyang is dressed. Let me repeat, Yuyang is wearing clothes. She did not steal the twenty yuan. It wasn't her." And that put her mind at ease. With Wei around, it didn't matter whether she was naked or not, because with his announcement, she would be clothed one way or the other.

She woke up early the following morning, and as she lay in bed she was sure she was sick. But she moved around a bit and did not feel any discomfort; except for the dull pain down below, everything else felt fine. She got up and took a few steps; she was fine. As she sat on the edge of the bed, she realized that she had dreamed all night, but she was unable to recall her dreams.

Yuyang really did feel fine, but she was exhausted. She had bled a lot the day before, but apparently nothing terrible had happened, and for that she was grateful. She had thought she'd be in terrible shape, but nothing seemed to be out of place. He'd fondled her again, that was all. Other than the bleeding, she didn't feel humiliated like she had the first time.

She actually felt better, since this was the first time in her life that anyone had actually knelt down to her, not to mention that the someone was her teacher. After this, it would be him, not her, who needed to fawn. Yuyang told herself that he had fondled her before, and since it was him again, she had lost nothing in the process. Once, twice, it was all the same, except that it took longer the second time. What did it matter if she bled? What girl doesn't bleed once a month? Besides, he had promised that he would never mistreat her and that he would try his best to keep her in town.

It might have been a transaction, but it was a substantial one, and well worth it, since she had come out ahead. With the teacher giving her his promise, she could not be unfeeling; and yet she felt bad. It wasn't pain, and it wasn't pleasure, just something that was hard for her to handle. She'd feel a lot better if she could scream. Yuyang might have been young, but no one needed to explain to her what went on between a man and a woman. She would never have consented if he'd asked her to do it. In fact, she would have threatened to scream if he'd asked, and she was grateful to him for not doing that.

It made a big difference to her. He was a man of his word. He hadn't taken off his clothes, so there was no reason to feel bad, just so long as he didn't make her do it with him. He was, after all, someone who had seen the world and weathered many storms; he knew how to take care of things. He showed his ample planning skills with the scheduling. No one would have expected him to ask Yuyang to come to his office every Sunday morning. Who'd have thought he was capable of doing that on a Sunday morning? No one would suspect a thing, which made it perfectly safe, and that put her mind at ease. Besides, her classmates' focus was on Pang Fenghua and the homeroom teacher; the more animated their gossip became, the less attention anyone would pay to Yuyang.

All along, she'd planned to wait till she'd gathered all the necessary intelligence before reporting to Wei Xiangdong, so she had no reason to hurry. One day—it made no difference when—she'd make that little bitch pay. Moving too soon could alert Fenghua, who might escape from her clutches. That would be a terrible loss. But Yuyang's youth betrayed her—she could not keep a secret.

One day, while she was sitting on Wei's lap, she could hold back no longer. She asked him if he knew the identity of the homeroom teacher's love interest. He produced the names of four or five young female teachers, but she shook her head and smiled.

"No, it's someone in my class," she said. His eyes lit up, a strange, eerie glint that seemed aimed at an invisible object. It was the glint of a tiger eyeing its prey. To Yuyang, that glare appeared to send steam into the air, to actually smoke.

"Really?" he asked. Encouraged by the light in his eyes, she nodded with certainty. "You're sure?" he asked.

Without a word, she went back to her dorm room to retrieve her diary and handed it to him. That was Yuyang's style. She'd rather act than talk, and let the facts speak for themselves.

"Why didn't you tell me earlier?" he asked sternly.

"The right to speak comes only after investigation," Yuyang said.

Nothing happened on campus for several days, which concerned Yuyang. The truly shocking event did not take place until Saturday night, though nothing out of the ordinary occurred during the day. After nightfall, not only did they not send for Pang Fenghua, they actually extended lights-out a full hour later and showed a couple of war movies. The teacher's weekend club was open, so lights blazed on campus, belying any sign of impending doom. At 9:30, the usual time for lights-out, Wei, flashlight in hand, made his move, followed by Director Qian, Teacher Huang of Student Affairs, Director Gao of Educational Affairs, Deputy Director Tang, several staff members who had applied for Party membership, and seven members of the school security team—a mighty contingent that headed to the dorm room of the homeroom teacher in charge of Section Three of the class of '82.

The lamps around the dormitory were not functioning; it was pitch black. Stepping lightly, the group moved so silently that the only sound was their heavy breathing, which they were having trouble keeping in check.

When they reached the darkened room, Wei stopped, turned around, and raised his hand to make sure that no one made any noise. The group stood still, like a grove of breathing trees. Wei curled the index finger of his right hand and tapped gently on the door, as if afraid to startle a child on the other side. Nothing stirred, so Wei craned his neck and whispered, "Teacher Peng, please open the door." As if making a deal with the doorframe, he repeated, "Teacher Peng, open the door now."

He waited, and then said, "Teacher Peng, I have a key, and I'll use it if I have to." Still nothing stirred inside. So Wei took out his key and inserted it into the hole, but the door remained shut—it was locked from the inside. Now everyone took a deep breath as Wei retrieved the key and raised his voice. "Smash it!"

He snapped on his flashlight, nailing the wooden door with a blindingly bright light. There was a thump on the other side, followed by the flickering of a fluorescent bulb. Peng opened the door, but he hardly resembled the Section Three homeroom teacher or the people's teacher of dialectical materialism, historical materialism, political economics, and the brief history of social development. Seemingly devoid of human form and skeleton, he looked like a chicken thrown into the pot or a dog fished out of the water.

The separate interrogations began that night. Pang Fenghua refused to talk until three in the morning, when, exhausted from crying, she confessed and took responsibility for everything, as if she were the one who had done all the unspeakable acts. Then she clammed up and resumed crying.

By comparison, the homeroom teacher had a better attitude. After seven or eight cups of boiled water, he responded to every question. But his interrogation was interrupted when he began spitting blood, thanks to the boiling water he'd gulped down.

How careless could someone be? How had he not sensed how hot the water was? And how had he managed to gulp it down like that? He must have been scared out of his wits. Fortunately, he cooperated by telling them everything, including the first kiss, the first embrace and who had initiated it, whose tongue had first entered the other's mouth, whether they had fondled each other and how, and who had begun fondling first and where. He told them everything, sometimes more than once because Wei kept repeating his questions, and Peng had to repeat his answers.

Wei's eyes lit up each time Peng responded, and Wei's skin twitched as if he were in pain or, perhaps, in ecstasy. He seemed to be enjoying himself, but Peng was less forthcoming when it came to sex. He hemmed and hawed, trying to evade the issue. Naturally, Wei would not let him off the hook, and he followed up with tough, carefully crafted questions, not giving Peng a chance to deny anything.

"When did you first go to bed together?" Wei asked.

"We didn't," Peng replied.

"The two of you had to be in bed because everyone saw how the sheets, the blanket, and even the pillows were all rumpled. How can you deny it?"

"We did go to bed, but not like that," Peng insisted.

"Like what then?" Wei was relentless.

"We were in bed, but we didn't do it. Honest, we didn't go to bed like that."

"Oh? What do you mean by 'like that'?"

"I mean sleeping together. We didn't sleep together."

"Who said you were sleeping? If you were, you wouldn't have been able to get up to open the door."

"I don't mean going to sleep. I mean having a relationship."

"What kind of relationship?"

"Between a man and a woman."

"And what is that?" Wei demanded.

"A sexual relationship. You can have her checked at the hospital," Peng said. In order to prove his innocence, he took a small box out of his pocket and opened it to show the contents— condoms, which he counted in front of everyone. There were ten, not one less.

In a burst of anger, Wei banged the table but was stopped by Director Qian, who signaled him with his eyes to keep the proper attitude.

"What does that prove?" Wei thundered. "I ask you, just what do you expect that to prove? Do you mean to say you can't have sex without one of those?"

Peng looked up. That's right. How could he prove he didn't do it by simply showing them that he didn't use the condoms? He couldn't stop blinking. Suddenly he fell to his knees in front of Wei and knocked his head on the floor repeatedly.

"It's true," he pleaded. "I'm not lying. We wanted to, but you showed up before we could do it."

"Did you two talk about it?"

"Yes."

"Who brought it up?"

Peng thought quietly for a moment before finally saying, "Not me."

"Who then?"

"She did."

"Who is she?" Wei was relentless.

"Pang Fenghua," Peng replied.

Five o'clock Sunday morning. The disappointing news came just before sunrise. The homeroom teacher had gotten away. He'd been guarded by two students of the school security team, but they were, after all, young and inexperienced. They'd dozed off and let the homeroom teacher of Section Three of the class of '82 sneak away right under their noses.

The security team searched everywhere on campus, even the toilets, but he was nowhere to be found. At 6:10 A.M., Wei Xiangdong gave a self-critical report to Director Qian, who quietly heard him out and then, instead of a reprimand, consoled him: "He didn't escape. How could he? He has simply fallen into the vast ocean of the people."

The homeroom teacher "had fallen into the vast ocean of the people." At 10:45, Yuyang heard Director's Qian's pronouncement from a classmate. Having never seen an ocean, Yuyang tried hard to imagine what it was like, but by lunchtime she still had not conjured up an image of an ocean. But she was convinced that, generally speaking, it must be vaster than she could envision. It must be infinite and boundless. She was sure of that.

Notes

1. Many rural villages are populated mainly by families with the same surname.
2. Here the author is showing how poorly educated Yumi is; she does not write well and her accented Mandarin causes her to choose the wrong words.
3. This is how country folk might comment that the government is up and running.
4. *People's Daily*, *PLA Daily*, and *Red Flag*.
5. A brand of alarm clock that refers to a somewhat obscure slogan from the 1950s.
6. If Little Tang's son marries Guo's sister-in-law, she would be considered a member of an older generation than Guo's, which would make her feel either awkward or proud.
7. Urban high school students and graduates were sent into the countryside by Mao during the Cultural Revolution to learn from the peasants. Their numbers were in the tens of millions.
8. A game resembling tag.
9. Refers to the Long March (1934–35) by Communist forces, which ended at their stronghold in Yan'an.
10. An expression denoting the ultimate humiliation.

11. A label forced on individuals who were critical of Mao's disastrous Great Leap Forward in the 1950s.

12. A Maoist slogan that means the East (essentially China) shall prevail over the West (mainly Europe and the U.S.).

13. A common phrase often used by Chairman Mao.

14. This is not a union in the style of a workers' organization; the responsibilities at a school are to furnish daily necessities.

15. An avant garde poetry movement of the 1980s.

16. On December 9, 1935, high school and college students in Peiping (Beijing) staged anti-Japanese protests, which are commemorated by the holiday 12–9.